The Physically Handicapped Child

The Physically Handicapped Child

An Interdisciplinary Approach to Management

edited by
Gillian T. McCarthy MB, MRCP, DCH
Consultant Neuropaediatrician, Chailey Heritage Hospital and
Royal Alexandra Hospital for Sick Children, Brighton

with a Foreword by
His Royal Highness The Prince of Wales KG, KT, GCB

ff

faber and faber LONDON · BOSTON

First published in 1984
by Faber and Faber Limited
3 Queen Square London WC1N 3AU
Typeset by Wilmaset, Birkenhead
Printed in Great Britain by
Redwood Burn Ltd, Trowbridge
All rights reserved

© *Faber and Faber Limited, 1984*

British Library Cataloguing in Publication Data

The physically handicapped child
1. Physically handicapped children
I. McCarthy, Gillian T.
362.7   HV903
ISBN 0–571–13263–4
ISBN 0–571–13204–9 Pbk

This book is dedicated to the children of
Chailey Heritage past and present
in love and admiration

Medicine has become increasingly complicated, particularly over the past 30 years. Up to that time a doctor could aspire to "know it all". He no longer can, and even those in specialties now could quite profitably spend all their time trying to keep up with new knowledge without ever seeing any patients. If this fragmentation has been bewildering for the professionals, it is even more so for their patients. Physically handicapped children are apt to become involved with a large number of "experts" and it can therefore become almost impossible for people to keep track of who is supposed to be doing what to them. This is particularly so for the children about whom this book is written.

The child is in contact with his paediatrician and family doctor, nurses, physiotherapists, occupational therapists, speech therapists, social workers and school teachers as a minimum. There will almost certainly be others; ophthalmologists, audiologists, orthopaedic and neuro-surgeons, orthotists and psychologists to mention a few. Somehow the people caring for him have to arrive at a shared and agreed picture of his current situation. This is the outcome of his inter-relationships with his school, family and friends. With this picture as complete as possible, a consensus must then be arrived at by the team as to what can be achieved next and with whose help.

Holistic medicine, as this overall approach is some-times called, is often spoken of as being a new approach. It is something, however, which good doctors have practised for thousands of years. They have realized that you cannot treat a kidney or a lung or a foot without regard to its owner, no matter how scientific you become. This book is written by a wide variety of dedicated professionals and the team approach to physical handicap outlined in the book exemplifies the advantages of this style of medicine and will, I hope, help to promote the standard of care, and hence the quality of life, for these children and their families. The team-work at Chailey Heritage is unusual and I recommend this book to anyone with an open mind working with disabled children that they may learn from the other disciplines.

Charles.

Contents

Contributors

Dr Margaret Borzyskowski MB, MRCP
Developmental Paediatrician
Newcomen Centre, Guy's Hospital, London

Andrew Brown Esq, MSc, MBES
Senior Electronics Engineer
Chailey Heritage Hospital

Miss Ruth Cartwright MCSP
Superintendent Physiotherapist
Chailey Heritage Hospital

Miss Pamela Charon MCSP
Superintendent Physiotherapist
Royal Alexandra Hospital for Sick Children, Brighton

Miss Morwenna Cork BA, SRN, HVTutCert
Senior Lecturer in Health Studies
Brighton Polytechnic

Mother Frances Dominica SRN, RSCN, FRCN
Helen House, Oxford

Steven Dorner Esq, MA
Principal Clinical Psychologist
Wessex Unit for Children and Parents, Middleton Ford, Portsmouth

John A. Fixsen Esq, MChir, FRCS
Consultant Orthopaedic Surgeon
St Bartholomew's Hospital, London; the Hospital for Sick Children,
Great Ormond Street, London
and Chailey Heritage Hospital

Dr Ian Fletcher MRCS, LRCP
Senior Medical Officer, Department of Health and Social Security,
Limb Fitting Centre, Roehampton
and Chailey Heritage Hospital

John Florence Esq, FBIST
Orthotist, John Florence Ltd, Orthotic Workshop,
The Chailey Heritage,
North Chailey, Nr Lewes, East Sussex

Mrs Christine Foster MCSP
Deputy Superintendent Physiotherapist
Chailey Heritage Hospital

Miss Nicola J. Gardner BSc, MEd (EdPsych)
Educational Psychologist
Chailey Heritage School and East Sussex Education Department

Mrs Rosemary Land BA (Hons), MPhil
Senior Clinical Psychologist
Chailey Heritage Hospital

Dr Gillian T. McCarthy MB, MRCP, DCH
Consultant Neuropaediatrician,
Chailey Heritage Hospital *and*
Royal Alexandra Hospital for Sick Children, Brighton

Mrs Valerie Moffat LCST
Senior Speech Therapist
Chailey Heritage Hospital

Timothy R. Morley Esq, MA, MB, BChir, FRCS
Consultant Orthopaedic Surgeon
King's College Hospital, London;
Royal National Orthopaedic Hospital, Stanmore *and*
Chailey Heritage Hospital

Roy Nelham Esq, BEng, CEng, MIMechE, MBES
Director, Rehabilitation Engineering Unit
Chailey Heritage Hospital

Michael Oddy Esq, MSc, PhD
Principal Clinical Psychologist
Department of Psychology, Larchwood Children's Unit,
St Francis Hospital
Haywards Heath, West Sussex

Mrs Jane O'Halleron DipCOT
Senior Occupational Therapist
Royal Alexandra Hospital for Sick Children, Brighton

Hugh Parrott Esq, CertEd, DipSpecEd
Headmaster
Chailey Heritage School

Nigel D. Ring Esq, MA, MSc, CEng, MIMechE
Consultant Rehabilitation Engineer

Dr Richard O. Robinson MA, MB, BCh, FRCP
Consultant Paediatric Neurologist
Guy's Hospital, London *and* Chailey Heritage Hospital

Miss Jill D. Rockey DipCOT
District Occupational Therapist
Chailey Heritage Hospital

Mrs Philippa Russell BA
Senior Officer, Voluntary Council for Handicapped Children
National Children's Bureau, London EC1V 7QE

Fred G. Sheppard Esq, DipVG
Senior Careers Officer (retired)
East Sussex Education Department

Miss Carolyn Shumway BSc, RPT (Massachusetts)
Senior Physiotherapist
Chailey Heritage Hospital

Miss Yenny Snider AIMSW
Social Worker
Chailey Heritage Hospital

Dr Michael Strode MB, BS
Associate Specialist in Paediatrics
Chailey Heritage Hospital

Mrs Patricia Vincent SRN
Ward Sister
Chailey Heritage Hospital

Editor's Preface

The care of physically handicapped children has developed enormously over the past 50 years and now involves a wide group of professionals interested in all aspects of the child and his family. Too often the individual carers operate in isolation and their efforts fail to have the effect they desire.

Chailey Heritage School and Hospital, founded in 1903, has been fortunate to be a centre where professionals have worked together to develop a multidisciplinary team. The purpose of this book is to show how a team approach can be effective, and the authors are drawn from all disciplines at Chailey and from our visiting consultants. We are also fortunate to have contributions from Mother Frances Dominica, Philippa Russell and Steven Dorner each of whom have brought special experience and wisdom from their particular fields.

Inevitably some background knowledge has to be assumed, and references and bibliography are provided at the end of each chapter to amplify the information.

The importance of the family to any child's development cannot be over-emphasised. Parents are part of the team, and if the family breaks down, parents must be replaced – not by an institution – if the psychological and spiritual development of the child is to reach its full potential.

The children at Chailey Heritage have played a major part in the development of the team approach by showing us what can be achieved physically and educationally, and telling us what they require emotionally and socially.

Most of all, physically handicapped children want to be thought of as children, to be given the same opportunities to develop as anyone else, and it is up to us to help them to do so.

Acknowledgements

A multi-author book is particularly difficult to draw together. I would like to thank all the contributors for their co-operation and patience throughout the book's gestation period. I also acknowledge the contribution of all the staff of Chailey Heritage, past and present, without whom this book would not have been written. In particular I wish to thank Mrs Janet Darby, Radiographer at Chailey Heritage, and Miss Diana Heath from the Department of Medical Photography and Illustration at the Royal Sussex County Hospital who have taken most of the photographs, also Larry Bray for the photograph on page 96.

My thanks also to Mrs Audrey Besterman for the beautiful line drawings.

Particular thanks go to the children and parents who have allowed us to publish photographs showing the children with unblocked features, also to those children who had photographs taken which we have been unable to use because of limited space.

The National Children's Bureau kindly gave permission for publication of Mrs Philippa Russell's contribution in Chapter 1, previously published in their journal *Concern*.

Finally, my thanks go to all the secretaries who have helped in typing the various chapters, but particularly to Mrs Liane Webster and Mrs Sally Parkes; and to my husband, Stephen Ramsay, for putting up with all the paper!

Glossary

acheiria Absence of a hand

adactylia Absence of fingers

achondroplasia A type of short-limbed dwarfism

amblyopia Absence of vision or poor vision not caused by any discoverable lesion in the eye

amelia Absence of a limb

amino-acid An organic acid in which one or more of the hydrogen ions are replaced by NH_2; any one of the hydrolytic products of protein breakdown some of which are indispensable to growth in higher animals

anterior horn cells The nerve cells present in the anterior horn of the spinal cord which connect with the motor nerves forming the lower motor neurone

antibody Specific constituent of serum proteins which develop in response to an antigen as part of the defence mechanism of the body

antigen Any substance which, after introduction into the body, is capable of producing an antibody and thus inducing immunity

apodia Absence of a foot

arthrodesis Surgical fixation of bone by the artificial production of bony union

arthrogryposis Curved stiff joints

ataxia Inco-ordination of muscular action caused by damage to the cerebellum or its nervous pathways

athetosis Slow, writhing involuntary movements of the limbs and trunk caused by damage to the basal ganglia

autosome One of the pairs of chromosomes numbered 1–22; a chromosome other than an X or Y

autosomal recessive inheritance A trait whose expression is dependent upon the homozygous state, i.e. inheritance of the gene occurs from both parents

bioengineer A person who combines engineering and life sciences in the study of biological processes

biofeedback Devices developed to assist control of body function by giving a recognisable signal of a particular function, e.g. head control

biopsy Removal of a small piece of tissue for examination under the microscope in order to make a diagnosis

bulbar signs Neurological signs caused by damage to the cranial nerves arising in the medulla causing swallowing and speaking difficulties

choroid plexus The highly vascular tissue derived from ependymal cells projecting frond-like into the cavities of the cerebral ventricles and producing cerebrospinal fluid (CSF)

complement A protein which takes part in the reaction between antigens and antibodies

concussion A state of unconsciousness or impaired consciousness usually caused by mechanical force applied to the skull, not causing disruption of tissue and usually followed by amnesia

congenital A disorder present at birth, not necessarily inherited

contusion A bruise from a blow by a blunt instrument inflicted without breaking the integument (skin)

craniosynostosis Premature fusion of the cranial sutures

creatinine phosphokinase An enzyme normally present in muscle which leaks into the serum in muscular dystrophy and other muscle disorders

cystogram A radiograph of the bladder

detrusor The main muscle of the bladder

detrusor sphincter dyssynergia Failure of co-ordination between detrusor muscle contraction and sphincter relaxation during bladder emptying

diplegia Paralysis of symmetrical parts. *Spastic diplegia*: spastic paralysis more marked in the legs, but also affecting the arms

dysarthria Impaired articulation arising from neuromuscular conditions affecting muscle tone and the action of the muscles used in articulation

dysmelia An imperfect or faulty limb

dysmorphic A structural abnormality resulting from a primary defect in the morphogenesis of a structure: it can range from an altered fingerprint pattern to complex congenital heart disease

dysphasia Incomplete language function caused by impairment of the dominant cerebral hemisphere serving the special intellectual functions concerned with the use of language

dysphonia Impairment of voice production caused by damage to the larynx or the control of voice

dyspraxia Impairment of motor performance

dysraphism Imperfect closure of the neural tube causing a defect of the spinal cord or its surrounding structures

electro-encephalogram (EEG) A record of cerebral action currents

electrocochleography   A test of hearing which records the effect of stimulating the 8th cranial nerve (cochlear) and measuring the cortical EEG responses over the temporal lobe of the brain

electromyogram (EMG)   A record of the action currents of muscle

fasciculation   Visible spontaneous contractions of groups of muscle fibres – a feature seen in the tongue associated with atrophy in spinal muscular atrophy

fibrillation   Localised irregular twitching of individual muscle fibres also seen in spinal muscular atrophy

hallux valgus   Deviation of the great toe towards the others

hiatus hernia   Protrusion of the upper part of the stomach through the oesophageal opening of the diaphragm into the chest

hemiplegia   Paralysis of the arm and leg on the same side of the body caused by an upper motor neurone lesion

infarction   Death of tissue caused by interruption of end-arterial blood supply

intravenous pyelogram/urogram (IVP/IVU)   A radiograph of the kidneys, ureters and bladder produced by excretion of injected dye

kernicterus   Damage to the basal ganglia caused by high level of circulating bilirubin in jaundice of the newborn

kinaesthesia   The sense by which movements of the body, weight, position or resistance are perceived by stimulation of specific receptor muscles, tendons or joints

kyphosis   Backward curvature of the spine (hump-back)

laceration   A tear or rupture

lordosis   Forward curvature of the spine

lower motor neurone   The motor nerve supply arising from the anterior horn cell in the spinal cord and terminating in the skeletal muscle

malleolus   Part of a bone shaped like a hammer, e.g. at the ankle, medial and lateral malleoli

Milwaukee brace   A spinal brace designed to exert distractive force between the pelvis and the head, incorporating a neck extension which takes weight through the occiput and chin

myelogram   A radiograph which outlines the spinal cord and its connections by injection of a radio-opaque dye or air

neural tube   The tube of cells in embryological development from which the brain and spinal cord develop

neuropathic bladder   Abnormality of the bladder caused by abnormality of its nerve supply

nystagmus   Involuntary, rhythmic movements of the eyeballs

optic fundus   The view of the optic nerve and retina obtained through the pupil with an ophthalmoscope

orthosis A splint for a disabled part of the body

osteotomy Division of bone or removal of a section of bone

paraplegia Paralysis of the lower half of the body

paraxial hemimelia Absence of one forearm or leg bone; the name of the deficient bone is used as a prefix

pes cavus A foot with very high arches

phocomelia A short flipper-like arm or leg

phonological Concerning the voice

proprioception The awareness of position in space and relationship of one part of the body to the rest

prosthesis An artificial substitute for a part of the body which is absent or has been surgically removed

quadriceps The large muscle on the front of the thigh made up of four parts

quadriplegia Paralysis of all four limbs of equal severity

radial club hand deformity Absence of the radius with acute deviation of the hand to the radial side of the wrist

rehabilitation engineering The branch of bioengineering associated with treatment of the disabled

renogram Radioactive isotope studies to show individual kidney function

recessive trait A characteristic which only manifests itself in persons who are homozygous for the mutant gene concerned, i.e. who have received a double dose of the gene

scoliosis Lateral curvature of the spine

siblings Brothers and sisters who collectively form a sibship

subluxation Partial dislocation of a joint

sub-talar joint The joint below the ankle joint between the talus and the calcaneus

syndrome A recognisable collection of abnormal features or symptoms

syringomyelia Dilatation of the central canal of the spinal cord causing pressure on the neural tissue

talipes Club foot

talipes calcaneus Bent upwards at the heel, i.e. dorsiflexed

talipes equinus (horse-like deformity) On the toes, i.e. the foot is plantar flexed

talipes valgus Turned outwards

talipes varus Turned inwards

tenodesis Fixation of a joint by fixation of tendons passing about the joint

tenotomy Division of a tendon

transverse terminal hemimelia (peromelia)   Absence of the distal segment of a limb in its entirety

Trendelenburg lurch   A waddling gait due to paralysis of the gluteal muscles

trisomy   The presence of a triple dose of a single chromosome such as the three No. 21 chromosomes in trisomy-21 – Down's syndrome

upper motor neurone   A nerve cell originating in the motor area of the cerebral cortex and terminating in the motor nuclei of the cranial nerves or in the central grey column of the spinal cord

ureter   The duct conveying the urine from the renal pelvis to the bladder

urethra   The channel through which the urine is excreted from the bladder

urodynamic studies   Studies taken during bladder filling and emptying to demonstrate bladder function

vesical   Relating to the bladder

visually evoked responses (VER)   A test of vision measuring the cortical EEG response to a visual stimulus

X-linked inheritance   A specific pattern of inheritance associated with transmission of abnormality via the X chromosome. The disorder is present in males and transmitted by females

Chapter 1

The Baby and the Young Child with Physical Handicap

by G. T. McCARTHY MB, MRCP, DCH *with* P. CHARON MCSP,
M. CORK BA, SRN, HVTutCert, V. MOFFAT LCST,
J. O'HALLERON DipCOT and P. RUSSELL BA

The birth of a baby with obvious physical abnormality evokes very strong feelings in parents and the staff caring for it. As abnormality is usually not expected the staff present at birth may be very inexperienced at handling the situation: their reactions are remembered very clearly by the mother years after. It is, therefore, important to develop a clear policy of management in the delivery room and to prepare junior staff who will most often be immediately involved.

If the baby needs resuscitation after birth, this must be done speedily and effectively. If he then needs to be removed from the delivery room for further treatment, it is important that the mother should be allowed to see her baby at least and, if possible, to hold him. Paediatric help may need to be called immediately for fuller assessment of the baby's condition. Both parents should be seen together by an experienced paediatrician as soon as possible after birth, so that they can be given accurate information about the problems and prognosis. Obvious severe abnormalities, like cleft lip and palate or absence of limbs, will have an immediate impact on parents, while a baby with spina bifida may not appear physically very abnormal.

It has been shown by follow-up studies that in the period of immediate shock, only a small fraction of the information given to parents is retained. More than one session will be required for them to understand what they have been told, and the help of an experienced and understanding member of the nursing staff is important to reinforce and continue discussion. If the baby requires surgery after birth, as in spina bifida or abnormalities of the bowel, there is often the added trauma of separation of mother and baby as transfer to a paediatric surgical unit is necessary. There may also be a period of waiting for a paediatric surgeon to be available for consultation. Most surgical units cannot care for the mother in the immediate postpartum period, but she should be transferred as soon as possible to be with her baby.

Spina bifida may present the added problem of having to decide whether or not to treat the baby surgically. The decision needs to be made by a paediatrician, paediatric surgeon and the parents, and is one that need not necessarily be made on the first day of life. Experience has shown that treatment of all babies with spina bifida and meningomyelocele by surgical closure of the back lesion and treatment of hydrocephalus results in an increased survival of children with very severe mental and physical handicap, and this is discussed more fully in Chapter 4.

Families who have been through the experience of deciding against active surgical treatment in the neonatal period, and who expect their babies to die, find it very difficult to establish a relationship with the baby who survives and is treated later. They need more help in coming to terms with the change in the situation. Spina bifida presents a particularly complicated picture and requires a multidisciplinary approach with the paediatrician co-ordinating care.

In situations where the physical abnormality is a rare one, such as arthrogryposis or limb deficiency, there is often the added problem of lack of experience of the condition by the general paediatrician. It is important to refer parents early to centres used to dealing with the rarer abnormalities so that they can learn about the condition and perhaps meet older children with it. It is very useful to show them film or video of children at different ages with a similar problem. It is also important to give them help in management in the early stages if this is required.

The nurse has a unique part to play in the early days of a handicapped child's life, particularly in giving the mother confidence in handling her baby. The mother with a first baby is especially vulnerable as she has to learn about babies as well as the problems of handicap. Additional barriers of incubators, tubes and infusions may make the bonding process more of a problem. The good nurse never forgets the mother and indeed thinks of mother and baby as one, encouraging her contact with the baby, feeding him, handling him as much as possible or, at first, just touching him in the incubator if that is all that is possible.

Nursing the sick neonate is becoming more technological, but is still dependent on the skill and observation of the nursing staff. Establishing feeding and sleep patterns as the baby recovers from surgery is important. The nurse also has to show parents how to care for anaesthetic skin, manage the neuropathic bladder and handle the baby with structural abnormalities.

The baby who presents with motor delay during the first or second year is most likely to be mentally handicapped. Cerebral palsy also presents in this way, and there is often a history of perinatal problems such as asphyxia, neonatal fits or jaundice, and usually these babies are followed up in a baby clinic so that help can be given as soon as the diagnosis becomes clear. The health visitor will often be the person who diagnoses the developmental delay in babies who present later in the first year. Referral should be made to the district assessment centre so that the baby can be fully assessed and management instituted. Professional intervention at an early age helps to support the family and gives the mother confidence in handling her baby. Local resources can also be brought into play at an early stage.

PAEDIATRIC DEVELOPMENTAL ASSESSMENT CENTRES

Centres vary in the composition of staff and in the way in which they relate to the local services. They may be community or hospital based, and directed by a paediatrician or a senior clinical medical officer. It is helpful if the assessment centre is closely linked with a children's hospital or department as this facilitates the exchange of information on children, medical investigations and also occasional hospital admission for surgery or acute illness. The staff may include nurses and nursery nurses, physiotherapists, occupational therapists and speech therapists, and social workers as well as doctors. A teacher may also be involved or linked with the educational services in a peripatetic role. It is also of vital importance to have a close link with the community medical services and the education department to ensure that everyone works together to provide optimum management.

Regional assessment centres provide specialist help with problems, and referrals are made from district centres, or direct from paediatricians or general practitioners (GPs). There may be a peripatetic role, with a developmental paediatrician visiting centres in the region.

DIAGNOSIS AND DEVELOPMENTAL ASSESSMENT

Dr Mary Sheridan (1973) defined a handicapped child as one who suffers from any continuing disability of the body, intellect or personality which is likely to interfere with his normal growth and development or capacity to learn.

The skill of carrying out a full paediatric, neurological and developmental examination can only be acquired with practice, and the initial examination may not include a full developmental profile although this is usually possible in babies and younger children. Analysis of the examination is important as neurological problems may impair developmental levels, and it is important to record findings and prognosis at each stage of development.

When a baby presents to the paediatrician it is important to determine:

1. If he or she is handicapped.
2. A cause for the handicap and, associated with this, genetic counselling.
3. A programme of management and continuing assessment.

A full neurological and paediatric examination should be carried out and a developmental assessment undertaken. Medical investigations should be done early with the aim of making a diagnosis if possible (Table 1).

NEUROLOGICAL AND DEVELOPMENTAL EXAMINATION

Before understanding variation from normal, it is vital to be aware of normal developmental sequences. It is not possible to give a full outline here, but the Stycar sequences, developed by Dr Mary Sheridan (1973), give a good working knowledge. These stepping-stones of normal development from one month to five years, cover the following areas:

1. Posture and large movements
2. Vision and fine manipulation
3. Hearing, speech and language
4. Social behaviour and play.

It is is important to take a family history as there may be evidence of a similar pattern of development in siblings or parents.

Posture and large movements

The examination of the baby normally starts with observation in the mother's arms. The posture of head and trunk and limbs is important, the level of alertness and social interaction can also be observed. Allow the baby time to get used to a new environment before a direct approach is made. Interesting toys help to distract attention and allow observation of hand function. The near vision test can also be done at this stage, using a Smartie or raisin and a 1mm 'hundred-and-

TABLE 1 Causes of physical handicap, associated problems, genetic implications and useful investigations

Cause	Abnormalities: complications	Leading to	Investigations
Neural tube defects i.e. failure of fusion of neural tube	Spina bifida: meningocele encephalocele meningomyelocele	Hydrocephalus Paralysis Loss of sensation Incontinence of urine / faeces	Skull ⎱radiographs Spine ⎰ IVP; cystogram Urodynamic studies CT brain scan *or* ultrasound scan of brain
	Spina bifida occulta	Weakness of legs Anaesthesia Bladder problems	Spinal radiographs Myelogram IVP; cystogram Urodynamic studies
Infection in utero 1. Virus infections, e.g. rubella, cytomegalovirus	Hepatosplenomegaly; purpura; pneumonia	Bleeding tendency	Virus antibody titres – baby and mother (Baby IgM antibody = intrauterine infection) Virus grown from urine or throat swab
	Microcephaly	Mental handicap Cerebral palsy	CT brain scan – periventricular lucency calcification
	8th cranial nerve damage	Sensorineural deafness (50%)	Radiograph bones–neonatal to 6 / 12 to demonstrate demineralisation of lower femur
	Cataract; retinopathy	Visual handicap (30%)	
	Congenital heart disease (CHD)	Persistent ductus arteriosus (PDA) 50%; pulmonary stenosis; ventricular septal defect (VSD); atrial septal defect (ASD)	Chest radiograph; ECG; echocardiogram; cardiac catheter
2. Protozoal organisms e.g. toxoplasmosis	Microcephaly Hydrocephalus Choroidoretinitis	Mental handicap Cerebral palsy; epilepsy Visual handicap	Complement fixation test Sabin-Feldman test – requires living protozoa X-ray skull – calcification CT scan – periventricular calcification
3. Other viruses	Anterior horn cell damage	Arthrogryposis	Antibody titres – mother / baby

TABLE 1 (*cont.*) Causes of physical handicap, associated problems, genetic implications and useful investigations

Cause	Abnormalities: complications	Leading to	Investigations
Drugs	*Thalidomide*: limb deficiency; deafness; congenital heart disease (CHD) *Phenytoin*: limb anomalies		
Perinatal insults Hypoxia Hypoglycaemia Intrauterine growth retardation Haemorrhage: ante or intrapartum	Microcephaly Diffuse cerebral damage	Cerebral palsy Visual handicap Deafness Epilepsy Mental handicap	Skull radiograph CT brain scan Full examination of optic fundi
Jaundice (hyperbilirubinaemia)	Athetoid cerebral palsy High tone deafness		Audiological investigations Electrocochleography in some cases
Prematurity **Traumatic delivery**, e.g. Breech delivery High forceps Multiple birth Cephalo-pelvic disproportion	Hypoxia; jaundice; haemorrhage; hypoglycaemia	Cerebral palsy (especially spastic diplegia) Epilepsy Mental handicap Visual handicap Deafness	CT scan Electro-encephalogram (EEG) Visual evoked responses (VER) Electroretinogram (ERG) Audiological assessment Electrocochleography in some cases
Genetic syndromes	Typical collection of anomalies Upper limb abnormalities Congenital heart disease (CHD) Radial club hand; thrombocytopenia Lobster claw	e.g. Down's syndrome Turner's syndrome X-linked mental retardation Holt-Oram syndrome Fanconi's syndrome Hand anomaly	Chromosome analysis: Trisomy 21 XO Fragile site on X chromosome Chest radiograph; ECG Full blood cell count; radiograph of arms Family history – 3 generations
Metabolic disorders	e.g. Lesch-Nyhan syndrome	Hypotonia: severe athetoid cerebral palsy Self-mutilation	Urine: uric acid / creatinine raised Hypoxanthine guanine phosphoribosyl transaminase (HGPRT) enzyme absent in red blood cells; X-linked Female carriers detected using hair

Cause	Abnormalities: complications	Leading to	Investigations
	Other metabolic disorders	Hypotonia: severe developmental delay epilepsy	Amino-acids in plasma and urine Organic acids in plasma and urine Mucopolysaccharides in plasma and urine
Anterior horn cell disorders	1. Anterior horn cell degeneration (Werdnig Hoffman disease); acute (Autosomal recessive)	Progressive muscle weakness before 6 months Areflexia; fibrillation; fasciculation of tongue. Death before 2	Electromyography (EMG) Creatinine phosphokinase (CPK) (usually normal) Muscle biopsy
	2. Intermediate form (Autosomal recessive)	Presents after 6 months. May sit and stand with calipers. Death, late teens / early 20s	Creatinine phosphokinase (CPK) usually normal may be slightly raised Electromyography (EMG) Muscle biopsy
	3. Late onset (Kugelberg Welander disease) (Autosomal recessive)	Usually ambulant, but weak; scoliosis may develop	Creatinine phosphokinase (CPK) usually normal may be slightly raised Electromyography (EMG) Muscle biopsy
Muscular dystrophy	Congenital	Early weakness – may be severe	Electromyography (EMG) Muscle biopsy Creatinine phosphokinase (CPK) raised
	Duchenne	X-linked: boys, present at 2½+ years	Creatinine phosphokinase (CPK) very high Muscle biopsy *Carriers* detected by CPKx3 raised in 70% Serial EMG
Skeletal disorders	Fragile bones Short stature	Fractures Typical features	Radiographs: skeletal survey Family history survey

thousand'; also measurement of the maximum head circumference.

The mother and baby can then move to the physiotherapy mat on the floor. At this stage, it is important to remove most of the baby's clothes in order to see full movement of the limbs and trunk. Assessment of head control from supine to sitting, prone function, balance reactions, parachute reactions and so on, can then follow and, where appropriate, neonatal reflexes can be elicited. Assessment of tone in the limbs, deep tendon reflexes and examination of hip abduction (after removing the napkin), observation of any joint contractures and examination of the spine can also be carried out. Some of this may need to be done with the mother holding the baby on her knees.

At the end of the examination a developmental level for motor abilities should be recorded.

Patterns of motor development are interesting, 90 per cent of children develop rapidly in prone, crawl and then walk. Nine per cent of children dislike being in prone, are sitters and shuffle on their bottoms, often walking later than the crawlers. One per cent of children roll, and stand and walk without crawling or shuffling.

GROSS MOTOR DEVELOPMENT IN PHYSICALLY HANDICAPPED CHILDREN
In the normal baby the smooth acquisition of motor function occurs rapidly in the first two years of life. Motor handicap may be caused by central brain damage, or by damage to the nervous system at spinal cord, anterior horn cell or lower motor neurone level. The muscles may be primarily affected and weak in muscle disorders, or the joints stiff and muscles weak in arthrogryposis.

Motor problems may be caused by absence of part or all of a limb, or by abnormalities of the skeleton causing deformity or abnormally short limbs, e.g. in achondroplasia.

Although each condition will need an individual approach, an understanding of normal development and intervention at an appropriate level is important, and the guidance of parents to help their children is central to any management programme. A more detailed discussion occurs in specific chapters.

Vision

Vision should be tested before hearing in babies and handicapped children. It is, of course, important to diagnose visual handicap in a child who has other problems, and the detection of a squint is also important as management can be instituted early and amblyopia prevented. It is important to refer babies with squints early for ophthalmological opinion and management. It is vital to examine the optic fundi and lens adequately, and it may be necessary to sedate a child and dilate the pupils sufficiently to obtain a good view of the fundi.

EXAMINATION OF VISION IN THE FIRST FEW YEARS OF LIFE

The Stycar fixed balls developed by Dr Mary Sheridan and Dr Dorothy Egan allow testing of vision from 6 months to $2\frac{1}{2}$ years. Each ball is the limb width of a Snellen letter and has the following Snellen equivalents: $\frac{3}{4}''$–6/60, $\frac{1}{2}''$–6/36, $\frac{3}{8}''$–6/24, $\frac{1}{4}''$–6/18, $\frac{3}{16}''$–6/12 and $\frac{1}{8}''$–6/9.

In the young child and baby, vision in each eye should be tested by occlusion, presenting the fixed balls at 10 feet under 1 year and, if possible, 20 feet over a year. After the age of 18 months it can be very difficult to hold attention. By $2\frac{1}{2}$ years children are usually able to match five letters, and the Sheridan Gardiner Single Letter Test can usually be carried out at 10 feet. Also, a near test card to the end. Occlusion of the eyes is exceedingly difficult between 18 months and $2\frac{1}{2}$ years, but should be attempted. A Catford Nystagmus Drum is sometimes helpful in obtaining a near visual acuity in small children.

Vision testing may be difficult in physically handicapped children with poor head and hand control. Solid plastic letters which can be separated for eye pointing are helpful. The use of electrodiagnostic tests – the electroretinogram (ERG) and visually evoked responses (VER) can sometimes help to demonstrate intact visual pathways when clinical assessment is inconclusive.

Manipulation

Precise hand function is unique to human development. In the normal baby the development of hand function correlates most closely with future intellectual development. In the neurologically damaged baby, however, it may give misleading information.

In the normal baby the involuntary palmar grasp is present from birth to about 10–12 weeks. The hand becomes more relaxed as the baby matures, and should be open and ready for voluntary grasp by 12 weeks when he will hold an object placed in the hand. At 16 weeks his hands come together as he plays, and between 11 and 20 weeks the baby constantly looks at his hands, turning them in front of the face and clasping them together. Persistence of 'hand regard' occurs in mentally handicapped children.

Before achieving grasp, the baby 'reaches with his eyes' and makes generalised anticipatory movements of the whole body and arms. Active grasp occurs between 4 and 5 months, and transferring an object from one hand to the other by about 6 months. At first the baby grasps with the whole hand, using a raking movement with all the fingers. Later a radial grasp develops, and finally he approaches objects with the index finger and opposes finger and thumb in a pincer grasp. The mature pincer grasp is usually achieved by 40 weeks. As the baby's hand function matures, his ability to play and therefore explore and learn increases.

Releasing objects from the hand occurs between 9 and 10 months, but casting – that is deliberately throwing objects to the floor, usually occurs between 12 and 15 months. By 13–15 months the baby is able to hold two cubes in one hand and build a tower of two one-inch cubes. Hand dominance does not develop until the second year of life.

The baby with cerebral palsy may have severe manipulatory difficulty. The palmar grasp reflex may persist, and active grasp and release may be difficult or impossible. The posture of the hand approaching a toy should be noted, and any persistent disregard of one hand, or asymmetry in approach. In movement disorders hand function may be severely impaired or impossible even in the presence of normal intelligence.

Hearing

It is important to test hearing in any handicapped child, but the presence of motor or visual problems or developmental delay may make the testing difficult. For example, a baby with cerebral palsy may not be able to turn his head to sound or produce normal babbling sounds.

TESTING HEARING – THE STYCAR DISTRACTION TEST
The baby sits on the mother's lap facing forward and is distracted by the showing of a toy for a few seconds. Sounds are presented at the level of the ear, initially at 18 inches and then 3 feet, the sounds include a high frequency rattle, cup and spoon and voiced S and O sounds and the baby's name. Localisation of sound below the ear usually occurs between 7 and 8 months. By 1 year the baby is able to localise sounds above and below the ear.

Older children can be tested using speech or pure tone audiometry, and later an audiogram can be done using head-phones.

ELECTRICAL TESTS OF HEARING
In some children it may be impossible to obtain a response to clinical tests, and electrical testing may be carried out to demonstrate the auditory pathways. The post-auricular myogenic responses are

brainstem evoked responses, the pathway tested passing through the brainstem. Electrocochleography involves insertion of a needle electrode through the ear drum under general anaesthesia and the measurement of cortical response by an EEG electrode over the temporal lobe. These tests only demonstrate the pathways of hearing, and give no indication of the way the hearing is used.

Speech development

The development of speech and language normally go hand in hand, but deviations in rate of speech development are common.

OUTLINE OF PHONOLOGICAL DEVELOPMENT

0–3 months	Cries and gurgles
3 months–1 year	Babbling, i.e. consonant and vowel and reduplication, e.g. bababa, nanana, etc
9 months–1½ years	First words – using consonants b, p, t, d, m, n, k, g, and open vowels
1½–2½ years	Consolidation of above consonants and all vowels
	Beginnings of 'harder' consonants – h, f, v, s, z, sh, w, y, l, th, ch, j, r
2½–3½ years	Consolidation of 'harder' consonants
2½–5 years	Development of consonant clusters, e.g. cr, pl, st, scr, etc

Source: Byers Brown and Beveridge, 1979

The normal development of language

It is necessary to have a basic knowledge of the normal acquisition of language in order to determine the extent of language delay or deviation. The knowledge of these levels of language will also act as a tool in planning programmes of treatment.

A. Comprehension of language begins with the development of early concept formation. Concepts are perceptions which have been generalised and classified. The child's first experiences occur as awareness of stimuli or sensations from the environment. He then learns to discriminate these stimuli so that they become meaningful, e.g. the sound of a spoon in a cup means drink.

B. Pre-verbal comprehension as described by Reynell (1977):
   (i) *Awareness of the permanence of objects*: by 9 months the child will search for an object that is hidden from him.

    (ii) *Situational understanding*: between 8–12 months the child understands familiar phrases as part of a sequence of events without the individual words having meaning.

    (iii) *Object recognition*: at 12 months the child demonstrates object recognition. He uses objects appropriately, i.e. drinks from a cup, brushes his hair with a brush.

    (iv) *Large doll-play*: from 14–15 months symbolic understanding develops with an understanding of representational objects, i.e. Wendy House material play.

    (v) *Small doll-play*: by 18–21 months the child will demonstrate the use of miniature toys, i.e. doll's house furniture and dolls.

    (vi) *Pictures*: between 18–24 months the child understands two-dimensional representations. The child can match object to pictures.

    (vii) *Matching symbol to symbol*: by 2–2½ years most children can match small toys to pictures.

C. Development of verbal comprehension

    (i) *Object recognition*: the child selects an object in response to naming.

    (ii) *Symbolic representation*: the child selects a picture or toy in response to naming.

    (iii) *Relating two named objects*: e.g. 'put the spoon in the cup'. This usually occurs between 2 and 2½ years.

    (iv) *Selecting objects by function*: e.g. which one do we go to sleep in? This stage is reached by most children at 2½ years.

    (v) *Abstract concepts* of size, colour, prepositions and negatives can usually be followed by children aged 3–4 years.

    (vi) *Recognition* of body parts and general information such as name, age, sex can also be used in determining the development of comprehension.

Social behaviour and play and normal emotional development

The area of social behaviour and play is often the most difficult to assess in babies and children with severe physical handicap, and depends on parental attitude and on the child's ability to explore his environment and be independent in it. Many handicapped children are over-dependent emotionally on their mothers, and their emotional immaturity persists into childhood and puberty. They and their parents need to be helped to develop independence and maturity in spite of severe handicap, as emotional problems and behaviour disturbance may develop.

THE ROLE OF THE HEALTH VISITOR

As a health professional working in the community, the health visitor has an established role in visiting families in their own homes. She may thus be seen as more socially acceptable by the family with a handicapped child because they do not feel they are being singled out for her visits. Health visitors are now generally working as members of a primary health care team, and take their case load from the general practitioner's list. They have a knowledge of services within their local community and should therefore be able to provide valuable information about local support available for the family, such as parent self-help groups, playgroups, toy libraries and the general health, social and educational services in the area.

Ideally, the health visitor's initial involvement with the family should be in the ante-natal period. This will allow a relationship to be established with the parents and for some insight to be gained into the family atmosphere before it has been affected by the trauma of the birth of a handicapped child.

If the handicap is diagnosed at birth, then a common reaction is one of grief at the loss of a 'normal' child (Gath, 1982; Darling, 1979). The parents may go through many of the stages associated with bereavement. These are outlined by Parkes (1975) and include shock and numbness, denial, anxiety and restlessness, searching, anger and guilt.

When visiting the family following the birth of a handicapped child, the health visitor must be prepared for the parents' grief reactions and accept that some of their anger and hostility may be directed towards the health professionals. In the past parents have been critical of health visitors for not responding appropriately to these normal grief reactions and withdrawing from the situation or keeping discussions at a superficial level, thereby not allowing parents to work through their grief (Ballard, 1976; Hannam, 1975). There is now an increasing emphasis on the health visitor's counselling role in relation to families with a handicapped child, and hopefully they will be able to meet the needs of parents more effectively.

If the handicap is not diagnosed at birth then the health visitor may be one of the first people the parents turn to if they are worried about their child's progress. Sheridan (1973) has stressed the need for health professionals to pay attention to any anxieties the parents may have – they are the ones in constant contact with the child, and if they are concerned about his development then he should be assessed. Increasingly, health visitors are being involved in programmes of developmental surveillance. They are therefore better equipped to respond promptly to any concern expressed by the parents. Even if the parents are not aware of any problems, the health visitor may detect developmental delay when carrying out routine developmental surveillance of the child. In either situation the health visitor has a responsibility to ensure that the child then has a full developmental assessment. The family will need continuing support from the health visitor while the child is undergoing tests, and when the diagnosis is made their reactions may be very similar to those of the parents whose child's handicap is apparent at birth.

In addition to the need to express their feelings, the family will want advice and guidance on the care and management of the child. The state of shock which follows the initial diagnosis may well result in the parents' taking in very little of what is said to them about the extent of the handicap, prognosis and future care needs. The need to go over the implications of the handicap and reinforce information given is well recognised. It is when parents return home with the child and assume full responsibility for his care that many questions are raised relating to day-to-day management. The parents face the same problems of adjustment to new roles and responsibilities as all parents but, for them, problems may be exacerbated by feelings of inadequacy, fear of handling their handicapped child and hopelessness about their child's future.

The health visitor should be able to provide support and guidance for them during this critical period of adjustment. As a visitor in the home, she is able to be flexible both about the amount of time she spends with the family and the frequency of her visits. In the familiarity of their own home the parents may be more relaxed and feel more confident about discussing the realities of the problems they face. The health visitor may be able to offer practical advice on coping with everyday problems, such as feeding difficulties, the crying baby, and disrupted sleep patterns. Her knowledge of the handicapping condition may need to be augmented and advice sought.

If the health visitor's contribution to the care of the family with a handicapped child is to be fully effective, it is essential she has good liaison with the other professionals working with the family. It is often helpful if she can accompany the family on some of their visits to the hospital or assessment centre. This will allow her to hear the advice and guidance given and she can then reinforce this in her home visits. She can also help the family prepare themselves for these visits by drawing up with them a list of issues they wish to discuss; often, when faced with the stress of a hospital visit, parents forget many of the things they intended to ask.

Recently some health authorities have started to train health visitors as home advisors for the Portage Home Intervention programme. This programme is designed to teach parents how to help their child to develop specific skills. It involves an assessment of the child's present level of ability and then, in consultation with the parents, specific teaching targets are decided upon. These targets are broken down into small steps and a learning goal is set for each week. The Portage home advisor demonstrates how to teach the child the activity and then observes while the parent practises teaching the child. An activity chart is left with the family, outlining the particular skill that is being developed, the manner in which it should be carried out and the number of times the activity should be done in one day. The chart also has space on which to record the child's progress over the week. The home advisor visits a week later to assess how the child has progressed with the activity, and, if it has been mastered successfully, will introduce a new learning goal. Where health visitors have been involved with the programme, they have found it increases the effectiveness of their work (Mansell, 1980).

The parents' need for a life of their own should be acknowledged and, if possible, the health visitor should try to find ways of providing short-term relief for the family. Liaison with social services is important here. In some areas it is possible to arrange a short-term admission to a hospital or residential unit. Alternatively it may be possible to arrange for foster parents to care for the child for the occasional weekend or while the parents and other children have a short holiday. Even arranging for a baby-sitter so that parents can have an evening out on their own can be invaluable in maintaining the parents' morale and ability to cope.

The extent to which the health visitors provide support for families with handicapped children is variable. In many instances their involvement with the family ceases once the child starts school, particularly if he goes to a residential school. Warnock (1978) emphasises the importance of the health visitor in providing a link between the home and the school, and with the introduction of the 1981 Education Act, health visitors may have an increasing involvement with the older child and his family.

The role of the health visitor can be very wide ranging. It encompasses information for the family about the handicapping condition, the services available, advice on the care and management of the child and support for the family through periods of stress. She is also concerned with the physical, social and emotional health needs of all family members.

The specialist health visitor

The need for a health visitor with special expertise in relation to the handicapped has been recognised. The emphasis is on the specialist being a resource person for the family health visitor (Twinn, 1981). She may be involved in joint visits to the family, or work intensely with them during a crisis period. However, it is the family health visitor who gives continuing long-term support.

In some health authorities there are specialist health visitors based in the children's hospital or in residential units or schools for the handicapped. These health visitors provide an invaluable link between the hospital or school and the child's home. They are readily available to discuss the special needs of the child with the family health visitor, and because of their expertise in the care and management of the handicapped child, can offer much practical advice.

THE ROLE OF THE PHYSIOTHERAPIST

The physiotherapist plays an important role in the management of the physically handicapped child and may often be the person to whom the mother confides some of her innermost feelings. The aim of the physiotherapist should be to help the parents to understand the child's physical needs and to handle him in an appropriate way. It is most important that the therapist does not take over the baby, but gives the mother confidence to handle the baby correctly as she is the one who will be most closely involved in his development. It is helpful to ask the mother to go through her daily routine with the baby, and to work out times that she would be handling him, playing with him and stimulating him. She can then work into this routine some of the planned practice movements and also, in the case of the immobile child, plan to change posture.

At the beginning the physiotherapist must remember that the family has suddenly been introduced to an alien medical situation. The parents need to be welcomed and given confidence and to have enough time for their questions to be answered. They need encouragement in learning different ways of handling, and awareness of opportunities. They are anxious to know what they can do to help, but we must remember that any analysis of movement is something quite new, as movement is automatic for most of us. It may be useful to demonstrate on the parent, for example:

Fig. 1/1

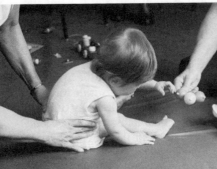

Fig. 1/2

Fig. 1/3

Fig. 1/4

1. How to assist a baby from the supine to sitting with one hand held in a diagonal direction to enable the child to place and push up with the free arm (Figs. 1/1 and 1/2).
2. How to get into the crawling position on hands and knees, either from prone or from sitting, the latter involving trunk rotation, hand placing, accommodation of legs as the weight is transferred from both hips to one, and finally to an equal distribution (between the shoulders and wrists and the hips and knees) with the appropriate head and trunk righting (Figs. 1/3 and 1/4).

It can bring greater emphasis to parents to ask them to stop and hold any one part of the sequence. This helps to bring a more meaningful feeling of movement which contrasts with watching the therapist.

The therapist has to learn the best way of helping each particular parent.

In developing the child's potential, it is important to be aware of situations that influence the alteration in tone, posture and performance so that suitable handling can be implemented, for example, an increased extensor pattern in a baby can be minimised and controlled at its very first signs by flexing the baby, by bringing the body to a right angle or more to the hips with counter-pressure on the front of the chest. Alternatively the baby can be sat with hips well flexed to the right angle or more by flexing the thighs (see Chapter 6).

Any treatment programme must take into account normal development and its milestone. A mother with a severely multiply-handicapped child, not having had physiotherapy counselling, may still be handling the child as a baby when it is 2 years old. The child needs to be treated on the day's findings, not necessarily repeating treatment done on the previous visit. The picture today could open up a different aspect of the developmental approach, and it is for the therapist to keep her horizons broad, and to view the child as a whole. The parents should leave a treatment session with the knowledge of a certain number of things to practise until the next visit. These can be written down if required, and the therapist should record what she has planned so that at the next session she can refer to what she has asked of the parent. Treatment should ideally be begun within the first weeks or as soon as any diagnosis is made. Valuable learning time can be lost with the 'wait and see' philosophy. Poor habit patterns become established, and the baby can be insecure and the parents anxious about handling difficulties. With any treatment technique it is essential to have experience of natural development, and the understanding of different avenues of treatment provides the appropriate selection. Many techniques and systems have been developed over the years and post-registration training is essential to enlarge the physiotherapy training (see p. 49).

THE ROLE OF THE OCCUPATIONAL THERAPIST

The occupational therapist (OT) should be introduced to the family as early as possible and must be aware of the emotional and physical pressures, as her early contacts are often made within the home. Treatment must always involve the parents, the needs of the child coming first, but always within the context of the family lifestyle and home. Any techniques and equipment must be discussed with parents and demonstrated so that they can continue their use effectively until the next session. There are two main aspects to the occupational therapy role: assessment and daily management.

The normal stages of development must be borne in mind and

activities chosen with a definite and realistic aim and broken down into small stages so that some success is ensured in the near future. Throughout her contact with the family, both at home and within the hospital, the OT is continually assessing the capabilities of the handicapped child, but it is even more important for her to provide practical and realistic solutions to the problems of his day-to-day management. This will not only make it easier for the family to cope but will ensure that the child reaches the maximum level of development and independence in activities ranging from feeding himself to dressing, bathing, toileting, purposeful play and, therefore, learning. In conjunction with other professionals and family, an appropriate daily routine should be developed as early as possible.

Seating

The first essential is for the child to be maintained in a position which prevents undesirable and incorrect patterns of movement and to allow him to use his present range of movement and motor control, thereby encouraging the next stage of development. The following offer some basic rules of seating for the baby and young child:
1. Observe and measure the child accurately so that the chair supports and fits where it should.
2. Select a variety of suitable positions for play, feeding and dressing, thereby preventing the child from remaining in one position for most of the day.
3. Provide stability using foot-rests, grip-bars, foam padding and trays.
4. Provide a tray at the correct height. For example, a high tray will not only prevent the child from leaning forward, but will give his arms stability while he feeds or plays.
5. Re-assess so that the child can progress to the next stage, for example from recliner chair or car seat type to corner seat to adapted high chair, the ultimate aims being to sit in as normal a chair as possible.
6. Suggest suitable positions on the mother's knee and on the floor by using wedges and general household seating.
Figure 1/5 illustrates a selection of chairs.

Fig. 1/5 A selection of chairs. *Top row* (L–R) Car seat with harness; Canvas corner seat; Action chair; *Middle row* (L–R) Tripp Trapp chair – adjustable seat and foot rest; Peto chair; Mountain chair; *Bottom row* (L–R) Watford potty chair; Sit-astride engine; Nursery chair with tray

Play

Play is essential for child development: it is through play that he learns.

Some basic interventions:

1. Select positions and seating, as described above.
2. Provide a play tray. Example: using non-slip surfaces, a border to prevent toys falling off, grip bars to stabilise one hand, while the other practises reaching, grasping and releasing, and so on.
3. Advise and introduce toys suitable for a child's age, stage of development and disability, but have a definite aim in mind.
4. Adapt or make special toys. Example: enlarging knobs, using magnetic boards, texture books, etc.
5. Advise parents on play, including the importance of limiting the number of toys at any one time to aid concentration and performance.

Daily living activities

Feeding: Management of feeding is discussed fully in Chapters 6 and 21. Once again, the importance of a good position on mother's knee, then in his own chair should be emphasised. Items of equipment that may be useful include shallow horn or rigid plastic spoons, two-handled beakers with cut-out rim, padded or adapted spoons, non-slip mats and suction bowls.

Dressing: The occupational therapist should advise on suitable clothes, particularly the advantages of loose all-in-one clothing, that include wide openings and few but easily accessible fastenings. Dressing is the time when the child can be taught the names of the different parts of his body and articles of clothing. Techniques and positions for dressing should be advised according to the disability.

Bathing: This is the time when the baby or young child is at his most relaxed, the water partially supporting the limbs, so that any aid must not prevent this by being too restrictive, but provide enough support for safety and give the parents free hands for washing and playing. When transferred to the big bath, a non-slip mat and some head support may be necessary, e.g. a dense foam head-rest, inflatable rings or special bath seats.

Toileting.
See Chapter 21 for full details of aids.

Throughout all the activities mentioned, the OT and the parents must encourage the child to participate to an ever-increasing degree so that he will achieve some measure of independence.

THE ROLE OF THE SPEECH THERAPIST

It is important that a child is referred early for speech therapy help as soon as there is evidence of problems. Parents are often concentrating on motor development and only later recognise the child's speech delay. Early language stimulation, correct breathing postures and feeding patterns should be stressed.

The physically handicapped child is prone to the normal incidence of speech and language disorders, whether it be a delay or a specific disorder as well as problems related to his disability. The level of language development will follow the normal pattern of development, but levels are often delayed as the physically handicapped child takes longer to acquire other milestones. For example, there is a period, at approximately 15 months which coincides with learning to walk, when the normal child will make little or no progress in speech and language development.

Early language stimulation experiences must be brought to the child if he is unable to move to explore his environment or even his own body in the same way as other children. He often lacks normal contact with other children, and he lacks stimulation when people stop talking to him because he is unable to respond.

The parents should be encouraged to change the child's position so that sometimes he is upright and sometimes on the floor, to give him opportunity to suck his fingers and mouth objects, to play simple body-image games which give rise to visual, tactile and kinaesthetic sensations, e.g. pat-a-cake, round and round the garden. Other important areas which help the child to develop are:

1. *Motivation*: do not anticipate the child's needs; give him choices to create in him a desire to communicate.
2. *Imitation*: in order to copy speech sounds and patterns the child first needs to imitate gross movements, e.g. copying actions in rhymes, waving bye-bye.
3. *Vocalisation*: to stimulate phonation by responding to the child's efforts to vocalise. Phonation is easiest when the child is relaxed or moving, so change of posture is again encouraged.
4. *Imagination*: teach the child to play imaginatively, e.g. hiding objects, feeding teddy, making a cup of tea.
5. *Develop concept formation*: encourage the child to listen to and

discriminate between familiar sounds, e.g. telephone, dog, television.

6. *Object recognition*: teach vocabulary relating to everyday objects and people; encourage the child to respond to the question: Where is?; point to parts of the body of the child, mother or doll; introduce action words, e.g. eating, jumping; put the thoughts of the child into words.

7. *Picture recognition*: build up a scrapbook with the child. This can act as a link between therapist and home.

These suggested programmes can be carried out by the parent within the daily routines of feeding, dressing, toileting and bathing.

Language disorders and their management

The aims of treatment are to:

(a) develop language concepts

(b) develop awareness of the social function of language

(c) improve verbal comprehension

(d) facilitate verbal expression

(e) if speech fails to develop consider use of an augmentative form of communication.

The earlier a programme of language stimulation is started, the more effective it is likely to be. Language programmes can be used with the child and parents at home, or in a group situation, and later in the classroom.

Articulation disorders and their management

The aims of treatment are to:

(a) Improve breathing patterns

(b) Encourage vocalisation

(c) Help with subsequent babbling

(d) Practise making facial expressions by moving facial muscles to link with emotion

(e) Help with correct feeding patterns to develop sucking, chewing and mature swallowing (see Chapter 6)

(f) Train auditory skills of memory, discrimination and sequencing

(g) Train oral sensory motor skills, e.g. tongue-tip exercises

(h) Associate sounds in words, phrases and sentences

(i) Reinforce and consolidate skills both at home and in the classroom.

SOCIAL WORK INVOLVEMENT

Reactions to the birth of a handicapped child

It is not by accident that pregnant women are said to be 'expectant'. They are expectant of a normal healthy baby who will fulfil at least some of their hopes for future family life. If the child is handicapped, there may be a great gulf between the dream and the reality. Many parents cannot handle the initial trauma and may go through a period of aggressive and irrational behaviour. Cliff Cunningham working from the Hester Adrian Research Centre described this shock reaction as a 'model of psychic crisis at the disclosure of handicap'. He noted that if parents did not get adequate professional support at this critical period, the shock reaction could be perpetuated through many months or even years. However, the provision of appropriate information, counselling and active involvement in care of the child would lead to 'adaption and orientation'.

Recent developments in services, including home teaching and visiting programmes and family support centres have demonstrated how these early needs may be met (Cunningham and Sloper, 1980; Pugh, 1981). The availability of services is also important since many families may conceal distress and ambivalence beneath an appearance of competence. The concept of parents as partners is not necessarily easy to implement. The growth of home-teaching programmes has clearly shown how parents can learn to monitor their child's development, to observe and assess and select and present the child with appropriate tasks. Equally, home-visiting programmes have enabled professionals to have an ongoing relationship with a family and to understand the particular constraints under which parents may have to work. It is hoped that home-based services will also involve fathers and siblings, as well as other members of the extended family who may be directly involved with the handicapped child.

Family relationships

Because services for children are often fragmented, it is possible for professionals to be unaware of pressures within the family and of the often differing expectations of members of the family. In a survey for the Welsh National School of Medicine, Kew (1975) found that the divorce rate among parents of severely handicapped spina bifida children was 10 times greater than the national average if the child lived and three times greater if the child died. Leiderman (1974) made similar observations with regard to an increase in the rate of divorce and separation after the birth of a baby nursed in a special care unit. In 1978 Gath's investigation of 104 families with Down's syndrome children did not find any major precipitation of divorce or separation, but did note that 33 per cent of the mothers in her survey suffered from clinical depression in the first 18 months.

Similarly there was some evidence that parents were more depressed a year after the birth of their handicapped child, which could have had some correlation with the drop-off of support services and home visits as the children reached their first birthdays. The Gath survey confirmed other evidence – that fathers also showed signs of considerable stress and that they often lacked the social network which was available for mothers in the community. All studies clearly demonstrated the importance of including fathers in the care of their children and in recognising depression and anxiety before starting programmes with the child. It should perhaps be noted that some parents, who have been late in accepting the permanence of a handicap, may still cherish hopes of a 'cure' and that final acceptance (with accompanying depression) may occur many months after the child's birth. Equally, the availability of a multidisciplinary service is only helpful if the family have their 'key therapist' or 'named person' who will ensure that they have access to the team and that they understand the nature of the advice and recommendations made by it.

Parents as partners

Parents may be very demanding of professional time. They will certainly benefit from demonstration of skills by which they can control and help their child. The Honeylands Home Therapy Programme noted that some parents have been very slow to accept that they can actually bring about progress in their child by working with him. Rubissow et al (1979), considering the first year of the project, noted that 'because we have encouraged parents' participation in observation and goal setting, we have somewhat deliberately created a tension of expectation of the parents which is trickier to work in than a customary clinic visit where the child is removed from the parents' arms for treatment and then returned'. Helping families to help themselves must take into account individual family backgrounds. Brazleton (1976) suggested that 'the success of any intervention programme should be measured not only by the child's development but by increased family comfort, decrease in the divorce rate, lower incidence of behaviour problems in siblings . . . perhaps by pretty soft signs but they may be a lot more important as measures of effectiveness of intervention than is a rise in IQ or increased motor capacity on the part of the child'. Brazleton described working with the family as the 'soft work of paediatrics' and queried how many paediatricians were willing to do this. Perhaps we should ask how many teachers and social workers are willing to do so.

Helping a parent to feel more confident in order to become more competent may be difficult. Parents' groups may be an invaluable way of establishing not only solidarity, but also a real recognition that a parent is a person with difficulties and *not* a failure.

Studies that examine the characteristics of parents related to *early education and development* tend to focus on differentials in cognitive and language achievement and emotional development. The relationship between birth stress and continued developmental problems is generally accepted. But the qualification is that birth stress and developmental problems have long-term adverse effects only if the family itself has additional problems. If the family unit is already unstable, then problems will result.

There has been a growth area recently in early intervention programmes such as the Portage Project, the Red House programmes and the USA Head Start. But early intervention programmes also create difficulties. First, the critical factor appears to be that of establishing some kind of change in the *parents' behaviour* which will carry over into the parents' relationship with the child and the family. Thus traditional education classroom techniques may provide *information*, but they do not necessarily offer *appropriate goals*. Models of parental intervention (like Portage), which teach the parent to be more effective and in turn teach the child, seem most successful. Because they are simple, they are likely to succeed. Equally importantly they ensure regular visits to the family from a committed home visitor.

REFERENCES

Ballard, R. (1976). Sharing the pain. Help for parents with a handicapped child. *Health Visitor*, **49**, 395–6.

Byers Brown, B. and Beveridge, M. (1979). *Language Disorders in Children*. The College of Speech Therapists, London.

Brazleton, T. (1976). *Case finding, screening, diagnosis and tracking*. Discussant's comments in *Intervention Strategies for High Risk Infants and Grandchildren* (ed Tjossem, T. D.). University Park Press, Baltimore.

Cunningham, C. and Sloper, P. (1980). *Parent counselling*. In *Tredgold's Mental Retardation* (12th edition). Baillière Tindall, London.

Darling, R. B. (1979). *Families Against Society*. Sage Publications, London.

Gath, A. (1978). *Down's Syndrome and the Family*. Academic Press, London.

Gath, A. (1982). The effect of a handicapped child on the family. *Midwife, Health Visitor and Community Nurse*, **18**, 506–15.

Hannam, C. (1975). *Parents and Mentally Handicapped Children*. Penguin, Harmondsworth.

Kew, S. (1975). *Handicap and Family Crisis*. Pitman Medical, London.

Leiderman, P. H. (1974). *Mothers at risk: potential consequences of hospital care of a premature infant*. In *The Child in His Family* (ed Anthony, E. J.). Wiley, New York.

Mansell, C. (1980) Portage – not just another course. *Health Visitor*, **53**, 426–7.

Parkes, C. M. (1975). *Bereavement*. Pelican, Harmondsworth.

Pugh, G. (1981). *Parents as Partners*. National Children's Bureau, London.

Reynell, J. K. (1977). *Reynell Developmental Scales*. NFER Publishing Co Ltd, Windsor.

Rubissow, J., Jones, J., Brimblecombe, F. and Morgan, D. (1979). *Handicapped children and their families: their use of available services and unmet needs*. In *Problems and Progress in Medical Care*, Series No. 12 Nuffield Provincial Hospitals Trust, London.

Sheridan, M. D. (1973). *Children's Developmental Progress from Birth to Five Years: The Stycar Sequences*. NFER Publishing Co Ltd, Windsor.

Twinn, S. (1981). The specialist health visitor for handicapped children: luxury or necessity? *Health Visitor*, **54**, 478–9.

Warnock, M. (1978). *Special Education Needs*. Report of the Committee on the Education of Handicapped Children and Young People. HMSO, London.

FURTHER READING

Lahiff, M. (1977). *The Needs of Specific Groups in Health Visiting*. In *Health Visiting* (ed Owen, G.). Baillière Tindall, London.

Sheridan, M. D. (1977). *Spontaneous Play in Early Childhood from Birth to Six Years*. NFER Publishing Co Ltd, Windsor.

Yeates, S. (1980). *The Development of Hearing*. MTP Press Ltd, Lancaster.

POST-REGISTRATION COURSES

The following centres hold regular post-registration training courses for physiotherapists and other professionals. Enquiries should be directed to the secretary unless otherwise indicated.

Western Cerebral Palsy Centre
Bobath Centre, 5 Netherhall Gardens
London NW3 5RN

Miss S. Levitt
Supervisor of Therapy Studies, the Wolfson Centre
Institute of Child Health
London WC1N 2AP

Cheyne Spastic Centre
61 Cheyne Walk
London SW3 5LX

Castle Priory College
Thames Street
Wallingford OX10 0HE

The Association of Paediatric Chartered Physiotherapists also holds meetings and post-registration courses. Full information regarding these can be obtained from the honorary secretary of this specific interest group c/o The Chartered Society of Physiotherapy, 14 Bedford Row, London WC1R 4ED.

Chapter 2

Nursing Care

by MOTHER FRANCES DOMINICA SRN, RSCN, FRCN

INTRODUCTION

The physical care of a child who is handicapped or who has a life threatening, chronic illness is only a small part of what one would describe as nursing care. It is just as much a part of the role of the nurse to recognise and meet the child's emotional and spiritual needs and indeed those of his family. Nursing care of such a child is about caring for the whole child and his family, helping them to achieve the optimum quality of life throughout, even though the life span may be short, enabling the child to meet diminution of health, or death, with dignity and helping the family to live on. The importance of being sensitive to the very different needs of each person and of being ready to respond in the way which is most appropriate to each individual cannot be over-stressed.

THE CHILD AND HIS FAMILY

The changing social pattern

The position of a family with a chronically sick or handicapped child is dramatically different now from the position of such a family in previous generations. Due to developments in preventive and curative medicine, the occurrence of some forms of chronic sickness and severe handicap in children is much less frequent, but many who would once have died now survive with varying degrees of dependency. Although there are more extensive and improved facilities offering support to these families, the pattern of family life has changed and the involvement of the extended family is less common. The nuclear family, not infrequently a single parent family, can suffer feelings of isolation.

Learning from the family

Anyone involved in the nursing care of a child must see him in the context of his family. Care of the handicapped or chronically sick is different from acute care and it is vital for the nurse to listen and learn from the family for it is the family who know best the individual characteristics and needs of their sick child. This is especially important where the child has difficulty in communicating.

The severity of children's disorders varies enormously as does the extent to which it involves and affects the family and, although in some cases the practical problems are immense, they are seldom the worst of the difficulties facing the parents; very often the secondary problems are the most taxing.

Prolonged anxiety and grief of the family

However imaginative and understanding we are, we can only begin to be aware of the strain and anguish which the family experiences physically and mentally. With an acute illness or accident followed by death, the grieving process and mourning have the potential of being resolved over a period of time. Objectively, at least, others accept this process. With chronic sickness or handicap the grief is terribly prolonged and may often begin from the moment of diagnosis, when it is recognised that there is no known cure and there is not the same possibility of resolving or completing the mourning. Every stage of diminished ability or independence, every loss of function and each new sign of deterioration is a further cause of mourning to the family and needs the acknowledgement of those around, not least those professionally concerned. This grieving may bring with it the feelings of denial, anger, remorse and guilt, as well as sorrow, common to all bereavement, and the need for the nurse to foster an honest and accepting relationship through all this is crucial.

Differing reactions of parents

It must be recognised that father and mother may react in very different ways to their distress, and the relationship may become strained because of the difficulty of one partner in understanding how or why the other is behaving in a certain way. Sheer physical exhaustion may affect communication and so things go from bad to worse. One or both partners may feel ashamed or guilty about their child's disorder and their own inadequacy in coping with it. It is generally easier and more acceptable for a woman to show her emotions than it is for a man and it is particularly difficult for him in the social or work context. It is also traditional for her to fulfil the nurturing, caring role which reinforces the bond between mother and child, sometimes to the apparent exclusion of the father. Both parents may have periods of time when they distance themselves from the child as a form of self-protection.

Arguments frequently occur as to the degree of protection the child needs, as to the best treatment or the management of behaviour. The nurse needs to try to make both partners feel valued and to include them both in communications concerning their child, showing a sensitivity to the difficulties each faces and making positive suggestions about activities they and their child may be able to enjoy together.

We must be aware that the difficulties and frustrations may cause such stress that they lead even the most caring parents to abuse their child physically and this needs to be seen as a symptom of the pain which they are suffering and handled in a cautious but sensitive way. There may be an isolated incident of physical abuse, causing the parents enormous guilt which, if talked over with someone who knows and understands the family, may be defused, thus preventing further incidents. Whatever the circumstances, signs of physical abuse are danger signals which cannot be ignored.

The effect on siblings

The disruption of family life inevitably affects other children in the family, who may feel neglected in favour of the sick child, and in some cases this can lead to strong resentment, resulting in disturbed behaviour. They may also carry around a huge burden of sorrow, which may manifest itself in many ways and therefore may not be recognised as such. A sibling may have fears that he himself will suffer the same illness or even die and he may well feel that he must protect his already overburdened parents from this and other anxieties or strong emotions. Here the nurse may have an important role to fill, just as friend and confidante. Explanation and involvement appropriate to the age and temperament of the sibling may help to overcome some of the difficulties. Siblings who do in fact suffer from the same condition, for example inherited progressive disorders, have their own very special needs.

The effect on others

Grandparents, aunts, uncles, cousins, friends, neighbours and professional care-givers are all affected by the child's suffering. We need to be aware that, as well as being a potential source of help, they are also potential casualties in the unfolding of a particular tragedy.

The importance of continuing social contacts

Friendships and social contacts outside the immediate family circle are of immense value for all members of the family to provide relief, diversion and support during the child's life and, should it occur, after his death. It is dangerously optimistic to think that old friendships which have been neglected during the child's life, often from simple lack of energy or reluctance ever to be parted from the child, can automatically be resumed later. Brothers and sisters should not be made to feel guilty about enjoying their own ordinary friendships, indeed these too should be encouraged.

Dependence and independence of the child

Members of the family may sometimes be helped to adopt a slightly different approach from the instinctive one which is to protect at all costs, sometimes to the detriment of the quality of the child's life. Every child is dependent on his parents or parent substitutes during the early years of his life; gradually this dependence diminishes in a well child and to a lesser extent in a handicapped child. Increasing independence is exciting and challenging for a young person, though some parents are reluctant to let go. How much more difficult for parents of a handicapped child to allow him to face the challenges of the outside world. Undoubtedly, a society which is geared to the normal imposes restraints on those who are different, so we must do all we can to help the child and his parents to meet and overcome these prejudices.

THE CHILD AND THE NURSE

Trust between child and nurse

There will be times when the nurse will be called upon to act as parent substitute. Trust and acceptance are essential to any satisfactory lasting relationship and this is certainly so between a nurse and a handicapped or sick child. Equally important to such a child is a feeling of self-worth and confidence which we must foster early on by an immediate readiness to accept him while acknowledging that it will take time for him to trust us. If this is to happen, our behaviour towards him must be consistent and our responses honest. If he trusts us enough, he may feel able to relax and perhaps to share some of his worst anxieties; it is remarkable how protective sick children feel towards their parents and they will often go to great lengths to spare them further pain, whereas someone they trust who is less closely related, but has some authority, may be taken into their confidence.

Flexibility in methods of treatment

Acute nursing care may often require textbook methods of treatment to ensure a satisfactory outcome. Nursing a chronically sick child however, allows and indeed demands a greater degree of flexibility and creative use of imagination. The child's own knowledge of the optimum way of coping with the disorder will most often be the way we must adopt. It is clearly not appropriate to carry out a task in textbook fashion, or even according to stated policy, if such action causes distress or unnecessary suffering, if only through its unfamiliarity. Commands and instructions issued by an apparently demanding and cheeky, chronically handicapped child can be irksome to say the least, but we must remember that a child who lives with a condition usually knows what is best for him. He is *not* a textbook case; he is a unique individual with his own idiosyncrasies and needs which he understands better than anyone. The child's agreement must be sought if we wish to try a new procedure, showing him that we are anxious to do the best for him and not just determined to do our own thing! All this assumes that his level of consciousness allows him to reason, relate and co-operate.

The need to be observant

There is a danger in caring for the chronically sick that we may not be sufficiently observant of changing needs, which may come about very gradually.

We need constantly to be assessing the child as he is and questioning whether our care remains appropriate. There is scope for imagination and resourcefulness, but always with consideration for the home situation if this is relevant.

Change in treatment may sometimes provide the opportunity of helping the parents to accept further deterioration in their child's condition, which they may not have noticed or indeed which they may have wanted to ignore or deny.

Basic physical care

The nurse must give meticulous attention to the physical needs of the child. Her standard of care can make all the difference between constant discomfort and nagging reminders of his plight and the possibility of freeing him to focus his attention on positive and outgoing thoughts and behaviour.

Care of skin and hair needs to extend to helping the child to feel attractive; well-fitting, pretty or 'fun' clothes which he enjoys wearing are also a boost to the morale and these should be chosen or adapted with a view to the ease of dressing or undressing.

Dental care is as important, if not more so, for a sick or handicapped child as it is for a well child. Cleaning the teeth, despite the difficulties that handicap may present, a good diet and regular dental check-ups are all important.

Diet needs to be imaginative and varied and it is not wise to give in to all his fads just because the child is handicapped. With loss of normal physical activity, bowel function is often impaired and if this is ignored it will cause added discomfort and anxiety to the child. Before resorting to large doses of aperients it is good to try added fibre in the diet, if this is possible.

Hydrotherapy, even just on the apparent level of play, can bring great relief to a child who has muscle contractures, paralysis, or who is emaciated. At its simplest, this can just take the form of the nurse's allowing extended play-time in the bath. Indeed, many forms of treatment or routine care can be transformed into fun-times if the nurse is prepared to adopt this approach.

The need for mental stimulation

Boredom and feelings of frustration may be overriding problems for the child whose activities seem so limited and a good nurse will enable him to explore positive avenues of interest which will stretch him, and will not be shocked by displays of anger which may be a direct result of his frustration, but rather will help him to channel his energies. Education and mental stimulation are vital for the child who is capable of benefiting to however limited a degree. Continuing relationships with peers can be a lifeline for the sick or handicapped child and with a little wise encouragement, the well child will be enthusiastic to include him in many ways to the benefit of both.

The danger of over-protection and over-indulgence

It is important to avoid over-protection and over-indulgence, not to swamp the child with material goods (which for many is the instinctive response to a child's suffering, especially where it is acknowledged that the life-span will be short) and to maintain discipline for the sake of the child. He needs to know that, as with other children, there are acceptable patterns of behaviour to which he is expected to conform. This structure is important to him for his own security in his world, where many things have deviated from the norm.

If he is over-indulged or spoilt in his behaviour, he may cause further problems in an already over-charged family atmosphere and may well become bewildered himself. His need is for physical and emotional love and strength, not material possessions.

THE CHILD WITH A LIFE-THREATENING DISORDER

Answering the child's questions

Most of what has been written applies to the child with a progressive, life-threatening disorder, as much as to the child with a chronic condition which is not progressive. There are, of course, special things to consider for the former. If the child is aware of his deteriorating condition, he may well ask questions. It is important to listen carefully to what he is actually asking, and adults easily fall into the trap of assuming that he is asking a more complex question than he really is. The cardinal rule is never to lie to a child. This does not mean to say that he must be given the whole stark truth in one blow, but one is often able to give truthful reassurance and allay the child's fears about the actual process of dying and death itself, always, of course, using terms which the child understands and being careful not to contradict beliefs held by his family. The small child has a natural capacity to live for the present moment and recognising this can be used to advantage by those responsible for caring for him. If he is free of pain and discomfort and is surrounded by people he loves and trusts, he is less likely to be fearful for the future. The older child will have taken on more of the fears and complexities of an adult in facing dying and death. It must be categorically stated that there are no hard and fast ways of answering his questions or set methods of helping him to come to terms with the truth.

So much depends on the nurse's own ability to absorb the impact of the emotional and spiritual implications and to cope with them within herself. Platitudes and pat answers are less than helpful. At times when there seems to be nothing helpful to say, it is better not to use empty words, but rather to try to communicate reassurance through physical presence – just being there alongside the child through it all.

Symptom control

With great advances in the right use of drugs for symptom control, pain and other distressing symptoms associated with the terminal phase of illness need no longer be a feature. In spite of the development of these skills, it must be admitted that there is still room for research into pain control in paediatrics, for it is an acknowledged fact that the child's absorption of, and response to, drugs is different from that of adults. Optimum use of drugs depends not only on the doctor's skill in prescribing and titrating, but also on the nurse's awareness of her responsibility to be acutely observant of symptoms and changes and to be prompt and accurate in reporting them. It should be remembered that optimum results in the use of drugs in pain control can only be achieved through regular and punctual administration.

The family can be spared some distress by seeing their child relieved of distress and, even where the child's level of consciousness renders him apparently unaware, it is important to continue to minimise the family's distress; for example the use of hyoscine can prevent the 'death-rattle'.

The family's involvement

The importance of the family's involvement throughout the child's illness cannot be stressed enough, but it is never more important than in the terminal phase. Communication between family and professional carers must be open and honest. The family may well feel particularly inadequate at this time and will need constant reassurance and encouragement to be involved on every level as far as they are able. Many people are afraid of how death itself will actually occur and relatives should be told as far as possible how the end may come. They may well have fears and fantasies unrelated to reality and if these can be dispelled, some of the anguish may be removed.

There are so many small, unobtrusive ways in which the sensitive nurse can help at this stage. The room can be kept fresh and comfortably tidy, the bed linen clean and the child cherished and tended lovingly. The family can be helped to talk to their child (they may not realise that hearing is one of the last faculties to be lost and he may continue to hear long after he has ceased to be able to respond, so they and others should be warned not to say things which may distress him). To hold him, or just hold his hand or stroke him is natural and right.

Through all the strain of caring for a chronically sick or severely handicapped child, there will almost inevitably have been moments when parents have wished it would all end. When the end of the child's life is actually in sight, this may result in great feelings of guilt. With the actual death of the child, the family may need to be helped through the appalling confusion of the mixture of relief and grief.

Relationship with the bereaved family

If the relationship has been one of trust and friendship, it will follow that it does not end with the death of the child. Bereavement, particularly where it centres around a child, can be a very lonely time. Friends and even relatives may find it an impossibly difficult task to be faced with the family's grief in all its varying forms of expression. They may be afraid of their own emotional reactions and the instinctive response is to stay away, hoping that the family will find support from others. Behaviour and remarks indicating that it is time the family 'got back to normal' can be devastatingly hurtful.

A family never gets over the death of a child, even though in time they may adjust. It may help to warn them of how other people may react and why. One of the most helpful things anyone can do is to allow them to talk about their child and even encourage them to do so. Their greatest need is to have a friend or friends who are prepared to stay alongside, not only through the tears but through the anger and accusations, the guilt and denial and all the bleak, inexpressible grief.

CONCLUSION

It is humbling to be entrusted with the care of a sick child and most especially one whose life is drawing to a close. As nurses, we may become deeply involved with members of the family and may see them at times when their defences are down and they are at their most vulnerable. We may be taken into the confidence of one or more members of the family and allowed an insight into problems and anxieties and patterns of family life which have not previously been shared. We are there not only as professional carers, but as fellow human beings who must be able to be trusted implicitly and with whom there need be no pretence. There will often be times when we have nothing wise to say and when all we can do is stand by, not trying to set ourselves up as having the answers; simply by sharing in the pain we may help to dissipate it a little.

Staff support is extremely important in this emotionally charged work. It cannot be denied that it is draining and there must be a regular opportunity for team members to share some of the joys and sorrows, perplexities and misunderstandings which inevitably occur. It should be added that a sense of humour in members of the team is invaluable!

There are chronically sick or handicapped children who will be cared for at home throughout; others may be in hospital or institutional care, and yet others move from one to the other at intervals. The nurse's involvement varies accordingly, but however full or limited her involvement may be, her role is one of great privilege and there can be few kinds of nursing more demanding or more fulfilling.

Chapter 3

Multidisciplinary Assessment

by G. T. McCARTHY MB, MRCP, DCH
with R. CARTWRIGHT MCSP,
N. J. GARDNER BSC, MEd(EdPsych), V. MOFFAT LCST,
J. ROCKEY DipCOT and Y. SNIDER AIMSW

The aim of assessment is to produce as full a profile as possible of the child and his family at a particular time, linking the findings with the past and using them to plan for the future. Assessment is carried out periodically:

1. To define problems
2. To plan treatment
3. To plan education and future placement
4. To provide support for the family, both practical and emotional.

There will be times when assessment is carried out to determine suitability for admission to school, and a specific assessment for a decision on admission to a residential school. The aims of these assessments will be slightly different. Nevertheless they have the same broad outline.

In this chapter headings and short notes are used in places where more detailed discussion of aspects of particular disabilities occur in the appropriate chapters.

Each member of the multidisciplinary team contributes to the assessment and there is inevitable overlap in some of the questions asked of the family.

SOCIAL WORK ROLE AND AIMS

The aims of a social work assessment are to establish where the family is in its understanding of the handicap, intellectually and emotionally; to assess the strengths and weaknesses of family functioning, and what kind of social work intervention might be necessary. It is important to assess whether problems within a family are due to the handicap and the feelings it gives rise to, or whether the handicapped member is merely the focus for pre-existing problems.

A social worker needs to feel comfortable working with handicapped children and to have knowledge of the implications of the condition presented. It is important never to overlook practical problems which may be creating difficulty and stress, and to seek for their solution.

The initial interview

Family structure: Including legal status (broken marriages), family health, employment, previous functioning.

Family attitudes: Understanding/acceptance of disability.
Levels of guilt, grief, rejection/over-protection.
Family view of short- and long-term future, aspirations and fears. Siblings' involvement.

Practical matters: Finance – welfare rights and allowances.
Housing – relevant to needs. Rate rebate if adaptations to property. Link with occupational therapist. Mobility in the locality. Access to shops.
Availability of car, phone, washing machine, etc. Family fund grants.
Outings and holidays possible with or without the child.
Local groups such as PHAB, Scouts, Guides.
Education/career – placement on leaving school.

Sources of support: Family; friends; social services department. Education welfare officer. Health visitor. GP. Group related to disability. Local church.

Follow-up: Plan work in revealed problem areas or referral to relevant professional help.

MEDICAL AND FUNCTIONAL ASSESSMENT

A combined assessment procedure involving paediatrician, physiotherapist and occupational therapist can be very helpful and avoids duplication of questions to the parents. It also enables the therapists to hear the full medical history. It should include:
Medical history, including family history.
Chronological list of surgery (amplified from previous hospital notes).

Intercurrent illnesses.
Immunisations.
Perinatal history.
Developmental history.
Vision; hearing; epilepsy.
Medication: past and present.
Present abilities. Parents' anxieties.

Physical examination:	Functional examination:
Height – centile Weight – centile OFC – centile Palpation of head for bony abnormalities and for valve system, where appropriate	
Eyes: eye movements, cover test for squint, examination of fundi	Vision test: near and distant. Colour vision
Ears and upper respiratory tract	Hearing and speech
Cardiovascular system heart sounds, pulses, blood pressure	
Chest: note any deformity	Vital capacity⎱where applicable Peak flow ⎰
Abdomen: palpation for enlargement of organs. Palpation of bladder Genitalia	
Skeletal system: spine and limbs for deformity, contractures, dislocations	Gait, motor function of legs and arms including co-ordination Examination of hands and fine manipulation
Central nervous system: cranial nerves Examination of limbs for tone, power, wasting, co-ordination and balance, sensation, abnormal movements Reflexes (as shown) R L Normal reflex is shown as ++ ++	Problems of manipulation, balance

Conclusions

1. Diagnosis and major physical problems.
2. Major functional problems.
3. Medical investigations required.

4. Referral for specialist opinion to orthopaedic surgeon or paediatric surgeon. Plan of possible future surgery.

The use of problem-orientated case records in children with continuing physical problems can be very helpful. Associated with this, a chronological chart of surgical operations and a chronological list of radiological procedures should also be made, as many children are exposed to a very high number of radiographs. Height, weight and head circumference charts should be started. Finally, the medical and functional aims should be made clear.

ROLES AND AIMS OF THE PHYSIOTHERAPIST AND OCCUPATIONAL THERAPIST

It is necessary to discuss with parents the areas of development which cause them most anxiety. The occupational therapist and, if possible, the physiotherapist, should visit the parents at home as soon as possible to look at the problems the mother has in caring for the child. The lifestyle of the family must be taken into consideration and also the number and ages of siblings, the father's work and attitude to the family and his involvement in the care of the child.

Physiotherapy assessment

This assessment is related to the child's age and physical disability. In the young child it is based on developmental progress. In the older child it is based on functional activities and interchange of the related movements. These will be defined in more detail in the individual chapters, but are outlined below.

Hand function   Wheelchair and transferring activities
Sitting   Travelling activities
Standing   Chest complications
Balancing   The use and fit of orthoses, and wheel-
Walking   chair and walking aids need to be
Climbing   reviewed regularly

CONCLUSIONS
1. Areas requiring particular help and remediation.
2. Short- and long-term aims for training.
3. Mobility in the home; at school; out of doors.

Occupational therapy assessment

This is based on the ability to carry out daily living activities.

Feeding: History of feeding abilities. Hand control or absence of hand or arm may need feeding aid.

Dressing: History of abilities and observation of undressing and dressing during paediatric examination.

Toileting: A history of present abilities and the training already undertaken. Cleansing difficulties may require an aid.

Management of incontinence and menstruation.

Management of bathing – need for aid?

Hand skills.

Correct seating.

Communication problems.

Home adaptations (see Chapter 21).

REHABILITATION ENGINEER

The rehabilitation engineer may be involved in the assessment process where applicable (see Chapter 15). The engineer brings a special expertise to the problems of rehabilitation, and his presence may be requested by any of the team members.

SPEECH THERAPY ASSESSMENT

It is extremely difficult to assess the language of a severely speech impaired child with severe motor involvement using standardised procedures as the child's responses are either unreliable or difficult to interpret, e.g. eye-pointing. More accurate results are obtained when tests are administered in the presence of other team members, such as psychologist, occupational therapist or teacher.

Language concepts often can be assessed only by using a battery of items from the verbal components of intelligence tests or by comparing levels of attainment with that of normal development. This is achieved by presenting the child with a series of tasks which require him to indicate Yes/No or look towards a certain object or picture.

Measurement of the child's progress

Subsequent or continuing assessment can determine the rate at which language skills are being learned. It is more important to know at what rate the child is progressing in comparison with normal development than to know at what level he is functioning at any one time.

Assessment of language development

Assessment of early concept formation, verbal comprehension and expressive language can be made on specially designed tests that have been validated and standardised.

The Symbolic Play Test (Lowe, 1975). This test evaluates the language potential of very young children who have failed to develop receptive and expressive language. The disadvantage for testing physically handicapped children is that the children must be able to manipulate the objects.

The Reynell Developmental Scales (Reynell, 1977). These scales provide a separate assessment of expressive language and verbal comprehension in children aged 1½–6 years. There is a separate verbal comprehension scale for children who are unable to use their hands, although this still has limitations with severely handicapped children.

Stycar Language Test (Sheridan, 1973). This test gives a series of clinical procedures for the differential diagnosis and management of developmental disorders of speech and language in young children. These procedures are: the Common Objects Test, the Miniature Toys Test and the Picture Book Test.

The Renfrew Action Picture Test (C. E. Renfrew, see p. 70). This requires the child to have intelligible speech to interpret a series of pictures. The short samples of spoken language are then evaluated in terms of the information given and the grammatical forms used. This test is useful for children aged between 3–7 years.

The Sentence Comprehension Test (Experimental Version) Kevin Wheldall, Peter Mittler and Angela Hobsbaum (see p. 70). This test assesses children's skills in receptive language from 3–5 years of age. The child shows he has understood a spoken sentence by identifying one picture out of four which corresponds to it. This is a useful test for the severely speech impaired child as he is not required to speak and eye-pointing responses are easy to interpret.

The British Picture Vocabulary Scales (Dunn et al, 1982). A quick estimate of verbal ability and often the only information relating to language that can be obtained from a severely speech impaired child is that of vocabulary. The test is easy to administer and covers an age range of 2½–18 years. The examiner shows a plate of four pictures and says the corresponding stimulus word. The child points to the picture which best illustrates the meaning of this word.

Assessment of articulation

The majority of articulation tests involve assessment by computing the standardised score for the child's correct pronunciations. The Renfrew Articulation Test gives a quick screening of the child's pronunciation. The Frenchay Dysarthria Assessment (Enderby, 1981) gives a reliable assessment when the different features of the articulators are presented in bargraph form. It is easy to see from this the relative strengths and weaknesses of a patient's speech, and structure therapy accordingly.

Assessment of aphasia (see p. 152)

PSYCHOLOGICAL AND EDUCATIONAL ASSESSMENT

The psychologist's main role in the multidisciplinary assessment of the physically handicapped child is to evaluate the child's present mental abilities and level of achievement in certain functional and educational skills. This assessment can then be used to devise a plan for treatment and/or appropriate education for the child.

Before conducting an assessment, the psychologist needs details of the nature of the child's handicap, including details of his vision and hearing. A physically handicapped child's opportunities for learning may well have been restricted both by the child's limited ability to explore all aspects of his environment and by neurological damage which may have affected his ability to interpret and respond to external stimuli. These factors must be taken into account when assessing a child, and it is essential to have a full developmental history and details of the child's family life.

The psychologist uses a number of techniques to assess the child's abilities. These include observational techniques, norm-referenced assessment, developmental assessment, applied behavioural analysis which includes criterion-referenced assessment and continuing evaluation of the child's rate of progress. The method of assessment will depend on the reason for the assessment and also on the nature and severity of the child's handicap.

Information concerning the child's concentration span, distractability and perseverance for chosen and given tasks can be noted from observing the child in his normal surroundings either at home, in the playgroup or in school. His interactions with his peers and with known adults can also be observed. Although it is preferable to observe the child in his familiar environment, limited information can be obtained from an interview with the child and parents or with the child alone.

A wide variety of norm-referenced tests is available. These tests compare the child's performance of certain tasks to the performance of a sample of the general population. The majority of these tests are standardised on the non-handicapped population and therefore great care must be taken when interpreting the results obtained from a handicapped child. The results of these tests should therefore be interpreted as a measure of the child's present skills, which may or may not reflect the child's potential. This type of assessment can be used to provide a profile of the child's present cognitive strengths and weaknesses, which should then be related to the child's functional and educational skills.

Norm-referenced tests are available which aim to measure a child's overall cognitive ability, specific abilities and educational attainments. The Wechsler Intelligence Scale for children, British Ability Scales and McCarthy Scales of children's abilities are all batteries of tests designed to investigate such skills as verbal ability, short-term memory, reasoning skills, visual-perceptual skills, spatial imagery and visual-motor skills. The tests provide information of the child's relative performance on each individual sub-test and also give verbal, visual/perceptual/performance and overall IQs.

Other tests are available which assess specific skills, for instance language abilities (see p. 33), scholastic attainments in basic skills such as reading, spelling, mathematics and specific perceptual/motor skills, e.g. the Frostig tests. Criterion-referenced assessment can be designed by the psychologist to investigate the child's performance on a particular functional or educational task. This assessment is concerned with describing in detail the aspects of a task that the child has mastered and which aspects he needs to learn. The tasks to be learned are analysed and a method of teaching based on behavioural principles designed. The child's rate of progress can then be observed in relation to the set curriculum and changes can be made as necessary to both the content and method of the teaching.

Developmental assessment places the child's behaviour in the context of normal developmental processes and is particularly useful when assessing a pre-school child or severely mentally handicapped child.

The basic methods of psychological assessment have been outlined and, as stated, the choice of method will depend on the reason for assessment and the child's handicap. For instance, when assessing a child with poor hand function combined with little or no speech, a combination found in many athetoid children, all the assessment will need to be by response selection, by fist-pointing, eye-pointing or where possible yes/no response. Examples of norm-referenced tests which are designed for response by eye-pointing are Reynell Verbal Comprehension Scale B and Columbia Mental Maturity Scale. The latter test requires the child to select the 'odd one out' of an array of items. The Raven's Matrices (a non-verbal reasoning test) and picture vocabulary tests can also be used for children only able to make a response selection.

If the child uses a communication system such as Blissymbolics or Makaton, then tests can be used as with a speaking child, provided the handicapped child has sufficient vocabulary or signs to answer the questions. It is always best to carry out this assessment with the help of someone who knows the child and his use of the communication system. When assessing a severely physically handicapped child it is advantageous to see the child with another team member such as the occupational therapist or doctor to advise on the child's physical responses to the assessment. In all cases the information obtained from psychological assessment should be discussed with the parents and the multidisciplinary team and used to plan appropriate strategies for intervention.

After an assessment has been carried out there should be full discussion among the team members to fill in the profile and to define aims for therapy, education, medical and social work involvement. A member of the team should be chosen to communicate the results of the assessment to the parents. The individual disciplines will frequently review the child from a particular point of view. For example, the psychologist and teacher may need to assess the child to aid remedial teaching, or the doctor arrange renal function tests for a particular child. The details of these will not involve all the team, and this type of work will continue alongside the wider team approach.

To date there is no single method of recording this type of multidisciplinary assessment – a multiplicity of forms is available. It is helpful to record daily living and social skills on a chart or graph which can be updated at regular intervals, and the older child should be encouraged to be involved in filling in the chart and deciding on the next aims. The members of the team have a great deal to learn from each other, hopefully for the benefit of the child and his family.

REFERENCES

Dunn, L. M., Dunn, L. M., Whelton, C. and Pintillie, D. (1982). *The British Picture Vocabulary Scale*. NFER/Nelson, Windsor.

Enderby, P. (1981). *Frenchay Dysarthria Assessment*, 2nd edition. Frenchay Hospital, Bristol.

Lowe, M. (1975). Trends in the development of representational play in infants from 1 to 3 years: An observational study. *Journal of Child Psychology and Psychiatry*, **16** (1), 33–47.

Reynell, J. K. (1977). *Reynell Developmental Scales*. NFER Publishing Co Ltd, Windsor.

Sheridan, M. (1973). *Children's Developmental Progress from Birth to Five Years: The Stycar Sequences*. NFER Publishing Co Ltd, Windsor.

The Renfrew Action Picture Test and the Articulation Attainment Test are by C. E. Renfrew of North Place, Old Headington, Oxford.

The Sentence Comprehension Test (Experimental version) is by K. Wheldall, P. Mittler and A. Hobsbaum and is obtainable from NFER, The Mere, Upton Park, Slough SL1 2D2.

FURTHER READING

Byers Brown, B. and Beveridge, M. (1979). *Language Disorders in Children*. The College of Speech Therapists, London.

Cooper, J., Moodley, N. and Reynell, J. (1978). *Helping Language Development*. Edward Arnold (Publishers) Ltd, London.

Crystal, D., Fletcher, P. and Garman, M. (1976). *The Grammatical Analysis of Language Disability: A Procedure in Assessment and Remediation*. Edward Arnold (Publishers) Ltd, London.

Fletcher, P. and Garman, M. (1979). *Language Acquisition*. Cambridge University Press, Cambridge.

Stackhouse, J. (1981). *What is Developmental Articulatory Dyspraxia*. The National Hospitals College of Speech Therapy, London.

Chapter 4

Spina Bifida and Hydrocephalus

by G. T. McCARTHY MB, MRCP, DCH
with R. CARTWRIGHT MCSP,
J. A. FIXSEN Mchir, FRCS, R. LAND BA(Hons), MPhil,
J. ROCKEY DipCOT and M. STRODE MB, BS

Spina bifida and hydrocephalus is a developmental defect caused by failure of fusion of the neural tube early in embryological life, around the 28th day. It is one of the conditions known as neural tube defects, which are among the commonest handicapping conditions of childhood at the present time. It has been noted that the prevalence of neural tube defects began to decline in England and Wales after 1972. Between 1972 and 1981 the national notification rate fell from 1.47 per 1000 live and stillbirths to 0.39 for anencephaly, and from 1.88 to 1.04 per 1000 for spina bifida (Leck, 1983).

GENETICS

There is known to be a genetic element which is multifactorial with a risk of a second affected child being 1 in 20, and with a similar risk of the affected person passing the defect on. After two affected children the risk rises to 1 in 10, and after three to as high as 1 in 4. A multicentre trial using multivitamins and folic acid suggests that prevention of neural tube defects is possible (Smithells et al, 1981). (See also Seller (1982).)

The neural tube may be affected anywhere along its length. If the forebrain fails to develop, anencephaly ensues and this is not compatible with life. Failure of fusion of the neural tube is associated with defective closure of the vertebral canal and often with other defects of the base of the brain, classified as the Arnold Chiari malformation, in which there is herniation of the medulla and often cerebellar herniation through the foramen magnum (see Fig. 4/5).

The commonest position of a spina bifida lesion is the thoraco-lumbar region, followed by the lumbo-sacral, thoracic and cervical lesions. Spina bifida occulta describes a lesion which is hidden from view. Skin covers the vertebral defect which is usually a simple failure of fusion of one or more of the posterior vertebral arches in the lumbo-sacral region. A defect limited to a single vertebra, usually L5 or S1, can be regarded as a normal variant (Laurence, 1969). If there is associated lipomatous mass or a hairy patch or naevus, or skin dimple, then the underlying spinal cord may be abnormal and occult spinal dysraphism may be present.

SPINA BIFIDA CYSTICA (APERTA) (Fig. 4/1)

Meningocele (Fig. 4/1a): The meninges form a sac lined by arachnoid membrane and dura containing cerebrospinal fluid (CSF) and, rarely, a small amount of nervous tissue. It is relatively uncommon (4 per cent of cases of spina bifida cystica) and may be associated with cutaneous lesions. The skin over the sac is usually intact.

Myelomeningocele (Fig. 4/1b): The neural tube is closed and covered by a membrane centrally and skin peripherally, but the spinal cord and all the nerve roots are outside the vertebral canal. In many cases there are associated anomalies of the cord with dilatation of the central canal, lipomata and other associated neural defects, such as split cord or tethering of nerve roots. In rachischeisis there is no sac and the spinal cord is flattened and lies wide open on the surface (Fig. 4/1c).

Assessment and management of the neonate with spina bifida aperta

Whether or not a policy of selection is carried out, all babies with spina bifida should be examined by a paediatrician or paediatric surgeon experienced in assessing such babies and in their long-term management.

NEUROLOGICAL EXAMINATION
The purpose of the examination is to determine, as far as possible, the level at which normal cord function ceases, and to assess the presence and degree of hydrocephalus.

Skull: The skull should be examined and the sutures and fontanelle palpated for evidence of distension and increased pressure. Measurement of the occipital frontal circumference (OFC) should be carried out and charted, and examination of the optic fundi also carried out, and eye movements noted by stimulation of the optokinetic responses.

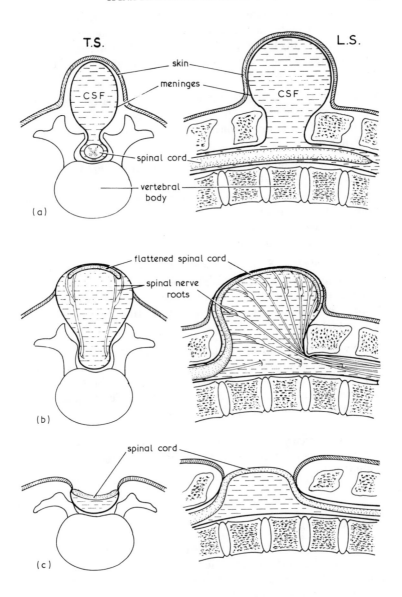

Fig. 4/1 (a) Meningocele; (b) myelomeningocele; (c) rachischeisis

Cranial nerves: The cranial nerves may be assessed by observation of the movement of the face, tongue and palate and by watching the baby suck. Occasionally bulbar problems can arise in the new-born period, especially immediately after back closure if hydrocephalus begins to develop more rapidly.

Spine: The spine should be palpated along its length as sometimes there are multiple lesions which are not always obvious. The length and width of the lesion should be measured and the position on the spine noted.

Limbs: The presence of active movements of the limbs should be looked for by stimulating the legs and eliciting neonatal reflexes. The power of the muscles may be assessed by making them operate both with and without gravity and with and without resistance, and it is useful to make a muscle chart. Deformities such as talipes and congenital dislocation of the hip should be looked for.

Bowel and bladder: Sphincter tone and bladder function should be assessed and anal reflex tested by stroking with an orange stick. A patulous anus and dribbling incontinence are associated with a lesion at the level of sacral(S) 2, 3, 4. Retention of urine is associated with a lesion at S1.

Sensory level: It is difficult to elicit a sensory level in a baby. If he is asleep, it may be possible to produce a level by stimulation with a pin, starting at the lower sacral territory perianal region, buttocks, thighs and legs and moving upwards over successive dermatomes of the anterior surface and on to the abdomen.

Radiological examination of the skull and spine and hips should be carried out, and bacteriological swabs taken from the sac and umbilicus.

Types of lesion

At birth, two types of lesion are recognisable (Stark and Baker, 1967). *Type 1* (one-third of patients): There is complete loss of the spinal cord function below a certain segmental level, which results in sensory loss and absent reflexes. These infants have characteristic deformities of muscle imbalance, the deformity depending on the level of the lesion. *Type 2* (two-thirds of patients): Associated with interruption of the corticospinal tracts. There is preservation of purely reflex activity in isolated distal segments.

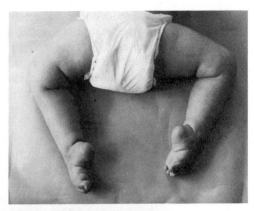

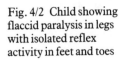

Fig. 4/2 Child showing
flaccid paralysis in legs
with isolated reflex
activity in feet and toes

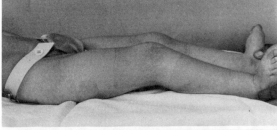

Fig. 4/3 Marked reflex
flexor activity:
(a) legs held,
(b) legs released.
No active muscle power

There are three sub-groups:
1. Below the level of spinal cord involvement there is a segment with flaccid paralysis and sensory and reflex loss and, below this, isolated cord function with reflex activity and spasticity. Toe clonus may be striking (Fig. 4/2).
2. A flaccid segment is almost absent and, therefore, there is virtually complete spinal cord transection with only reflex activity below the level of the lesion (Stark and Drummond, 1971) (Fig. 4/3a and b).

On the basis of evidence of clinical and electrodiagnostic studies, it is likely that paralysis in myelomeningocele is due to a lesion of the upper motor neurone (UMN) rather than the lower motor neurone (LMN). In high lesions the UMN lesion tends to occur above the plaque. In low lesions it may occur elsewhere, e.g. within the plaque itself. The UMN lesion may be a primary developmental anomaly, but is more likely to be related to secondary changes occurring before, during or shortly after birth.

3. Incomplete transection of the long tracts occurs, so the child has a spastic paraplegia with some preservation of voluntary movement and sensation. There is also a small group of patients, 5 per cent, with a hemi-myelomeningocele in whom one leg is more or less normal, but the other leg is affected by a type 1 or 2 lesion.

Selection for treatment

It is known that the majority of untreated infants with myelomeningocele die early in life (Laurence, 1969; Mawdsley et al, 1967). The policy of treating all affected infants in Sheffield from 1959–69 resulted in a unique record of the outcome (Lorber, 1971; 1972), and was followed by a policy of selective treatment (Lorber and Salfield, 1981). A careful study of the results leads to the outline of four prognostic criteria.

1. *The degree of paralysis*: The greater the paralysis the worse the prognosis, not only in terms of mobility, but also IQ, associated spinal deformity, and severe renal complications.
2. *Excessive head circumference*: If the infant's head circumference is at or over the 90th centile at birth and disproportionate to weight, the degree of hydrocephalus is usually gross, with poor prognosis in terms of IQ.
3. *Kyphosis*: Kyphosis present at birth has a very poor outlook in terms of later severe deformity, paralysis and incontinence.
4. *Associated gross congenital anomalies or major birth injury*: The presence of gross congenital anomalies such as heart disease and severe birth injury is of the gravest prognostic significance.

CLOSURE OF THE BACK

As soon as the decision to operate has been made, the back should be closed. Wound breakdown may occur, but healing is best effected by keeping the wound clean and allowing healing by secondary intention, unless a CSF leak is present, in which case a shunt needs to be inserted.

HYDROCEPHALUS

Hydrocephalus occurs in about 80 per cent of children with spina bifida. It may be of the obstructive type, at the aqueduct, or caused by malabsorption or over-production of CSF and termed communicating hydrocephalus (Fig. 4/4). In many cases, the hydrocephalus is caused by a mixture of these factors. The type III Arnold Chiari malformation is common: it consists of prolongation of the cerebellar vermis and 4th ventricle into the cervical spinal canal and kinking of the inferiorly placed medulla. This may produce obstruction of the

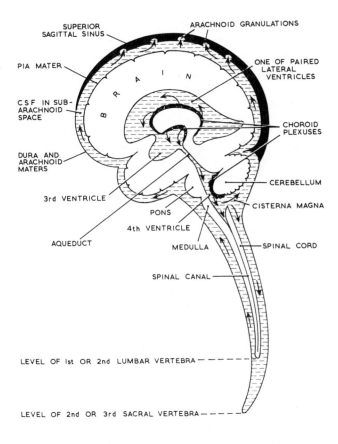

Fig. 4/4 Ventricular system of the brain

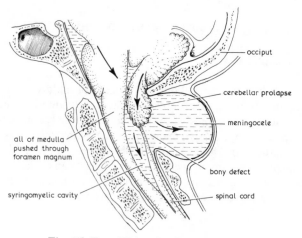

Fig. 4/5 Type III Arnold-Chiari malformation

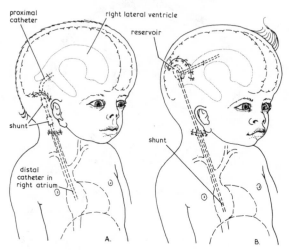

Fig. 4/6 Shunt systems for treatment of hydrocephalus.
(a) Spitz-Holter; (b) Pudenz

4th ventricle. Figure 4/5 shows the mechanism of production of
syringomyelia in type III Arnold Chiari malformation.

Hydrocephalus may be present at birth or become overt after back
closure, when the head circumference rapidly increases, and there
may be associated feeding problems, vomiting and swallowing
difficulties. In most cases, it is necessary to insert a by-pass valve to
carry the excess CSF from the ventricles of the brain into the
circulation or the peritoneal sac. Different types of valve are used: the
commonest ones are the Spitz-Holter valve and Pudenz (Fig. 4/6). A
useful addition to the system is a reservoir which allows the ventricles

to be tapped easily and pressure measurements to be carried out. A multi-purpose valve has recently been developed, which allows closure of the system and insertion of intrathecal antibiotics. The advent of computerised axial tomography (CAT: CT scan) makes it possible to demonstrate ventricular size easily, and serial scans can be used if there is any doubt about shunt function. In theory, the valve system allows the brain to grow at a normal rate without the internal pressure of the CSF. In practice, it had not been possible to monitor ventricular size, until the CT scan became widely available, and recent studies have shown that many children have persistent dilatation of their ventricular system, or the ventricular system becomes very small and the ventricles almost disappear (Figs. 4/7a and 4/7b). The common complications arising from valves (shunts) are either obstruction or infection.

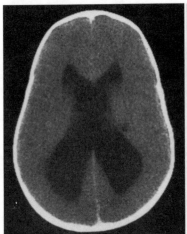 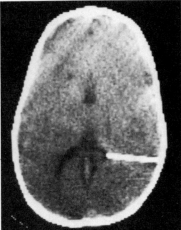

Fig. 4/7(a) CT scan showing marked hydrocephalus

Fig. 4/7(b) CT scan following shunt insertion; the ventricles are now very small

On rare occasions the valve itself is the cause of obstruction.

Upper end block: The choroid plexus of blood vessels may become wrapped around the ventricular catheter, or the catheter may simply become submerged in the brain tissue due to changes in the size of the hydrocephalus. The valve may fail to refill or do so very slowly.

Lower end block: (a) Ventriculo-atrial (VA) shunt: This may simply be caused by withdrawal of the atrial catheter from the fast moving blood flow by growth. Once in the great veins the irritant effect of the CSF on the wall of the vein will lead to inflammation, at first partial and

. finally complete. (b) Ventriculo-peritoneal (VP) shunt: The peritoneal catheter may be wrapped round by the surrounding tissue and become enclosed in a pocket, causing slowly rising pressure.

The catheters may break or become disconnected, and this is visible on a radiograph only in the radio-opaque varieties.

CLINICAL PRESENTATION OF SHUNT OBSTRUCTION

The clinical picture in shunt blockage can be extremely varied and it is important to remember that if the build-up of intracranial pressure is gradual, dangerously high pressures can be reached with very little in the way of clinical signs or symptoms. These are shown in Table 1.

TABLE 1   Clinical symptoms and signs of valve malfunction

Symptoms	Signs
Headache	
Vomiting	Neck stiffness
Drowsiness	Papilloedema
Irritability	Slow pulse
Epilepsy	Distension of spinal defect
Pain in the neck or back	Limited neck flexion
Neck retraction	
Visual problems, diplopia	Increasing 6th nerve palsies
Slowing performance – often noticed by teachers	Optic atrophy
Personality changes	Chronic papilloedema
Onset of epilepsy which is difficult to control	Slowing performance, school failure
Swallowing difficulties and intractable bronchitis	Bulbar and brainstem signs
Weakness of the arms or loss of dexterity	Appearance of spasticity; cerebellar ataxia
	Dissociated sensory loss and weakness of arms with loss of reflexes due to syringomyelia

PHYSICAL EXAMINATION

Apart from the signs associated with the complications mentioned, the following points in the examination of the child may be helpful:
1. An increasing skull circumference which falls outside the normal growth rate can be a valuable indicator. It is, therefore, important

to have serial head circumference readings and a chart on each child. Tension of the anterior fontanelle in the infant may give direct reference to the pressure, and in some older children an artificial fontanelle may be useful in determining where the pressure is raised.

2. Irregularities of the pulse, as well as classical slowing of the pulse, may indicate raised intracranial pressure.
3. Pumping the reservoir in suspected cases of blockage can temporarily overcome partial obstruction of the distal catheter with relief of symptoms. It is a manoeuvre worth trying providing the reservoir appears to be refilling instantly.
4. The feel of the valve may be misleading.
5. Investigations: skull and chest radiographs are helpful if a radio-opaque valve system is in situ. Only the tip of the Pudenz catheter has a radio-opaque marker. A CT scan may be helpful, particularly if a previous record has been made.

TREATMENT

Any child suspected of having a blocked valve should be transferred to a neurosurgical centre for observation and possible treatment. Some valve blockages can right themselves, but others cannot, and it is impossible to say how much time can be safely allowed for observation. If the clinical assessment suggests a severe rise of pressure, emergency aspiration of CSF via the valve or ventricle may be a life-saving measure before transfer to the neurosurgical centre. If a Rickham reservoir is present, aspiration should be carried out using full aseptic techniques and the intracranial pressure can be measured.

In the absence of a valve reservoir and a rapidly deteriorating child, a lumbar puncture needle may be passed along the side of the ventricular catheter. Aspiration of the valve reservoir using a fine hypodermic needle and full aseptic precautions may also be indicated. Sudden death may occur in children with hydrocephalus and valve systems.

Preventive surgery: Many surgeons prefer to lengthen the distal atrial catheter at intervals as the child grows to prevent the complications of lower end block. This may prevent exposing the child to episodes of uncontrolled pressure.

Shunt infection

In those systems which drain into the circulation, the tip of the distal catheter acquires a coating of fibrin and blood clot which provides an ideal culture medium for circulating bacteria. An episode of bacteraemia can thus infect the tip of the catheter and infection may spread up into the valve and to the cerebral ventricles. Infection may be introduced at the time of operation and, commonly, is associated with low-grade bacteria, which normally inhabit the skin. The presence of these organisms in the circulation may also produce a sensitivity reaction, resulting in the development of nephritis or nephrotic syndrome. Occasionally embolic phenomena occur, with the development of bacterial endocarditis and patchy areas of pneumonia.

The catheters draining into the peritoneal cavity, although less likely to become infected, can do so if the catheter tip lies in close proximity to the wall of the bowel for any length of time. The irritant effect of the CSF may produce inflammation in the wall of the bowel, which allows the passage of bowel organisms into the peritoneal cavity. Infection of the distal catheter and eventually the whole valve system and brain may follow.

CLINICAL PRESENTATION OF SHUNT INFECTION

Pyrexia: Caused by escape of organisms into the circulation. This may take the form of isolated spikes of temperature, a continuous swinging temperature or a low-grade pyrexia associated with failure to thrive and chronic anaemia. In the rare case this is complicated by bacterial endocarditis. A systolic murmur may be heard, patchy consolidation of the lungs, enlargement of the spleen and finger clubbing may occur.

Meningism: Headache, vomiting, drowsiness and neck stiffness may occur.

Shunt nephritis: Oedema, proteinuria, haematuria and hypertension may occur. Unrelieved, this will ultimately lead to chronic renal failure.

INVESTIGATIONS

Blood cultures should be carried out at intervals, preferably at the time of pyrexia, and a positive culture will usually be obtained.

Blood counts typically show anaemia with some degree of leucocytosis.

CSF aspirated from the valve will culture the organism, but there will be no cellular response in the CSF until the brain becomes infected.

TREATMENT

Successful treatment almost invariably involves the removal of the entire valve system and the insertion of a new one, once the infection has been overcome by means of systemic and intrathecal antibiotics, the latter only being required in ventriculitis.

Preventive treatment: In those valves which drain into the circulation, prophylactic antibiotics should be given to cover any procedures such as dental extraction which may provoke a bacteraemia.

Other shunt complications: These include over-drainage of the ventricles with overlapping of the sutures and craniosynostosis, producing rather similar symptoms to those of raised intracranial pressure. Occasionally the catheter perforates the heart or abdominal viscera, or becomes detached from the valve, causing pulmonary embolism. Skin necrosis over the valve can also occur.

MANAGEMENT OF ANAESTHETIC SKIN

From birth the mother has to be vigilant in the care of anaesthetic skin. Friction from crawling, hot liquids and pressure from shoes and appliances may cause problems. Poor skin and tissue cover over a prominent kyphos may easily be damaged by pressure and lead to ulceration. Regular inspection of the anaesthetic areas must be carried out by the mother while the child is young, and as soon as the child is able to take responsibility he must learn to examine himself, using a mirror for the back and bottom. Bathtime is a good time for this.

Pressure sores

Pressure sores almost inevitably develop in some children. The factors involved are:
1. Excessive pressure localised to a small area, caused by deformity and asymmetrical posture.
2. Poor circulation of both blood and lymph.
3. Optimum micro-climate – wet skin, contaminated with urine or faeces.
4. Abnormal skeletal structures, e.g. prominent kyphosis, scar tissue over excess callus formation following orthopaedic surgery.
5. Scar tissue associated with poor subcutaneous tissue following closure of back lesion.

All of these factors are exacerbated by the absence of sensation which normally stimulates alteration of posture before tissue necrosis occurs.

PREVENTION

Buttocks: Good basic hygiene, with a daily bath, combined with control of incontinence is the first consideration. The sitting posture is also of great importance, and the use of a cushion carefully chosen to minimise the danger of excessive pressure localised to a small area. In addition the child should be encouraged to lift the pelvis off the seat several times each hour.

Lower limbs: Great care should be taken in the fitting of orthoses and in providing extra padding for postoperative plasters. Paralytic toes should be uncurled before the shoe is laced up.

Spine: Pressure areas related to spinal deformities can be protected by the use of Stomahesive applied directly to the skin.

Lumbar sympathectomy in some cases improves circulation in the legs.

MANAGEMENT

Conservative: The essential is to provide effective relief of pressure. In the buttock area this can sometimes be achieved by the use of a chip-foam cushion with a cut-out area over the vital point, but it will often be necessary to avoid sitting until sound healing has occurred; the use of a self-propelled prone trolley can be a useful aid in such circumstances. For the legs plaster of Paris or Baycast splints – changed weekly – can be a most effective aid in relieving pressure.

Local preparations: Initially, when necrosis and infection are present, the twice-daily application of eusol and paraffin emulsion is most effective. Once the area is clean, sterile petroleum jelly gauze impregnated with chlorhexidine (Bactigras) provides a mild stimulus to the formation of granulation tissue; excess granulation will need the application of silver nitrate.

Once the ulcer is well healed careful massage with grease can mobilise adherent scars, so reducing the risk of recurrence.

Minor surgery: The healing process can be accelerated by the excision of necrotic tissue and fibrotic areas. Traumatising the edge of an indolent ulcer will stimulate the inflammatory reaction and so promote healing.

Plastic surgery: While most pressure sores arise from without, others are due to shearing forces. The latter can cause a deep breakdown of tissue, with the formation of bursae which can be very extensive. Final ulceration through the skin will then lead to communication into the bursa. Surgical excision of the bursa, combined with a rotation flap, is then required. This can be a very extensive procedure, which alters the blood supply to the skin, and so may not be repeatable in any given area.

INTELLECTUAL DEVELOPMENT OF CHILDREN WITH SPINA BIFIDA

General intelligence

Surveys have shown that children with hydrocephalus have lower IQs than their brothers and sisters. There are also interesting differences between spina bifida children with and without shunts. Table 2 shows the results of assessment using the Wechsler Intelligence Scales for Children (WISC) at age 11 years in the Greater London Council (GLC) survey.

TABLE 2   WISC mean IQs at 11 years (standard deviations in parentheses). *From* Halliwell et al (1980)

	Number	Full Scale IQ	Verbal Scale	Performance Scale
Controls	45	112.0 (11.9)	110.4 (11.5)	111.3 (13.0)
Shunt	67	80.0 (17.4)	84.3 (18.8)	77.4 (16.5)
No shunt	30	100.1 (16.1)	99.8 (15.0)	100.4 (17.1)

The distribution of intelligence within the whole group is slanted towards the lower end of the IQ range and intelligence is particularly affected in the shunt-treated group, who also had average performance scale scores lower than verbal scale scores. This is particularly true for low ability children. The presence of a shunt indicates an initial degree of hydrocephalus, though some children without shunts may have had some degree of hydrocephalus. A recent large survey by Lonton (1979) relating intellectual skills and CT scans in children with spina bifida and hydrocephalus showed that even large degrees of hydrocephalus had insignificant effects on the verbal IQ, but there was a small but statistically significant effect upon performance scale IQ on the WISC. The abilities most affected were motor and perceptuo-motor skills.

Children with shunts were only found to be substantially inferior in skills to those without if their ventricles were very large or abnormally small. The highest proportion of children with shunts was found in the group with the smallest ventricles.

Visual perception

Several studies show a general trend towards inferior functioning in visual perception in hydrocephalics. The type of task the children find difficult is the embedded figure test, where a simple figure like a triangle or a star has to be picked out from a group of overlapping shapes (Miller and Sethi, 1971; Tew, 1973).

Scanning ability

Hydrocephalic children may have difficulty in rapidly surveying a visual array before responding. Tasks like working from left to right, looking between their work and a key, or finding their place on a page may be particularly difficult for them.

On tasks combining perceptual and motor skills hydrocephalic children may have marked difficulties from an early age. Impaired hand function may also be present as a result of cerebellar involvement in the Arnold Chiari malformation (Fig. 4/5).

Verbal ability

Most children with spina bifida give the impression of having normal verbal ability by being 'chatty' and using quite complex language structures, but on the other hand there can be an apparent lack of understanding. Several studies show that spina bifida children have normal verbal memory and development of vocabulary.

Hyperverbal behaviour is an extreme form of fluent speech coupled with poor understanding. Not all children show it although the label can get widely applied. Tew and Lawrence (1972) found evidence of hyperverbal behaviour in 28 per cent of their sample. In the GLC survey 40 per cent of the children at 6 years were rated clinically as hyperverbal, although only 20 per cent showed it to a marked degree.

ORTHOPAEDIC MANAGEMENT

Myelomeningocele produces a bewildering variety of orthopaedic problems in the lower limbs. It has also become clear that in the majority of spina bifida patients the neurological deficit can progress and alter with increasing age. As a result early operations based on the principles used in poliomyelitis are likely to fail or need revision.

Originally, orthopaedic surgeons advised early surgery to correct the limb deformities before the age of 18 months to 2 years, when the child would be ready to walk. This doctrine resulted in a large number of operations being performed which later proved to be ineffective and of no benefit to the child. The present approach is best summarised by the title of the Casey Holter Memorial Lecture given by Mr Menelaus in 1976 – *A Plea for Realistic Goals to be Achieved by the Minimum of Surgery.*

The patient should be seen and assessed from the orthopaedic point of view as soon as possible after birth. A muscle chart, at this stage, is useful to provide a baseline. However, it is essential to realise that some or all of the movement observed in the lower limbs may be involuntary or reflex. Such movement, far from being of use to the child, is often a handicap and a major deforming force which may require both conservative and surgical treatment.

Until the general condition and prognosis of the child can be accurately assessed, the lower limb deformities should be treated by passive stretching and careful splintage. Surgery is rarely indicated until it is clear the child is going to be capable of standing and walking. Sometimes a simple *tenotomy* of the adductors at the hip or a specific deforming tendon around the ankle or knee is worth while to allow effective conservative treatment to continue and prevent gross progressive deformity. Major operations should rarely be done until it is clear that the child is going to be a useful walker, or if deformity prevents satisfactory positioning in a wheelchair.

The foot

The whole range of foot deformities may be seen in spina bifida patients. The deformity is frequently quite different in each limb.

TALIPES EQUINOVARUS (TEV)

It is important not to think that the neurological *talipes equinovarus* seen in spina bifida will behave in the same way as the so-called idiopathic congenital talipes equinovarus (CTEV). Initial treatment is the same in the two conditions by careful stretching and strapping or serial plasters. Great care should be taken to avoid pressure sores due to the disturbance of skin sensation in these patients. Early operation is rarely indicated unless the deformity is completely incorrigible, when a simple tenotomy of the deforming tendon will usually allow further effective correction by conservative means to continue.

Sometimes an arthrogrypotic type of limb is encountered in spina bifida. In these patients, early radical surgery may be necessary, but must be followed by diligent and continuous splintage for many years. The problem of anaesthetic skin can make this difficult to achieve. Once the child shows his potential to walk or is already standing on his deformed feet, then definitive surgery can be undertaken, if possible in combination with any other surgery necessary in the limbs. Surgery should be done in as short a time as possible to avoid long periods of immobilisation in plaster which results in disuse *osteoporosis* and frequent fractures when the child starts to mobilise again.

CALCANEO-VALGUS FOOT

The *calcaneo-valgus* foot is also common. A mild degree is little disability. If the deformity is severe, division of the overacting dorsiflexors is worthwhile. Gross valgus instability of the sub-talar joint is sometimes controllable by transferring the tendon of peroneus brevis into tibialis posterior. A below-knee orthosis and boot, usually combined with an inside 'T' strap, will also support the calcaneo-valgus foot very successfully. If necessary, the sub-talar joint can be fused by the Grice-type sub-talar arthrodesis once the bones have reached a reasonable size.

In the older child with a calcaneo-valgus deformity, it is very important to assess the ankle joint. Much of the valgus of the foot may be due to a valgus tilt at the ankle joint itself. This can be corrected by a supramalleolar medially-based wedge osteotomy at maturity.

Triple arthrodesis can be considered at maturity. However, this produces a rigid foot which can be cosmetically pleasing, but its rigidity may lead to sores and problems with walking. Arthrodesis at the ankle joint is not recommended as this usually fails and forms a mobile pseudarthrosis or Charcot joint.

CLAWING OF THE TOES AND PES CAVUS DEFORMITY

Clawing of the toes and cavus deformity can be a considerable problem in a good walker. The resulting high pressure areas on the sole and the toes predispose to sores. It is vital to keep the foot plantigrade, if possible, to avoid intractable skin ulceration. For this reason, surgical correction is often necessary in older children who remain good walkers.

The knee

At the knee, flexion is the chief problem although hyperextension can also occur. In the first 1–2 years passive stretching and splintage should be used to try and mobilise the knee and get as good a passive range of movement as possible. When the child wants to walk, and particularly if he needs an orthosis, significant knee flexion should be corrected. It is difficult to fit a satisfactory orthosis with a knee flexion deformity of 25 degrees or more. Correction by posterior soft tissue release at the knee is the simplest and best operation. Transfer of the hamstrings to the quadriceps apparatus is rarely indicated and may result in stiff, extended knees. This is fine when the child is small and can sit down with his legs straight out, but is of no help to the older child who has to spend most of the day sitting in a wheelchair. Similarly, patients born with stiff extended legs manage very well until about the age of 8–10, when their inability to flex becomes an increasing nuisance and *quadricepsplasty* may be necessary.

Supracondylar osteotomy of the femur to correct flexion deformity should be avoided in the early years, as it can produce a very awkward anterior angular deformity with growth. At maturity, however, it can be a very useful and successful method of correcting persistent and recurrent flexion deformity of the knee, plus any *varus* or *valgus* deformity.

The hip

Dislocation, subluxation and dysplasia of the hip are extremely common. Nowhere has the attitude to orthopaedic treatment changed so much in the last few years. It is vital to remember that the dislocation is neurological in origin and not a congenital dislocation of the hip (CDH). In the 1960s an aggressive approach to reducing and stabilising the hips by surgery in the first two years of life was strongly advocated. However, this led to large numbers of stiff and sometimes painful hips which were of no benefit, or even a positive disadvantage to the children.

Nowadays, if both hips are dislocated, they should nearly always be left alone unless the child has a pure lower motor neurone lesion and is going to be an active community walker, probably without any aids at all. A single dislocated hip should be replaced if the child is going to be a good walker, but not otherwise. Splintage in the traditional frog position can lead to severe contracture in this position. If a child has a dislocated hip at birth which is not reducible, it should be left alone until it is clear that he is going to be a good walker. If it is then causing problems, operative reduction can be considered. If a hip is dislocated, but reducible at birth, a simple abduction broomstick-type splint can be used, as advocated by Professor McKibbin.

If the hip adductors are tight and tending to cause subluxation or dislocation, then closed adductor tenotomy is all that is necessary, followed by passive stretching. The iliopsoas tendon transfer which was widely used in the past is now rarely indicated, except in children with a lower motor neurone lesion, a powerful iliopsoas, and who walk with a Trendelenburg lurch, i.e. the same type of patient who responded well to this operation when it was described by Dr Mustard for use in poliomyelitis.

Many of these children have an *upper motor neurone lesion* and spasticity of the adductor muscles. This can lead to progressive subluxation, and open *adductor tenotomy* (as in cerebral palsy) will be necessary. Hip dysplasia is very common in spina bifida and may require treatment by operation on the acetabulum if the child remains a good walker, but otherwise surgery is unnecessary. Flexion deformity at the hip is also common. If this fails to respond to the conservative stretching, surgical flexor release may be indicated to allow the hip to extend so that the child can stand in an orthosis. Abduction deformity can occur, but is usually correctible by passive stretching and physiotherapy. However, if this fails, soft tissue release at the hip can be used.

Orthoses

Orthoses of some kind will be necessary for the majority of patients. In general, a pelvic band is often necessary to start with; if a patient continues to have to use a pelvic band he is very unlikely to use his orthosis as an adult, as it is too cumbersome. These patients will almost invariably prefer to use a wheelchair as adults. It is most important to be realistic about the aims in these children. Once it is clear that elaborate orthoses are not going to be used as an independent means of locomotion as an adult, then time and effort should not be wasted on further training with these orthoses, but should be directed towards encouraging independence in a wheel-chair. Patients who are independent in long-leg or short-leg orthoses will normally continue to use these as adults if walking does not become too laborious and exhausting.

The aim of orthopaedic surgery is to allow the child to be as independent as possible within his limitations at maturity. This should be achieved by the minimum of surgery, backed up by regular physiotherapy done by the parents under the supervision and guidance of the physiotherapist.

PHYSIOTHERAPY AND OCCUPATIONAL THERAPY MANAGEMENT

The pre-school period

The aim in the first year of life is to help the baby to develop as normally as possible within the limitations of his neurological problems and to attain the normal developmental milestones of head control, grasp, sitting balance, rolling and pulling to sitting and movement on the floor, either shuffling or 'commando' crawling. The anaesthetic legs may be in danger of friction damage if not covered, and sheepskin bootees can be made to protect the feet.

Different positions for play will give the child experience in spatial awareness, and a suitable highchair with a tray or table at the right height, with knees and feet supported at right angles, will allow the child to play. Obviously the level of the spinal lesion will affect the degree of sitting balance; for some children sitting balance is not attainable without using arms, and therefore suitable support for the back will enable them to use their hands properly in play. Even babies with low lesions (lumbar 5 to sacral 1 (L5–S1)) have problems with hip stability and need more support than usual.

Babies with hydrocephalus may have the added problem of ataxia which interferes with their balance and makes them anxious about sitting and standing with support. It is important to progress at the pace of the child and decide for the individual when to stand and begin the process of learning to walk with support. For the toddler stage, the Chailey Chariot enables the child to move around rapidly at his own level (Fig. 4/8). The Oswestry swivel walker is helpful in giving the toddler the experience of standing and moving in an upright position.

Fig. 4/8
Chailey Chariot

The general care of the baby may initially be frightening for the parents and they may need advice. The repaired area of the back may need protection. The skin must be regularly inspected for poor circulation and signs of pressure sores. A good time to do this is at bathtime. The parents need to be aware that these problems can occur however carefully the baby is handled. If the baby is very immobile, changes of posture are necessary.

TOILETING
Even though the baby may be expected to be doubly incontinent and need to wear nappies, it is important to establish a regular routine for bowel evacuation at around the age of 2 years, to try to produce a pattern of bowel management. A potty chair with a bar across the front will give the child confidence and allow him to lean forward and push, either to empty the bowel or bladder (see p. 42). There are large nappies and a variety of protective pants on the market. The pants need to be well-fitting around the thighs, but not so tight as to restrict the blood supply (see Chapter 5).

BATHING AND DRESSING
As the child gets older and heavier, a shallow bath insert can be used to lessen the strain on mother's back (see Chapter 21). The empty surface of the insert makes a convenient site for drying and dressing the child. It can be hung on the wall above the bath when not in use. When the child has learnt to transfer from one surface to another, he can begin to get in and out of the bath by himself. Great care is needed to ensure that the temperature of the bath water is not too hot and the hot water tap is fully closed, as a dripping tap can easily scald a toe.

Undressing is usually achieved before dressing, and the clothing is more easily discarded from the top half of the body, particularly if the child wears high orthoses.

A joint home visit by the occupational therapist and social services department needs to be arranged so problems of access in the home can be assessed and plans for future adaptations and additions to the house can be started.

AMBULATION
When the child is ready to stand, usually between 18 months and 2 years an assessment needs to be made of the degree of support required from the orthosis. At first, more support may be necessary, and can be removed gradually as the child becomes stronger and more confident. Table 3 shows the usual degree of support needed according to the neurological level of the lesion, and Figure 4/9 the segmental nerve supply to the legs.

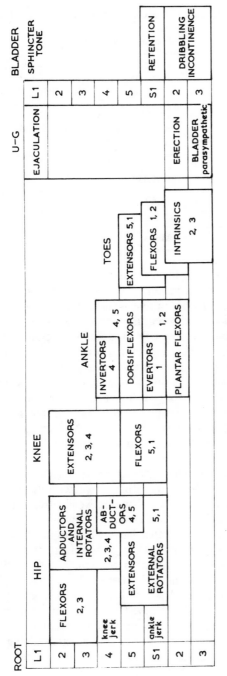

93

Fig. 4/9 Segmental nerve supply to legs

TABLE 3   Ambulation support according to neurological level

Level of paralysis	Equipment required
Above L1	Thoraco-lumbar-sacral orthosis (TLSO) with knee-ankle-foot orthoses (KAFOs) Hip-guidance orthosis (HGO) (Rose et al, 1981)
Below L2	TLSO with KAFOs or lumbar-sacral orthosis (LSO) LSO with KAFOs
Below L3–4	LSO with KAFOs or KAFOs
Below L5	KAFOs or AFOs
Below S1	AFOs

ORTHOSES (Figs. 4/10, 4/11, 4/12, 4/13)

If they are to be used successfully, orthoses must become as much part of the child's daily living routine as his clothing. It has been clearly shown that children who require orthoses with pelvic support or higher are very unlikely to use them as adults. They almost invariably prefer to use a wheelchair, and it is important to be realistic about the aims in these children. There are however positive gains to standing and walking, even for a short time in childhood. Circulation is improved as the child starts to move and kidney function is also facilitated. A change of posture is important so that standing, even without walking, is worth while in a small child, and a standing table may be used for him to play on or to be used as a desk in the schoolroom when he is older.

The child with the high lesion requires a pelvic or thoracic band for support, and he usually needs a Rollator walker initially; he learns to move by a swivel movement, changing weight from one leg to the other (Fig. 4/14). He may then go on to a 'jump-to' gait, either using the Rollator walker or parallel bars. The length of time taken to progress to using quadripod sticks, independent sticks or crutches varies tremendously according to the child's self-confidence and personality, and also to the enthusiasm and encouragement given to the child by the parents. A swing-through gait using crutches allows for rapid movement and is achieved by many children, even with high lesions (see Fig. 15/2, p. 280). Some very active children may damage their ankle and knee joints by over-enthusiastic walking, especially using a swing-through gait. Parents need to be informed and realistic

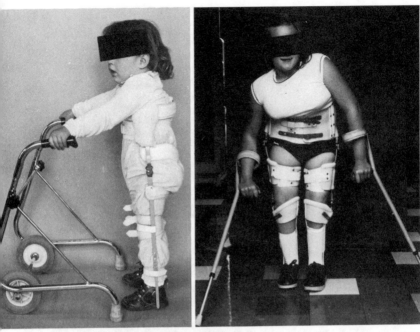

Fig. 4/10 (*left*) TLSO with KAFOs. Child using a Rollator walker
Fig. 4/11 (*right*) Polypropylene TLSO with KAFOs. Ring-topped crutches

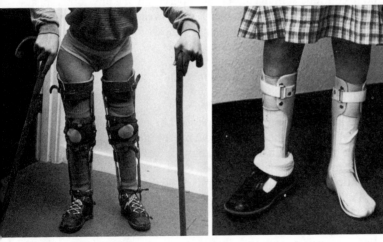

Fig. 4/12 (*left*) KAFOs
Fig. 4/13 (*right*) Polypropylene AFOs worn with sandals

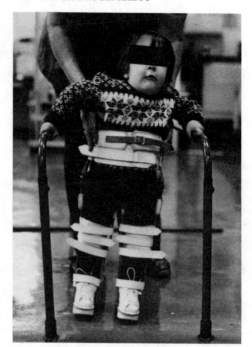

Fig. 4/14 Child learning to walk in parallel bars with a swivel movement

about the aims of walking and the use of orthoses, and encourage the child to continue at home under the supervision of a physiotherapist.

The hip guidance orthosis (HGO) was developed for children with high lesions with a relatively poor prognosis for long-term walking (Rose et al, 1981). It permits low-energy-cost ambulation at a reasonable speed. The brace incorporates:

1. hip articulation during ambulation which is mechanically satisfactory;
2. very rigid body-brace and leg-brace;
3. fixed adduction angle of 5 degrees at hip level;
4. limitation of flexion at hips (from 5–10 degrees);
5. lateral rocking with a shoe rocker.

In the more severely handicapped child, a wheelchair will be used and seating must be looked at regularly as the child grows (Chapter 14). Transfers and press-ups must be practised daily and the child taught to transfer from one position to another when on his feet or in a wheelchair.

Before starting primary education, the therapist (occupational therapist (OT) or physiotherapist) and the parents will need to visit the chosen school to look at access to toilets, classroom and playground and talk to the teachers and school helpers. A supportive role is then established so that when difficulties arise the therapist will be contacted.

Parents need advice and encouragement in the management of the orthosis.

1. Toes may become curled inside a boot and produce pressure sores.
2. A regular check of boot size needs to be made.
3. Orthoses, jackets and boots can rub sores very quickly and regular inspection of the anaesthetic areas must become a routine. Red areas will develop and need to be distinguished from true pressure sores.
4. Clothing must be pulled down to prevent pressure under the orthosis.
5. Nappies are difficult to apply, especially when the child is wearing a thoraco-lumbar-sacral orthosis (TLSO), and nappies need to be well out of the way of orthoses.

The school child from 5–11 years

OCCUPATIONAL THERAPY

Learning to dress is a continuing process, and parents and children need encouragement to persist in gaining independence in this skill. The rush of getting the child ready for school in the mornings makes this difficult during the week, but should be practised at weekends when the family is more relaxed. The aim should be complete dressing in 20 minutes, including orthoses and boots. The choice of clothing is important. Plain wool socks without heels eliminate pressure sores and keep the child's legs warm. Open-to-toe boots are desirable so that the position of the feet can be checked easily. High equipment must be put on next, and at first mother will need to support the child's legs as he transfers into the orthosis, and to check that the spurs are fitted into the sockets of the boots, and that ankle, knee and thigh straps are at the correct tension. Protective underpants will then need to go on over the orthosis, together with a pair of loosely fitting trousers. The trouser fly needs to be lengthened down to the crutch seam so that it will be easier to empty the urine bag, and the waist band may need enlarging to accommodate the equipment.

Special care needs to be given to the type of clothing to be worn, as some materials cause friction which can produce pressure sores. There needs to be a compromise between suitable clothing which the child can put on himself, and fashion.

Children with hydrocephalus often have perceptual problems and these may be highlighted by their difficulty in learning daily living activities like dressing and teeth cleaning and in learning to move about, either walking or in a wheelchair.

It is very important to develop problem-solving concepts and manipulative skills at primary school age as a foundation upon which further new skills can be built. If a child does not develop a work method of his own he will be unable to relate any new task to previous experience and each new skill will be seen as an isolated task, needing to be broken down into small stages and gradually built up. Many teachers in primary schools are unfamiliar with the hidden disability, and the OT may have an important role in working with the child on this type of splinter-skill training and building of self-esteem as well as his abilities (Ayres, 1972).

PHYSIOTHERAPY

Where a child is attending a normal school, it may be easier for staff to manage him in a wheelchair, and it is important that his walking ability is not neglected and that he is encouraged to spend at least part of the day on his feet. This can be achieved by using a standing chair (Fig. 4/15) thus eliminating the necessity of manipulating hip locks. If

Fig. 4/15
Standing chair

small wheels are attached to a standing chair it can be transported between classrooms by the school helper, the child walking if possible.

A great deal of encouragement is needed to keep the more severely handicapped child on his feet. It is worth while in the early years, particularly in keeping weight down and strengthening arms and shoulders. Equipment will need to be checked regularly or at six-monthly intervals; the physiotherapist needs to see the child and encourage the parents to work with him on walking, transferring from one position to another, getting up from sitting to standing, and from standing to the floor, managing steps and stairs.

Independence from a wheelchair is also important, and advice needs to be given to allow the child to participate in gym lessons, swimming and games. The individual problems of the child can be pointed out at a school visit. The problems of spastic arms, anaesthetic skin, fractures, friction and pressure sores must be brought to the attention of teaching staff. Out-of-school activities with able-bodied children of their own age can include participation in PHAB clubs (Physically Handicapped and Able-Bodied), swimming, archery, riding for the disabled, Brownies and Cubs.

Adolescence

Towards the end of primary education, consideration of the next type of school requires consultation between the parents and the team. This is often the point at which a child can no longer manage in a normal school because of problems of access, frequent changes of classroom and occasionally educational problems. It may also be the time when the family decide that a boarding school might be appropriate. It is vital that therapists pass on relevant information about the children.

At this stage of the child's development it is easier to see what permanent alterations to the home are necessary, and the requirements of the family need to be discussed with the social services so that suitable alterations to the house can be organised.

Independence in dressing, bathing and toileting need to be stressed at this stage with the emphasis on personal hygiene. Many of the youngsters are unaware of their body odour, and the occupational therapist can help to overcome this by pointing out its social unacceptability.

From the age of 14, it has been found useful to assess the independence of the teenagers when not being prompted by their family or care staff. Short stays when they can look after themselves in a bungalow or flat with an OT as an observer can often pinpoint the areas of independence on which most work needs to be done. At Chailey Heritage independence training is carried out in pairs, and the youngsters are responsible for themselves in every stage of the procedure; packing, menu planning, shopping, cooking, housework and the taking of medications are among the expected activities. At the end of the two- or three-day session the occupational therapist prepares a report on each child which can be used by the family, care staff and teaching staff as a basis for continued activity. The Association for Spina Bifida and Hydrocephalus organises independence holidays with the aim of pinpointing problems and promoting individual independence.

PHYSIOTHERAPY AND THE ADOLESCENT

The onset of puberty is often early in children with spina bifida and this aggravates the problems of adolescence because of the associated immaturity. Parents need even more patience and tolerance in dealing with their child at this stage of development. It is often a time when a decision needs to be made about continued walking. The less severely handicapped need to be encouraged to overcome problems in order to stay on their feet.

During the growth spurt of adolescence, spinal deformities increase and this may interfere with balance, both in sitting and standing. It may be necessary to support the spine with a polypropylene jacket (TLSO) and if there is instability in sitting a flanged jacket or one fixed to the back of the wheelchair may be used. Both these types of jacket are bulky, and clothing may need to be adapted, but with careful planning and some dressmaking this can be overcome. It is possible to attach the straightforward polypropylene TLSO to KAFOs (Fig. 4/11), or it may be easier to fit the equipment over the TLSO; but as the child becomes older, walking with high equipment may be found to be impractical and a decision to use a wheelchair may be taken. At this stage the physiotherapist's role is a supervisory one and the parents need to continue to encourage their child if he is able to maintain mobility.

REFERENCES

Ayres, A. J. (1972). *Sensory Integration and Learning Difficulties.* Western Psychological Services.

Halliwell, M. D., Carr, J. G. and Pearson, A. M. (1980). The intellectual and educational functioning of children with neural tube defects. *Zeitschrift Fur Kinderchirurgie*, **31**, 4.

Laurence, K. M. (1969). The recurrence risk in spina bifida cystica and anencephaly. *Developmental Medicine and Child Neurology*. 11, Supp 20, 23.

Leck, I. (1983). *Epidemiological clues to the causation of neural tube defects*. In *Prevention of Spina Bifida and Other Neural Tube Defects* (ed Dobbing, J.). Academic Press, London.

Lonton, A. P. (1979). The relationship between intellectual skills and CAT scans of children with spina bifida and hydrocephalus. *Zeitschrift Fur Kinderchirurgie*, 28, 4.

Lorber, J. (1971). Results of treatment of myelomeningocoele. An analysis of 524 unselected cases. *Developmental Medicine and Child Neurology*, 13, 279.

Lorber, J. (1972). Spina bifida cystica. Results of treatment of 270 consecutive cases with criteria for selection for the future. *Archives of Disease in Childhood*, 47, 854.

Lorber, J. and Salfield, S. A. W. (1981). Results of selective treatment of spina bifida cystica. *Archives of Disease in Childhood*, 56, 822–30.

Mawdsley, T., Rickham, P. O. and Roberts, J. R. (1967). Long term results of early operation of open myelomeningocele and encephalocele. *British Medical Journal*, 1, 663.

Menelaus, M. B. (1976). Orthopaedic management of children with myelomeningocele: a plea for realistic goals. *Developmental Medicine and Child Neurology*, 18, Supp 37, 3–11.

Miller, E. and Sethi, L. (1971). The effect of hydrocephalus on perception. *Developmental Medicine and Child Neurology*, Supp 25, 77–81.

Rose, G. K., Stallard, J. and Sankarankutty, M. (1981). Clinical evaluation of spina bifida patients using hip-guidance orthoses. *Developmental Medicine and Child Neurology*, 23, 30–40.

Seller, M. J. (1982). *Paediatric Research: A Genetic Approach. Neural Tube Defects: Cause and Prevention* pp. 197–211. (Spastics International Medical Publications) William Heinemann Medical Books Limited, London.

Smithells, R. W. et al (1981). Apparent prevention of neural tube defects by periconceptional vitamin supplementation. *Archives of Disease in Childhood*, 56, 911–18.

Stark, G. D. and Baker, C. W. (1967). The neurological involvement of the lower limbs in myelomeningocoele. *Developmental Medicine and Child Neurology*, 9, 732.

Stark, G. D. and Drummond, M. (1971). The spinal cord lesion in myelomeningocele. *Developmental Medicine and Child Neurology*, 13, Supp 25, 1.

Tew, B. J. (1973). *Some psychological consequences of spina bifida and its complications*. In *Proceedings of the 31st Biennial Conference*, ASE, London.

Tew, B. J. and Lawrence, K. M. (1972). The ability and attainments of spina bifida patients born in South Wales between 1956–62. *Developmental Medicine and Child Neurology*, Supp 27, 124–31.

FURTHER READING

Anderson, E. M. and Spain, B. (1977). *The Child with Spina Bifida*. Methuen, London.

Chapter 5

The Neuropathic Bladder and Bowel

by M. BORZYSKOWSKI MB, MRCP *and* M. STRODE MB, BS

There are many causes of a neuropathic bladder in childhood. Spina bifida is the commonest, and others include spinal cord tumours and trauma, sacral agenesis, myelitis and a small group in whom a cause is not found. In some of these children, the neuropathic bladder is the major handicap. Defective bladder innervation results in inefficient bladder emptying, incontinence and recurrent urinary tract infections with the risk of impairment of renal function. The aims of management are preservation of renal function, continence and social integration. The method used has to be acceptable to both the child and those looking after him.

INITIAL ASSESSMENT

In the baby with spina bifida, assessment of bladder function should be made during the neonatal period. It is important to observe the baby during micturition, to see whether he is able to pass urine in a stream, whether he is incontinent on crying, and whether the bladder is expressible manually. Intermittent filling and emptying of the bladder begins as early as the third month of fetal life and continues after birth until maturational development of the suprasegmental pathways permits increasing control both by day and night, but even then the pattern of complete dryness, then a steady powerful stream until the bladder is empty, followed once more by dryness without dribbling, continues. In a normal infant the bladder cannot be emptied by external pressure except under general anaesthetic.

Bladder and renal function should be fully assessed in any child in whom a neuropathic bladder is suspected. Assessment of renal function includes measurement of plasma creatinine, glomerular filtration rate and an intravenous urogram (IVU). If renal function is impaired, more sophisticated tests may be required. Bladder function is assessed by means of a video-urodynamic study (combined micturating cysto-urethrogram and cystometrogram). Urine should be cultured regularly for evidence of infection.

LONG-TERM SUPERVISION

The main problem in the maintenance of normal renal function is that many neuropathic bladders do not drain adequately. The commonest cause for this is an inco-ordination between the main bladder muscle (detrusor) and the muscles controlling the bladder outlet – the latter failing to relax when the detrusor muscle contracts (detrusor-sphincter dyssynergia). The semi-stagnant urine is liable to recurrent infection, and over a period of time – unless the problem is relieved – a series of structural changes take place in the urinary tract, i.e. bladder trabeculation and later diverticulation, being followed by *incompetence* of the uretero-vesical junction with back-flow of urine up one or both ureters (ureteric reflux), with progressive stretching of the ureters and collecting systems of the kidneys (hydro-ureters and hydronephrosis). Renal reflux – back-flow of urine into the kidney substance itself particularly in the presence of infection – will finally lead to chronic renal failure (Fig. 5/1). There may also be *obstruction* to urine drainage at the uretero-vesical junction leading to back-pressure effects on the kidney.

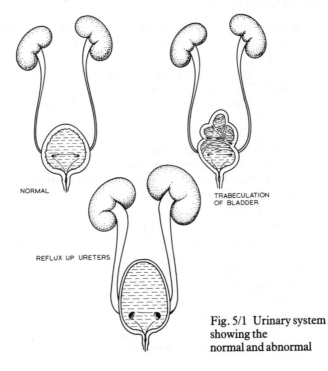

NORMAL

TRABECULATION OF BLADDER

REFLUX UP URETERS

Fig. 5/1 Urinary system showing the normal and abnormal

Clinical observations

It follows from the above that regular supervision of the urinary tract is essential at three- to six-monthly intervals in the first instance. Danger signals that the bladder is not draining adequately include:

1. Recurrent urinary infections, which may be overt with illness and pyrexia, or sub-clinical, the latter being assessed from the results of carefully taken clean-catch specimens every few weeks.
2. A history that the child is always wet may indicate a dribbling overflow incontinence, or conversely, long periods of dryness may be due to a dangerous degree of retention.
3. On examination, the discovery that the bladder is always distended, or that it is difficult to express, can be of real significance, especially if associated with priapism (penile erection), as the latter may be indicative of too much sphincter activity at the bladder neck. Routine recording of blood pressure is essential for early detection of hypertension, often caused by earlier attacks of pyelonephritis.

Special investigations

(a) Regular checks on the urine with carefully taken clean-catch specimens (using the dip-slide method) every one to three months.
(b) Six-monthly estimations of blood urea and creatinine.
(c) Serial IVUs (the intervals between which should not exceed two years). These give vital information of bladder and renal function.
(d) Renal function tests including estimations of the glomerular filtration rate (GFR) which gives the production of urine in millilitres per minute (ml/min) from both kidneys.
(e) Renograms which estimate the percentage contribution made by each kidney to the total output; such tests can be of great value in selected cases.
(f) Simple measurement of the residual urine – after an attempt at bladder emptying has been made (by voluntary effort, manual expression, or a combination of the two) is of value in itself.
(g) Video-urodynamic studies, i.e. combined micturating cysto-urethrogram and cystometrogram. These provide information on bladder size, shape and capacity; residual urine; the presence or absence of vesico-ureteric reflux; detrusor pressure at rest, during filling and during a detrusor contraction. These studies enable one to plan the most appropriate management in each

child. If it is not possible to carry out such studies, a micturating cysto-urethrogram should be performed.

(h) Ultrasound examination of the kidneys, ureters and bladder can be useful in management.

Control of infection

Whatever other methods are being employed, the control of infection is of basic importance if the first aim of management – the preservation of renal function – is to be achieved.

Clearly any overt urinary tract infection associated with clinical symptoms of illness and pyrexia must be treated with an adequate course of the appropriate antibiotic. With sub-clinical infections – detected by the bacteriology alone – indications for treatment are not so clear, for the light-hearted use of antibiotics can lead to the emergence of highly resistant strains of bacteria which are of particular danger in a closed community, due to the risk of cross-infection. It is therefore necessary to adopt some criteria for the treatment of sub-clinical urinary tract infections if this danger is to be avoided.

The present policy includes two requirements:

1. A concentration of pathogenic organisms of 100 000 organisms/ml or over, confirmed by a second carefully taken clean-catch or catheter specimen culturing the same organisms.
2. The presence of back-flow (ureteric reflux) up one or both ureters.

Prophylaxis: The use of drugs given in suppressive doses once or twice daily, usually co-trimoxazole (Septrin), trimethoprim or nitrofurantoin. Prophylactic treatment should be reserved for cases with ureteric reflux or recurrent urinary tract infections.

Other measures include a good fluid intake which helps to reduce the concentration of organisms in the urine, but this measure should be used with discretion, especially in those children who are using intermittent self-catheterisation as a means of controlling their incontinence.

Adequate drainage of the bladder is of fundamental importance in the prevention of urinary tract infections and lies at the heart of the problem.

MANAGEMENT OF URINARY INCONTINENCE

1. *Manual expression of the bladder*, at approximately two-hourly intervals during the day, should be *the routine* for infants and young children, unless investigations have revealed that there is a

significant out-flow obstruction from the bladder, in which event attempts at expression may hasten the onset of ureteric reflux. It is important to adopt the correct technique for expressing the bladder:

(a) The child must be relaxed, as effective expression is impossible if the abdominal wall muscles are contracted, when bruising may be the only result.

(b) The pressure should be increased gradually, with a *warm* hand and in the right direction, i.e. downwards into the pelvis (as for an expression of the placenta after childbirth).

(c) If possible, the pressure should be a continuous one until the manoeuvre is completed, rather than a series of attempts, but the latter may be necessary if the child is not relaxed.

Bladder expression may be difficult in infants, who dislike the procedure.

In some cases reflex emptying of the bladder can be achieved by tapping the skin over the lumbo-sacral area, or pinching the skin of the lower abdomen or thighs.

2. *Time training.* When the child is old enough to co-operate, it is always worth recording whether periods of dryness can be achieved, with regular attempts at bladder emptying – whether by voluntary effort, manual expression or a combination of the two. It is usual to start with an hourly interval, and simply record how much urine is passed, and whether the child is wet, damp or dry. If there is enough success at hourly emptying, the interval can be increased. It is best to carry out this test for limited but well-supervised periods of time – morning and afternoon over a two-day period – as this will be quite long enough to decide whether it is worth persisting. It is sometimes worth repeating this test as the child grows older, for just occasionally – and to everyone's surprise and delight – it is found that a supposedly incontinent spina bifida child can be controlled in this way!

3. *Indwelling catheterisation* is a useful short-term measure in management of chronically dilated upper tracts from obstructed outflow; it can also be used as a long-term method of control (Rickwood et al, 1983). Silastic balloon catheters are far better tolerated than other varieties, and need only be changed every six to eight weeks. Catheterisation should be carried out with full aseptic precautions, and it is important to keep the balloon size as small as possible (not exceeding 10ml), as larger balloons interfere with drainage; the calibre of the catheter should not exceed 18FG. One difficulty with this method is that the urethra stretches over a period of time, allowing leakage of urine round the catheter. When

this happens it is best to remove the catheter for 48 hours, during which time the urethral tone is improved; a smaller catheter can then be introduced with success.

While some children can be well maintained by the prolonged use of silastic balloon catheters, the problems of leaking round the catheter, and the generally decreasing bladder capacity (of particular danger in the unstable bladder), coupled with the impossibility of keeping the urine free from infection, make the method very unsatisfactory in many cases. In a few children recurrent misplacements of the balloon into the posterior urethra can lead to the creation of a false pocket into which the balloon can readily slip. In this confined position the catheter acts more like a cork than a drain, leading to back pressure damage to the upper tracts.

4. *The use of urinals.* The problem with urinals in children is to obtain a water-tight fit between the appliance and the skin. With adults, the use of a skin adhesive – with disposable condom sheaths – presents no such problem, and the same holds true for the mature adolescent, for whom a condom sheath provides a reasonably close fit. With smaller children the problem is much more difficult, and becomes increasingly so the younger the child.

The Pubic Pressure Urinal (Down Bros) depends for its competence principally on the pressure of the flange on to the suprapubic pad of fat. While working well in the standing position, when sitting or in bed it is exceptional for this urinal to prevent some leakage.

The best method at present depends on the use of disposable penile sheaths of graded sizes attached to the penis by rolling over an adhesive strip of Stomahesive (Seton type) or Uriliner (Conveen type) which is wound round the base of the penis. Where necessary adhesive spray can improve the effectiveness of the skin seal; the free end of the sheath is attached to a thigh bag.

Whatever urinal is used it is important that *regular attempts at bladder emptying* should be maintained during the day, and the urinal not simply used as a method of controlling incontinence, if damage to the upper tracts is to be avoided.

5. *Pads and napkins.* In some severely handicapped girls incontinence pads may be the only method which is effective. In the past few years a number of manufacturers have co-operated in trials to produce more effective and acceptable products. An example of this is the Ancilla incontinence pad which is designed to have a high absorption capacity and keep the skin dry. Kanga pants and Molmycke pants and pads have also proved useful in both sexes.

6. *Clean intermittent catheterisation.* This has proved to be a major advance in the management of this condition since it was introduced by Lapides et al (1972). It is a clean and not sterile technique, and is performed every two or three hours during the day. A bladder capacity of about 50ml together with some urethral tone are required in order to achieve continence. This technique can be used in both sexes, and self-catheterisation is encouraged from the age of 6 years. Clean intermittent catheterisation can also be useful in the management of children who will never be able to catheterise themselves.

Method: Prior to catheterisation the hands are washed. When the bladder is empty the catheter is slowly withdrawn and washed in soapy water. It can be kept in a plastic or polythene container and should be changed approximately weekly. It does not need to be kept in an antiseptic solution. The stiffer Portex catheter has proved popular, although a short metal catheter can also be used. The child should always be encouraged to pass urine spontaneously prior to catheterisation if this is possible. The aim is that the child should be able to catheterise himself or herself in an ordinary toilet and that special facilities are not required. A mirror can be a useful aid to a girl who is learning the technique.

There have been many reports claiming improvement in renal function, continence and infection rate. A recent study, the first in the form of a controlled trial, confirmed that treatment with clean intermittent catheterisation, supplemented where necessary by drugs, gives a highly significant improvement in continence (Borzyskowski et al, 1982). There was no significant difference in infection rate between the intermittently catheterised children and those who were not catheterised. Results regarding renal function were encouraging, although long-term follow-up is required.

7. *Drug therapy.* Four groups of drugs can be used in the management of the neuropathic bladder, based on the findings of the video-urodynamic study. These are:

(a) Anticholinergic agents such as propantheline in a dose of 1mg/kg/day in three doses up to 12 years, and 15mg every eight hours thereafter (to reduce detrusor contractility and therefore indirectly increase bladder capacity). Oxybutynin 2.5mg nocte increasing to 5mg three times a day from 10 years is effective in the same way as propantheline, and has been shown to be more effective than the latter in several trials in the USA (Mulcahy et al, 1977). It is not yet freely available in the UK but looks like a useful drug for future use.

(b) Cholinergic drugs such as bethanecol in a dose of 0.6mg/kg/ day in three doses (to increase detrusor contractility).

(c) Alpha adrenergic stimulants such as ephedrine in a dose of 2.5mg/kg/day in three doses up to the age of 12 years, and 30mg every eight hours thereafter (to increase the resistance of the bladder neck).

(d) Alpha adrenergic blockers such as phenoxybenzamine in a dose of 0.3 to 0.5mg/kg/day in two doses up to the age of 12 years, and 0.5 to 1mg/kg/day in two doses thereafter (to reduce the resistance of the bladder neck).

Drugs can be used on their own or in combination with other forms of management, particularly clean intermittent catheterisation.

Clean intermittent catheterisation should always be given a trial on its own as some children will achieve satisfactory continence with this alone. In those in whom satisfactory continence is not achieved, the most appropriate drug (based on the findings of the video-urodynamic study) should then be given a trial. This will usually be either propantheline (to decrease bladder instability or irritability) or ephedrine (to increase the resistance of the bladder outlet). In the study mentioned above, propantheline was found to be the most commonly used and most effective drug in both groups of children, i.e. whether intermittently catheterised or not.

In some children clean intermittent catheterisation with or without drug therapy is either unsuccessful or not feasible as a form of management, and in those children the other forms of management available should be considered. It may also be felt after video-urodynamic assessment that the child would benefit from some other procedure such as colposuspension, artificial sphincter implantation or urethrotomy. If so, the ability to empty the bladder should be carefully reassessed following such a procedure, and if unsatisfactory, clean intermittent catheterisation can then be introduced.

It is felt that where possible, clean intermittent catheterisation with the selective use of drugs is the management of choice for these patients. Careful initial assessment of bladder and renal function together with regular follow-up and reassessment are mandatory.

Surgical procedures

The place of surgery in the management of the neuropathic bladder can be an important and decisive one, and is closely related to the urodynamic problems of the bladder, often complicated by varying degrees of back-pressure damage to the ureters and kidneys.

Operations designed to alleviate an outflow problem at the bladder neck such as transurethral or open bladder-neck resection, external sphincterotomy or bilateral pudendal neurectomies are of considerable importance in improving bladder drainage and so of preserving the upper tracts. It is probably best to defer such procedures until a thorough trial has been made with intermittent catheterisation.

Surgery to improve the retentive capacity of the bladder, such as tightening the bladder outlet (urethral plication) or providing a sling for a weak bladder neck (colposuspension) may be needed if success is to be achieved with intermittent self-catheterisation, and recently the introduction of artificial sphincter implantation makes continence attainable in some adolescents or adults. Internal urethrotomy is being performed with success in cases where the bladder neck is tight but continence can be preserved.

In the presence of significant ureteric reflux, re-implantation of the ureters to re-establish competence at the junction of the ureter with the bladder should be undertaken in conjunction with whatever method is likely to succeed in overcoming a bladder outflow problem, such as intermittent catheterisation, or the ureteric reflux is likely to recur.

Urinary diversions were introduced both as a means of controlling incontinence and of preserving the upper tracts from increasing back-pressure damage. In such procedures a loop of terminal ileum, or colon, is isolated with its blood supply. The proximal end is closed, and the other end brought out on to the abdominal wall. The ureters are implanted into the bowel, which acts as a collecting system; a bag is then attached to the skin over the externalised bowel (stoma).

The difficulty in maintaining ileostomy apparatus in children with severe spinal deformity was apparent at an early stage, but other disadvantages of this method are becoming more apparent with time. Initially the expectations of preserving, and even improving, renal function were fully justified, and many children have benefited from the great social advantage of controlled incontinence; but in the longer term a significant proportion appear to develop progressive dilatation of the upper tracts.

The reason for this appears to be that over a long period of time (10 years) the loop tends to lose its peristaltic activity, perhaps due to lack of physiological stimulus, thus changing its character from an active mechanism for expelling urine into a passive sac in which increasing amounts of residual urine collect. If this is associated with ureteric reflux, which is often the case, the scene is set for progressive hydronephrosis and chronic renal failure. Conservative treatment of this problem includes the use of short indwelling balloon catheters –

inserted into the stoma and changed regularly–to provide freer drainage and reduce the residual urine in the loop. Reversing the diversion (undiversion) may be necessary, i.e. restoring and possibly increasing the size of the original bladder in the hope that intermittent or indwelling catheterisation will be effective in controlling the incontinence. Urinary diversion is no longer being carried out purely to treat incontinence, but still has a place in selected cases, especially when there is severe damage to the upper tracts.

The management of urinary incontinence is a continual problem, and it is important to teach the child to be independent. The smelly, soggy child *has* to learn that he is socially unacceptable, and to take responsibility for himself. This is a battle which may take years to achieve in the dull adolescent.

MANAGEMENT OF BOWEL INCONTINENCE

The underlying difficulty is deficient sensation in the lower bowel, rectum and anus, often associated with a patulous or atonic anal sphincter. This lack of sensation leads to diminished reflex, peristaltic activity in the bowel and constipation. Very occasionally the colon is unduly irritable, with consequent diarrhoea, unassociated with constipation, but it should always be remembered that a chronically constipated bowel may present with symptoms of diarrhoea due to softening of some of the bowel contents around the faecal rocks.

Bowel training

If satisfactory control of the bowels is to be achieved–which is within the reach of the majority in the long term–the ability to develop an effective push is the key to success, and without this ingredient other measures are likely to fail. The problem is to get the co-operation of the child in what is a very boring and effortful exercise, and until the child is concerned in trying to keep clean, and confidence begins to dawn that this is attainable, one is fighting a losing battle! Quite young children should be encouraged to push down–this exercise often being carried out on a couch or bed in the first instance, rather than on the lavatory. Later, bowel-training sessions should not usually exceed two 10-minute periods a day, but be an active time, with plenty of encouragement.

Physical assistance

Invariably at the outset, physical assistance on the part of mother, nurse or care staff will be needed to augment the child's own efforts. Initially this takes the form of a manual evacuation, but later perianal pressure, synchronised with the child's own efforts can be effective. With maturity and fuller co-operation, this too often becomes unnecessary, a satisfactory evacuation being obtained by voluntary effort alone. Should this not be achieved, the child can then be taught to provide his own physical assistance with the use of a disposable glove. Recently a biofeedback method of bowel training has been tried and may prove helpful in future management (Whitehead et al, 1981).

Suppositories. These can take the place of physical assistance, the child then making a voluntary effort on the lavatory 20–30 minutes after the insertion of the suppositories. One or two Dulcolax (bisacodyl) suppositories (10–20mg) are usually found to be the most effective. Like physical assistance, the use of suppositories is intended to be a passing aid until such time as voluntary pushing down becomes more effective. The long-term use of suppositories may continue to be a necessary aid in some adolescents.

Laxatives. The use of laxatives is most important in the bowel-training programme, using drugs from the following categories either singly, or more often in combination:

(a) *Bulk-forming drugs* act by increasing the faecal mass which stimulates peristalsis, e.g. unprocessed bran taken with food; ispaghula husk (Isogel); methylcellulose (Cologel) and sterculia (Normacol).

(b) *Faecal softeners* act by lubricating or softening the faeces, e.g. dioctyl sodium sulphosuccinate (Dioctyl-Medo); lactulose (Duphalac) and danthron (Dorbanex). It should be remembered that too much softness makes evacuation by voluntary effort more difficult.

(c) *Stimulant laxatives* act by increasing intestinal motility. The most commonly used are standardised senna preparations (Senokot) and bisacodyl (Dulcolax). The principle to be followed when using drugs in this group is first to clear the bowel thoroughly by the use of enemata, and then to increase the dose every few days until the desired effect is produced. In practice it is not possible to increase the scale of dosage very far in these children, or diarrhoea – with increased bowel incontinence – may result. The combination of a bulk-forming laxative such as Isogel, with a stimulant laxative such as Senokot may give the best results.

Enemata. In a minority of children, muscular weakness, severe spinal deformity, or a combination of the two, makes it impossible to attain bowel control by the methods described above, in which event the regular use of enemata can be an alternative. A Micralax enema (5ml) can be self-administered on a daily or alternate day basis. A phosphate enema every few days may be effective, while for the more resistant cases a 'King Size' enema saponis can provide the answer. The technique for the latter is to mix a large volume of warm water (6 pints) with enema soap, then run it in, a pint at a time, until the returned fluid has a distinctly faecal content, at which point the procedure is stopped. The enema fluid is not retained, due to anal incompetence, but the insensitive colon is finally stimulated into activity by what is, in effect, a prolonged wash-out. This method seldom fails to produce a satisfactory evacuation, and in exceptional cases can be successfully used on a weekly basis to control bowel incontinence.

Rectal prolapse can be a problem in some children, often associated with bleeding. When it occurs excessive straining should be discouraged, constipation treated and manual assistance used. If it persists, a sclerosing injection may be helpful. Occasionally a suture needs to be inserted into the subcutaneous tissue around the anus and tied in a purse-string while a finger is held in the anus. This may make bowel evacuation more difficult and stenosis may occur.

Bowel training in the child with spina bifida is usually a very slow, uphill grind, but in the long term – given perseverance and a willingness to co-operate – satisfactory control of the bowels, by one means or another, can usually be achieved.

REFERENCES

Borzyskowski, M., Mundy, A. R., Neville, B. G. R., Park, L., Kinder, C. H., Boyce, M. R. L., Chantler, C. and Haycock, G. B. (1982). Neuropathic vesico-urethral dysfunction in children. A trial comparing clean intermittent catheterisation with manual expression combined with drug treatment. *British Journal of Urology*, **54**, 641–4.

Lapides, J., Diokno, A. C., Silben, S. J. and Lowe, B. S. (1972). Clean intermittent catheterisation in the treatment of urinary tract disease. *Journal of Urology*, **107**, 458–61.

Mulcahy, J. J., Hector, E. J. and McRoberts, J. W. (1977). Oxybutynin chloride combined with intermittent clean catheterisation in the treatment of myelomeningocoele patients. *Journal of Urology*, **118**, Part 1, 95–6.

Rickwood, A. M. K., Philip, N. H. and Thomas, D. G. (1983). Long-term indwelling catheterisation for congenital neuropathic bladder. *Archives of Disease in Childhood*, **58**, 4, 310–14.

Whitehead, W. E., Parker, L. H., Masek, B. J., Cataldo, M. F. and Freeman, J. M. (1981). Biofeedback treatment of early faecal incontinence in patients with meningomyelocoele. *Developmental Medicine and Child Neurology*, **23**, 313–22.

FURTHER READING

Withycombe, J., Whitaker, R. and Hunt, G. (1978). Intermittent catheterisation in the management of children with neuropathic bladders. *Lancet*, **2**, 981–3.

Chapter 6

Cerebral Palsy

by R. O. ROBINSON MA, MB, BCh, FRCP
and G. T. McCARTHY MB, MRCP, DCH,
with J. A. FIXSEN MChir, FRCS,
V. MOFFAT LCST, J. ROCKEY DipCOT
and C. SHUMWAY BSc, RPT(Mass)

Cerebral palsy is a term used to describe motor handicap arising from cerebral dysfunction which is non-progressive and present at, or shortly after, birth. Although the neurological deficit is unchanging, its expression may not be. Thus, children with generalised types of cerebral palsy are frequently hypotonic initially, but then after a short interval develop spastic quadriplegia, or after a longer period dystonic choreo-athetosis.

The causes of cerebral dysfunction may vary from maldevelopment, infection, vascular accidents, hypoxia and trauma. However, the proportion of cases of cerebral palsy associated with a potentially damaging perinatal event is now considerably less than one half – probably about one third. Genetic factors have subsequently emerged so that about half the cases with symmetrical involvement with spasticity, ataxia or choreo-athetosis are recessively inherited with a recurrence risk of one in four, giving an overall risk of about one in eight. Asymmetrical cases, for example hemiplegia, remain arbitrary events, and the risk of recurrence in subsequent siblings is low (less than one in 200) (Bundy, 1981 (personal communication)). As the mechanisms for the cerebral dysfunction rarely select only those areas of the brain concerned with movement, it is important to look for and treat other commonly associated handicaps such as mental handicap, deafness, visual impairment, educational problems and fits.

GENERAL APPROACH

Each of the adults concerned with the child with cerebral palsy will be involved primarily with one area of his difficulties. The areas have complex and two-way functional relationships, for example, improvement in vision may provide the incentive for movement; improvement in mobility may widen the child's visual horizons. The importance of teamwork therefore cannot be over-emphasised. In addition, the personality of the child and the home background may critically affect the form of management and its likely results. In the early stages the physiotherapist, occupational therapist and speech therapist have an obvious role in management, but the social worker, teacher and psychologist are also important members of the team. Each professional needs to explore how his specialty overlaps with the others and to show each other possible ways of handling the child. These practical recommendations *must* be shown to parents, residential care staff, voluntary helpers and nursing staff. Combined treatment by different therapists or working with the teacher in the classroom should be encouraged.

AIMS OF TREATMENT (Levitt, 1977)

1. Development of independence in daily living activities of feeding, dressing, washing and toileting.
2. Development of communication by speech, gesture, symbols, writing, sign-language, typing.
3. Development of some form of mobility.

SYSTEMS OF TREATMENT

Many different systems of treatment for cerebral palsy have been developed, but it is not possible to detail them here. All the methods claim good results, but clinical experience does not confirm the superiority of any one approach. However, two approaches are outstanding and deserve full study.
1. The use of reflex inhibition and facilitation developed by Karel and Berta Bobath. The method is based on the principle that the fundamental difficulty in cerebral palsy is lack of inhibition of reflex patterns of posture and movement (Bobath, 1980).·
2. Conductive education developed by Dr Andras Petö. The method is based on the principle that movement in the cerebral palsied child has to be consciously learned and reinforced by continuous effort. The traditional division of roles of therapist and teacher is abolished. Adults specially trained in all aspects of treatment and education work with the children mainly in groups led by a 'conductor'. The aim is to encourage children to do as much as possible for themselves while at the same time educating them.

Speech is used to express intention, followed by movement carried out rhythmically accompanied by speech to reinforce the movement (Cotton, 1974).

THE SPASTIC CEREBRAL PALSIES

Spasticity is a disorder of tone characterised by an initial increased resistance to stretch which may then lessen abruptly. The degree of spasticity varies with the child's general condition, emotional state, temperature and health; it also depends on the correct positioning and degree of support of the child.

If the spasticity is severe, the child is more or less fixed in a few typical patterns due to the severe degree of co-contraction of the involved parts, especially around the proximal joints – shoulders and hips. Some muscles appear weak due to tonic reciprocal inhibition by their spastic antagonists, for example the gluteal and abdominal muscles by spastic hip flexors, the quadriceps by spastic hamstrings and the dorsiflexors of the ankles by spastic triceps surae. True weakness may develop in some muscle groups from long-standing disuse or immobilisation in plaster casts or apparatus.

HEMIPLEGIA

Hemiplegia occurs when spasticity involves the arm, trunk and leg on the same side of the body. A typical posture is seen in standing: the lower limb is adducted and internally rotated, the knee slightly flexed and the foot in equinus. The arm is adducted and internally rotated at the shoulder, flexed at the elbow, the forearm pronated and the wrist, fingers and thumb in flexion. A proportion of children have 'dystonic' postures overlying this with adduction and extension of the shoulder, flexion of the wrist and extension abduction of the fingers and thumb (Fig. 6/1).

Causes of hemiplegia

1. *Occlusion of the internal carotid or middle cerebral artery.* This occurs prenatally, and being rarely fatal, our knowledge of its acquisition is limited. Acute hemiplegia also occurs in the first few years of life and may result from trauma, malformation, occlusion or inflammation of the internal carotid artery, hypertension, or associated with blood disorders.

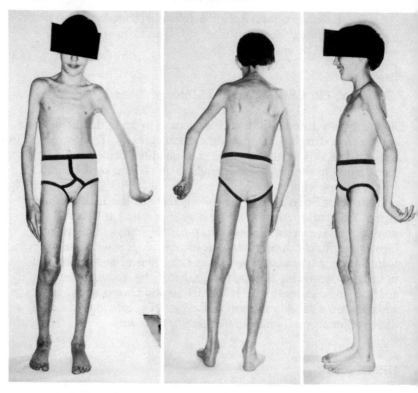

Fig. 6/1 Hemiplegic posture: anterior, posterior and lateral views

2. *Direct cerebral involvement such as trauma or infection leading to necrosis.* This is often associated with mental handicap, the other hemisphere being involved, but to a lesser extent.

Diagnosis

Asymmetry is quickly recognised by parents who may express this by saying a baby is strongly left- or right-handed. If this occurs within the first year suspicions of hemiplegia should be aroused. Another early sign is continued 'fisting' on the affected side. The leg is said to be typically less affected than the arm. This is true in so far as the leg and foot have less precise functions than the arm and hand. Most of these children walk and use one hand well. They usually achieve independence and are not precluded from leading useful and satisfying lives by their handicap. By comparison with many of the children considered in this book therefore, their handicap is relatively mild. It is obviously helpful if the parents can be brought to a sense of perspective early.

In addition to the motor loss, there are two other components to the disability. One is of sensory loss or inattention to the affected side. This may be suspected early if the function of the arm is worse than the degree of handicap would predict. The other is hemianopia (loss of half of the field of vision on the affected side). Undergrowth of the affected limbs may occur and correlates well with cortical sensory loss – both reflecting parietal lobe involvement.

Management

ENCOURAGING SYMMETRICAL MOVEMENT AND AWARENESS OF
HEMIPLEGIC SIDE

In infancy two-handed holding of a bottle, larger bricks, the feeding beaker, etc, should be encouraged. Symmetry is also aided by using patterns of handling which elicit non-preferred postures and movements. As the child gets older 'sit and ride' toys, then tricycles, wheelbarrows which put the grasp reflex to good use, large balls for two-handed throwing all promote maximal two-handed use. Swimming is a good activity in hemiplegics for this reason. Talking about the arm and hand during washing, bathing and dressing, holding the toddler by the hemiplegic hand and using it maximally in rough play will all help promote awareness. Always dress the affected side first. Later this helps the child to learn to dress himself.

The focus of treatment should change according to the results achieved. If a child treated early and adequately is still not using the hand by 2 years, the function of the hand will always be very limited. Recognising this saves therapists, parents and not least the child from continuing frustration. Thus, occupational therapy following this early period accepts and uses limited function. In feeding, a padded handle and strap may be necessary for utensils used by the affected hand. Early feeding attempts may be facilitated by the use of a non-slip mat and plate guard. A point should be made of propping the affected arm on the table during feeding, drawing and later at school in order to discourage retraction of the shoulder and encourage symmetrical sitting postures. Similarly, during dressing the child should be in a symmetrical position with the feet on the floor. This also assists in retaining flexion in the hips, knees and ankles necessary for dressing. During toileting the body may be stabilised against a wall in order to assist clothing adjustment. During bathing the abnormal leg should be put in first from a sitting position on a bath stool. A wall rail may be necessary as may non-slip patches on the bath base. If the child cannot be stabilised, the object he is working with can. Thus at school the affected arm can be used as a paperweight. Rulers mounted on a magnet used with a metal sheet underneath the paper can be useful, as may spring-loaded left or right-handed scissors. Other aids for one-handed use are described in Chapter 21.

In the leg good function and movement promote awareness. While the child can afford to be one-handed, he cannot afford to be one-footed. Therefore the aim is efficient weight-bearing and transfer in a variety of situations. It is as well for physiotherapy to be one stage ahead of the child's achievements. To be encouraging crawling when the child is sitting, and standing when the child is crawling. Once one stage is reached, the previous stage should not be ignored as it is rarely perfect, and promotion of balance and weight distribution at one level will favourably affect that ability at a higher level. At the stage of standing, great attention must be paid to the foot posture as this has a profound effect on the static and dynamic posture of the whole body. The usual equinus tendency can be controlled by bracing for 12–18 months after walking starts. This can be achieved in a variety of ways:

(a) A moulded polypropylene ankle-foot orthosis (AFO) (Fig. 6/2).
(b) A below-knee iron with a T-strap.
(c) A below-knee iron with a 5–10 degree backstop.
(d) The use of corrective plaster boots intermittently as described on page 121.

If the foot is satisfactorily held and comfortably positioned by one of

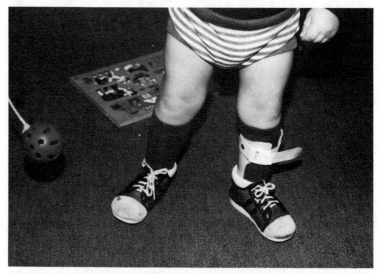

Fig. 6/2 Ankle-foot orthosis (AFO)

these devices physiotherapy can concentrate on the hemiplegic side of the pelvis rotating forward and down in sitting, standing and walking in order to achieve a more effective (and 'normal') gait pattern.

PREVENTION OF FIXED DEFORMITY

The major role in preventing fixed deformity is borne by physiotherapy preventing postural deformity. This is most effectively achieved by positioning the child correctly for long periods, such as in standing to prevent equinus and knee and hip flexion deformities. The position is reinforced by weight-bearing. Passive stretching once or twice a day, while it may theoretically augment the stretch reflex, may also prevent the formation of soft tissue contractures at extremes of movement.

Orthopaedic management

If, despite physiotherapy, a *handicapping* deformity persists or progresses, an orthopaedic opinion should be sought. It must be clearly understood by all concerned that operations do nothing for the central (neurological) problem, and can only work within the confines of the patterns of movements dictated by it. Even the simplest surgical procedure may upset the child with cerebral palsy for several months. The results of surgery should not be assessed until at least 6–12 months after operation.

The greatest contribution of orthopaedics in the hemiplegic child is in the lower limb. In most patients the hip and knee deformities respond well to non-surgical treatment and the equinus remains the persistent problem. A below-knee plaster can be used very effectively to stretch the tendo calcaneus. The toes should be supported to prevent excessive flexion. The plasters are usually changed after 2 or 3 weeks and the child encouraged to stand and walk as much as possible. This can defer the need for surgery for some time and can be repeated with success. Once the contracture cannot be overcome under general anaesthetic, or recurs rapidly after plastering, then formal lengthening of the tendo calcaneus should be considered.

ELONGATION OF THE TENDO CALCANEUS

Elongation of the tendo calcaneus by the slide method is the most commonly performed procedure. It is relatively simple and allows the child to stand and walk in the plasters 24–48 hours after operation and only requires 4 weeks in plaster. Opinions vary about night splintage. In general, if there is good active dorsiflexion prolonged night splintage is unnecessary, but if the dorsiflexors are weak then it is probably advisable.

Relief of equinus may be sufficient in itself to correct valgus or varus of the foot. If varus (the commoner deformity) persists and presents a functional difficulty, the tibialis posterior may be elongated or divided. Lateral transfer of the tibialis posterior is an attractive operation, but tends to lead to over-correction of the foot in time, and should be used with great caution. Valgus can be treated by elongating the peronei tendons and providing a medial arch support. If it persists a Grice-type extra-articular fusion of the sub-talar joint can produce a stable and satisfactory result.

Correction of shortening is always a consideration in the lower limb. Traditionally 1.25cm ($\frac{1}{2}$in) or less is ignored. More than this may be treated by raising the sole of the shoe. However, in a child who is using an equinus deformity for support, this is merely a nuisance to be compensated for by further flexing the hip and knee. Raising the heel alone merely promotes equinus, but since this is often the most efficient posture for the hemiplegic child when 'abnormal' walking patterns are established, it might be accepted. Surgical lengthening is rarely if ever indicated.

ARM AND HAND

Proximal control, as well as awareness of the hand should be present before any surgery is contemplated to hand or forearm.

Flexion/adduction deformities of the thumb may be prevented or deterred by the use of soft, firm plastic splints. Release of the permanently adducted thumb can be achieved near or at maturity by fusing the carpometacarpal joints. Abduction of the thumb can be corrected by releasing the thumb adductor from its origin on the metacarpals.

Similarly, correction of fixed finger flexion contractures and forearm pronators can be achieved by mobilisation, release or transfer of appropriate muscles or tendons. This is usually a cosmetic procedure and is best performed after puberty.

Scoliosis may develop and management is described in Chapter 10.

DIPLEGIA

In this type of cerebral palsy the spasticity affects all four limbs, but the legs are more involved than the arms (when the converse is true the pattern is referred to as double hemiplegia). It is frequently associated with prematurity, and is thought to be caused by damage to corticospinal fibres as they pass by the outer angle of the lateral ventricle. They are particularly vulnerable at this point due to the effects of ventricular expansion, hypotension or hypoxia. The damage being thus localised, mental handicap or fits occur in only a minority of this group.

The increased tone in the lower limbs is frequently noted during the first few months by the mother. This may be a problem when trying to abduct the legs during nappy changing, but usually does not interfere with development until sitting positions are attempted. The true extent of the handicap becomes apparent when weight-bearing starts. The extent to which hand function is affected is highly variable. The greater the degree of upper limb involvement, the greater the incidence of accompanying mental handicap and fits.

In the early stages the unwanted postures and movements can be inhibited by nursing in the prone position, and later by having the child sit with hips astride (abducted, externally rotated) on the floor or on a lap. From there, progression to rotational movements of the trunk in sitting, and then in standing can be made. Thereafter the aim is acquisition of a useful stable gait (Fig. 6/3).

If the hips and knees are mobile, the physiotherapy approach is to encourage useful standing with the feet plantigrade. This by itself (as

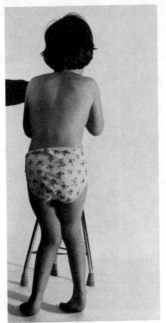

Fig. 6/3 Typical diplegic posture demonstrating weakness around the hips and knees with adduction of hips and flexion of knees

with hemiplegia) may be sufficient to inhibit extensor posturing and allow the emergence of stable patterns of movement. The Flexistand or standing box may help at home. Because the abductors and extensors of the hips are functionally weak, good standing balance should be achieved before walking. In general, appliances help these children relatively little and are best avoided. If Rollators or crutches are used, the weight tends to go through the arms rather than the legs. Apart from limiting hand function, any tendency to spasticity in the arms or legs is increased. These 'aids' also tend to increase adduction and internal rotation at the hips by allowing hip flexion – the position one is trying to avoid in order to increase stability. If an aid is necessary it is preferable to use the least stable one that the child can manage so that he is less able to put weight through the arms and use them to counterpoise. If waiting becomes impossible quadripod sticks used at the side encouraging extension, abduction and external rotation at the hips should be used for preference. The height of the sticks should be such that flexion is avoided (Fig. 6/4). The use of aids must be reassessed frequently. Hip abductors which strap to each thigh with a hinged joint between may be useful temporarily as a teaching aid.

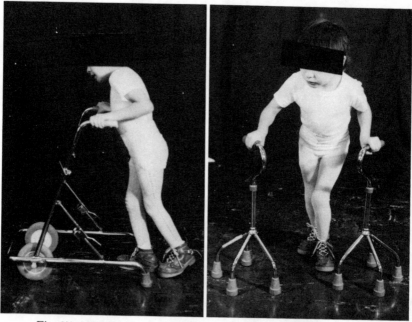

Fig. 6/4 (a) Walking with a Rollator. (b) Walking with quadripod sticks

Orthopaedic management

In most of the children the ability to bring the weight forward over the base (i.e. the bottom in sitting and feet in standing) is lacking. To compensate for this they poke their heads forward, round their shoulders and flex their hips. Instead of using dorsiflexors to get their weight forward to initiate walking they launch themselves by plantar flexion. Analysis of all these factors and the child's abilities and disabilities is required in order to decide what, if any, surgery will be beneficial.

If contractures of the hips and knees have been acquired by the time weight-bearing and walking is contemplated, they must be released. Abduction is improved by an open adductor tenotomy with obturator neurectomy. This is obviously important if there is evidence of progressive subluxation of the hips as seen in serial radiographs. Simple valgus of the femoral neck and a break in Shenton's line are not of themselves indications for surgery, as any child with delay in weight-bearing and limited walking will inevitably show these radiological features. An iliopsoas release should be considered if hip extension is not improved by adductor tenotomy.

Persistent and disabling femoral anteversion may have to be dealt with by external rotation osteotomy which involves a bony operation with internal fixation and usually six weeks in plaster. This should not normally be considered under the age of 10 years otherwise recurrence is extremely common.

Flexion deformity at the knees may be adequately dealt with by serial plasters, gaiters or back-slabs. In the presence of fixed flexion deformity distal hamstring release is indicated. Occasionally proximal hamstring release can be considered in a small group of patients who show very tight hamstrings, less than 30 degrees of straight leg raising, a short stride when walking, but less than 5 degrees of fixed flexion at the knees.

MANAGEMENT OF EQUINUS DEFORMITY

Dealing with flexion contractures at the hips and knees may be sufficient to correct equinus at the foot. The foot equinus may have been necessary as the centre of gravity may be abnormally far forward due to the flexion of the trunk on the hips. In this situation correction of equinus by lengthening the tendo calcaneus makes walking more difficult and frequently impossible. Careful consideration of the child's necessity for various postural or fixed deformities for function, as well as assessment of alternative mechanisms, is required when contemplating surgery.

Valgus everted rocker-bottom foot: Once the equinus deformity has been overcome the commonest foot deformity is the valgus everted rocker-bottom foot. The sub-talar joint is always hyper-mobile in these children. The standard operation to stabilise the sub-talar joint is the Grice sub-talar arthrodesis which can be carried out from the age of 4 years upwards. This is a bony operation and requires three months in plaster. Other options are discussed in the section on hemiplegia, page 120.

Hallux valgus: In association with a pronated forefoot these patients frequently develop increasing and troublesome hallux valgus. This can be corrected by osteotomy of the first metatarsal and release of the adductor hallucis from the base of the proximal phalanx of the big toe. This operation should probably be delayed until the age of 13 or 14 unless absolutely necessary, otherwise recurrence with growth is likely to occur.

Where hand function is significantly compromised, the aims and techniques of occupational therapy are as outlined in the sections on dystonic choreo-athetosis and hemiplegia.

QUADRIPLEGIA

Where the arms as well as the legs are severely spastic, there is widespread bilateral hemispheric dysfunction; generally this affects both cortex and white matter, and the incidence of associated mental handicap is higher in this group than in any other (in the region of 80 per cent). Perinatal events over-represented in this group include major intraventricular haemorrhage with distension of ventricles with blood, and often an intracerebral component to the bleeding; or severe asphyxia with presumed post-hypoxic cerebral oedema and secondary cerebral hypo-perfusion. Management is discussed on page 128.

ATAXIA

This is a relatively uncommon form of cerebral palsy which is usually characterised by generalised cerebellar signs. These are: disturbance of balance, inco-ordination, dysarthria, intention tremor, hypotonia, and sometimes nystagmus. Ataxia may occur as part of a dysmorphic syndrome, or be associated with intra-uterine infection. Mixed ataxia and spasticity occurs in a diplegic pattern and may be caused by prolonged hypoglycaemia in the neonatal period.

The hypotonic component of cerebellar involvement is the predominant feature in the early months – although in many instances this is also related to the accompanying mental handicap.

Early motor milestones are frequently delayed either because of or in association with the hypotonia, but the majority of children with ataxia alone acquire independence in walking as in all other aspects of life.

There is as yet no specific technique of handling or drug therapy which inhibits the involuntary movements. Management consists of encouraging the child and parents through the normal sequences of development and providing aids for stability as necessary. Providing a firm base itself may help to inhibit excess movements. Thus, weight-bearing should be encouraged early. Similarly, in sitting, a stable seat should be provided at a height for the feet to be resting on the floor. A Watford potty chair at the same height with a bar for stabilising arms is useful in the early stages (see p. 42). Rails should be attached as appropriate by the toilet and bath.

Dressing is best started by concentrating on the lower half. Here the child can sit on the floor with his back against the wall. For the upper half a small table is useful to stabilise the arms when donning vest and T-shirt. When this is achieved dressing can be attempted when sitting on a chair or bed. Fussy straps and buttons are obviously best avoided.

When feeding, the stable seat at the appropriate height for the feet must not be forgotten. In addition, the non-dominant hand placed well forward may give added stability (see p. 134).

The more delicate movements for writing may be impossible and an electric typewriter should be used early.

DYSTONIC CHOREO-ATHETOSIS

Involuntary movements (choreo-athetosis) are so frequently combined with dystonic posturing that they are conveniently classified together. Here the brunt of damage has fallen on the basal ganglia. Although much overlapping pathology exists, choreo-athetosis is most frequently found with damage to the caudate nucleus and putamen, and dystonia with damage to the globus pallidus. Since kernicterus as a cause for this has receded, the mechanism is obscure in the remainder, but probably involves sub-acute regional hypoxia rather than acute total asphyxia (which gives rise to brainstem and thalamic damage), or periodic hypo-perfusion (which gives rise to damage in 'watershed areas').

Athetosis is defined as irrepressible, slow writhing movements, the result of imperfectly co-ordinated activity of agonists and antagonists which are exacerbated by attempting voluntary movement.

Choreic movements are rapid involuntary jerks present at rest which are increased by voluntary movements.

Dystonia is a disorder of muscle tone expressed as postural abnormality, intermittent contractile spasms and complex action dystonias where purposeful movements are deformed.

Voluntary movements are partially or totally disrupted anywhere in the body including the lips and tongue. The tone varies so that the baby is usually markedly hypotonic and only exhibits athetosis in the second or third year. The adult may have muscle tension which develops to control posture. Mixed cerebral palsy occurs when an involuntary movement disorder is combined with spasticity.

Intelligence is usually good in the pure athetoid, but in the group as a whole mental handicap occurs in as many as 50 per cent (Crothers and Paine, 1959).

Oesophageal reflux and hiatus hernia may occur with athetosis and may cause abdominal pain, acute or chronic haemorrhage, stricture or ulceration of the oesophagus. Medical treatment involves drugs which inhibit acid secretion, e.g. cimetidine and antacids, and treatment of anaemia, which may be severe. Surgical treatment is indicated if medical treatment is unsuccessful, but postoperative management may be difficult.

Sandifer described a group of normal children who developed odd head postures and trunk movements construed as dystonia and were found to have oesophageal reflux. (This is known as the Sandifer syndrome.) The movements disappear once the reflux has been dealt with by antacids or surgery (Kinsbourne and Oxon, 1964; Werlin et al, 1980). However, the oesophageal reflux and hiatus hernia associated with athetosis may add to the movement disorder.

A rare cause of athetosis in boys, associated with self-mutilation is the Lesch-Nyhan syndrome. This is an inherited disorder of purine metabolism associated with a high serum uric acid. The condition is X-linked.

Management of spastic quadriplegia and dystonic choreo-athetosis

Many children with basal ganglia damage also have a degree of underlying spasticity. Although the causes of neuronal damage in these groups are different, the disability and aims of management overlap sufficiently for them to be treated together in this section.

In the young severely spastic or athetoid child it is possible to see uninhibited reflexes more easily as they dominate all other activity. It is important to understand the ways in which primary reflexes are elicited or inhibited in order to develop ways of handling the child to allow more functional patterns to emerge. There are many such reflexes, the commonest and most powerful being:

1. *The tonic labyrinthine reflex* (TLR): This reflex is never seen in the normal baby. It is evoked by changing the position of the head in space. In supine a massed extensor posture results; the head extended, the back arched, the arms at the side, forearms pronated, legs adducted and internally rotated and feet in equinus. The chest is usually expanded because of the extended posture. In prone, flexor activity predominates.

2. *The asymmetric tonic neck reflex* (ATNR): This does not occur as an obligatory response in a normal baby, but is seen as a normal posture in the first five months of life. In the abnormal response, turning the child's head to one side results in increased extensor tone to the same side and flexor tone in the opposite side (the fencing position) (Fig. 6/5). It causes marked asymmetry and may

Fig. 6/5 Asymmetric tonic neck reflex (ATNR)

prevent normal grasp while looking at an object. It is usually stronger to the right so most children appear left-handed. In the severe form it may be responsible for development of dislocation of the hip and scoliosis, and prevent eye/hand co-ordination.

3. *Symmetric tonic neck reflex* (STNR): Active or passive extension of the head produces increased extensor tone in the arms and flexor tone in the legs. Flexion of the neck has the opposite effect.

4. *Associated reactions*: Tonic reflexes spreading from one limb to the rest of the body producing hypertonus in all parts of the body not directly involved in the intended movement.

5. *Extensor thrust*: Antigravity muscles contract when the sole of the foot comes in contact with a surface. This results in a rigid leg with hip and knee extension and plantar flexion of the foot.

6. *Grasp*: Palm contact provokes whole hand involuntary grasp, precluding development of pincer grasp or release.

7. *Startle reactions*: Generalised paroxysmal responses involving the whole body, caused by sudden noises or loss of balance.

These unwanted reflexes:

(i) Prevent normal movements
(ii) Prevent the acquisition of a secure base for sitting or standing
(iii) Impose fixed postures and induce secondary structural deformity.

Early management depends on full assessment of motor development and the presence of reflex activity. The physiotherapist may manage reflex activity in a variety of ways:

(a) Use reflexes where they facilitate a skill. Not all reflexes are 'bad'. The extensor tone of the hemiplegic leg, for example, may serve a vital supportive function.

(b) Inhibit reflexes where they impede motor development (more commonly). This may be done in several ways:

1. *Use other, more powerful reflexes to induce new motor patterns.* For example, pulling a child forward from supine with one hand induces a propping reaction in the other arm with abduction, supination of the forearm, dorsiflexion of the wrist and extension of the fingers (see p.39). This may effectively counter the opposite posture of the spastic arm.

2. *One abnormal reflex may be used to inhibit another.* This is particularly useful in facilitating handling. For instance, changing a nappy may be extremely difficult because of the adduction and extension induced by the tonic labyrinthine reflex. Flexion of the neck – evoking the symmetric tonic neck reflex – may suffice to allow hip flexion, abduction and external rotation (Finnie, 1974). A strong extensor thrust may be a major interruption to feeding. It

can be inhibited by avoiding support to the feet, and flexing the hips, trunk and knees.

3. *Breaking up abnormal reflex sequences* can sometimes be done with equipment – this is the logical rationale for the use of orthoses in cerebral palsy. For example, the extensor thrust induces equinus of the foot and tends to throw the standing child off balance backwards. This thrust may be inhibited by a below-knee orthosis fitted to a Piedro boot with a backstop, or even by a lightweight ankle-foot orthosis. This allows the child to stand stably and acquire walking. Giving the child experience of new movement patterns may allow him to initiate them himself. Increasing his postural repertoire not only prevents the acquisition of secondary fixed structural deformities, but also allows the build-up of sequences of voluntary movements.

It is also important to realise *what physiotherapy cannot do*. Involuntary movements may be minimised by reducing stress and giving confidence and stability, but not eliminated. Passive stretching exercises may help to prevent secondary deformity; they will not cure, and may actively elicit spasticity.

Building up the movement repertoire in the child with generalised cerebral palsy is best done initially by encouraging symmetrical movements thereby inhibiting the asymmetric tonic neck reflex. Balls, rolls and wedges encourage head extension and two-handed play. Gaiters on the arms used temporarily at this stage give increased control for eye/hand co-ordination.

Drugs

The long-term use of drugs in cerebral palsy is rarely helpful, but in certain situations can be worth while for a short time with a definite aim in mind.

Baclofen: acts mainly as a gamma amino butyric acid (GABA) mimetic in the spinal cord blocking the excitatory effects of the sensory input from limb muscles.

Diazepam: probably acts by enhancing the response to locally released GABA. Its action on the spinal cord is independent of any action in the brain, although doses which reduce muscle tone are often sedative. It has a longer action than baclofen, and the sedative action can be overcome by giving a single daily dose at bedtime; it is particularly useful for night spasms.

CLINICAL STUDIES

Assessment of effects has proved difficult because no simple way exists of making an objective measurement of spasticity. Also relief of spasm may remove the means by which posture is maintained. In cerebral palsy, baclofen is most useful in reducing spasm to allow the use of splints for improvement in walking. Side-effects may be distressing, particularly diurnal enuresis.

Diazepam given at night is particularly useful as a short-term measure in controlling severe spasm in the young spastic child.

Both drugs can cause drowsiness, and baclofen can also produce a confusional state and headaches; hallucinations have occurred on withdrawal. It is important to introduce the drugs slowly to avoid side-effects.

DEVELOPMENT OF INDEPENDENCE IN DAILY LIVING ACTIVITIES

Sitting

When progressing to sitting, several techniques and facilities are available. A corner seat with a fitting tray can be carried without difficulty from room to room. Later a chair with arms, and again a tray, is appropriate. A ladderback chair (Joncare) can be used to encourage head and trunk control. A high chair allows the child to join in what may be the family's main social activity – mealtimes (see Fig. 1/5, p. 42). Other aspects of feeding are dealt with below. A pushchair which allows the child to face the mother is preferable to one in which he must twist his head and neck in order to see her talking. Stability while sitting on a toilet seat may be difficult (see Chapter 1). Independence and therefore privacy during toileting is an important part of social maturity. Two other aspects of sitting require emphasis: (1) sitting for relaxation which should be an enjoyable activity in itself, and (2) if sitting is all a child can do he deserves change from time to time. A beanbag may encourage unwanted postures, but as an alternative experience may be a sufficient end in itself. Mountain chairs may serve the same function (see p. 42). Seating priorities may need to be thought through and are discussed in Chapter 14.

Dressing

For the child who can sit independently, dressing and undressing should be attempted. A chair and table at chest height are useful props, stabilising the arms and back when sitting for dressing the top half. The lower half can also be dressed while sitting, the clothes being pulled up over the bottom by leaning first to one side then the other. Clothing should be loose and uncomplicated. Putting on socks and shoes is usually achieved last. Currently, trainers with Velcro fasteners are popular among boys and obviate the need for laces or buckles.

Bathing

Bathing is an important time for play and learning. A bath/swimming aid to support the child's head while floating in supine will give him confidence and free the mother's hands for washing him (see Fig. 21/8, p. 357). When a baby bath becomes too small to put on a table, a bath insert will save excessive stooping. A non-slip insert may give a feeling of added stability. Later, independent bathing may be impossible, although access to a shower may be possible using a special chair.

Feeding

Feeding and speech are closely linked because the complex movements required for speech are superimposed on those patterns already acquired in breathing, eating and drinking. It is therefore important that the 'correct' lip, tongue and jaw positions for feeding are learnt as early as possible.

The development of feeding is via sucking, chewing and mature swallowing (with closed lips) to independent feeding. This process will be delayed or hindered for the handicapped child with generalised cerebral palsy by a combination of weak and unco-ordinated movements of oral and pharyngeal muscles and the various early reflexes that persist. These normal immature feeding patterns are:

1. The rooting response, which is present from birth and disappears at about 3 months.
2. The sucking/swallowing reflex appearing shortly after birth and disappearing by 5 months.
3. The bite reflex which is present from birth and usually has disappeared by 5 months.
4. The gag reflex, which is present from birth and begins to weaken once chewing begins.

Other difficulties include:
(a) A hypersensitive palate.
(b) An abnormally high palate.
(c) Tongue thrust.
(d) Weak lip closure.
(e) Extension and involuntary head movements.
(f) Lack of head and trunk control.
(g) Poor eye/hand co-ordination.

An interdisciplinary approach is essential to overcome these problems. The speech therapist must work closely with the parents, occupational therapist, physiotherapist and nurse to ensure that correct feeding patterns are maintained throughout the child's life at home, at school or on the ward.

HEAD AND TRUNK CONTROL

Positioning of the child to attain maximum head and trunk control is the first priority and will be determined by the age and type of handicap. The *aim* is to position:

1. *The baby*, sitting on the lap so that the head is supported in an upright position to prevent swallowing of air and to keep him in a flexed position and unable to extend.

2. *The child* must also have the head erect and in the mid-line, but with back well supported and arms extended forward to prevent extensor spasm.

Appropriate seating is important. The aim is to transfer from lap feeding to a chair as soon as possible so that the child gains a greater degree of independence and becomes part of the family group at mealtimes.

DRINKING

The tongue thrust often hinders drinking, and the child must be helped to develop a more mature sucking pattern.

1. *The baby* may have a very poor sucking reflex and will need help to initiate natural sucking. Swallowing can be promoted by pressing up under the chin gently with thumb and forefinger, making circular movements to help the tongue move up to the gum ridge, and then by stroking under the chin and upper part of the throat to help swallowing. He may require a softer teat with a larger hole initially, but as sucking improves the size of the hole can be reduced. The teat should not be too long as this may trigger off the gag reflex, and also limits the tongue movements necessary for sucking.

2. *The older child* can be encouraged to suck liquid through a straw as

an exercise to promote better lip and palate function. Polythene tubing can be used for this. As well as strengthening the lips it improves the mobility of the soft palate. The size of the bore is decreased and the length of the tube increased as the child's sucking improves. The child may need some assistance at first to close the lips round the straw. A straw with a non-return valve is now available.

There is a variety of mugs and training cups that can be used when the child is ready to try drinking from a cup (see Chapter 21).

Games to promote lip and tongue movements can be used, such as blowing bubbles, feathers, candles; licking gummed paper, lollipops or sweet substances.

DESENSITISATION TECHNIQUES

The cerebral palsied child is often hypersensitive around the face and mouth. Desensitisation of lips, tongue and palate can be done indirectly through play where the child learns to tolerate touch around the face and mouth. This can be done by techniques such as touching, stroking, rubbing, tapping and brushing, and also by encouraging the child to put his own fingers in his mouth or to suck toys. The child should include cleaning his teeth as part of his daily routine. Greater awareness of movements of the lips and tongue can be made by using different flavoured foods such as honey, jam, 'hundreds and thousands', and placing these sweet substances on lips or gum ridge and encouraging movement by licking the food off (Fig. 6/6).

More direct methods, e.g. proprioceptive neuromuscular facilita-

Fig. 6/6 Group of children practising tongue movements licking chocolate spread from around their lips

tion techniques (PNF) (brushing and icing techniques) should be attempted only under the direction of a qualified person.

BITING AND CHEWING

The diet of a cerebral palsied child is extremely important, not only from a nutritional point of view, but also to lay a foundation of good biting and chewing patterns.

Weaning from a liquid or purée diet to solid food is a slow process for the physically handicapped child with a gradual introduction of new flavours, textures and temperatures. Prolonged bottle feeding only strengthens the infantile sucking and swallowing patterns, while prolonged feeding of liquidised or puréed foods encourages the tongue thrust to persist. The *aim* is to reduce the amount of soft mashed foods and increase the amount of rusks, crusts, apples and small pieces of meat so that the child learns to tolerate more solid food. Chewing helps to eliminate the gag and bite reflexes and tongue thrust.

Tongue thrust prevents food from moving to the back of the mouth for swallowing. To help overcome this, depress the bowl of the spoon on the front of the tongue and gently move it backwards.

The *aim* is to promote chewing and tongue movement, and lip closure by:

(i) Placing food either side of mouth between back teeth.
(ii) Gently moving child's jaw up and down.
(iii) Holding the lips together and rubbing the fingers round the outside of the cheeks.
(iv) Demonstrating chewing using exaggerated movements.

ASSISTED FEEDING

The helper should be on a level with the child and either at the side or opposite him. It is useful to stabilise the plate on a non-slip mat to prevent it sliding off the table. The spoon should not be too large as this often encourages the bite reflex, nor should it be made of a brittle material. The spoon should be held level so that the handle is not raised to scrape the food off against the teeth or to drop the food into the mouth. When hand to mouth movements are impaired, the right trajectory can be acquired using a Tommy Tippee spoon. The *aim* is for the child to take the food off the spoon with his lips and not his teeth, and to graduate from passive to independent feeding as quickly as possible (Fig. 6/7).

Fig. 6/7 Assisted feeding. The child's wrist should be bent well back to help in grasping the spoon, and the elbow must be kept firmly on the table so that it acts as a lever bringing the spoon from the plate to the mouth. The other arm is extended on the table, and sometimes a bar or handle is used to keep the arm straight. In the motivated child viscous damped feeding devices which may be custom designed can be adapted (see Fig. 21/3)

INDEPENDENT FEEDING

The child is now encouraged to use a fork as well as a spoon. Games can be used as a pre-feeding activity to encourage better eye/hand co-ordination and the actions necessary for feeding. It is inevitably going to be slow and messy. The child should be given time and praised when he succeeds. Above all, remember that this is a social occasion and an ideal time for babbling, sound imitation and general conversation.

Dribbling

Dribbling is a problem for a large number of cerebral palsied children, and is often the most offensive aspect of the disability. Dribbling interferes with feeding, speech, classroom activities, social activities and the ultimate placement of the child.

TRADITIONAL TREATMENT

The three methods which have been used traditionally to treat dribbling are drugs, surgery and intensive speech therapy. All have their limitations, and often improvements are not maintained.

MODERN METHODS

More recently other methods have been studied in the treatment of dribbling:

1. *Orthopaedic appliances have been used to encourage lip closure.* The chin cup is an example of this, and although it was originally used to retard the forward growth of the mandible, is now used effectively in programmes to control dribbling.

2. *The Exeter Lip Sensor* was developed to give an audio-feedback to children with an open mouth posture and poor lip closure. With careful patient selection it is felt that it may be a valuable aid in reducing the problem (Huskie et al, 1981).

3. *Behaviour modification techniques* are used where cerebral palsied children are trained to associate an auditory cue with swallowing. An electronic dribble-control device, which is in a small box pinned to the child's clothing, emits a bleep at regular intervals, giving the child an auditory signal to swallow or alternatively, if unable to swallow, to wipe the mouth. This method reduces the professional time involved and encourages the child to control his dribbling.

General aims before the above techniques are introduced are:

(a) To take baseline recordings of the amount of dribbling before treatment.

(b) To make the child aware of his own appearance. This can be done by showing the child his wet chin, soiled clothing or looking at himself in the mirror.

(c) To promote lip closure by exercises such as sucking, blowing and holding objects of decreasing size between the child's lips or during feeding (pp. 134–5).

(d) To establish reflex swallowing (p. 134).

(e) To condition the child to wearing the device.

SURGERY

Transposition of the submandibular ducts to the tonsillar fossa can be very helpful in the older child by reducing the volume of saliva in the front of the mouth.

Disorders of speech

The ability to co-ordinate the processes of respiration, phonation and articulation is basic to speech development. Controlled exhalation of air is required for speech.

Voice: Phonation is dependent upon laryngeal control of voice affecting pitch, volume and appropriate voice inflections.

Dysarthria: The child finds it difficult to synchronise the movements of lip, tongue and palate necessary for articulation and may also be unable to co-ordinate respiration, phonation and articulation.

Fluency: The fluency of speech may be interrupted by irregular inco-ordinated movements of breathing, phonation and articulation so that speech becomes scanning or fades completely at the end of a phrase.

Breathing may be too shallow so that the child only manages one word per breath, or reversed so that he speaks on an inhaled breath. Breathing patterns should be improved as early as possible by:
1. Improving sitting posture to aid function of diaphragm and abdominal muscles – working towards unsupported sitting.
2. Good seating – to ensure correct posture of head, neck and trunk, if support is necessary.
3. Practising voluntary control of inhalation and exhalation. Imitation of sighing, and blowing or vocalising on exhalation. Inhalation can be stimulated by momentarily interfering with inhalation by holding a tissue over the child's mouth and nose.
4. Exercises to promote vocalisation. Breathing-in is associated with extension – the child's arms should be brought up and out during inhalation and down and across the chest during exhalation.
   Vocalisation can be improved by:
(a) Changing the child's position – movement stimulates phonation.
(b) Vibration of the chest stimulates phonation.
(c) Putting the floppy child into a weight-bearing situation – vocalisation increases as tone increases.
(d) Encouraging laughing, coughing, crying.

Standing and walking

Standing balance should be developed before moving on to walking. The development of hip extension and trunk balance and rotation is important, and the use of rolls, wedges, large balls, is helpful. Weight-bearing may need to be encouraged by preventing knee flexion with gaiters or splints. Apparatus for standing is useful in

Fig. 6/8 Flexistand
giving support around
the chest, behind the
hips, at the knees and feet

school such as a standing frame, box and cut-out table, or Flexistand
(Fig. 6/8). The use of standing poles in development of balance is very
helpful, particularly if asymmetry is marked.

Ideally, walking should be achieved without aids, but the principle
should not be pursued at all costs or frustration may ensue. Correction
of abnormality of gait or posture of course continues, and problems
need to be analysed in order to work out the correct solution (Levitt,
1977).

Where walking aids are required stabilisation of arms in gaiters or
hands in gloves can be helpful (see Chapter 13).

The decision to abandon attempts at walking usually becomes
apparent during treatment. It is important to have realistic aims and
review them. A formal decision may need to be made involving both
child and parents so that the child can concentrate on mobility from a
wheelchair for which training and practice is required. Movement
must still be encouraged and seating considerations are important (see
Chapter 14). A powered wheelchair should be considered if the child
is unable to propel himself so that learning through the experience of
mobility can occur.

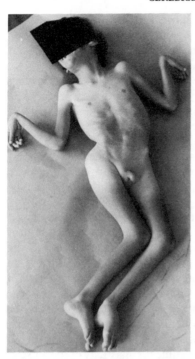

Fig. 6/9 Severe deformity with windswept hips which are both dislocated; there is scoliosis; *note* the wrist and ankle deformities

SECONDARY STRUCTURAL DEFORMITY

Despite much handling and movement experience, secondary structural deformity which may be damaging and painful can develop (Fig. 6/9). It is here that the orthopaedic surgeon has most to offer. The major deformity in spastic quadriplegia involves the hips which frequently take up the windswept position described as a result of the ATNR. The problem, if this position is maintained, is that the adducting hip becomes subluxed and then dislocated and painful. In addition the pelvis tilts up on the side of the adducting hip with consequent formation of a secondary scoliosis to the abducting side with further postural instability and pain. Early recognition of an asymmetrical seating habit and correction of this can postpone or even avoid surgery (p. 262). The adducted hip may be released with an open adductor tenotomy and obturator neurectomy combined with release of the iliopsoas which, in the flexed adducted position, can produce increasing internal rotation and subluxation. Sometimes if bony deformity has become too great, then the severe anteversion of the femoral neck has to be corrected by external rotation osteotomy of the upper femur. Finally, if the hip is actually dislocated or is so severely subluxed that it cannot be relocated by soft tissue procedures, then open reduction combined with femoral, and sometimes pelvic, osteotomy is necessary.

Early soft tissue surgery and the awareness of the dangers of leaving such a position may avoid this type of extensive bony surgery. At times patients present with established dislocation and severe pain. If possible the hip should be replaced in the socket, but sometimes the cartilage of the femoral head has been severely damaged and the socket is grossly dysplastic. In these patients it is sometimes necessary to excise the upper end of the femur to below the level of the lesser trochanter, producing a flail hip, which is pain-free and can be positioned comfortably.

Rarely, the surgeon is presented with a patient who has developed extreme extension and external rotation of the hips. This produces anterior subluxation of the hip with a characteristic bulge in the femoral triangle. These patients are in a parlous situation as they are usually unable to stand, and can lie only either prone or supine with their legs in the extended position. In such a case excision of the upper portion of the femur to below the lesser trochanter is probably the only way of getting mobile hips which allow the patient to sit up and be positioned in a chair. It is essential that at least the upper quarter of the femur is excised, otherwise with time the spasticity of the muscles will cause the femoral shaft to ride up thus impinging on the pelvis causing further problems with sitting and pain. Although this type of surgery may seem very major in often severely handicapped children, results are extremely gratifying in terms of comfort for the patient and improvement in the ease of management for those who have to look after him.

Flexion at the knees, provided it can be kept reasonably under control, is not such a problem in a child who is not going to progress to standing and walking. However, sometimes the flexion contractures can become very gross with subluxation and distortion of the knee joints. If this cannot be controlled by conservative means, then excision of the hamstring tendons distally, plus division of the two heads of the gastrocnemius muscle at the back of the knee is probably the only way of preventing recurrent flexion contractures at the knees.

In these patients it is usually not necessary to correct the foot deformity surgically unless the position of the foot is a great nuisance when the child is sitting in a chair.

Fig. 6/10 Athetoid boy using a two-input POSM switch for typing

THE CEREBRAL PALSIED CHILD IN THE CLASSROOM

Seating is important so that the child's posture is ideal for the proposed activity, with the chair and table at the correct height. The use of non-slip mats helps to prevent equipment sliding. A large-handled pencil (or an ordinary one invested with a soft-tube grip) will assist defective grasps. Chailey spring-loaded scissors assist cutting. Electronic teaching aids may be required (see Chapter 17) (Fig. 6/10).

Educational problems

Children with cerebral palsy often have visuo-spatial and visuo-motor difficulties which interfere with their educational development. Attention control may also be a problem. Full assessment by an educational psychologist is required. Many educational games are available, designed to assist perceptual problems, eye/hand co-ordination, two-handed activity, weight conception, body image, laterality, etc.

Leisure activities are available and should be encouraged, PHAB clubs, Guides and Scouts are examples. Citizens' Band (CB) Radio has provided an exciting new form of social outlet.

EMOTIONAL DEVELOPMENT IN CEREBRAL PALSY

The child with cerebral palsy is often immature in emotional development. The degree of motor delay may increase the child's dependence on the mother. In spastic children the poor balance and marked startle-response make them vulnerable to any change in posture or sudden noise. Poor hand function makes play difficult and exploratory behaviour is inhibited. These children often go through a period of resistance to being handled by anyone but the mother. Home treatment and group therapy using play may be more effective than individual therapy for a time. It is particularly important to involve parents in therapy so that they are able to continue at home.

Children with athetoid cerebral palsy may be more vulnerable to stress because their physical activity is so dependent on conscious effort. In strange situations they lose control. The severely affected athetoid may have the additional problem of poor or absent speech and be even more dependent on his family for interpretation of his needs. In spite of this, athetoid children are often outgoing in personality.

Behaviour disturbance may occur at any age, but particularly at adolescence, when counselling of both child and family is required.

Depression may develop during adolescence producing apparent physical deterioration: it can be treated effectively. Problems of social integration and the need for counselling and sex education are discussed in Chapter 19.

REFERENCES

Bobath, K. (1980). *A Neurophysiological Basis for the Treatment of Cerebral Palsy*. (Spastics International Medical Publications) William Heinemann Medical Books Limited, London.

Cotton, E. (1974). Improvement in motor function with the use of conductive education. *Developmental Medicine and Child Neurology*, **16**, 637.

Crothers, B. and Paine, R. S. (1959). *The Natural History of Cerebral Palsy*. Oxford University Press, Oxford.

Finnie, N. (1974). *Handling the Young Cerebral Palsied Child at Home*, 2nd edition. William Heinemann Medical Books Limited, London.

Huskie, C. F., Ellis, R. E., Flack, F. C., Selley, W. G. and Curle, H. J. (1981). The Exeter lip sensor – a preliminary report. *The College of Speech Therapy Bulletin*, 355 and 356.

Kinsbourne, M. and Oxon, D. M. (1964). Hiatus hernia with contortions of the neck. *Lancet*, **1**, 1058–61.

Levitt, S. (1977). *Treatment of Cerebral Palsy and Motor Delay*. Blackwell Scientific Publications Limited, Oxford.
Werlin, S. L., D'Souza, B. J., Hogan, W. J., Dodds, W. J. and Arndorfer, R. C. (1980). Sandifer syndrome: an unappreciated clinical entity. *Developmental Medicine and Child Neurology*, 22, 374.

FURTHER READING

Blencowe, S. M. (1969). *Cerebral Palsy and the Young Child*. E. and S. Livingstone, Edinburgh. (This book can be obtained from the Cheyne Spastics Centre, 61 Cheyne Walk, London SW3 5LX.)
Bundy, S. and Griffiths, M. (1977). Recurrence risks in families of children with symmetrical spasticity. *Developmental Medicine and Child Neurology*, 19, 179–91.
Cotton, E. (1975). *Conductive Education and Cerebral Palsy*. The Spastics Society, London.
Levitt, S. (1982). *Treatment of Cerebral Palsy and Motor Delay*, 2nd edition. Blackwell Scientific Publications Limited, Oxford.
McDonald, E. T. and Chance, B. Jnr (1964). *Cerebral Palsy*. Prentice-Hall, Englewood Cliffs, N. J.
Rapp, D. L. (1980). Drool control: long-term follow-up. *Developmental Medicine and Child Neurology*, 22, 448–53.
Rapp, D. L. and Bowers, P. M. (1979). Meldreth dribble control project. *Child Care, Health and Development*, 5, 143–9.
Ryan, M. *Feeding Can Be Fun*. The Spastics Society, London.
Warner, J. (1981). *Helping the Handicapped Child with Early Feeding*. Demscoprint Ltd, London.

Chapter 7

Rehabilitation after Acute Neurological Trauma

by G. T. McCARTHY MB, MRCP, DCH *with*
R. CARTWRIGHT MCSP, V. MOFFAT LCST, M. ODDY MSc, PhD,
R. O. ROBINSON MA, MB, BCh, FRCP, J. ROCKEY DipCOT,
P. RUSSELL BA, and P. VINCENT SRN

Acute injury to the brain in childhood has a variety of causes, trauma being the major problem.

HEAD INJURY

Accidents in the home are the major cause of head injury in children up to the age of 3 or 4. Road accidents start to be a problem at 3 years, reaching a peak between 6 and 7 years, and are the major cause of death between 5 and 14 years. Baby battering may result in severe head injury. Comninos (1979) found that falls lead to 68 per cent of head injury in children under 14. In general, twice as many boys as girls are involved in accidents. The most severe injuries are associated with road traffic accidents.

Severe head injury may result in concussion, contusion or laceration of the brain. The immediate effect is severe brain swelling causing raised intracranial pressure, often followed by apnoea with secondary damage then occurring from hypoxia and impaired blood flow. The use of artificial ventilation in the early stages of brain injury is justified in order to assess the potential for recovery.

It may be necessary to open the skull in order to decompress the brain and stop bleeding. Intracranial pressure monitoring is usually carried out in severe cases, and the use of hyperosmolar intravenous drugs, e.g. urea or mannitol, and steroids, will also reduce brain swelling. Epilepsy may occur during the acute phase, or complicate recovery, and anticonvulsants are commonly used to prevent severe seizures.

Post-traumatic hydrocephalus, subdural haemorrhage or effusion may develop and require treatment, and serial CT scans of the brain are very helpful in monitoring the acute situation.

OTHER CAUSES OF CEREBRAL DAMAGE

1. Meningitis or acute encephalitis.
2. Severe status epilepticus associated with hypoxia.
3. Following cardio-respiratory arrest or operative or postoperative shock.
4. Acute infarction of the brain may accompany other medical conditions such as sickle cell disease or accompanying cerebral oedema in severe diabetic coma.
5. Severe brain damage may also occur as the result of vascular accidents in children with vascular malformations or blood clotting defects, but these are rare.

The association of bleeding following removal of ventricular shunts in hydrocephalus is not uncommon.

Progression of recovery

COMA

Coma is defined as the state of disturbed consciousness during which there is no meaningful psychological interaction with the environment.

The level of consciousness is measured using a number of responses to stimuli such as the voice, response to pain and the presence of reflexes. The pupillary responses are important, and in the deepest level of coma the pupils may become fixed and dilated, the corneal reflex is lost and the child assumes decorticate and decerebrate patterns of movement. He may be in a flaccid areflexic state, and assisted ventilation is usually required.

In contrast to adults, children experiencing coma have generally been thought to have a better outcome than adults (Bruce et al, 1978), but the outcome is more difficult to predict (Plum and Caronna, 1975). The cause of the coma may have a direct bearing on outcome. Duration of coma is considered to be predictive of outcome in adults, but in children its prognostic significance is less well defined. In a recent study by Johnston and Mellits (1980), coma duration had predictive value in outcome, particularly for language and intellectual function. There appears to be a definite difference between coma caused by brain trauma as opposed to damage from severe hypoxia.

FAILURE TO RECOVER MOTOR FUNCTION

The persistent vegetative state: After an initial comatose period the child is in a state of wakefulness without awareness and often never regains recognisable mental function. Gillies and Seshia (1980) presented data on 17 children who showed features of the vegetative state following non-traumatic brain injury. Prognosis for this group is poor.

Decerebrate or decorticate responses, roving eye movements and spontaneous blinking occurred early in its evolution and preceded the appearance of clinical sleep/wake cycles.

Akinetic mutism: Patients fix and follow visually, may obey commands, but are mute and inert (Cairns, 1941).

The locked-in syndrome: The child is quadriplegic and mute, but fully alert and responsive. Lateral eye movements are impaired, but vertical eye movements are preserved (Plum and Posner, 1972; Golden et al, 1976).

As the level of consciousness lightens, movement will be seen which may be generalised and uncontrolled, and the child may be confused and disorientated. Epilepsy may occur. Asymmetry of movement may become apparent. Correct positioning of the child is important and, of course, may be affected by other injuries. Chest physiotherapy carried out by the therapist and nurses is important to keep the airways clear. A change of posture and passive movements of the limbs is required regularly to maintain circulation and prevent pressure sores and contractures developing. Neurological examination is required at each stage as evolution of motor problems occurs during recovery. A CT scan of the brain may be helpful in localising damage.

Long-term management

After severe head injury or cerebral damage it is important to stimulate the child appropriately by talking to him, singing and playing music which he knows. Sensory stimulation is important and should include tactile stimulation with different textures, visual stimulation using simple clear objects and pictures, and olfactory stimulation using different smells and tastes.

Physiotherapy

If there is a severe motor problem, it may be necessary to pass through developmental stages of head control, trunk balance, sitting and standing, stimulating recovery by giving the child appropriate motor experience. Physiotherapy assessment is therefore important so that the therapy is aimed at the correct developmental level. Spasticity of limbs may become more obvious at this stage and dystonic postures may develop as the child attempts to regain motor function. As in cerebral palsy, the therapist must aim at helping the child to regain function, and where possible eliminate patterns of movement that will lead to deformity. Unlike cerebral palsy, however, there will be a progression of recovery in motor function which may be rapid even after prolonged coma and continue for the first two years or so following an accident. It must be remembered that the child is having to relearn motor function, having been previously normal. Ataxia can be a very severe disability, again becoming obvious during recovery when the child starts to move. A mixed pattern of ataxia and spasticity is common, and the use of bracing to the legs or serial plasters may be necessary to give postural support. The rate of recovery is variable, and it is helpful to keep detailed records and review aims at intervals according to progress. Often one is surprised by the degree of recovery. Orthopaedic surgery may be helpful, particularly elongation of the tendo calcaneus in the spastic leg. Timing of surgery is important. The natural progression of recovery and good physiotherapy may make it unnecessary.

Occupational therapy

At the same time as physical and motor recovery occurs, recovery of daily living skills will emerge. The occupational therapist (OT) has an important role in stimulating the child. Feeding may be a problem, and introduction of solid feeding, chewing and swallowing is important. If this is impaired, speech production may be difficult and the speech therapist will be helpful in showing nursing staff how to feed and give advice on encouraging chewing, swallowing and lip closure (see Chapter 6). Often speech graduates from mouthing to whispered words *before* voice returns.

As recovery occurs, the child needs to play with appropriate toys for the developmental level and the level of hand function. Self-feeding may need to be retaught, and dressing and toileting should be introduced at the appropriate time according to the degree of neurological damage.

Seating is important, and the child may progress from a chair with head support to one with trunk support and arm rest, and finally to a normal chair.

VISION

Vision may be severely damaged in acute trauma and may also often go through a recovery phase, so the assessment needs to be progressive. At first the use of Stycar graded balls may be helpful, moving on to letter matching as recovery occurs (see Chapter 1). Visual field defects may be suspected from the visual attention and the CT scan findings and demonstrated during recovery. Optic atrophy may have been caused by direct injury to the optic nerve or as the result of raised intracranial pressure. Eye movements may also be paralysed and it is important to involve an ophthalmologist in the recovery programme at an early stage. Double vision may be a disturbing feature for the child.

HEARING AND SPEECH

Loss of hearing may be suspected during recovery because of the child's lack of responsiveness. The use of everyday sounds in the Stycar hearing test is helpful, starting on the level of the ear at 18 inches and progressing to 3 feet and below and above the ear. As recovery occurs the child may be able to co-operate for audiometry, or electrodiagnostic tests may be required (see Chapter 1).

Speech therapy

The importance of early involvement of the speech therapist in the management of the child has already been mentioned, as recovery of feeding, swallowing and chewing is important to the recovery of speech.

Speech may have been affected by damage to the control of the muscles of articulation, producing slurring of speech, or may be affected by cerebellar damage producing ataxic (scanning) speech, or it may be affected by damage to the speech and language centre of the brain producing aphasia. Of course, there may be a combination of factors operating.

Aphasia. This is language impairment following injury to the dominant, usually left, cerebral hemisphere. It is a term applied to all disturbances of language, motor or sensory, due to damage to the language centre in the cerebral cortex. *Aphasia* indicates a complete loss of function, whereas *dysphasia* implies only partial loss. Aphasia can affect all aspects of language. For example, there may be failure to understand written words (dyslexia); gesture (asymbolia); or music (amusia); or it may impair the ability to write (agraphia), as well as to speak or listen.

Expressive dysphasia is caused by damage to the cortex in the region of the inferior frontal convolution of the dominant cerebral hemisphere (Broca's area) or of its connections. When severe, the person may be unable to speak at all, but in less severe forms, there may only be difficulty in forming words. A telegrammatic style may be used, picking out the key words in a sentence or making grammatical errors, confusing articles, prepositions and conjunctions. There may be a disorder of word and sentence formation, faulty pronunciation, word-finding difficulties and inability to name objects (nominal dysphasia) or perseveration where there is inappropriate repetition of the same reply to different questions.

Receptive dysphasia results from a lesion in the posterior temporal or temporo-parietal region of the dominant hemisphere or of its connections. In the severe form, the person hears, but does not understand speech (word deafness) and any speech is unintelligible (jargon). In a mild form individual words may be recognised, but the complete meaning of the sentence is not understood.

It is not surprising that the damage producing aphasia is likely to cause associated neurological disabilities.

Auditory agnosia is an impairment of sensory function, resulting in the person having difficulty in making sense of what he hears. This could be an agnosia for words or sounds.

Apraxia is an impairment of motor function when the person may know what he wants to say, but has difficulty formulating the correct sounds (or agraphia where he is unable to write what is intended).

Speech requires the combined activities of cerebral function, and recovery of speech after severe lesions of the dominant left hemisphere may also depend on the function of the right hemisphere and the corpus callosum, the main connection between the two hemispheres, i.e. the person may retain some non-intellectual speech.

(a) Automatic speech: e.g. songs that have been learnt by heart.
(b) Serial speech: e.g. counting days of the week, etc, which are the result of rote learning.
(c) Social phrases: e.g. 'hello' and 'goodbye'.
(d) Recurrent utterances: i.e. repetition of words or phrases.
(e) Emotional utterances: e.g. 'Oh dear'.
(f) Primitive words: i.e. words that were among the first to be learnt, like 'yes' and 'no'.

PROGNOSIS
The degree of recovery from aphasia will depend on:
1. The site and extent of the lesion, e.g. which part and how much of the speech area has been affected, or whether the non-dominant hemisphere and commissures have been damaged.
2. (a) Associated non-language defects, e.g. impairment of other mental functions, particularly memory, apraxia and agnosia.
   (b) Other disabilities, e.g. defects of visual fields, ocular movements, motor functions, sensory functions, epilepsy, dizziness.

3. (a) Psychological factors, e.g. inability to concentrate, to co-operate or to adjust to the limitations, depression, emotional lability.

   (b) Environmental factors, e.g. home and social conditions, help from relatives, encouragement and reassurance.
4. Age.
5. Cerebral dominance.
6. Pre-morbid language and intellectual ability, personality and temperament.
7. The stage at which speech therapy starts.

The most rapid recovery occurs within the first few weeks, but can continue for some years. The younger the child, the more likelihood of complete recovery. Left hemisphere lesions in young children under age two are often no more injurious than right hemisphere lesions.

Management

ASSESSMENT

The speech therapist's role is to observe and assess the nature of the speech and language disorder in order to obtain a detailed profile of the patient's abilities and disabilities on which to base treatment. For the older child whose language is developed, assessment can be done using recognised tests of aphasia, e.g. Minnesota Test for Differential Diagnosis of Aphasia (Schuell, 1965); An Aphasia Screening Test (Whurr, 1974); Porch Index of Communicative Ability (PICA) and the Boston Assessment and Evaluation of Aphasia. For the younger child, observation of achievement and use of test material for delayed language development (see Chapter 3).

TREATMENT

Rehabilitation must involve an interdisciplinary approach. This is essential in order to understand the diffuse problems of the head-injured patient.

(a) *Posture*: The physiotherapist will advise on good head, neck and trunk positions.
(b) *Breathing*: It may be necessary to teach correct breathing patterns in order to improve voice (see Chapter 6).
(c) *Motor problems* such as dyspraxia: The speech therapist will need to work closely with physiotherapist, occupational therapist, nurse and parents to promote awareness of speech musculature by feeding (see Chapter 6).
(d) *Cognitive and perceptual problems* will require close liaison with psychologist and class teacher.

(e) *Communication*: The patient will probably need a period of intensive speech therapy at the onset. Frequency of treatment will depend on the severity of speech and language disorder, the patient's general health and emotional stability, availability of patient and speech therapist. The speech therapist will advise on the handling of rehabilitation of speech and language.

(f) *Alternative methods of communication*: The speech therapist may feel that the introduction of an alternative method of communication may be beneficial to the patient as an interim measure to augment his speech. This may be a sign or symbol system (see Chapter 17).

(g) *A communication aid* may be necessary, and the speech therapist will advise on the selection and introduction of a suitable aid (see Chapter 17).

Psychological aspects of recovery

INTELLECTUAL DEFICITS

There is now strong evidence for a direct relationship between severity of injury and intellectual deficit (Brink et al, 1970; Levin and Eisenberg, 1979; Chadwick et al, 1981a). Chadwick et al (1981a) suggest that cognitive deficits are normally transient in children who have had a period of post-traumatic amnesia (PTA) of less than three weeks and that even transient deficits are extremely unlikely after injuries leading to a PTA of less than a day.

Recovery of intellectual function appears to continue for as long as five years after injury (Klonoff et al, 1977). The rate of recovery slows down as time from the accident increases and slows down earlier in less severe cases (Chadwick et al, 1981a).

There is surprisingly little evidence concerning the effects on recovery of sustaining a head injury at different stages in childhood. One study (Woo Sam et al, 1970) found that despite the fact that the younger children were less severely injured (in terms of coma duration) they suffered more severe intellectual deterioration. Chadwick et al (1981a) found few differences in course or extent of recovery but there were indications that the younger group (those aged less than 10) made a more rapid recovery.

As yet no clear definition of the typical patterns of deficit in children has been reached. The Wechsler Intelligence Scale for Children (WISC), which has 10 sub-tests, has frequently been used to assess intellectual deterioration. Chadwick et al (1981b) employed more specialised neuropsychological tests in addition to the WISC but found only a small number of deficits not identified by the WISC. In a sub-group of children who showed no deficits on the WISC, tests of speed of visuo-motor or visuo-spatial functioning were able to pick up specific deficits.

A crucial question concerns the influence that such deficits exert on scholastic achievement.

Once again the degree of disruption will depend upon the severity of injury and consequent cognitive deficits. However, even among a group with relatively mild head injuries Chadwick et al (1981a) found that among children with more severe injuries (PTA more than three weeks) there was a pattern of reading impairment followed by recovery but residual impairment was found only among those who also showed persistent intellectual impairment. The final follow-up in this study was two years after injury and it is possible that this is too short a period in which to judge possible accumulating effects on scholastic attainment. Indeed, in an unselected sample of children with head injury Klonoff (1977) found that 25 per cent of younger children and a third of the older children were still not making normal progress in school five years after injury. For the most severely injured this frequently results in attendance at a special school.

PERSONALITY CHANGE AND PSYCHIATRIC DISTURBANCE AFTER HEAD INJURY IN CHILDHOOD

Assessing the influence of head injury in childhood on behaviour and personality is complicated by evidence that there is a considerably higher incidence of pre-morbid behaviour problems in head injured children compared to controls (Craft et al, 1972). Such children do appear to be more likely to develop new psychiatric disorders following head injury than those with no such history of disturbance (Brown et al, 1981; Harrington and Letermendia, 1958). However, there does appear to be a relatively high rate of behaviour disorders even among those without such a history. Estimates of the frequency vary from 10 per cent of head injured children (Rune, 1970) to 52 per cent (Brown et al, 1981) depending in part upon the severity of injury. Recovery appears to continue for up to three years, although there is a suggestion that the problems can recur at later stages of development.

The form of behavioural or psychiatric problem that follows a head injury in childhood is normally of a kind that commonly occurs in child psychiatric practice (e.g. hyperactivity, temper tantrums, sleep disturbance, eating problems, discipline problems). However, Brown et al (1981) identified a small group of five cases who showed a pattern they named a 'disinhibited state'. These children showed a variety of disinhibited behaviours, such as making very personal remarks, asking embarrassing questions or getting undressed in inappropriate social situations. All the children in this group had received severe injuries, none had a history of psychiatric disturbance prior to injury and in each case the disturbance was evident from the earliest stages of recovery from the accident. The authors therefore suggested that this form of disturbance could be attributed directly to the brain damage. However, with this notable exception, the increased frequency of psychiatric disorder found among children following head injury appears to be a function of the stresses associated with head injury rather than brain damage per se.

Behavioural disturbances disrupt relationships between children, their parents, their teachers and their peers. Such relationship difficulties are worst about a year after injury and usually resolve thereafter (Klonoff and Paris, 1974). Brown and colleagues in an unpublished study (cited in Oddy, 1983) have suggested that parents err in the direction of an under rather than over use of discipline. One year after injury, 20 per cent of parents were rated as using too little discipline. This tendency was particularly marked when the child was on anticonvulsive medication. As parental handling did not differ according to the type of disturbance, Brown and colleagues concluded that the parent's behaviour was not reactive to the child's disturbance but may in fact increase the risk of disturbance developing in the child.

The recoverability of the child's brain

It is often said that the brains of children recover better from injury than those of adults. Since, as in adults, the neurones of children cannot, once killed, be replaced, this idea needs qualifying. There are certain areas of the brain which perform unique functions. For example, the left occipital lobe serves sight for the right field of vision in both eyes. If this is damaged in a child, he will lose vision permanently in this area just as would an adult. Similarly, strokes in children appear to cause the same degree of motor handicap to the relevant area as in adults.

However, the idea has some validity. Obviously a young, active exploratory child will compensate, using the unaffected side to better advantage than will an infirm, demoralised elderly person. Immediately after trauma, children can develop cerebral oedema faster and more extensively than adults, and for a period of time appear worse with a worse prognosis than is borne out by their subsequent good recovery.

Additionally, however, another mechanism may be at work. Some functions, although carried out by both cerebral hemispheres, are predominantly served by one. Language concentrated in the left hemisphere in most people is one example. It appears that if a child receives left hemisphere damage relatively early – say within the first six years of life – language function can, to a large extent, be transferred successfully to the right cerebral hemisphere. It is conceivable that right cerebral hemisphere functions, less well documented, could be similarly transferred to the left. Adults on the whole are less capable of making this kind of intracerebral adjustment. While attempts to take advantage of this facility in children have not been systematically explored, this offers one possible therapeutic approach (Robinson, 1981).

ACUTE SPINAL CORD INJURY

The spinal cord may be acutely damaged by trauma, vascular accident, tumour or infection. There is potential for recovery, but long-term effects are similar to those of spina bifida. Depending on the level of injury, there is paralysis, loss of sensation, incontinence and impotence.

An increasing number of children with high cervical lesions (above C3 level) are surviving on long-term ventilation. Sadly, many remain in acute paediatric units. For them, integration into the community and environmental control is possible to improve their quality of life. It must be recognised that their continued existence is precarious, but nurses and, indeed, parents can be trained to manage their various problems.

Nursing management

MANAGEMENT OF THE AIRWAY

A permanent tracheostomy is necessary and the individual arrangements of tracheostomy tubes will vary. However, the long-term management requires modification of short-term tracheostomy care. For example a non-cuffed tube may be used to allow speech. The attachment of the tube to the ventilator is vital, and a stainless steel screw fitting inserted into a disposable Portex tracheostomy tube works well. The tracheostomy tube is held in position by tapes inserted through rubber tubing and tied around the neck.

Local infection may occur at the tracheostomy site and is treated appropriately.

Rubber whistle-tip catheters should be used for both tracheal and pharyngeal suction as long-term use of plastic catheters causes trauma and scarring of the tissues. After use the catheters should be soaked in sodium bicarbonate solution and syringed through with the solution. They can then be sterilised in Cidex solution by immersion for at least 10 minutes, then rinsed through with sterile water and allowed to dry, covered by sterile paper towels until re-used.

The tracheostomy tube has to be sucked out and changed regularly, and changing is done after hand ventilating with an Ambu-bag. The nurse caring for the child must be confident of the procedures to follow if the tube blocks or the ventilator fails, and the child must also feel confident in his carers.

Tracheal suction is usually only required twice daily, but needs to be increased if the child has a cold.

CHEST PHYSIOTHERAPY

Routine chest physiotherapy consists of vibration and percussion during manual hyperventilation as the child is moved from side to side and on to his back. This is done by the physiotherapist with the assistance of a nurse. A cough mechanism may be developed using the expiratory phase of manual hyperventilation and this is encouraged to minimise the trauma of the mucous membrane while using a rubber suction tube. The chest clearing is assisted by suction if coughing is not sufficient. Suction techniques need to be clean but not sterile. Changes of position are encouraged during the day and 'sucking out' is done on average six times a day (after meals and drinks) and twice a night by the nursing staff.

When there is a chest infection and/or lung collapse, chest physiotherapy is increased to two-hourly during the day, and evening cover is provided by the physiotherapy staff if necessary, but where possible the night is left free for sleeping. Normal postural drainage positions are used bearing in mind the tube to the tracheostomy. Because it is impossible to position the patient in prone position due to the tube, the patient should not be allowed to lie on his back in order to prevent collapse of the dorsal segments of the lung. Coughing is encouraged, but obviously more suction is required. If the secretions are viscous, 2ml of saline can be inserted by a syringe through the tracheal opening to help loosen the secretions; suction should then be done immediately. For techniques of suction see *Cash's Textbook of Chest, Heart and Vascular Disorders for Physiotherapists* (Downie, 1983).

A Milwaukee type jacket is used when in the sitting position to maintain the airway.

Passive movements are carried out daily to every joint in arms and legs for ease of handling, and exercises are also performed during dressing and undressing. A cage over the bed helps to prevent foot deformities.

MANAGEMENT OF THE VENTILATOR

More than one ventilator is required if the child is able to sit in a wheelchair. A portable ventilator needs to be attached to the chair. A humidifier may be used in the system during the night as it is difficult when the child is up and about. Readings of the ventilator need to be taken on a regular basis (usually two-hourly at night only), measuring the minute volume and tidal volume.

Phrenic nerve pacing has been developed in the USA. This enables the patient to be removed from a ventilator for several hours at a time (Glenn, 1978). Ventilation is maintained by diaphragmatic movement produced by electrical stimulation of the phrenic nerve. This device will certainly aid management, but has not yet been fully evaluated in the UK.

TEMPERATURE CONTROL

This may be a problem in high cervical lesions. The temperature tends to drop rapidly and maintenance of a normal temperature is difficult. A sheepskin can be used in bed and a space blanket added. An electronic thermometer allows temperature readings to be made without removing the covers or disturbing the child during the night. Adequate clothing should be worn in bed, and it is important not to remove the clothing completely when putting the child back to bed. Outdoor clothing is fully insulated ski wear including hat and gloves; underwear is thermal.

BRACING

A Milwaukee brace is necessary, suitably adapted in order to allow the child to sit in the wheelchair safely. It is important to check that the brace does not produce pressure ulcers or compress the colostomy.

SEATING

Contoured or special cushions may be necessary to prevent pressure sores (see Chapter 14).

BOWEL CONTROL

This may be a problem, and a colostomy makes bowel management much easier.

BLADDER CONTROL

This can be maintained using a urinary appliance (see Chapter 5), or an indwelling catheter.

CONTROL OF CONTRACTURES AND SPASTICITY

Varying degrees of spasticity occur in the limbs, and it is important to manipulate the arms and legs passively. The use of baclofen, an anti-spastic drug, can be helpful (see p. 131): it is most effective in spinal spasticity. The dose needs to be adjusted to the response, and it is important to avoid side-effects, particularly emotional problems and lowering of blood pressure. In spite of regular passive movements contractures may develop.

Obviously the maintenance of a child on permanent ventilation requires skilled nursing. It also requires great imagination in order to allow the child to live a reasonable life. With the assistance of the interdisciplinary team it is possible for such a child to move in his own electric wheelchair, and by the use of movement in the face and neck, to manipulate by electronic control his educational and social environment (Fig. 7/1).

Since it is possible to keep children alive who would have otherwise died, it is important that we do give them a reasonable quality of life.

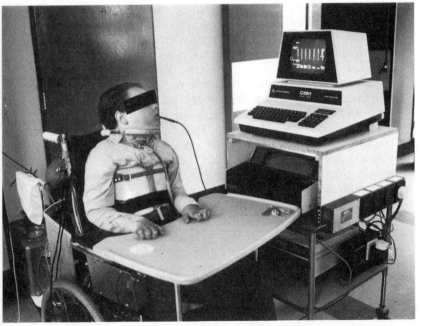

Fig. 7/1 Child in a modified attendant-operated powered wheelchair with portable ventilator. Note the Milwaukee brace. The computer is being operated by means of a suck-blow technique

SOCIAL WORK INVOLVEMENT

Disability presenting in the adolescent period provokes very special problems. Firstly, the young person concerned will have a 'lost identity'. Not all disabled people have the intellectual ability to compensate for a physical disability through higher education and a rapid realignment of job prospects. Many will have seen themselves as essentially 'physical' people, interested in sport and a full social life. Others, on the brink of leaving home, will have to adapt to renewed and greatly increased dependency. Conversely, even loving parents will have begun to anticipate the freedom of the post-parenting period, perhaps looking forward to career changes, moving house, a shift in responsibility. Few families will willingly talk about their new problems unless there is sensitive and non-judgemental counselling. Emotional problems may be concealed behind demands for new pieces of equipment or house modifications. Parents may not even admit to each other what the re-organisation of family life may mean.

Re-organisation may not only mean widening the bathroom door so that a wheelchair can get through. It may mean accepting the performance of duties which are less than acceptable to both parent and child. Parents in correspondence with the Voluntary Council have highlighted some of the difficulties. One mother noted that 'He [the father] has to help me bath Susan. Even with a hoist, we can't manage alone. But he has to travel as part of his job and I think an incontinent girl needs a bath *every* day. He says he'll have to give up work to help me.' Another father wrote, 'She [the mother] finds it very difficult looking after John. He's 18 and acutely embarrassed about his mother having to help him all the time. I don't suppose she saw him naked after he was 9 or 10 – and now they both have to face it all the time. It's not like a nurse you don't know – they both feel uncomfortable. If only we could get our bathroom adaptations through quickly, it wouldn't be necessary.' A third parent told of how the hospital consultant described her son after a major car accident as 'just a head on a bed – he'll never do anything. He meant to be kind to me, he didn't want me to hope for too much. In a way maybe he was right. Everything my son has done has amazed and pleased me. But if I had been a different sort of woman, I might have gone off and drowned myself!'

The Spinal Injuries Association finds that parents of young people in this category of disability – and their families – are often singularly ill-informed about their rights and availability of services. Many do not know of the existence of voluntary agencies which can provide appropriate information and peer counselling. Indeed, parents of 'new' disabled young people seem at a particular disadvantage in having to cope with a threatening situation with an immediacy which is not present in other disabilities. The expertise of spinal injuries units is seldom available in the community unless there are active attempts to continue liaison and for the *professionals* to learn from their hospital-based colleagues before discharge.

REFERENCES

Brink, J. D., Garrett, A. L., Hale, W. R., Woo-Sam, J. and Nickel, V. L. (1970). Recovery of motor and intellectual function in children sustaining severe head injuries. *Developmental Medicine and Child Neurology*, 12, 565–71.

Brown, G., Chadwick, O., Shaffer, D., Rutter, M. and Traub, M. (1981). A prospective study of children with head injuries: III Psychiatric sequelae. *Psychological Medicine*, 11 (1), 63–78.

Bruce, D. A., Schut, L., Burns, L. A., Wood, H. H. and Sutton, L. N. (1978). Outcome following severe head injuries in children. *Journal of Neurosurgery*, 48, 679–88.

Cairns, H. (1941). Akinetic mutism with an epidermoid cyst of the 3rd ventricle. *Brain*, 64, 273–90.

Chadwick, O., Rutter, M., Brown, G., Shaffer, D. and Traub, M. (1981a). A prospective study of children with head injuries: II Cognitive sequelae. *Psychological Medicine*, 11 (1), 49–62.

Chadwick, O., Rutter, M., Shaffer, D. and Shrout, P. E. (1981b). A prospective study of children with head injuries: IV Specific cognitive defects. *Journal of Clinical Neuropsychology*, 3 (2), 101–20.

Comninos, St. C. (1979). Early prognosis of severe head injury. *Acta Neurologica*, Supplement 28, 144–7.

Craft, A. W., Shaw, D. A. and Cartlidge, N. E. F. (1972). Head injuries in children. *British Medical Journal*, 4, 200–3.

Downie, P. A. (ed) (1983). *Cash's Textbook of Chest, Heart and Vascular Disorders for Physiotherapists*, 3rd edition. Faber and Faber, London.

Gillies, J. D. and Seshia, S. S. (1980). Vegetative state following coma in childhood: evolution and outcome. *Developmental Medicine and Child Neurology*, 22, 5, 642.

Glenn, W. W. L. (1978). Diaphragm pacing – present status. *PACE* 1, 357–70.

Golden, G. S., Leeds, N., Kremenitzer, M. D. and Russman, B. S. (1976). The locked-in syndrome in children. *Journal of Paediatrics*, 596–8.

Harrington, J. A. and Letermendia, F. J. J. (1958). Persistent psychiatric disorders after head injuries in children. *Journal of Mental Science*, 104, 1205–7.

Johnston, R. B. and Mellits, E. D. (1980). Paediatric coma: prognosis and outcome. *Developmental Medicine and Child Neurology*, 22, 1, 3.

Klonoff, H. and Paris, R. (1974). Immediate, short-term and residual effects of acute head injuries in children. Neuropsychological and neurological correlates. In *Clinical Neuropsychology: Current Status and Applications*, (eds) Reitan, R. M. and Davison, L. A., John Wiley, Washington.

Klonoff, H., Low, M. D. and Clark, C. (1977) Head injuries in children: a prospective 5-year follow-up. *Journal of Neurology, Neurosurgery and Psychiatry*, 40, 1211–19.

Levin, H. S. and Eisenberg, H. M. (1979). Neuropsychological outcome of closed head injury. *Child's Brain*, 5, 281–92.

Oddy, M. (1983). In *Psychological Recovery from Head Injury* (ed Brooks, D. N.). Oxford University Press, London.

Plum, F. and Caronna, J. J. (1975). *Prognosis and medical coma*. In *Head Injuries* (ed McLaurin, R. L.). Grune and Stratton, New York.

Plum, F. and Posner, J. B. (1972). *The Diagnosis of Stupor and Coma*, 2nd edition. Davis Co, Philadelphia.

Robinson, R. O. (1981). Equal recoverability in child and adult brain? *Developmental Medicine and Child Neurology*, 23, 379.

Rune, V. (1970). Acute head injuries in children. *Acta Paediatrica Scandinavica*, Supplement, 209.

Schuell, A. (1965). *The Minnesota Test for the Differential Diagnosis of Aphasia*. University of Minnesota Press, Minneapolis.

Whurr, R. (1974). *An Aphasia Screening Test*. Available from 17 Canonbury Square, London N1 2AL.

Woo-Sam, J., Zimmerman, T. L., Brink, J. D., Uyehara, K. and Miller, A. R. (1970). Socio-economic status and post-trauma intelligence in children with severe head injuries. *Psychological Reports*, 27, 147–53.

ACKNOWLEDGEMENT

Figure 7/1 is reproduced by kind permission of Action Research – The National Fund for Research into Crippling Diseases, Vincent House, Horsham RH12 2PN.

Chapter 8

Neuromuscular Disorders and Muscular Dystrophy

by R. O. ROBINSON MA, MB, BCh, FRCP *with*
R. CARTWRIGHT MCSP, J. ROCKEY DipCOT and P. RUSSELL BA

This is a group of disorders characterised by slowly progressive weakness due to a gradual degenerative muscle process. There are several varieties which differ according to the age of onset, patterns of muscles affected, speed of deterioration and association with related conditions. They are all inherited disorders – although again the mode of inheritance differs – and all (save one and hence called congenital muscular dystrophy) are characterised by an initial period of apparently normal power and motor development. The basic cause or causes of the muscle degeneration is not known.

DUCHENNE MUSCULAR DYSTROPHY

The Duchenne variety of this group of disorders is the commonest type, and for practical purposes is only seen in boys. The child appears normal initially. Walking may be achieved at the usual time but is frequently a few months delayed. By this time weakness can be detected. The gait, even in the early stages, is abnormal. There is no spring from the weight-bearing foot, and the first signs of the characteristic rolling movements of the hips can be detected. The child jumps and hops inadequately. Running is not properly acquired. It is at this stage that the child is usually referred.

Diagnosis

The diagnosis can be made with a fair degree of confidence from the characteristic pattern of weakness on a careful clinical examination. The calves, though weak, may appear bulky. This 'pseudo-hypertrophy' is due in part to replacement of functioning muscle by fat and fibrous tissue. Rising from the floor is difficult from the supine position. The child rolls to prone, pushes up to a bear-walking

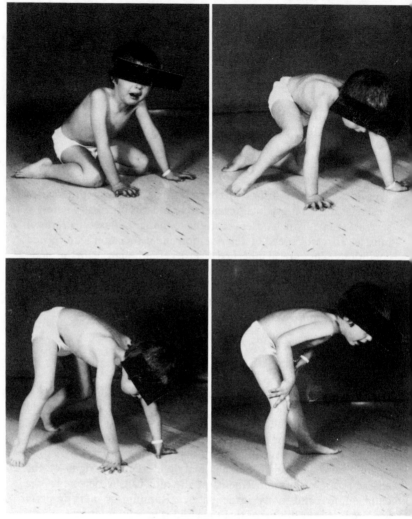

Fig. 8/1 Gowers' sign

position and then extends his trunk on his pelvis by 'walking his hands up his legs' (Gowers' sign) (Fig. 8/1).

An enzyme called creatine-phosphokinase (CPK), normally concentrated in muscle, leaks from dystrophic muscle into the bloodstream. In Duchenne muscular dystrophy the CPK blood level is very high. This is not only of value in helping to establish the diagnosis, but it is also of value in screening families (see below).

Further evidence of muscle disturbance can be obtained by recording the electrical activity directly from the muscle – an electromyograph (EMG).

The diagnosis is confirmed by muscle biopsy. A small piece of muscle is removed, either at operation or by using a wide bore needle, and then examined histologically. The appearances are characteristic. While this procedure may be transiently uncomfortable, it should be carried out for it is the only way sufficient certainty can be obtained to enable the doctor to talk to the parent confidently about the future.

Genetic aspects

Duchenne muscular dystrophy is an X-linked recessive condition. This means it is carried by asymptomatic females whose sons have a 50 per cent chance of inheriting the condition and whose daughters have a 50 per cent chance of themselves being carriers. In addition, if the mother is a carrier the mother's sisters also have a 50 per cent chance of being carriers and clearly need to know the risks for any future children they may plan to have. Not all mothers are carriers; the condition may arise *de novo* in the son. Such women are not at an increased risk of having further affected sons. However, at the present time the carrier state can be detected in about 70 per cent if up to three serial CPK levels are estimated. Unfortunately at this time prenatal diagnosis has not been reliable. The poor best that can be offered the pregnant carrier is selective abortion of the male fetus. Nevertheless screening and appropriate counselling of the family can achieve a great deal in terms of prevention. Equally important is early diagnosis of the first affected male. A CPK estimation is good practice in the investigation of a boy of 2 who is not yet walking – particularly if he also seems generally somewhat delayed. In this way the disaster of the birth of a second affected brother may be prevented.

Progress of the condition

Once the diagnosis has been established, the family can be told that the child will become progressively weaker. He will stop walking at 7–13 years (Dubowitz, 1978), and can be expected to die in the late teens or early twenties. Grim though this picture is, much can be done to alleviate the condition and improve the child's quality of life.

Walking

As weakness advances, walking becomes more difficult and unstable. Continuation of walking is important for some boys and their families.

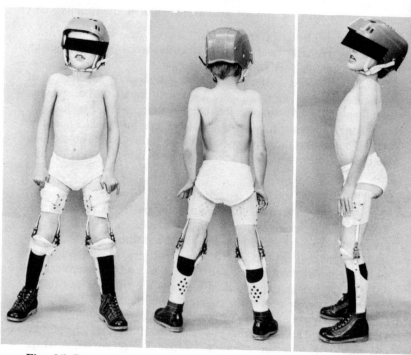

Fig. 8/2 Polypropylene orthoses, anterior, posterior and lateral views. *Note* the lordotic posture

It usually depends upon a reasonably plantigrade foot. Progressive talipes equinovarus frequently develops towards the end of the walking period. It may be retarded, but rarely prevented altogether, by daily passive dorsiflexion of the feet combined with either polypropylene ankle-foot orthoses inside the shoes, or night splints. Similarly, as more time is spent in sitting, hip and knee flexion contractures begin to occur. If prolongation of walking is going to be attempted, these contractures must be relieved. This can usually be achieved by percutaneous tenotomy. When walking is abandoned contractures are almost inevitable. Bed rest, even for only a few days – for whatever reason, frequently causes a decline in power which may prove impossible to reverse. After surgery the children should be mobilised in a walking long-leg plaster. Light polypropylene orthoses are then fitted (Fig. 8/2). This form of walking can continue up to 13 years of age.

During walking, however achieved, preparation should be set in hand for the inevitable transition to a wheelchair. Ramps for access to the home should be laid, doors should be widened, toilet and bathroom facilities should, if possible, be provided downstairs. A chairlift for the stairs is an alternative option. The possibilities of providing appropriate education – by this time usually secondary – in a suitable architectural setting must be explored. Pre-empting problems in this way smooths the transition to a wheelchair. The change does not then assume the proportions of a crisis.

Sitting

The wheelchair should be self-propelled for as long as possible, although a powered chair is eventually inevitable. Around the time of abandoning walking, transfers from wheelchair to bed, car, lavatory, and so on should be taught, to maintain independence for as long as possible. The wheelchair should be fitted with a lap-strap to prevent the child being tipped out. Transferring to a bed depends on the correct bed height; it is made easier by a firm mattress with a board underneath.

Similarly, sitting on the toilet can be stabilised using a Sanichair with straps, or an individually moulded toilet seat can be provided. Cleansing can take place from the front while sufficient sitting balance and hand strength are retained. For micturition a wide-based urinal with a U-shaped cut-out cushion can be used.

Scoliosis

As the condition progresses, breathing exercises, postural drainage and percussion of the chest need to be taught to parents so that they may carry them out when necessary.

Walking is associated with an exaggerated lumbar lordosis. When seated, the majority of boys tend to slump forward and lose this lordotic curve. It is thought that in this position the back is more susceptible to forces from the side; the posterior articular facets become unlocked. A progressive scoliotic curve adds greatly to these children's difficulties (Fig. 8/3). Asymmetric ischial pressure makes comfortable seating progressively more difficult. One arm becomes dedicated to propping, with loss of two-hand function. With increasing instability the back becomes less comfortable; the problems of seating become overwhelming whereupon a bed-bound existence begins. Thoracic involvement in the curve causes a pulmonary ventilation perfusion mis-match with additional vulnerability to hypostatic pneumonia. By this time hip and knee flexion contractures have frequently been acquired which prevent self-turning in bed. Since this is necessary every two hours, it is this

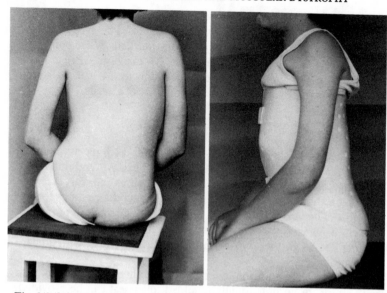

Fig. 8/3 (*left*) Progressive scoliotic curve. *Note* the pattern marks from the jacket

Fig. 8/4 (*right*) Polypropylene jacket (TLSO) accentuating the lumbar lordotic curve

additional strain which frequently overbears the family's ability to cope. Institutional life begins therefore at a time when the patient most needs the comfort and support of his home and family. This catalogue of deterioration may not be inevitable if scoliosis can be prevented. One way of attempting this is to fit the child with a light polypropylene jacket (TLSO) which accentuates the lumbar lordotic curve (Fig. 8/4) (see Chapter 12). Such a jacket can be worn under ordinary clothes and prevents neither wheelchair mobility nor school activities. It is hoped that this method may retard or even prevent altogether the development of scoliosis.

Continuing weakness

Hand and arm function can be assisted, even in the face of profound weakness, by correctly positioned arm supports. These may take the form either of overhead gantries with slings on springs (or knicker elastic), or of ball-bearing arm supports attached to the wheelchair. These will continue to allow the use of electric typewriters or micro-writers when using a pen is no longer possible. Similarly, lightweight cutlery and a beer mug with a straw incorporated into the lid allow independent feeding to a late stage. Once the child can no longer transfer for himself, the height of the bed may need to be raised so that the parents may the more easily turn him at night and dress or undress him on the bed. Parents' backs are always at risk. They should be taught early how to lift with bent hips and knees but straight backs. Hoists may need to be provided by the bed and bath. Bath seats and rails are useful initially, and later a bath care insert may be invaluable (see Chapter 21).

With increasing immobility, obesity is a not infrequent problem in these boys. It need hardly be said that this compounds the effects of muscle weakness, and obesity places an additional burden on those caring for him. This occurs for four reasons: (1) many do not reduce their intake with decreased activity; (2) over-eating may assuage depression and anxiety; (3) over-feeding may be a mother's response to her child's condition; and (4) perhaps most commonly, over-eating may be a response to boredom – particularly in those boys with limited intellect. Appropriate hobbies to encourage include CB radio, television games, chess, fishing and photography. Swimming may continue for a period after walking becomes impossible. Eventually the weight of the water induces dyspnoea at which point it should of course be abandoned.

Intelligence

An accompanying feature of this disorder is mental handicap. The normal distribution of intelligence is shifted 15–20 points 'to the left'. The average IQ therefore is around 80–85. The mental handicap is, unlike the weakness, non-progressive and is present before the weakness. It has been shown that the performance level is better than the verbal level; reading may be retarded. Not surprisingly there is also a high rate of emotional disturbance (Leibowitz and Dubowitz, 1981).

Social and psychiatric aspects

This condition is different from most others treated in this book since it involves gradual progression and relatively early death. These families are entitled to informed discussion and well co-ordinated help. Much appreciated advice on practical aspects can be found in *With a Little Help* published by the Muscular Dystrophy Group of Great Britain. Many families find sharing problems with others in a similar situation a great source of strength. It is sometimes said that these boys and their families face three crises. The crises of diagnosis, stopping walking, and dying.

The shock of diagnosis is a little different from that of breaking the news of most forms of handicap. First of all, the child may be relatively little affected at the time of diagnosis, and incredulity may predominate. Second, the repercussions of only one partner transmitting the condition can lead to guilt on the one hand and recriminations on the other. These feelings need to be ventilated, together with the usual bereavement for the loss of the normal child, before the parents can be expected to cope realistically.

Stopping walking is a crisis in the sense that this is the most inescapable evidence of continuing deterioration and all that is implied by that. Its effects may be ameliorated for the child by suitable forward planning as outlined above.

The realisation of the reduced life expectancy usually comes slowly to the children. Death itself is rarely feared, although the mode of dying may be. This needs careful exploration with the child, usually at a time he chooses with the person he chooses. He needs to know that death is neither painful nor uncomfortable, taking place in the setting usually of increasing drowsiness associated with a chest infection. This not infrequently relieves unspoken fears.

PROGRESSIVE NEUROMUSCULAR DISORDERS

There are a great many of these. Most are rare, but the group of spinal muscular atrophies is the commonest. This presents a spectrum of severity. The most profoundly affected (those with Werdnig Hoffman disease), present at, or shortly after, birth with severe hypotonia and weakness. Such children do not have enough strength to overcome gravity with their proximal muscles, and consequently they do not achieve independent sitting and may not be able to reach out. Rehabilitation as such is not a realistic goal for this group. Swallowing and ventilatory weakness combined make death from hypostatic pneumonia inevitable within the first two years.

At the other end of the spectrum is the Kugelberg-Welander type. Here weakness does not become apparent until, at the earliest, the second year. Initially this may be confined to the lower limbs and pelvis, with subsequent involvement of the arms. The course is relatively static, with a continued waddling gait and lumbar lordosis identical to that seen in the more mild dystrophies and myopathies. Respiratory insufficiency is not a problem.

Between these two extremes fall a number of children who achieve sitting unaided at the normal time, but who do not acquire standing or walking alone. As in the other varieties, the arms are not as involved as the legs. Reaching is possible but may be obviously weak. As with the most severe forms, fasciculation of the tongue, a hallmark of the disease, when present is unmistakable. A number of children have been seen who initially resemble the Kugelberg-Welander type, acquire walking but subsequently deteriorate more rapidly and become unable to walk and have greater arm weakness within a few years. It is in these two latter groups that rehabilitation has most to offer.

The diagnosis is supported by EMG findings of the denervation characteristic of anterior horn cell disease and the muscle biopsy which typically shows large muscle group atrophy.

Rehabilitation

This consists of:

Prevention of scoliosis. This happens relatively soon after loss of independent sitting and can occur very rapidly. Anything less rigid than a polypropylene jacket seems ineffective. This should be applied at the earliest sign of a postural curve (irrespective of whether it corrects fully on suspension). It would seem logical to incorporate a full lumbar lordosis as for the children with muscular dystrophy (p. 168). Should this fail to prevent progression, an extensive anterior and posterior spinal fusion, if necessary with Harrington distraction rods, may be necessary.

Promotion of walking. If the child can bear some weight on his feet he may acquire walking using lightweight polypropylene orthoses. He will almost certainly need a pelvic band, and possibly higher support, depending on trunk strength and the presence or otherwise of scoliosis. In either case confident balancing is only likely with the aid of some kind of support sticks. There must therefore be enough residual arm strength for these. If the child is too weak even with this support, an ORLAU swivel walker may be considered (Stallard et al, 1978). This depends on the ability to shift weight from one leg to the other. With this movement the apparatus swivels around an eccentric hinge bringing the non-weight-bearing leg with it. It can be fitted if necessary to a child wearing a spinal jacket. While it may produce a kind of 'walking' and be of benefit for that reason alone, the child with spinal muscular atrophy who cannot walk in long calipers with support sticks is unlikely to be able to get into or out of the swivel walker independently. In addition, the swivel walker is useful only indoors on very flat surfaces, and cannot at this time mount door sills or other minor hurdles.

An alternative to walking is a powered chair. This can be fitted with adapted hand controls with micro-switches as necessary. Adequate support must be given, particularly to the neck to prevent any whiplash effect from rapid acceleration or deceleration forces.

In the event of limited arm strength, an overhead gantry with slings on elastic or springs above a tray can permit independent feeding, play and writing (see p. 351).

SOCIAL WORK INVOLVEMENT

Living with the long-term prospect of death taxes any family's ability to care. If a child has muscular dystrophy, parents may not only see a loved child deteriorating, but be fearfully watching other siblings who may or may not have the condition. In these cases, they may also have to cope with the other children's fears and anxieties as well as their own. Many parents cope magnificently with an intolerable situation. But, as one mother said, 'to provide such love and security is enormously costly. It is fought for as parents are themselves struggling to cope. There is anger; the anger of impotence, born of the knowledge that you can do little or nothing to change the situation; there is anger at other people's insensitivity and at the endless waiting and frustration which is part of the whole business of treatment.'

Burton (1975) highlighted the need not only for social services support during the terminal process, but actually *after* death when all too often the final offering is 'his clothes and teddy bear wrapped in a plastic sack – like I put my rubbish in'. Common reactions in the mourning process include shock and numbness (often confused with acceptance); sleeplessness and lack of appetite; guilt for opportunities lost, cross words said and preoccupation with the dead child's image. He is 'seen' in his room, on the stairs.

One unit which has run a number of parents' groups for families whose child is dying or has died, has highlighted the need to provide support at critical times. Birthdays, or indeed anniversaries, are often terrible reminders of what is lost. Many parents desperately need to share their anxieties, but cannot talk to family or neighbours. Although many get invaluable support from the medical profession, most are desperately aware of pressure of time. Parents' groups, with the non-directive guidance of a skilled social worker, are an invaluable means of providing continuity of care and support. Some voluntary organisations, like the Compassionate Friends or the individual disability organisations, can also run group sessions and self-help. While the parents will invariably be the major contributors to groups, the needs of siblings should never be forgotten. Many specialist hospitals offer brothers and sisters a chance to talk to a social worker. If such support is not given, not only may other children bitterly blame themselves, but they may perceive the parents' grief as indicating regret that they are the survivors and not the dead brother or sister.

Support of the dying child or young person is particularly difficult in a society which has largely lost the traditional framework of support from the church. We do not expect children to die and, in an age of technological medicine, few adults have personally experienced the loss of a close relative in childhood, or early youth. One result is that the child is often caught up in a collusion of pretence about the non-existence of death. Bluebond-Langner (1978), in her study of the private worlds of dying children, found that 'mutual pretence' was the general shield against pain. Although social work support cannot remedy the situation, it can ensure that families are supported through the often protracted period of dying and bereavement.

Experience of feedback from a series of Voluntary Council seminars on this theme has suggested that not only parents, but also *professionals* have personal needs and emotional stress when working in this field. A characteristic of work at child development centres like Charing Cross and Honeylands is that professionals support each other, and that the personal involvement is recognised and discussed on a team basis. Personal feelings about handicap may vary, but feelings about death will almost invariably be painful, and to a certain extent incapable of satisfactory resolution. After all, death may be a relief, but it is never a happy solution in childhood. Medical, nursing staff, therapists and teachers, especially those in junior positions, will be particularly vulnerable also. Their training is coupled with society's anticipation that they are people who cure: they are too young to have had much experience of pain and grief, and they are the 'grassroots workers' who will deal most frequently on a day-to-day basis with anguished parents. 'Who cares for the carers?' is a question insufficiently asked. Yet it is directly concerned with the quality of care offered, and greater social work involvement in the professional team could go some way to providing it.

REFERENCES

Bluebond-Langner, M. (1978). *The Private World of Dying Children*. Princeton University Press, USA.
Burton, L. (1975). *The Family Life of Sick Children*. Routledge and Kegan Paul, London.

Dubowitz, V. (1978). *Muscle Disorders in Childhood*. W.B. Saunders Co, Philadelphia.

Leibowitz, D. and Dubowitz, V. (1981). Intellect and behaviour in Duchenne muscular dystrophy. *Developmental Medicine and Child Neurology*, 23, 577–90.

Stallard, J., Rose, G. K. and Farmer, I. R. (1978). The Orlau swivel walker. *Prosthetics and Orthotics International*, 2 (1), 35–42.

ACKNOWLEDGEMENT

Figure 8/1 is reproduced from *An Introduction to Paediatric Neurology* by G. P. Hosking, by permission of the publishers, Faber and Faber Limited, London.

Chapter 9

Arthrogryposis Multiplex Congenita

by R. O. ROBINSON MA, MB, BCh, FRCP *with*
R. CARTWRIGHT MCSP,
J. A. FIXSEN MChir, FRCS and J. ROCKEY DipCOT

Arthrogryposis is a word derived from the Greek meaning 'curved joint'. It refers to the clinical condition of babies born with stiff contractures of the joints. These contractures arise from prolonged fetal immobility. It is important to make as exact a diagnosis as possible, for very occasionally these conditions are not only genetically inherited (with the attendant risks for future children), but also carry their own additional complications. Examination should therefore be directed towards the integrity of the central nervous system and the exclusion of other congenital abnormalities. Investigations should include nerve conduction velocities, EMG and muscle biopsy (which is often most conveniently performed during other surgery). When all the evidence is in, the majority are found to be sporadic, belong to the neuropathic group and have in common selective depletion of anterior horn cells in a greater or lesser number of spinal cord segments (Wynne-Davies and Lloyd Roberts, 1976). The cause of the anterior horn cell depletion is unknown. An analogous condition with a similar pathology occurring in a variety of domestic animals is caused by the Akbana virus (Whittem, 1957). While a virus aetiology would furnish an explanation for the apparently world-wide epidemic of arthrogryposis which occurred during the 1960s, symmetrical involvement of affected joints is harder to understand on this basis.

CLINICAL FEATURES

In approximately equal numbers either all four limbs are involved or the legs only are involved, with a minority having affection of the arms only. The pattern of deformity depends ultimately on the length of affected spinal cord segments. A muscle with a long length of innervation, for example pectoralis major (C5–T1) is likely to escape total paralysis, whereas a muscle with a restricted segmental innervation such as the quadriceps (L3–4) or pronator (C7) is more likely to be selectively involved. If not all muscles across a joint are affected, the joint will tend to become locked in a position dictated by the residual muscle mass in a manner similar to the lower limb deformities occurring in spina bifida. If, however, all the muscles across the joint are affected so that the joint is flail, it will become stiffened in the position dictated by fetal folding.

This provides some justification for the suggestion that myopathic cases of arthrogryposis (generalised muscle weakness) are characterised by flexion contractures (fetal folding), whereas neuropathic cases more frequently have fixed extension, particularly in the arms. Similarly clinical clues afford a basis for speculation about timing of the presumed insult. Many joint spaces exist seven weeks after conception, and by eight weeks the limbs are seen to move. At 11–12 weeks skin creases form across the plane of joint movements. It may be inferred therefore that when the skin creases are abnormal, the fetus became affected between the eighth and the twelfth weeks. A characteristic feature of arthrogryposis are the dimples seen near joints. These imply close fetal contact between skin and bone secondary to an early fetal failure to develop subcutaneous tissue. The muscles of the head and neck are usually spared. However the temporo-mandibular joint may be ankylosed leading to early feeding and speaking difficulties. This may be accompanied by micrognathia and sometimes small larynxes – a point sometimes of considerable anaesthetic significance. While scoliosis can happen and be progressive, this is unusual. Longitudinal growth is frequently reduced.

MANAGEMENT

Arthrogryposis from any cause is rare – 0.31 per 1000 according to one estimate (Wynne-Davies et al, 1981). Its management depends on a delicate balance achieved between therapists, orthotists and orthopaedic surgeons. The right balance is most likely to be struck by drawing upon the experience of following a number of individuals throughout childhood and adolescence. It follows therefore that the best results will be obtained only by involvement of referral centres with this experience. This may take the form of an initial assessment, major intervention in the form of surgical correction, fitting of orthoses and intensive physiotherapy, or minor interventions in the form of advice about dressing or feeding aids. Rare though the condition is, sufficient experience has been acquired to achieve a consensus about certain aspects of management.

With the exception of lower limb flexion contractures (see below), less emphasis should be placed on straightening limbs than on maximising the functions of residual movement, for the fact is that an independent existence is possible with trunk and head mobility alone.

In the newborn the joint surfaces themselves are remarkably little affected. However, they become distorted with time and lack of movement. Initially the deformities are caused by peri-articular soft tissue contractures which are often amenable to considerable stretching, particularly in the young. Thus, at birth the limbs often appear very stiff, but daily passive stretching by the parents with supervision by a physiotherapist usually gains a considerable increase in joint mobility (but not strength). This may be continued for the first year, at the end of which time a decision is necessary about how best to tackle lower limb deformities prior to walking.

Lower limb

Further correction to that achieved by passive stretching can be obtained by serial plasters. Hip abduction and flexion and knee flexion can be corrected simultaneously. The plaster is applied with the limb in the 'best' position obtainable and then removed two weeks later. It will then be found that further correction can now be gained. However, serial plasters rarely correct deformities sufficiently to allow conventional equipment to be worn to aid walking. One of two possible approaches – both having their merits – can be made at this point.

SURGICAL CORRECTION AIMED AT ACHIEVING A PLANTIGRADE FOOT AND EXTENDED BUT REASONABLY FLEXIBLE KNEES AND HIPS
If this approach is followed it is best to start with the foot which is usually either in severe talipes equinovarus or is of the rocker-bottom variety (vertical talus).

For the former a posterior or postero-medial release may be sufficient. If adequate correction is obtained, then rigorous splintage is essential to hold the correction at least until the child is ready to stand. This can be achieved by well-fitting Denis Browne hobble boots incorporating a heel-retaining strap, or, alternatively, by specially moulded splints. However, frequently the foot deformity is so severe that adequate correction can only be achieved by talectomy. The position of the foot on the tibia is maintained postoperatively for eight weeks by a Kirschner wire and plaster, following which long-term splintage is applied as above. This may correct the hindfoot very well, but further surgery to the forefoot may be necessary later.

A rocker-bottom foot (vertical talus) does not of itself preclude walking. However, it is likely to give rise to severe problems later and can only be corrected surgically. Once the child is established in walking, then surgical correction can be considered. The heel equinus is corrected by soft tissue release. The navicular, which is dislocated dorsally on the talus, is returned to its correct alignment. Sometimes this makes the medial border of the foot too long, and the navicular may have to be removed altogether. If the lateral border of the foot is very contracted, a lateral release of the foot may also be necessary.

Surgical correction of knee flexion is difficult as the anatomy behind the knee is frequently very abnormal. For this reason a tourniquet is best not used so that vascular structures remain identifiable. It is usually necessary to divide everything save the nerves and blood vessels behind the knee, including the posterior capsule of the knee joint. Even after this, further serial plasters to get full extension may be necessary. This must be followed by rigorous long-term splintage to try and prevent recurrence. It is always tempting to perform a supracondylar osteotomy of the lower femur in a resistant case. This temptation must be resisted if at all possible until near maturity, otherwise subsequent growth produces a disabling and unsightly anterior angulation of the femur.

A hyperextended knee which does not respond to serial plastering will probably require a quadricepsplasty to release the tight quadriceps and achieve a functional position with some joint mobility.

At the hip, resistant flexion and abduction may require, as in the knee, extensive soft tissue release down to and sometimes including the joint capsule. Deformity is frequently accompanied by dislocation. Since this is already of long standing at birth it is irreducible. If it is unilateral it should be reduced surgically to avoid the problems of leg length inequality. If the dislocation is bilateral it should probably be left alone since the extensive surgical programme required frequently leaves stiff, poorly functional hips and risks the complications of myositis ossificans or femoral fracture secondary to immobilisation osteoporosis.

THE DEVELOPMENT OF LIGHTWEIGHT EXTENSION PROSTHESES ENABLES WALKING IN THE PRESENCE OF CONSIDERABLE RESIDUAL DEFORMITY (Fig. 9/1)

Provided extension of the hips and knees can be obtained to within 30 degrees, no further surgery is necessary. The position of the foot is accepted, and weight-bearing shared between a number of sites on the orthosis. The use of the limb in the prosthesis is then encouraged by physiotherapists either with or without under-arm crutches depend-

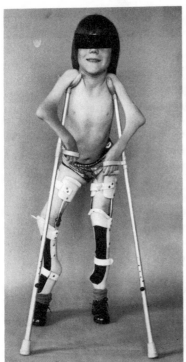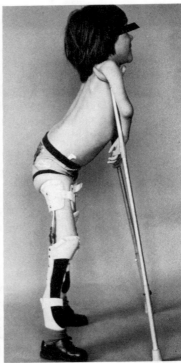

Fig. 9/1 Boy with 4 limbs affected wearing lightweight extension prosthesis and using lightweight underarm crutches with custom-made handpieces

ing on the extent of arm involvement (see below). These prostheses have the added advantage to the child that he thereby achieves the same head height as his peers. Normal shoes fitted to the prostheses appear at the end of trousers.

SUMMARY
Which of these two approaches is adopted must depend on the availability of orthopaedic and orthotic expertise. The merits of the extension prostheses have been outlined. The surgical approach has the merit of getting the child into conventional calipers, and is of particular benefit for selected problems where residual functional muscle is available.

Upper limb

These children rarely have a single problem in the upper limb. It is most important to observe them very carefully before considering surgery. Often a child will use his deformity to function well, in which case 'correction' of the deformity may be unhelpful. Usually therefore surgery in the upper limb is not undertaken until at least the age of 3 or 4, and only after very careful and repeated functional assessment.

Ideally active extension of one elbow for toileting and menstruation hygiene, and active flexion of the other for feeding is desirable. Whether or not this can be achieved obviously depends on the extent of muscle involvement. Thus, if both elbows are stiff in extension, a posterior soft tissue release on one can be followed by either a Steindler flexorplasty (which may leave an increased flexion deformity at the wrist), or anterior transfer of the triceps tendon to the radius, or the pectoralis muscle can be transferred to the biceps (which, however, creates a very extensive chest wall scar). Since the humerus is frequently internally rotated at the shoulder, elbow surgery can be usefully combined with external rotation osteotomy at the humerus to get the arm into a more functional position. Sometimes, in the more severely involved child, none of this is possible due to lack of functioning and accessible muscles.

Flexion deformities of the wrist are common, but may be a positive advantage with limited elbow flexion for feeding. Stiff hypoplastic flexed fingers are rarely amenable to surgery, but severe adduction deformity of the thumb in the palm may be worth correcting in order to obtain a palmar grasp. Arthrodesis of the wrist may be requested by the older patient for cosmetic reasons and may be of some functional benefit; it can be considered at about 12–14 when the wrist nears skeletal maturity.

The majority of the remainder of the therapeutic endeavours are directed towards solving a whole range of difficulties, usually by a combination of trick movements and individualised items of equipment. Since the form of these solutions is determined by the distribution of residual power and mobility, they are rarely the same from child to child. Management proceeds by trying out a variety of what would appear to be best options. Many children with arthrogryposis possess considerable ingenuity and motivation, and discover solutions for themselves before their therapists do so (Fig. 9/2). What follows therefore is a list of devices that we have found of value.

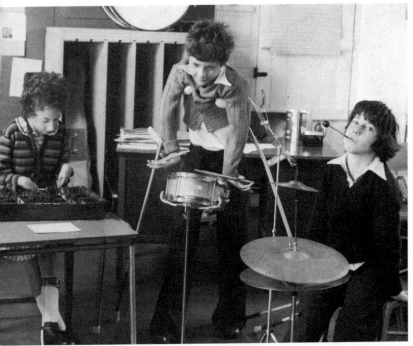

Fig. 9/2 The school band

Mobility

Initially, one of the commonly available prams, and then a pushchair or Baby Buggy will nearly always be found suitable without further adaptation. Meanwhile the parents are taught how to encourage the baby to roll, sit and then progress by whatever method seems most likely to succeed. Even at this stage the emphasis is less on the mode of movement than on the motivation for movement. Toys, for example, can be placed just out of reach. The reward afforded by play for acquisition of movement cannot be over-emphasised. Sitting is seen to have a point if the nursery chair is provided with a tray with overhead slings on springs for arm support (see Chapter 21). Progression to standing (with or without orthoses as necessary) (Fig. 9/3) is facilitated by a play table on castors which can move around and out of the room. Support at the table with a saddle seat may be necessary initially. It should not be forgotten that orthoses are frequently relatively task specific, and in the young they should be discarded for periods in the day for play on the floor when other forms of learning may take place. Under-arm lightweight crutches with custom-made

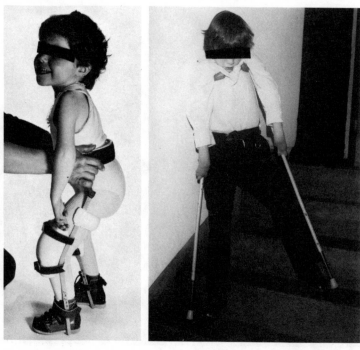

Fig. 9/3 (*left*) LSO (free hip joints) with KAFOs and moulded Plastozote knee caps accommodates some hip and knee flexion. Child is standing for the first time

Fig. 9/4 (*right*) Negotiating stairs

handle pieces may be required if the arms are straight and weak (see Fig. 9/1). Stairs may be negotiated with these by first getting the back against the wall, next by wedging the uppermost crutch, and then moving the uppermost leg on to the next step and finally, after adjusting the second crutch for maximum support, lifting the second leg on to the step followed by the second crutch (Fig. 9/4). For longer distances wheelchairs, either self-propelled, powered or propelled by crutches, may be necessary.

Feeding

Frequently extraordinarily delicate clean feeding is achieved directly from the plate by children with little effective use of the arms. This is rarely socially acceptable however. A rocker spoon or a pivoting block with a specially adapted spoon, the plate being held on a non-slip mat, may provide the answer (Fig. 9/5). A straight-sided bowl is frequently

Fig. 9/5 Feeding, using a pivoting block and adapted spoon

helpful, and may also be used as a pivoting block, as is a long-handled spoon. Drinking from a light mug directly with the edge gripped between the teeth is not usually difficult and is quite acceptable.

Toileting

A potty chair fitted with castors is also an opportunity for movement. Lavatory adaptations may take the form of rails for support in getting on and off, or pimple rubber mats on the floor to prevent feet or crutches slipping. A raised toilet seat may be required. Cleansing may take place from the front using a toilet paper aid. Menstruation can be managed by stick-on pads or tampons with a tampon aid depending on the degree of arm function (see Chapter 21).

Dressing

This is frequently best learnt as undressing to start with. Clothing should be relatively loose with rings on zips and loops on socks and

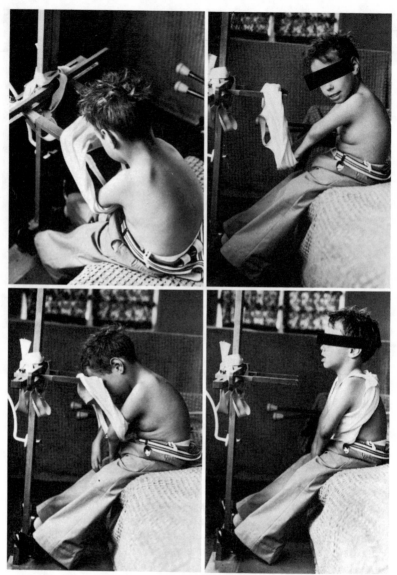

Fig. 9/6 Using a dressing stand. The vest is draped in correct position and the arms and head inserted. The feet are stabilised on the base of the stand

pants for insertion of a mouth or hand stick with an S-shaped hook. Many of the dressing difficulties can be met by initially draping the clothes on a hook or extended window-stay (Fig. 9/6).

Schoolwork

The relative positions of seat and work surface need to be checked. The desk top and/or the chair should be adjustable – the chair if necessary with a spring-loaded mechanism. For mouth-writing an orthodontic mouthpiece may be required, but a piece of polythene tubing over the pencil may suffice. Hand-splints incorporating the pencil may be necessary, and metal boards and magnets for stabilising the paper can frequently be useful. Later a microwriter or electric typewriter can be used, if necessary with a mouth-stick. Spring-loaded scissors may be needed for cutting out (see Chapter 21).

Bathing

Initially a swimming aid allows the mother two hands for more efficient washing, and a bath insert can be useful (see Chapter 21). Frequently the children learn to swim without aids. Taps may need to be long-handled, or tap aids may be used.

Domestic activities

A shelf attached to the cooker door may be of value. Cooking utensils should be light; trays should be one-handled with non-slip surfaces and trolleys can be used to advantage. Tucking in of bedclothes can be obviated by using duvets.

REFERENCES

Whittem, J. H. (1957). Congenital abnormalities in calves: arthrogryposis and hydrancephaly. *Journal of Pathology and Bacteriology*, **73**, 375–87.

Wynne-Davies, R. and Lloyd Roberts, G. C. (1976). Arthrogryposis multiplex congenita: search for prenatal factors in 66 cases. *Archives of Disease in Childhood*, **51**, 618–23.

Wynne-Davies, R., Williams, P. F. and O'Connor, J. C. B. (1981). The 1960 epidemic of arthrogryposis multiplex congenita. *Journal of Bone and Joint Surgery*, **63B**, 76–82.

Chapter 10

Spinal Deformity in the Physically Handicapped

by T. R. MORLEY MA, MB, BChir, FRCS

The term scoliosis is derived from the Greek, meaning curvature, and is used to describe any lateral curvature of the spine. Scoliosis may be associated with exaggerations of the normal curve in the anterior or posterior plane, producing either lordo-scoliosis (forward curvature) or kypho-scoliosis (backward curvature).

CLASSIFICATION

Spinal deformities are either structural or non-structural.

Structural curves are characterised by loss of normal flexibility, and do not correct, either anatomically or radiologically on side bending. In addition to the lateral curvature, the spine is rotated about a vertical axis into the convexity of the curve, producing rib prominence. The rib hump remains on forward flexion.

Non-structural curves correct fully on forward flexion, and are not associated with vertebral rotation on lateral bending (Fig. 10/1).
    The commonest causes for non-structural curves are:
(a) Postural: due to poor posture and can be corrected by active muscular effort. These curves correct on forward flexion; there is no rib rotation. Postural curves correct on lateral flexion, structural curves do not (Fig. 10/2).
(b) Compensatory curves are solely a response to pelvic obliquity, and can be corrected by equalising leg lengths.
(c) Pressure on nerve roots, either by adolescent discs, or by spinal tumours.
    The differentiation of structural and non-structural curves is vital. Non-structural curves disappear when the underlying cause is corrected (these will not be discussed in this chapter).

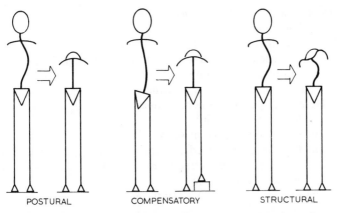

Fig. 10/1 Postural curves correct on forward flexion; there is no rib rotation. Compensatory curves are solely a response to pelvic obliquity and can be corrected by equalising leg length. In structural curves there are anatomical changes with rotation around the vertical axis causing rib rotation and a rib hump on forward flexion

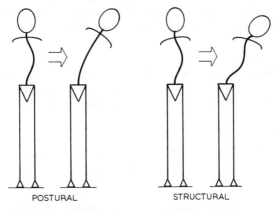

Fig. 10/2 Postural curves correct on lateral flexion. Structural curves do not

STRUCTURAL CURVES

NEUROPATHIC
Upper motor neurone
(a) Cerebral palsy
(b) Syringomyelia
(c) Spinal cord trauma

Anterior horn cell and lower motor neurone
(a) Myelomeningocele
(b) Poliomyelitis and other viral myelitedes
(c) Spinal muscular atrophy – anterior horn cell degeneration
    (i) Werdnig Hoffman disease
    (ii) Kugelberg-Welander syndrome
(d) Hereditary peripheral neuropathies
    (i) Motor neuropathies
    (ii) Peroneal muscular atrophy
    (iii) Degenerative disorders affecting peripheral nerves and spino-cerebellar tracts – Friedreich's Ataxia – Charcot-Marie-Tooth disease
(e) Dysautonamia (Riley-Day syndrome)

MYOPATHIC
(a) Arthrogryposis
(b) Muscular dystrophy – progressive degenerative myopathies
    (i) Duchenne muscular dystrophy
    (ii) Limb girdle dystrophy
    (iii) Facio-scapulo humeral muscular dystrophy
(c) Congenital myopathies – specific structural abnormalities in the muscle. Only occasionally progressive (Dubowitz, 1978).

CONGENITAL
These may be either failure of formation or of segmentation of the vertebrae. Congenital abnormalities are commonly seen in myelomeningocele in addition to the laminar defects.

IDIOPATHIC
Typical idiopathic curves may also occur in the physically handicapped.

OTHERS
Scoliosis has been described as a feature in the number of genetic and metabolic disorders associated with physical handicap.

Spinal deformities in the handicapped are only one facet of a complicated whole, and therefore physical examination and a full assessment are vitally important. Disaster attends treatment of these curves without a full understanding of all the complicating factors.

A complete history is taken. It should include information on the pre-natal and perinatal history, development both physical and mental, development of the spinal deformity and of course a past history both medical and surgical. In addition to this the picture should be built up of the patient's general condition, his health and disability associated with other physical handicaps. In the adolescent years it is important to make an assessment of maturity. A careful family history is taken and also some assessment of family circumstances.

Physical examination

There are three important areas to be recorded: the deformity, the aetiology and the complicating factors.

The patient is evaluated, and the presence of abnormal body development such as dwarfism or excessive height is noted, as are abnormal facies and evidence of other generalised disease.

Depending on these findings, specific areas such as the heart or eyes may need to be examined in more depth.

Examination of the spine includes the level of curve, i.e. thoracic, thoraco-lumbar or lumbar, the direction of the convexity of the curve and the presence of kyphosis or lordosis. Following this, clinical assessment of the mobility of the curve and the degree of rotation is made. This may be done by side bending or by suspension. The degree of rotation can be measured, albeit somewhat crudely. Information must be recorded on fixed deformities of other joints, particularly the hips and also the degree of pelvic tilt.

A full neurological examination is carried out and some assessment made of mental maturity and ability. In addition to this it is important to have some idea about functional ability, particularly such factors as sitting stability and ability to transfer.

Cardio-pulmonary function may also be important, and a general assessment is made by such simple methods as singing and holding a note, and also by spirometry. If there is anxiety about cardio-respiratory function full assessment should be undertaken in a specialist unit.

Building a complete picture is complicated and may not be immediately possible without the aid of a team who know the child well and have had a chance to assess him out of the clinic surroundings and over a period of time. It is vitally important to assess spinal deformity as a team effort, providing a complete profile of the child and family (see Chapter 3).

RADIOGRAPHIC EVALUATION

The standard views, i.e. a standing antero-posterior (AP) and lateral view of the whole spine, may need to be supplemented. If the child cannot stand, radiographs may be taken sitting or in suspension, or even prone with passive bending to evaluate mobility of the deformity.

Incidence and natural history

The incidence and progression of deformity in some of the more common conditions causing physical handicap will be discussed.

CEREBRAL PALSY
Approximately 25 per cent of patients with cerebral palsy will have a structural spinal deformity of more than 10 degrees. Many of these curves are severe, i.e. between 90 and 180 degrees, especially in the non-ambulatory quadriparetic and in the more severe diplegics (Fig. 10/3).

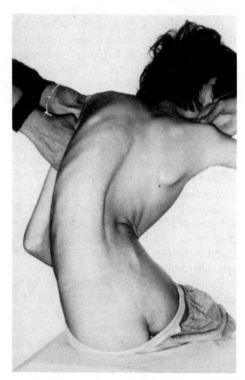

Fig. 10/3 Severe scoliosis in an athetoid quadriplegia

Postural deformities, particularly kyphosis, are common in the very young, with loss of the normal truncal reflexes. The curves in cerebral palsy are typically long 'C' curves and may impair walking ability and sitting stability.

MYELOMENINGOCELE

Of all the causes of spinal deformity these are the most severe and difficult to treat. There are two separate types of deformity, which may well exist together: (a) paralytic and (b) congenital.

The *congenital curves* are due to failure of formation or segmentation of the spine and are present at birth. The *paralytic curves* are related to muscle imbalance and appear later. About 75 per cent of patients with myelomeningocele will develop a curvature, the majority being paralytic curves or mixed, with less than one-third being purely congenital.

The incidence of scoliosis is related to the level of paralysis, and generally speaking one can expect 100 per cent incidence of spinal deformity with defects at T12 or above, reducing steadily to 25 per cent at L5.

All these curves are progressive, particularly in the adolescent growth phase. The congenital curves are particularly severe, and never respond to bracing.

The *paralytic curves* are usually 'C' curves from the mid-thorax to the sacrum, frequently with pelvic obliquity. Many are associated with deformity in the anterior posterior plane, i.e. lordo-scoliosis (Fig. 10/4) or kypho-scoliosis (Fig. 10/5). In a case where there is a wide open spina bifida there is a loss of posterior stability and kyphosis

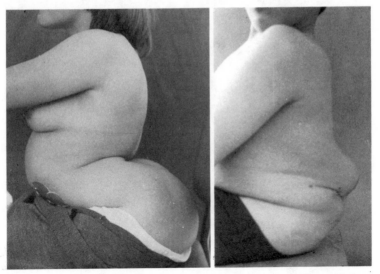

Fig. 10/4 (*left*) Child with myelomeningocele showing gross lordo-scoliosis
Fig. 10/5 (*right*) Child with myelomeningocele showing gross kypho-scoliosis

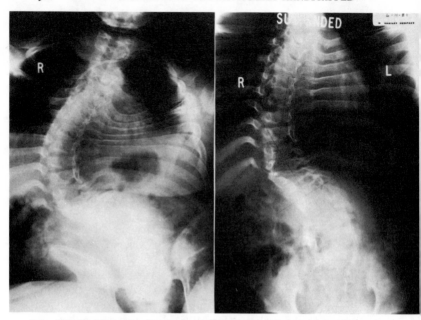

Fig. 10/6 Radiographs showing a mixed congenital and paralytic curve producing lordosis, scoliosis and kyphosis. *Left*: Sitting. *Right*: Suspended

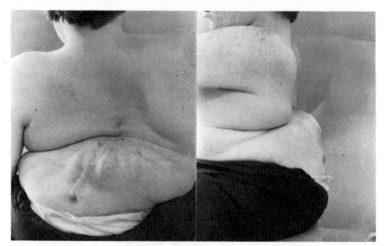

Fig. 10/7 Posterior and lateral views of boy in Fig. 10/6

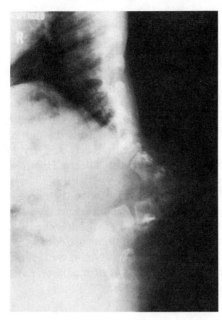

Fig. 10/8 Lateral radiograph showing gross kypho-scoliosis (same boy as Fig. 10/5)

tends to occur. Where the laminae are partly formed, there is a posterior tethering, and lordosis occurs in association with a scoliosis (Figs. 10/6 and 10/7). Deformities in the antero-posterior plane alone may occur producing kyphosis (Fig. 10/8). Congenital deformities present at birth may complicate closure of the myelomeningocele. These curves are severely progressive, unresponsive to conservative treatment and require early surgical intervention.

GENERAL CONSIDERATIONS
Respiratory function is often limited due to the collapsing spine and abdominal muscle paralysis. Careful evaluation is required, both to try to prevent respiratory failure and also in patients being considered for surgical intervention.

In the presence of a neurogenic bladder, intercurrent infection and renal hypertension may complicate any surgical treatment. Renal function should be fully assessed.

The presence of urinary tract diversion may also make bracing difficult, and can interfere with any surgical treatment done from the front.

If the child has hydrocephalus, the function of the valve must be considered. Treatment of the spine can affect the relative length of the catheter and produce obstruction postoperatively.

SPINAL MUSCULAR ATROPHY

Spinal muscular atrophy causes a wide spectrum of clinical manifestations. Scoliosis is more common in the less progressive types, i.e. in the children living into adolescence. Only 20 per cent of children with spinal muscular atrophy have scoliosis before the age of 5, increasing to 85 per cent in children beyond the age of 12.

These curves are collapsing in type and are associated with respiratory problems. Early bracing is important, with the aim of increasing lumbar lordosis in order to lock the facets and try to prevent the lateral collapse. Braces are often poorly tolerated by these children and careful adjustment is necessary.

Surgical treatment should be considered early, when the curve is not more than 30 or 40 degrees, because if the curve remains easily correctable then surgical techniques can be used which allow the child to sit up immediately postoperatively and without the use of bracing. If the opportunity to correct the spinal deformity is missed, rapid progression may occur in adolescence with loss of sitting balance and death from progressive respiratory failure.

Management of spinal deformity

Conservative	Surgical
Observation	Minor localised fusion
Bracing	Anterior fusion
Electrical stimulation	Posterior fusion
Plaster correction	
Seating	

Where possible treatment should always be conservative. Operative treatment involving fusion of the spine in a corrected position is a traumatic undertaking for both child and parents, and has the disadvantage of halting spinal growth. In order to have any hope of treating these deformities without operation they need to be diagnosed early and referred to a specialist clinic. Most physically handicapped children are already under medical supervision, but despite this *deformities are regularly ignored* until they are far too advanced, making any form of conservative treatment impossible. Children are not referred, either in a mistaken desire to protect the child from more forms of bracing or because of the lack of understanding of what can be achieved conservatively by treating small curves.

OBSERVATION

Small curves under 25 degrees can often be treated by observation alone, particularly if the child is nearly at maturity. It is not true that curves stop progressing at the end of growth, but the rate of progress does dramatically decrease. Neuropathic and myopathic curves particularly progress in adult life because the imbalance causing the deformity persists.

Most curves are observed initially in order to develop an overall picture of the child in relation to the deformity, and also to develop a picture of the individual natural progression. Not all curves behave predictably.

BRACING

Aggressive bracing is the mainstay of non-operative treatment. Bracing is not a new innovation, indeed apparatus was described by Hippocrates. Ambrose Paré was the first to describe body shells in 1579; these were made by armourers. The landmark in effective bracing control was the Milwaukee brace, originally described by Blount and Schmidt in 1946 (Blount and Moe, 1973).

The principle of bracing is to exert force, either lateral or distractive, to the spine. The force is indirect and is transmitted via the pelvis, the ribs and the paraspinal muscles. The force over the apex of the curve is opposed by two other forces in the opposite direction. The correction is both active and passive, but where possible should be active, the child coming away from the brace and correcting its own spine. In cases where there is paralysis of the paraspinal muscles, then only passive correction is possible. Although normal skin sensation is desirable, lack of this should not exclude the use of braces.

Modern braces tend to avoid the neck rings which are associated with the Milwaukee and which are much disliked and are often a considerable disadvantage to the physically handicapped. Under-arm braces either taken from the mould of the child or by the use of 'off the shelf' moulds can be used. An example of the latter modular brace is the Boston brace, which is widely used with idiopathic curves but is of less value in the physically handicapped. Whichever form of brace is used, careful follow-up is necessary in collaboration with an orthotist, physiotherapist and occupational therapist together with the co-operation of the nursing staff if the child is in hospital. It is quite wrong to believe that a well-fitted brace disturbs the development of a handicapped child. On the contrary, it may enhance developmental potential significantly by allowing the child to hold up his head and use both hands instead of using them for support.

The general indications for bracing are: (a) a small curve under 45 degrees which remains flexible; and (b) in a child with remaining growth potential.

Relative contra-indications for bracing are: (a) large curves, over 50 degrees, which are stiff; and (b) where growth has ceased. Special care must be exercised where sensation is abnormal.

Since many of the curves in the handicapped result from an imbalance that persists, the indications for bracing may continue into adult life. In this situation the aim is to prevent a slow downward progression.

Bracing the physically handicapped has been associated with poor results, mainly because braces have been used inappropriately. There is no hope of holding a progressive congenital curve or a stiff neuropathic curve of over 90 degrees.

In certain situations a brace may be used as the only realistic method of control in the severely handicapped, in which case the predicted result and outcome must be modified.

Usually the brace is applied having corrected the lumbar lordosis in order to control rotation. In some specific situations such as spinal muscular atrophy, the lordosis may be increased to lock the posterior facet joints and prevent spinal collapse.

In all situations one must be prepared to be flexible and to listen to the views of all the supportive staff as well as to the child and his parents.

ELECTRICAL STIMULATION

The indications for electrical stimulation are very much the same as for bracing. A small electrical stimulus is applied to the paraspinal muscles in order to 'pull' the spine straight. So far the results are very much the same as for bracing, and there is very little experience in the physically handicapped. This is partly due to the problems of control and acceptance, and partly due to the fact that abnormal muscles cannot be stimulated.

PLASTER CASTING

Plaster corrective techniques were first described in the latter part of the nineteenth century. The techniques have become more sophisticated, combining both distraction and lateral pressure.

Plaster correction is called 'localising', and involves correcting the curve maximally, often under sedation, and then holding the corrected position for 6–12 weeks before repeating the procedure. This is often done in conjunction with a bracing policy. Localising is particularly effective in the young child with a mobile curve, but also may be useful and acceptable in long 'C' curves such as in cerebral palsy.

SEATING

Specialised seating should *not* be considered as a method of spinal control. All that seating can do is to contain the child in the optimum position for function; it cannot alter the progress of deformity. In the severely handicapped this aim may be a justification in itself, as no active treatment may be possible or acceptable (see Chapter 14).

Surgical techniques

Spinal fusion is a crude concept, and indicates that the deforming forces are out of control and that the only way of stabilising the situation is to fuse the spine.

The spinal surgeon dealing with these deformities in the physically handicapped should first be experienced in the treatment of idiopathic scoliosis. When surgery is contemplated children are best managed in centres well versed in the competent care of the problems of the physically handicapped as well as the spinal surgery. The decision to operate should be taken only after careful consideration of all the inter-related factors, and where possible should include a team approach.

Having made the decision to treat a curve operatively, then the general condition should be re-evaluated, particularly in relation to the cardiovascular and respiratory systems, and also an overall view of the renal function. Complications during surgery and the immediate postoperative phase are common, but with careful planning can be predicted and in most cases avoided.

In some instances, minor surgery may prevent serious progression. Attempts to modify spinal growth on one side, usually on the convex side, have been tried without noticeable success. These operations to modify spinal growth must be done very young, as half the spinal growth has been achieved by the age of $2\frac{1}{2}$. There are situations where the operation is indicated, particularly in congenital curves, with a localised area of uneven growth. In this case, by fusing on the side with normal growth potential, the uneven growth can be neutralised.

More extensive fusion procedures must wait for greater spinal growth, or a very short trunk may result. In order to avoid this complication, attempts are being made to use extendable rods. At this stage the problems, both of repeated surgery and biomechanical failure remain considerable.

Spinal corrective procedures are usually carried out between the ages of 10 and 13. In neuropathic and myopathic curves, because the deforming force will continue into adult life, the fusion procedures must be based on the principle of achieving a correction which is as straight as possible, and then producing a really strong fusion. This usually involves both anterior and posterior surgery.

The most common and well-tried form of posterior surgery is to use a Harrington rod to distract the spine and then to fuse the spine posteriorly by excising the posterior joints and laying on graft (Harrington, 1962). If there is a significant degree of kyphosis, failure is almost inevitable if this procedure alone is carried out, particularly where the spinal deformity is 'collapsing' and associated with neuropathy or myopathy.

Where the curve is small, but remains easily correctable and is of the collapsing type, the technique described by Luqué in Mexico may be used, in which two steel rods are laid up either side of the spine and at each level the vertebrae are wired to the rods. This is a technique which is particularly applicable to the neuropathic collapsing spines such as poliomyelitis and spinal muscular atrophy. The great advantage is that there is no need for postoperative bracing and the child can be sat up immediately.

The alternative is to do both anterior and posterior staged surgery. Initially the spine is approached from the front by a transthoracic, retroperitoneal or combined thoraco-abdominal approach. The spine is exposed and the discs are excised at each level from within the curve. Following this the spine may be instrumented by using screws and a cable, a technique described by Dwyer and Schaffer (1974), or alternatively the spine may be left mobile with bone chips inserted, and then put on traction in preparation for a second stage procedure. The Dwyer technique is indicated if there is an element of lordosis, but is contra-indicated if there is kyphosis as this tends to increase with the operative technique.

If the spine is to be treated by traction, then at the same time a halo is applied and fixed to the skull and traction applied through this and pins inserted through the lower tibia. At a second stage the spine is approached posteriorly and is instrumented in the normal way. This method of anterior release, followed by posterior instrumentation and fusion, gives an excellent correction and firm fixation, but remains a very big procedure.

The risks of damage to the spinal cord must always be borne in mind. Pre-operative assessment of the spinal cord by myelography is indicated where there is any possibility of cord tethering. During the operation the integrity of the cord can be monitored electrically using a modified electromyogram.

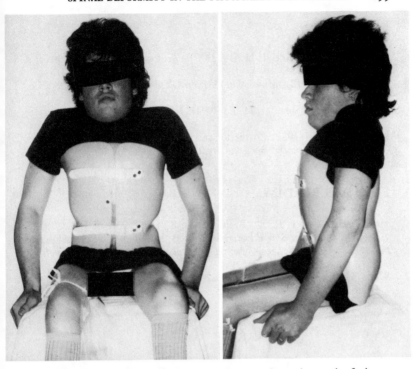

Fig. 10/9 Postoperative bracing following anterior and posterior fusion

POSTOPERATIVE TREATMENT

Postoperative treatment is simplified as far as possible. Immediately postoperatively no form of spinal brace is used, and where possible the child is allowed to get up after a period of two weeks. At the end of this time the child is mobilised wearing a plastic removable brace, and this is maintained until fusion is solid, and worn at all times (Fig. 10/9). This may be anything between 10 and 12 months.

Great advances continue to be made in the treatment of scoliosis. These can now be particularly applied to the physically handicapped where surgery has always been daunting, because of the severity of the deformity and also other associated problems. Having said this, the rewards of spinal surgery and correction may be even greater in these children. The future lies in being able to isolate the cause of these curves and hopefully to prevent them. Meanwhile we must rely on early detection and more aggressive conservative measures, always with the aim and hope of avoiding major surgery in children who cannot be expected to co-operate fully in these procedures.

REFERENCES

Blount, N. P. and Moe, J. H. (1973). *The Milwaukee Brace*. Williams and Wilkins, Baltimore.

Dubowitz, V. (1978). *Muscle Disorders in Childhood*. W. B. Saunders Co, Philadelphia.

Dwyer, A. F. and Schaffer, M. F. (1974). *Journal of Bone and Joint Surgery*, **56B**, 218.

Harrington, P. R. (1962). Correction and internal fixation by instrumentation in scoliosis. *Journal of Bone and Joint Surgery*, **44A**, 591.

FURTHER READING

Moe, J. H., Winter, R. B., Bradford, D. S. and Lenstein, J. E. (1978). *Scoliosis and Other Spinal Deformities*. W.B. Saunders Co, Philadelphia.

Nash, C. C. (1980). Scoliosis bracing. *Journal of Bone and Joint Surgery*, **62A**, 648.

Watts, H. G. (1976). *The Boston Brace*. Children's Hospital Medical Centre, Boston, Mass.

Chapter 11

Limb Deficiency

by I. FLETCHER MRCS, LRCP *with*
R. CARTWRIGHT MCSP and J. ROCKEY DipCOT

A child may be born with one or more limbs either partially or completely absent. The person responsible for breaking the news to the parents must do so with considerable care, for whatever is said will be permanently ingrained upon their minds. Experience has revealed that it is essential for the mother to see *and hold* her baby as soon as possible. Failure to do so adds to the maternal torment and may even lead to rejection. The majority of limb deficient children are quite normal in all other respects and compensate well for their handicap, often excelling in a wide variety of activities.

NOMENCLATURE (Fig. 11/1)

A widely accepted classification of the various types of limb anomaly was devised by Frantz and O'Rahilly (1961). They consider that a convenient term, embracing all conditions, is *dysmelia* (Gk: *dys* imperfect or faulty, *melos* limb). Complete absence of a limb is designated *amelia*, while the term used to denote a very short arm or leg with a 'flipper-like' hand or foot is *phocomelia* (Gk: *phoca* seal).

The term 'transverse terminal hemimelia' is used when there is absence of a *distal* segment of a limb in its entirety, whether above, below or at the elbow (or knee) joint. In gross appearance the limb is similar to an amputation stump and in some parts of Europe the neater name *peromelia* is used (Gk: *peros* maimed). Absence of *one* forearm or leg bone is a type of paraxial hemimelia and the name of the deficient bone is used as a prefix, e.g. absent fibula – 'fibular hemimelia' – and when only part of this bone is missing – 'partial fibular hemimelia'.

STATISTICAL ANALYSIS

Of 800 dysmelic patients dealt with by the author the ratio of males to females was 3:2. Those with defects, of one or both upper limbs

Complete absence of a limb = amelia

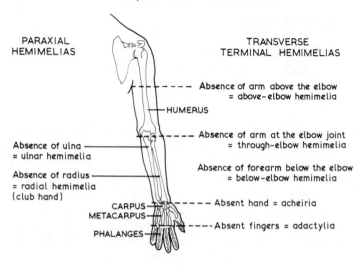

PARAXIAL
HEMIMELIAS

TRANSVERSE
TERMINAL HEMIMELIAS

— — — — Absence of arm above the elbow
= above-elbow hemimelia

— HUMERUS

— — — — Absence of arm at the elbow joint
= through-elbow hemimelia

Absence of forearm below the elbow
= below-elbow hemimelia

Absence of ulna —
= ulnar hemimelia

Absence of radius —
= radial hemimelia
(club hand)

CARPUS — — — — — Absent hand = acheiria
METACARPUS
— — — — Absent fingers = adactylia
PHALANGES

LOWER LIMB

Absence of half the pelvis and the whole limb (rare) = hindquarter amelia

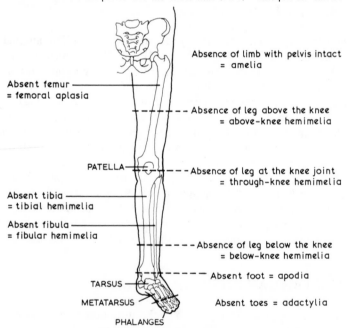

Absence of limb with pelvis intact
= amelia

Absent femur —
= femoral aplasia

— — — — — Absence of leg above the knee
= above-knee hemimelia

PATELLA — — — — — Absence of leg at the knee joint
= through-knee hemimelia

Absent tibia —
= tibial hemimelia

Absent fibula —
= fibular hemimelia

— — — — Absence of leg below the knee
= below-knee hemimelia

— — — — Absent foot = apodia

TARSUS —
METATARSUS — Absent toes = adactylia
PHALANGES

Fig. 11/1 Upper and lower limb deficiency nomenclature

accounted for 70 per cent; lower limb deficiencies *alone* 14 per cent, and there were 16 per cent with a combination of upper *and* lower limb anomalies.

AETIOLOGY AND FAMILY HISTORY

The majority of limb deficiencies are idiopathic and only about 1 per cent are hereditary, split (or 'lobster claw') hands and feet, for instance. Most mothers have uneventful pregnancies and a family history of the same condition is extremely unlikely. The affected child may be the eldest or youngest and may even be one of twins. Thalidomide and its derivatives (withdrawn in 1961) accounted for approximately 11 per cent of all the dysmelic patients dealt with by the author (I.F.).

ARTIFICIAL LIMB AND APPLIANCE CENTRES (ALAC)

There are a number of Artificial Limb and Appliance Centres in Britain each with full-time doctors experienced in dealing with dysmelia. In England they are under the aegis of the Department of Health and Social Security, in Scotland they come under the Scottish Home and Health Department and in Wales the Welsh Board of Health.

A neonate with a malformed limb should be referred to the nearest centre as soon as possible after birth. *Both* parents should be present at the first consultation so that a detailed history may be obtained and the baby examined. The doctor is then able to outline a programme which will include tne wearing of a prosthesis (if indicated), the type of schooling, sporting activities and other leisure pursuits. It may also be possible to allay any fears regarding hereditary factors being responsible. All these matters are of vital importance to the family.

UPPER LIMB DEFICIENCIES

Below-elbow terminal hemimelia

The commonest major limb deficiency is absence of one hand and approximately two-thirds of the forearm. The ratio of left to right being 2:1. The stump is rounded at the end, but despite its appearance it is not a congenital amputation. Close inspection will reveal the presence of rudimentary digital buds (Fig. 11/2). Elbow flexion is

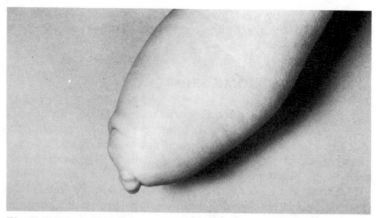

Fig. 11/2 Below-elbow transverse terminal hemimelia showing ridge of rudimentary digital buds. *Note* the invaginated fold of skin near the tip

normal but an excessive degree of hyperextension is common. Pectoral muscles should be examined as, very occasionally, they are deficient on the affected side.

The end of the stump is often considerably cooler than the skin of the normal forearm and cyanosis is frequently present. Despite this, problems rarely occur. There is an exquisite sense of touch terminally and 'two-point discrimination' is similar to that of a normal finger pulp (2–3mm).

PROSTHESES

A lightweight one-piece prosthesis with a little cosmetic foam hand should be supplied at about the sixth month. This accustoms the infant to limb wearing. A socket, which encloses the stump, is similar to that used on the functional prosthesis, which is supplied during the second year. The latter has a wrist mechanism allowing rotation and removal of the hand so that a gripping device may be easily interchanged. This operates from a cord which is attached to a ribbon-like appendage used for suspension of the prosthesis. Opening of the gripping device is achieved by extension of the elbow coupled with shoulder flexion.

At about $3\frac{1}{2}$–4 years of age a myo-electric hand prosthesis may be substituted. This is substantially heavier than the foregoing and children with very short stumps (less than 5cm) may experience difficulty due to the weight. Two gold-plated electrodes are incorporated in the socket of the prosthesis and sited over the extensor and flexor muscles just below the epicondyles. Activation of these muscles produces, respectively, opening and closing of the mechanical hand. The index and middle fingers are pivoted as a single unit which 'opens' and 'closes' against a fully opposed thumb which moves simultaneously. A 6-volt rechargeable battery is connected by a trailing flex to the prosthesis and located in a convenient pocket or special pouch. Provided the stump is not too long the battery may be incorporated in the forearm of the prosthesis, which makes the unit completely self-contained and less liable to damage; it does, however, add to the overall weight.

Acheiria and adactylia

The second commonest limb deficiency is either complete or partial absence of one hand and again the ratio of left to right is 2:1. Often there is a strong, fully mobile wrist, although a radiograph may show a deficiency in the number of carpal bones. The forearm is minimally shorter than its fellow in infancy and in full maturity may be 1–2cm shorter. Pronation and supination are usually normal. Very rarely these movements are lacking due to radio-ulnar synostosis.

Digital buds can always be identified, but vary in maturity in different individuals, from small nodules to pedunculated rudimentary fingers bearing tiny nails.

Other hand anomalies include absence of the distal portion of the palm and one or more digits. The latter, however, may be represented as proximal stumps looking very much like amputations or rudimentary fingers (Fig. 11/3).

TREATMENT

Because of the excellent sense of touch, a prosthesis should *not* be fitted, certainly during the early years. The lack of grip, which seems to cause great concern to surgeons and other people dealing with the child, is of *no consequence*! Surgical intervention (to form a cleft) should not be undertaken. It is mutilating and ugly and can seriously interfere with the highly developed sense of touch. Experience in dealing with a large number of children and adults with acheiria has revealed that the handicap is negligible, but a few who have had the misfortune to undergo surgery have requested a cosmetic hand to hide the mutilation!

APPLIANCES

In rare instances an opposition device may be supplied and is of some use in carpentry, e.g. for holding a chisel. One social problem is the inability to hold two eating utensils at the same time. To overcome this, the author (I.F.) has devised two simple types of wrist band. A

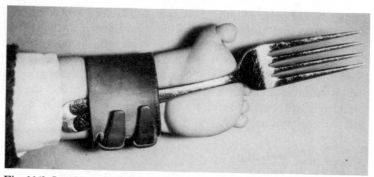

Fig. 11/3 Leather wrist band used to hold a fork when there is either partial or complete absence of the left hand. *Note* the rudimentary thumb and finger buds

plain one with two strap-and-buckle fastenings to secure the handle of a fork, normally used when the left hand is missing (Fig. 11/3). A similar one with a slot and pocket to take the handle of a knife is supplied for those with right acheiria. These are extremely well accepted by a large number of people who were first issued with the appropriate band at about $3\frac{1}{2}$ years of age.

In the early teens some boys and girls request a cosmetic hand for occasional social use.

Bilateral below-elbow hemimelia and acheiria

Because of the excellent degree of sensation at the end of the stumps, prostheses are rejected by children born with absence of *both* forearms and hands and by those with bilateral acheiria. Left to their own devices these individuals becomes very adept with their stumps. Fastening quite small buttons can be accomplished in two to three seconds. Writing is performed with the pen held between the two stump ends and is as speedy as normal. A fork or spoon can be dextrously swivelled between the two stumps so that eating presents no problem.

Those with acheiria may adopt the same method or use two of the wrist bands described above. One youth, with no hands, is able to tie his shoe laces within 30 seconds, using his stumps and gripping with his teeth.

Above-elbow and through-elbow hemimelia

A transverse terminal hemimelia above the elbow is very rare, particularly as a single entity. When it does occur, it is usual for the condition to be either bilateral or for one or both lower limbs to be dysmelic. As growth proceeds, the end of the arm stump becomes very pointed. Despite this, surgery on the end of the *congenital* humeral stump should be resisted as ulceration does not usually occur. If the bone *is* trimmed, repeated surgery will be necessary until growth has ceased. Slightly more common is the unilateral absence of the complete forearm. The humeral epicondyles are poorly developed and the stump end is well rounded and the presence of a dimple may be observed.

PROSTHESES

One year of age has proved to be the best time to supply a prosthesis for both the through-elbow and above-elbow stumps. For both, it is advisable to prescribe a one-piece prosthesis (without either elbow or wrist joint). The socket extends from the shoulder to the stump end and is blended with a gentle curve at the elbow, to become continuous with the forearm to which is attached a little cosmetic hand. The prosthesis is secured by a ribbon-type harness which passes across the nape of the neck to encircle the opposite shoulder and axilla. At about the age of 2–2½ years the child should be ready for a limb with an elbow joint incorporating a locking mechanism. A wrist unit is also fitted allowing the hand to be removed and a gripping device substituted when necessary. This is activated by means of a Perlon cord attached to the back of the harness.

Amelia

Although amelia is rare, absence of *both* arms occurs more frequently than the unilateral condition. The scapulae are small and the acromion processes upward pointing and very mobile. A firm grip can be achieved between jaw and shoulder (a method often used for carrying objects). A small dimple is nearly always present in the approximate position of the glenoid and, at puberty, hair is present in this area. Some individuals have complete amelia while others have a single flail digit at shoulder level, almost invariably on the right side, which should *not* be removed.

Children with either unilateral or bilateral amelia will, almost invariably, reject prostheses. Not because they have little to offer, but because they are, inevitably, cumbersome and limit activity particularly during play-time. It is extremely difficult to convince the parents (and others intimately involved) that provided the lower limbs are normal, a child with bilateral amelia will become very adept with its feet. Prehension comes naturally and should never be discouraged

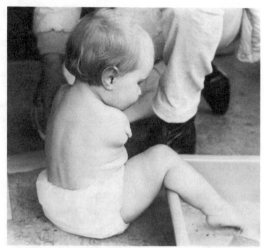

Fig. 11/4
Baby using
feet for play.
Note the
hip mobility

(Fig. 11/4). Hip mobility, which allows either foot to reach the back of the head, must be maintained. During the growing years, the child will exhibit dominance for one or other foot, usually the left and the opposite hip will lose much of its flexibility unless checked. The importance of maintaining the extreme degree of movements of both hips is a safeguard for the child should the dominant limb be injured.

In the early days parents may be worried in case the child is late in walking. Some amelic babies have shown no inclination to stand until 20 months or more, because the child is unable to support himself when learning to stand and, while on his feet, cannot use them for prehension. The baby often moves about by shuffling on his bottom. Ultimately, balance is excellent and many of the boys become keen footballers. Swimming is another activity in which these youngsters excel, but it is advisable for them to learn a backstroke prior to attempting any face-down methods.

Both unilateral and bilateral amelics can usually manage at ordinary schools. In the early days children prefer to sit on the floor when writing. However, it is important that they learn to sit on a chair and be able to write comfortably with the appropriate foot on a table or desk a little higher than the chair. When the child is very young parents have to be more indulgent, but independence must be encouraged (see Chapter 21).

Short-term admission to a specialist unit for periodic training in aids to daily living is essential.

Paraxial hemimelia

Radial hemimelia: Partial or complete absence of the radius (a pre-axial defect) results in a 'radial club-hand' deformity, the hand being acutely deviated to the radial side of the wrist and the thumb is often rudimentary or absent. Sometimes the elbow lacks normal mobility in which event it is usually in the extended position.

SURGICAL CORRECTION
Unless the elbow can be flexed to at least 90 degrees *no* attempt should be made to correct the wrist deformity. To do so may well prevent the child from reaching its mouth. Attempts to achieve active elbow flexion and wrist correction have often been unsuccessful and any such surgery should be undertaken with extreme caution (Lamb, 1972).
Ulnar hemimelia: Partial or complete absence of the ulna is often associated with a short radius which is completely fused to the humerus (radio-humeral synostosis). The hand is never complete and it is usual for only one or two fingers to be present. These are often rudimentary and syndactyly is an additional feature. There is a wide variation in the types which exist. Some forearms are almost normal in length, while others are devoid of a hand with one or two digits which may appear to be an extension of the humerus (Figs. 11/5a and 11/5b). When severe shortening exists, it is likely that the condition is bilateral and quite often one or both legs may also be involved.

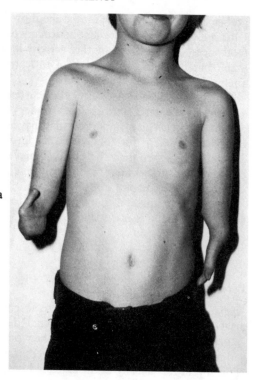

Fig. 11/5(a) Boy with bilateral ulnar hemimelia and radio-humeral synostosis. There is a single digit on the right, and two fused digits on the left arm

PROSTHESES

When the forearm is only moderately short and one or two fingers exist, it is best to allow the free use of the limb. A cosmetic prosthesis may, however, be requested during the teens.

An extremely short radio-humeral synostotic hemimelia which is devoid of digits resembles an elbow disarticulation. It can, therefore, be fitted with a prosthesis suitable for the latter condition unless both arms are similar, when *no* prosthesis is advised for *either* side.

Phocomelia

This is a very rare intercalary deficiency originally defined as a 'flipper' hand (or foot) without any intervening long limb bone. Many of the thalidomide victims had either bilateral or quadrilateral phocomelia. Sensation is normal, but lack of reach is the main physical problem. Only rarely is an arm prosthesis accepted since it deprives the wearer of natural hand function. However, some people with unilateral phocomelia may wish to wear a purely cosmetic limb.

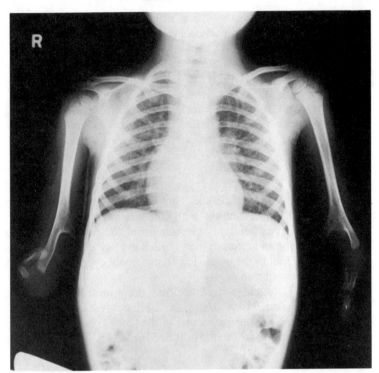

Fig. 11/5(b) Radiograph of 11/5(a). The medial spur-like projection on each humerus is likely to be the medial epicondyle

(In the author's (I.F.) experience the vast majority of people, bilaterally affected, discarded prostheses at an early stage and it is clear that they should not be supplied as frustration will be inevitable.)

ARM TRAINING

Many of the limb centres have facilities for arm training. Instruction in the use and care of an upper limb prosthesis consists of showing the parents how to undertake stump hygiene and clean the socket of the prosthesis. (Only about 50 per cent of upper limb prosthetic wearers like to use a stump sock.) The application and tensioning of the harness suspension is also explained.

Bi-manual activities encourage the use of the prosthesis and frequent short sessions in the arm school are strongly recommended during the growing years. At least one parent should be present throughout the early sessions. It is usual for children to attend the clinic and possibly the arm school every three months.

LOWER LIMB DEFICIENCIES

The commonest form of dysmelia affecting the lower limbs is shortening due to a long bone deficiency. The bones involved may be aplastic (absent) or hypoplastic (poorly developed) and short.

Fibular hemimelia

Isolated lower limb deficiencies are rare. The type most often encountered is absent fibula with a short tibia usually curved anteriorly, the apex being at the junction of the middle and lower thirds of the bone and referred to as a 'tibial kyphos'. Overlying this is a dimple, adherent to the bone. The foot is small, everted and devoid of the lateral one or two rays.

The tendo calcaneus is thin and has the appearance of a tight subcutaneous cord which draws the heel upwards causing fixed equinus. Because the bony structure of the foot has been distorted in utero, an elongation of the tendo calcaneus usually fails to improve the deformity.

EXTENSION PROSTHESES

An artificial foot, ankle and possibly shin, may be supplied to fit over and beyond the short leg, to achieve the correct length. Reasonable cosmesis must be achieved. For the extension prosthesis to be acceptable both functionally and cosmetically, the natural limb needs to be shorter than the length of the natural foot since this has to be set in equinus. Provided it lies neatly in the long axis of the tibia, the cosmetic effect with the prosthesis is very good. So often the foot is everted and as growth proceeds the deformity becomes more obvious and difficult to mask.

The first prosthesis should be supplied at about 10–12 months and consists of a light leather 'bootee socket' extending to the knee and holding the foot comfortably in equinus. Duralamin side struts connect the socket to a wooden platform beneath which a foot and lower part of shin has been fitted. No ankle joint is included for children under 8 years of age.

For the older child an enclosed extension prosthesis may be fitted. This is very cosmetically acceptable and consists of a leather bootee socket as in the foregoing with either a zip or lace fastening for its

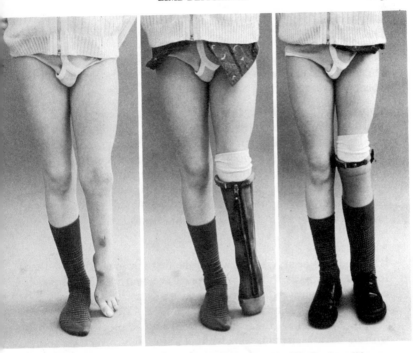

Fig. 11/6(a) (*left*) Boy (10 years) with fibular hemimelia. His foot is well in line with the long axis of the tibia. Shortening is only just sufficient for a metal enclosed prosthesis

Fig. 11/6(b) (*right*) Same boy as 11/6(a) with a leather bootee socket and zip fastening

Fig. 11/6(c) (*right*) Same boy with the bootee completely contained within a metal shin complete with foot. Owing to the length of the natural limb an ankle joint could not be incorporated

entire length. The whole is then put into a shin casing contoured to match the natural leg as far as is possible (Figs. 11/6a.b.c). If there is room, an ankle joint is incorporated. The enclosed type is not recommended for very young children because pressure areas may develop as the child grows and it is essential for the wearer to identify these immediately so that adjustments can be made.

If the amount of shortening is less than the length of the foot, the latter will protrude and be unsightly and a raised boot will be necessary unless surgery is performed.

SURGERY
The options are:

Leg equalisation: (This is not recommended unless full correction can be guaranteed and the foot plantigrade so that a normal shoe may be worn. Odd-sized shoes are *not* acceptable.)

Amputation: If at birth the rudimentary foot is markedly everted then disarticulation should be performed at the ankle, so that a prosthesis may be fitted before the first birthday. Disarticulation should also be considered when there is no likelihood of the foot being plantigrade and there is insufficient shortening to allow the fitting of an extension prosthesis. There are, however, intermediate degrees of shortening and deformity which must be individually assessed, preferably by a medical practitioner working in the field of prosthetics.

PROSTHESES
If the foot has been removed within the first few months of life then the first prosthesis should be supplied at about 10–12 months. It consists of a lightweight plastic shin with a detachable soft liner, and the foot has a toe joint, but no ankle joint.

Children who have the foot amputated and are subsequently fitted with a prosthesis not only walk without a limp, but run and are able to play all the usual games. Many of the boys become keen footballers or rugby players. Also, of considerable psychological importance, is the fact that ordinary shoes can be worn and the general appearance is excellent.

Tibial hemimelia

Absence of the tibia is rare except in thalidomide deformities and it is usual for the fibular head to lie alongside the lateral femoral condyle. The foot is reasonably well formed, but inverted.

TREATMENT
When the defect is unilateral or bilateral, disarticulation at the knee is the ideal method of treatment *provided* the hips and upper limbs are normal. The prosthesis is the same type as that used for through-knee dysplasia.

Femoral dysplasia

The femur may be entirely absent or exhibit varying degrees of hypoplasia and in nearly all instances it is the proximal portion of the bone which is deficient. The tibia, fibula and foot are usually normal, but deficiencies of these are sometimes encountered. A radiograph is essential to determine the state of the hip joint as this influences the treatment very considerably.

EXTENSION PROSTHESES

1. When the hip joint is *stable*.

A platform type extension prosthesis extending up to the knee is all that is necessary. This may consist of a leather bootee socket embracing the leg and maintaining the foot in equinus. This is supported on a wooden platform duly shaped down to an ankle and foot. Metal supporting struts are fitted either side of the appliance, extending from the top of the socket to the base of the platform. An alternative extension prosthesis is the enclosed type as described for fibular hemimelia.

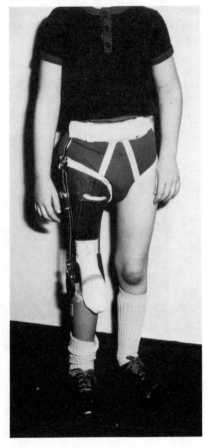

Fig. 11/7 Boy with complete absence of the right femur fitted with an extension prothesis. Full weight is taken on the ischial tuberosity and the foot is unsupported. A joint, with a lock, is situated level with the left knee and is released when sitting

2. When the hip joint is *unstable*.

An extension prosthesis with a blocked leather socket is made from a cast of the *whole limb* and buttock. Full ischial tuberosity bearing is essential. The socket is attached by means of jointed side steels to an artificial shin and foot. A pelvic band with a hip joint is usually incorporated to prevent excessive rotation and abduction of the limb when walking (Fig. 11/7).

Transverse terminal hemimelia

Although transverse terminal hemimelia is the commonest type of dysmelia affecting the upper limb, it is rarely seen in the lower. However, when it *does* occur other limbs are often involved.

The foot: The whole foot, the forefoot, or merely the toes may be absent. It is of interest to note that when the forefoot is missing, there is no equinus deformity as so often occurs when an amputation is performed at the same level.

PROSTHESES

For complete absence a standard Syme prosthesis is supplied. As the child grows there is a likelihood of slower development of the tibia and the two malleoli. Paradoxically, the cosmetic effect is therefore

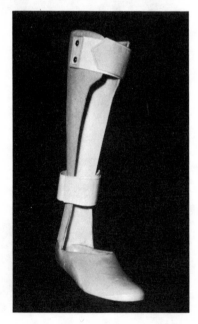

Fig. 11/8 Dropped-foot type of prosthesis for a forefoot deficiency. Made from Ortholen which is flexible and allows the ankle to move when walking or running

excellent. There are two types of prosthesis for absence of the forefoot:

1. A plastic dropped-foot type with a blocked toe-piece will fit neatly into an ordinary shoe (Fig. 11/8). Some very active youngsters, however, maintain there is insufficient support with this type when they play rugby or football.
2. A Chopart type of appliance is the alternative. This consists of a soft leather bootee with central lacing and a polished beech insole.

Below-knee hemimelia

The end of the tibial stump is pointed and may eventually require trimming. The fibula is frequently deficient.

PROSTHESIS
The conventional below-knee prosthesis as described on page 214 is supplied.

Through-knee and above-knee hemimelia

When a child is born with absence of one or both legs, whether at or above the knee, it is advisable to have a radiograph of the hips. Quite often there is either congenital dislocation or proximal femoral focal deficiency causing a hip flexion deformity. If this exists, walking will be extremely slow and difficult to accomplish, particularly if bilateral. The stumps are well rounded at the end with a fleshy pedicle either at the side or posteriorly. The femoral condyles are lacking, but children with *normal* hips and bilateral defects have no problem when running on the bare ends of the limbs.

PROSTHESIS
During infancy, a simple non-articulated prosthesis is supplied. This may have a metal socket with an end-bearing pad and light hip joint incorporating a pelvic band. A foot may be fitted or, if the stump is short, a small 'rocker' may be preferred since it is lighter and easier to use. In due course, a knee joint is fitted and only a minimal limp is evident. Most youngsters can take part in many of the usual games.

Bilateral deficiencies

The prostheses are similar but when knee joints are supplied a locking mechanism is incorporated initially. Provided the hips are normal, balance is quickly acquired and the locks may be omitted on subsequent limbs.

For recreational purposes a pair of short leather sockets, with stout soles, can be issued. These enable the youngsters to play football and run more easily on asphalted playgrounds.

Amelia

Type (a): Complete absence of the lower limb with an intact pelvis, but unformed acetabulum on the affected side.

Type (b): A hemi-pelvis in which the whole of the limb and the associated half of the pelvis is missing. This is an extremely rare phenomenon and may be associated with an absent kidney and testis on the affected side.

In the former type, it is usual to find a small fleshy nodule on the lateral side of the pelvis, which is probably a rudimentary limb bud.

Although early radiographs show no evidence of any long bone, a palpable mass is occasionally present in the region of each hip. By the time the child reaches adolescence, a radiological examination may reveal a nodule of bone with an epiphysis. This is most likely to be a *distal* end of femur. (Femoral deficiencies are almost invariably proximal.)

PROSTHESES

(a) *Unilateral amelia*: At about 10–12 months a lightweight non-articulated prosthesis is fitted with a socket embracing the lower portion of the trunk and both hips. Because artificial hip and knee joints are, of necessity, heavy, it is inadvisable to incorporate them until the child is walking well. They may be added some time between the third and fifth years of age and it should be possible to walk with a 'free' knee within a short space of time.

(b) *Bilateral amelia*: Because an infant without either lower limb is unable to maintain a sitting posture a special supportive device is necessary. This is based on the original Chailey 'flower-pot' design and is supplied at the sixth month (Fig. 11/9).

SWIVEL WALKERS

At about 10–12 months a new socket is made, beneath which are two non-articulated legs with a spring-loaded swivel action. In order to walk the child sways from side to side.

The age at which separate prostheses are supplied varies considerably with the development of the child and initially these limbs are non-articulated. Each socket fully embraces the hip and buttock and the two prostheses are connected back and front by

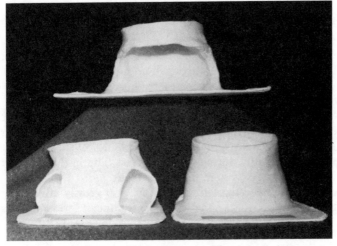

Fig. 11/9 Plaster of Paris 'flower pots' for sitting balance

adjustable straps. Having been securely fastened into the prostheses, the child should be able to achieve a 'swing-through' gait with the aid of crutches. As the height is increased, there may be a need to introduce hip and knee joints, but these will add very considerably to the weight of the limbs. It will be appreciated that the child is in a permanent sitting position despite the appearance of standing. Removal of prostheses for transfer to wheelchair or private car is a simple matter and therefore the non-articulated limbs may be used until the child is in the teens.

MULTIPLE ASYMMETRICAL LIMB ANOMALIES

There are a number of people with multiple limb deficiencies which do not fit into any recognised pattern. There are, however, certain specific features: always three and often four limbs are affected; they tend to be different from one another and asymmetrical, quite unlike the thalidomide deformities which are pre-axial deficiencies, bilateral and usually symmetrical.

TREATMENT
Because of the diversity of the limb conditions it is not possible to outline a specific method of treatment. However, experience has shown that the greater the malformation, the less likely it is that multiple prostheses will be accepted.

'Lobster-claw' deformity

The bifid hand or 'lobster-claw' deformity is considered to be hereditary, due, possibly, to an autosomal dominant trait (Temtamy and McKusick, 1969). Functionally, the hands are capable of excellent grip but, for psychological reasons, surgical closure may be advisable at an early age.

When the feet are also affected (which is usual) standard shoes can rarely be worn. Corrective surgery should, however, be tempered with caution since discomfort may result. Surgical shoes should be prescribed, certainly during the early years, and in due course the patient may have a say in ultimate treatment.

Very occasionally the lower limbs are also grossly affected with distal tibial hypoplasia, the proximal rudiment presenting as a separate entity and covered completely by skin (Fig. 11/10).

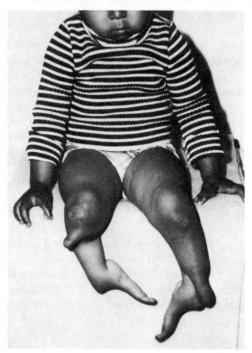

Fig. 11/10 Hereditary lobster-claw hands, tibial hypoplasia and single-ray feet

TREATMENT
When this condition exists, the feet are far from normal and the removal of whatever rudiment exists is the treatment of choice. Fusion of the tibia to the fibula is ideal if it can be achieved, but when there is a wide separation between these two bones, considerable difficulty is experienced when surgical approximation is attempted. Reasonably standard below-knee type prostheses can be fitted, but great care has to be taken to prevent pressure sores if the tibial segment starts to migrate.

Ring constrictions

A baby may be born with one or more fingers (or toes) only partly formed and giving the appearance of an encircling constriction band. Although a deep sulcus is present, there is never any evidence of an actual ligature. The condition is almost invariably multiple and the terminal part of one or more limbs may also be missing or, if present, without any bones distal to the constriction.

TREATMENT
When the ring constriction is around either the leg or forearm it may be advisable to remove the pendulous distal portion of the limb and fit an appropriate prosthesis.

Absence of the lumbar spine and sacrum

When a baby is born with absence of the lumbar spine and sacrum the lower limbs are usually paralysed, abducted and externally rotated at the hips. The knees are acutely flexed often with webbing of the skin between the thighs and calves giving a frog-like appearance. The two iliac bones are joined posteriorly and double incontinence is the rule. There may be rectal atresia and hypoplasia of the pelvic organs.

TREATMENT
Provided the popliteal webbing is not too severe it should be possible for the infant to have a 'sitting socket' at about 6 months and later a pair of swivel walkers (see p. 218).

SURGERY
Major surgery has something to offer for the severely flexed lower limbs. Bilateral disarticulation at the knees may be performed and followed by subtrochanteric osteotomies to correct the abduction and rotation. Prostheses may then be fitted but *heavily* padded pelvic

bands are essential since they will impinge upon the rib cage. Because of the paralysis from the waist level the child will not be able to take any effective stride with either leg but should be able to achieve reasonable walking speed, over short distances, with the aid of crutches and resorting to a tripod gait.

STUMP CARE AND HYGIENE

Whenever a lower limb prosthesis is worn it is usual to wear a stump sock and these may be woollen, nylon or cotton and are supplied by all ALACs. Owing to the difficulty of manufacturing the great variety of shapes and sizes of socks for the lower phocomelic limb, stockinette is frequently used and cut into the shape of a pair of trousers and then sewn. As many of the patients with two-limb (and certainly with four-limb) phocomelia perspire very considerably they find the stockinette most acceptable. Whatever type of sock is worn, it is advisable to have a clean one each day and to avoid using detergents when washing the socks as rashes have occasionally resulted.

The inside of plastic sockets should be wiped with a damp cloth each evening and then carefully dried ready for morning use. Leather sockets and others which are lined with leather should be exposed to the air overnight. The affected limb should be washed night and morning and thoroughly dried prior to donning the prosthesis. This, together with suspension straps, should be inspected periodically thus minimising serious breakages. Tell-tale cracks can usually be seen and then an early appointment at the appropriate limb centre should be requested for repairs to be undertaken.

PSYCHOLOGICAL EFFECTS

It is understandable that parents will be very upset when they know they have produced a malformed baby. There are usually feelings of guilt and one parent may blame the other. Turmoil of this nature, if it persists, will become apparent to the child even though not fully understood. The child will then feel unwanted and insecure. The majority of children with a good home background and parents who do not *show* anxiety over the limb condition are usually very well adjusted. Comments *will* be made by other children, but if a rational explanation is given to an enquiring child, without anger, it is likely to have a good effect. To hide the affected part and make a mystery of the condition will only arouse curiosity and invite numerous comments.

Malformations most likely to cause psychological problems are those affecting a hand rather than more proximal deficiencies. A well-rounded stump seems to be accepted by the lay public better than a deformed hand. Many people with limb deficiency, and others with an amputation, tend to compensate by indulging in a variety of sporting activities at which they usually excel. This should be encouraged and some of the many youth organisations are beneficial in this respect. The psychological trauma experienced by a limb-deficient person varies quite considerably. It is clear, however, that the greater the understanding and acceptance by the parents and others, coupled with a good stable home, the happier the child will be. Those closely involved with limb-deficient children should make light of their handicaps and encourage independence while steering them towards as normal a life as possible and remembering that over-protection causes frustration. Recognition of any potential, however bizarre it may seem, should be fostered to the full. Life has presented a great challenge to limb-deficient people and they will meet it and overcome it, often having a greater determination than the so-called able-bodied. What handicapped persons want more than anything else is acceptance and recognition of their *ability* not an emphasis of their *disability*.

OCCUPATIONAL THERAPY AND PHYSIOTHERAPY

General principles

Full movement in all remaining joints is essential and must be encouraged from the beginning to achieve independence in daily living later. Not only do the parents need to be taught how to handle their child, but also to be shown how to help the baby overcome the difficulties in attaining the normal developmental milestones.

Children with severe limb deficiencies have reduced sweating surfaces and so need to be lightly clad in loose cotton clothing as they feel the heat excessively. Dehydration also occurs very quickly if the child is unwell, therefore the fluid intake must be increased. Babies with short or absent legs find difficulty in attaining sitting balance. This was overcome at Chailey by making a plaster of Paris 'flower pot', a shell which totally enclosed the lower half of trunk and pelvis with apertures for feet (Fig. 11/9). The device was mounted on a base and fitted into a chair with castors so that the parents could push it from room to room. Now, sitting sockets of plastic or leather are made and fitted like a saddle on a little wooden animal, also mounted on castors.

Changes of position and play are vital so that the child can investigate his environment using hand, stump, mouth, body and feet – he may even be taught to roll (Fig. 11/11). Teeth take undue strain, so regular dental appointments are essential. Once sitting balance is attained, play needs to encourage bottom shuffling. This can be augmented by climbing into a low trolley with canted wheels for self-propelling.

Bony areas around the feet of phocomelic children may become painful, and socks continually wear out due to constant shuffling, and may need protection in the form of polypropylene 'spats'. Leather patches on the seats of trousers help to prevent undue wear.

Children with short or absent arms take longer learning to stand and may be nervous of falling without arm protection. Supported standing in a baby-walker or using adapted reins will give confidence until they are ready to take the plunge. Falling needs to be taught. Chins and heads are vulnerable and a crash-helmet can be worn. A potty chair may be necessary to aid balance for toileting. Another reason for late walking is that the feet are used for prehension and open-toed socks and shoes are necessary for these babies.

Children with abnormalities of all four limbs learn to walk on their own feet, if present, but there are a few who need to have the experience of the upright position in prostheses before they do this. Crutches tend to upset the balance, and the length of the stump of the

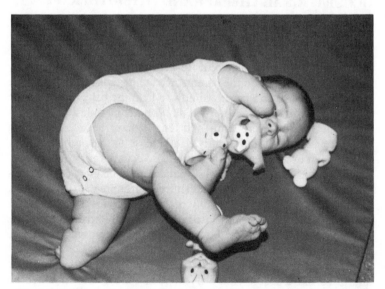

Fig. 11/11 Baby with multiple limb deficiencies exploring his environment

upper limb will determine whether the child is able to control a prosthesis for the lower limb at an early age. Those with long arm stumps can use adapted crutches to aid walking. When balance is precarious, a standing table can be used. Gradually, independent standing and walking are encouraged. As these are achieved, mobility is increased to include kerbs, steps and stairs. When a child is wearing two rigid artificial legs and has very short or absent arms, the best way to go up and downstairs is sideways using the wall, but this depends on the width of the stairs. It may also be helpful to have a high banister with stops on it, so that a chin or short upper limb can help a child going up and downstairs forwards. Mobility should be continually encouraged, for example, sitting to standing, rising from the floor to standing, so that these lead to functional activities such as being able to get in and out of the bath, on and off the toilet, also in and out of the car.

FEEDING

The relationship between chair, tray or table needs to be adjusted according to the disability of the child. Modifications to cutlery can include metal rings attached to the knife and fork for children without fingers, and bent sundae spoons with extended handles for foot use. Upper limb prostheses with spoon and fork attachment can be used with a non-slip mat and a straight-sided bowl.

REFERENCES

Frantz, C. H. and O'Rahilly, R. (1961). Congenital skeletal limb deficiencies. *Journal of Bone and Joint Surgery*, **43A**, 1202–24.

Lamb, D. W. (1972). Treatment of radial club hand. *Hand*, **4**, 22.

Temtamy, S. and McKusick, V. A. (1969). *Synopsis of hand malformations with particular emphasis on genetic factors*. In *Clinical Delineation of Birth Defects*, vol IV (jt eds Bergsma, D. S. and McKusick, V. A.). Williams and Wilkins, Baltimore.

FURTHER READING

Burtch, R. L. (1966). Nomenclature for congenital skeletal limb deficiencies: a revision of the Frantz and O'Rahilly Classification. *Artificial Limbs*, **10**, 1, 24.

Fletcher, I. (1980). Review of the treatment of thalidomide children with limb deficiency in Great Britain. In *Clinical Orthopedics and Related Research* No. 148, 18–25. J.B. Lippincott Co, Philadelphia.

Fletcher, I. (1982). The management of limb deficient children. *Maternal and Child Health*, **12**.

Henkel, L. and Willert, H-G. (1969). Dysmelia – a classification of congenital defects of limbs. *Journal of Bone and Joint Surgery*, **51B**, 399–414.

Kuhne, D., Lenz, W., Petersen, D. and Schoneberg, H. (1967). Defekt von Femur und Fibula mit Amelie Peromelie oder ulnaren, Strahldefekten der Arme – Ein Syndrome. *Humongenetik*, **3** (3), 244–63.

Mallinson, V. (1980). *None Can be Called Deformed*. Arno Press Inc, USA. (Previously published in 1956 by William Heinemann Limited, London.)

Mazoyer, D. (1975). L'amputé congénital du membre supérieur. Réflexions à propos de 50 cas. *Annales de Médicine Physique*, **XVIII**, 3.

Robertson, E. (1978). *Rehabilitation of Arm Amputees and Limb Deficient Children*. Baillière Tindall, London.

Chapter 12

Orthotics

by J. FLORENCE FBIST

FOOTWEAR AND INSOLES

Wherever possible, the physically handicapped child should wear shoes that are similar to those worn by normal children. Ordinary shop-bought shoes can be modified and adapted in numerous ways to accommodate abnormal feet or to attach to orthoses. With modern adhesives the majority of soles can be raised, sockets can be fixed and inserts moulded to fit in the shoes or to reinforce the uppers.

For the less fortunate who cannot be accommodated in normal shoes, there is a range of specially constructed footwear in stock sizes with different width fittings and depths, and these are available on the NHS. Insoles for correction of deformities can be made in a variety of materials today, ranging from man-made plastics to rubber, leather and cork. The expanded polyethylene (Evazote, Plastazote, Texlon) can be purchased in varying densities and used for correction and pressure problems.

The child with grossly abnormal feet will need custom-made surgical footwear to a specially-built cast. Care in selection of style of uppers can greatly enhance the appearance. Anaesthetic feet, for example in spina bifida, need to have boots that lace low for easy access so that toes can be straightened out when they are applied. It is far easier for the boots to be made from a plaster of Paris (POP) cast where there is a severe deformity such as equinus.

Non-weight-bearing feet may be accommodated in soft boots lined with lambswool, or these can be moulded in expanded polyethylene and covered with stretch plastic or gloving kid. Even when special shoes or boots have to be made, it is possible to copy the style of a standard shoe upper to make the wearing of these more acceptable. Raises to accommodate shortening can be made in cork, microlite or high-density expanded plastic.

ANKLE-FOOT ORTHOSES (AFOs)

These are below-knee bracing for correction of ankle-foot deformities or stabilisation of ankle and foot. They are made of conventional steel or aluminium alloy, and may be either single or double sided.

Single medial or lateral strut with calf band and round spur. This is used in conjunction with a T- or Y-shaped strap for the correction or stabilisation of a varus or valgus condition of the ankle. It is important that shoes should be adapted correctly and reinforced where necessary with inserts, otherwise the foot will turn inside the boot or shoe (Fig. 12/1).

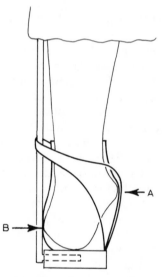

Fig. 12/1 Adapted boot for an AFO (viewed posteriorly). Unless the boot is reinforced at B, the corrective force A will distort the upper, and the foot will turn inside the boot

Double medial lateral struts with calf band and round spurs. This is used for the same condition as the single AFO. This double AFO can control both varus and valgus and stabilise the heel of a shoe. Both single and double AFOs can be used with dorsi-plantar flexion stops, either with round spurs or ankle joints. Toe-raising springs can be fitted either to the AFO ankle joints or attached to the toe of the shoe. Springs should never be used on a spastic limb as this will only antagonise and increase the spasticity. This will not be effective unless the sole of the shoe is reinforced. Better control of the ankle and foot can be achieved by fixing the angle of dorsi-plantar flexion. With the small child or infant, steel AFOs attached to foot-plates can be used. As the weight of the individual increases, the sole-plates tend to break due to the leverage on the footpieces. All conventional steel AFOs rely on the footwear for stability.

With the availability of high density plastics much better control of ankle-foot deformities can be achieved. Polypropylene is the most adaptable plastic currently in use. A cast is taken of the leg below knee with the child seated and the knee flexed. In this way the orthotist can hold the foot in the correct position controlling varus or valgus and angle of dorsiflexion and plantar flexion. This cast is removed from the leg and filled with POP to form the positive cast of the limb. Careful rectification of the cast is needed, emphasising any prominences such as the malleoli and reducing soft tissue areas. Polypropylene is heated to 190 degrees centigrade (190°C) and can be drape-formed or vacuum-formed over the cast. This should be left on the cast for 12 hours before removing. The trim line can be varied either to eliminate ankle-foot movement or to allow dorsiflexion and plantar flexion (Fig. 12/2).

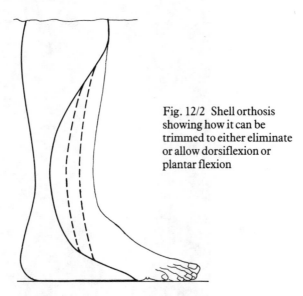

Fig. 12/2 Shell orthosis showing how it can be trimmed to either eliminate or allow dorsiflexion or plantar flexion

The fixed ankle AFO is used extensively for a spina bifida low lesion, i.e. below sacral 1–2 where there are no active plantar flexors. The child is unable to stand still and dorsiflexion gives rise to knee flexion. Accurate positioning of the feet can enable the child to stand still and can influence knee control. This fixed ankle orthosis is also useful for spastic hemiplegia and quadriplegia and muscle disorders, and can be worn both day and night. However, reaction to a rigid splint may be more difficult with spastic children, and spasm may produce more problems with pressure sores.

A modification of the polypropylene AFO is the patellar tendon bearing orthosis. This can be used in two ways:

1. A reinforcement to the standard AFO which gives both stronger anterior support and can extend to take a bearing on the femoral condyles. This is particularly useful for the heavier lower lesion spina bifida child for helping to control genu valgum (Fig. 12/3).

2. A suspension orthosis for relief of weight from the tibia or fibula or for relieving pressure from the plantar surface of the foot. This has been used very successfully in the treatment of ulcers under the heels of children with vertical talae and absence of plantar flexors.

Contra-indications for the use of polypropylene AFOs are oedema and severe spasticity.

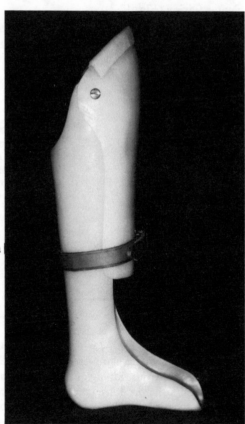

Fig. 12/3 Patellar tendon bearing orthosis

KNEE-ANKLE-FOOT ORTHOSES (KAFOs)

These are above-knee bracing for correction of knee-ankle-foot deformities or stabilisation of knee, ankle and foot. KAFOs are an extension to the thigh of AFOs, the ankle and foot being controlled as described with AFOs. Knee deformities may be flexion, recurvatum, varus and valgus. With conventional steel or aluminium alloy construction these are corrected with slings at the knee using the medial lateral struts for correction (see Fig. 4/10, p. 95).

Knee joints may be fitted and can be used to allow flexion, but resist hyperextension or lock at 180 degrees to eliminate movement when weight-bearing, but unlock to allow the child to sit with the knees flexed. These locking joints can be either locked or unlocked by hand or can be spring loaded to lock automatically when the leg is straightened. All knee locks are difficult to operate under load and where flexion spasm is present. It is almost impossible for the child to operate knee locks. A useful aid to make this easier has been designed by research in the Rehabilitation Engineering Unit at Chailey. This is a boss added below the ring of a standard ring-catch joint. It works on a cantilever principle and can be used on each individual joint or can be connected by an anterior bar to operate both joints in unison. It is useful for children with weak hands, for example those with muscular dystrophy or arthrogryposis (see Figs. 8/2, p. 166 and 9/1, p. 179).

If recurvatum control only is needed, it may be possible to have an extension to the thigh on the lateral side only with a free joint allowing flexion, but resisting hyperextension by stopping the joint at 10 degrees of flexion. This is particularly useful for children with spina bifida at the level of lumbar 4–5 where the quadriceps are active and the hamstrings weak.

Steel or aluminium constructions are heavy and, apart from mass production of joints facilitating speedier construction, little has been done to improve the design, which has not changed for over 100 years. In the late 1960s experiments were carried out using high density plastics for shell construction and carbon fibre to replace steel or alloy side-members. One significant factor to emerge from this research was that half the weight of a conventional KAFO was leather, and replacing side-members with lightweight materials did not alter the weight of the complete orthosis significantly. Considerable advances have been made over the last decade in the use of high density plastics for shell construction. The Stanmore Cosmetic caliper highlighted the use of high density polyethylene (Ortholen) (Tuck, 1971) and polypropylene vacuum-formed shell orthoses (Yates, 1971).

Polypropylene shell KAFOs are widely used in paediatric orthotics for poliomyelitis, spina bifida, muscular dystrophy, spinal muscular atrophy and arthrogryposis. Some of the advantages over conventional construction are listed below:

Lightweight
Easy to take off and put on (doff and don)
Speedy construction
Easy to adjust
Long lasting
Normal footwear can be worn
Cosmetically more acceptable.

Skill is required in taking an accurate cast of the limb and techniques of rectification of the positive cast and the moulding of the orthoses are time consuming, but the end result is so much better (Fig. 12/4). Contra-indications for the use of shell KAFOs are

Fig. 12/4
Polypropylene KAFO

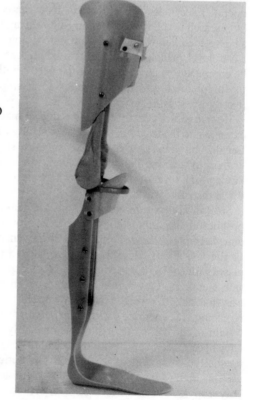

oedema, severe spasticity, gross deformity of the knee. It may be necessary to attach KAFOs to some form of body orthosis (Fig. 12/5).

Reciprocal gait is difficult and almost impossible in complete paraplegia. The only method of ambulation is swing-through or jump-to gait. This involves high energy consumption and consequently nearly all children requiring stability at this level become wheelchair bound when they reach adolescence. Strong shoulders and arms are required for this method of ambulation.

The same design of orthoses with thoracic and pelvic bands are used as standing frames for muscular dystrophy and spinal muscular atrophy, but ambulation is not possible. Recent advances in design of hip joints and rigid thoraco-lumbar bracing have made reciprocal gait more possible (Rose and Stallard, 1979). Polypropylene can be used as the thoraco-lumbar brace and attached to KAFOs with hip joints. This reduces the weight of the orthoses, but does nothing to improve the problem of high-energy-consumption ambulation (Fig. 12/5).

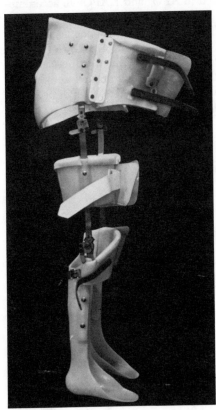

Fig. 12/5
Polypropylene TLSO+KAFOs

EXTENSION PROSTHESES

Extension prostheses are widely used in paediatric orthotics:
  For congenital limb deficiency
  As compensation for shortening
  As an aid to diminutive height.

Ultra lightweight construction using polypropylene has led to a higher acceptability of extensions for limb deficiency. Joints at knee level facilitate sitting and can be added to enable patients to use public transport.

Compensation for shortening can be made much more cosmetically acceptable. Equinus deformity of feet can be used to good effect to replace unsightly block raises on surgical footwear (Fig. 12/6). Extensions can be incorporated in AFOs and KAFOs to accommodate shortening from as little as 1cm to a gross shortening of 20cm or more. In many cases this will enable children with one normal limb and one disabled limb to wear ordinary footwear (Fig. 12/7). Feet that have resisted operative correction, as is frequently the case with arthrogryposis during growth, can be accommodated comfortably and cosmetically in bilateral extensions attached to KAFOs or AFOs. These can also be used as an aid to diminutive height (see p. 182).

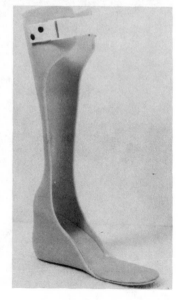

Fig. 12/6 Equinus deformity
accommodated in an AFO

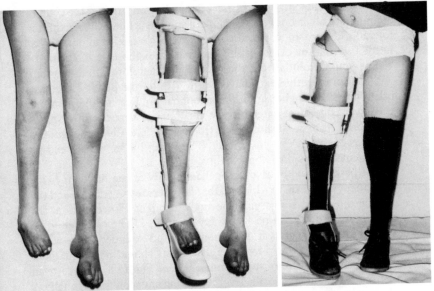

Fig. 12/7 To show how the short leg can be accommodated to match the normal leg

The child with achondroplasia, although able to walk on his feet, has many disadvantages to people of normal height apart from appearance. Inability to reach normal-height electrical fittings, water taps, shelves and even door handles restricts the activities of daily living in the normal community. Short lower limbs also mean short length of step and the child is consequently slow in ambulation. Bilateral extensions can both enhance appearance and provide a better chance of acceptance in the community.

THORACO-LUMBAR SACRAL ORTHOSES (TLSO) AND CERVICAL THORACO-LUMBAR SACRAL ORTHOSES

With the advance in moulding thermoplastics, conventional steel spinal orthoses are rarely used in paediatric orthotics. Accurate casting techniques and correct postural seating methods have led to a better understanding of the correction of spinal deformities.

The spinal orthosis invariably used is the total contact moulded plastic TLSO. Polythene or polypropylene can be used, although the former in lower density will need reinforcing for stability. The orthosis is the same for all thoracic and thoraco-lumbar support. Cast rectification and trim lines will vary depending on whether the child is ambulant or chair bound. The aim is always to achieve the maximum tolerable degree of correction, and comparison of radiographs is needed so that the orthotist can see what the orthosis is achieving.

The spine extends from the pelvis, and therefore it is important with all spinal orthoses to have a firm grip on the pelvic structure, otherwise it is like a house without a foundation. Bearing this in mind, the lower edge must extend below the anterior superior iliac spines anteriorly, fit close to the greater trochanters laterally and extend to the level of the coccyx posteriorly. The upper limits will depend on the extent of the spinal abnormality.

The best method of casting for the majority of conditions is to lay the patient supine on two blocks, the shoulders resting on one and the seat on the other. By varying the angle of hip and knee flexion, the amount of lordosis can be accurately controlled. The cast should be started round the pelvis at trochanter level and extended to the waist. As this sets, a firm grip over the iliac crests should be maintained, emphasising the anterior superior iliac spines (Fig. 12/8). The cast can then be extended up to axilla level correcting any scoliosis manually as the bandages are applied. The patient can then be sat up with the hips and knees flexed and the cast extended to rest on the platform.

If there is a gross degree of lateral pelvic obliquity with a compensating scoliosis, it may be necessary to extend the TLSO to rest on the chair seat to give more stability. Casting by this method

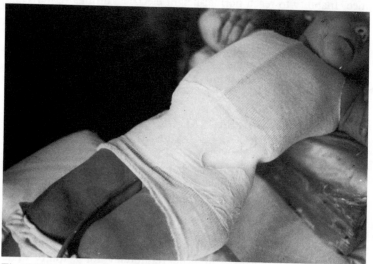

Fig. 12/8 Casting a TLSO. *Note* the emphasised anterior superior iliac spines

will give a clear indication of the limits required. Casting supine has advantages over casting under traction:

1. The maximum degree of tolerable correction can be achieved.
2. The rectification of the positive cast is assisted as the abdomen flattens naturally.
3. It is more comfortable for the patient.
4. Seating posture can be checked before removal of the cast.
5. Where there is poor muscle tone, as in muscular dystrophy and spinal muscular atrophy, traction is incompatible with casting an orthosis.

The negative cast should be sealed immediately after removal to avoid distortion. The positive cast needs careful rectification, which should be supervised by the orthotist. The trim line of the orthosis should be marked clearly on the cast. In the case of Duchenne muscular dystrophy it is wise to fit a TLSO as soon as the child becomes non-ambulant. Experience has shown that if a good lumbar lordotic posture can be maintained, this will prevent lateral pelvic obliquity and discourage the onset of scoliosis. The first TLSO need therefore only be extended to mid-thoracic level. Lumbar kyphosis must be avoided as this results in unacceptable pressure over the thighs and makes the wearing of a TLSO impossible. The higher the curve, the higher the orthosis must be carried. It is important to note that axillary pressure for spinal distraction is rarely, if ever, acceptable. There is no point in carrying the support high above the apex of the curve (see p. 168).

The more complex the shape, the more difficult it will be to spring open, and a hinge may be necessary. Where a hinge is to be added, the cast is examined to find the flattest area to place the hinge as it will only work in one plane. A low density lining is first moulded, and a flat area created to place the hinge (Fig. 12/9).

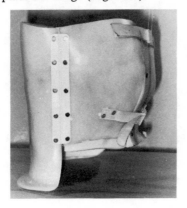

Fig. 12/9 Hinged TLSO
with extension
to rest on seat

Where there is a high cervical thoracic curve, or where head support is needed, the orthosis will need to be extended to chin and occiput. This can be achieved either by a standard Milwaukee brace, or by moulding a plastic extension. The principle of the Milwaukee brace is one of self-traction; the patient must be able to lift his head away from the neck ring. Where there is muscle weakness in the neck, the TLSO should be carried high to make this possible. In some cases of spinal muscular atrophy or congenital muscular dystrophy, the head piece may not need to be worn continually or may only need to support posteriorly. This can be made detachable and need only be worn when necessary (Fig. 12/10).

No matter how careful the orthotist may be, some scoliosis will progress, and, with rotation, gross rib abnormality may occur which will make the wearing of a plastic orthosis impossible. In these cases moulded leather is the best alternative as it is more tolerable to wear. The disadvantages are mainly hygienic as it is not possible to clean and will absorb perspiration. Plastic orthoses can be perforated for

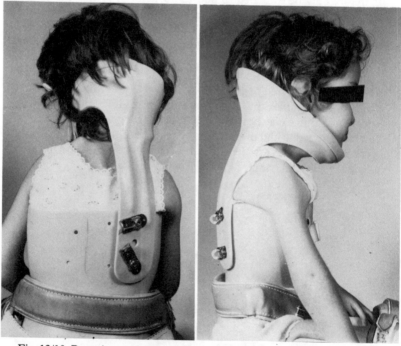

Fig. 12/10 Posterior and lateral views of a TLSO with specially designed neck piece to correct the head tilt

ventilation. It is important not to perforate in areas that are taking the most pressure as sores may develop. The perforations should be not less than 6mm in diameter and not more than 9mm. Plastic TLSOs may be lined with low density expanded polyethylene, but wherever possible this should be avoided as this makes the orthosis very hot to wear.

REFERENCES

Rose, G. and Stallard, J. (1979). The principles and practice of hip guidance articulations. *Journal of Prosthetics and Orthotics International*, **3**, 37–43.

Tuck, W. H. (1971). In *The Advance in Orthotics* (ed Murdoch, G.). Section 3, *Recent Advances*, part 2 Lower Extremity, 187–93. Edward Arnold, London.

Yates, G. (1971). *A modular system of exoskeleton bracing*. In *The Advance in Orthotics* (ed Murdoch, G.). Section 3, *Recent Advances*, part 3 Modular Orthotic Systems, 211–17. Edward Arnold, London.

Chapter 13

Wheelchairs and Mobility Aids

by C. FOSTER MCSP

Choosing the right wheelchair can greatly increase a child's ability to move around, and for some it is the only means of mobility. Others who are able to walk short distances indoors may need a chair to cover greater distances and for outdoor use. A wheelchair may give the child greater independence at home, at school and with his friends. In some cases a chair is only required for occasional use – for a shopping trip, a walk, or on holiday – times when the family act as a unit.

It is important that the chair looks good, moves easily and does not produce a barrier between the child and the world. There is a tendency to talk down to people in wheelchairs; remember to sit down if possible when meeting a child in a wheelchair so that you are able to see his face. Encourage children to play team games and do wheelchair dancing – this can be great fun, especially if able-bodied peers are put into wheelchairs and join in. They then discover how skilfully the disabled move.

CHOICE OF WHEELCHAIR

When prescribing a wheelchair there are some basic principles to be applied in all cases:

Size: The child should sit comfortably, the seat width and depth should be adequate to allow for winter clothing and additional cushions if required for support. The back should be high enough to support the shoulders, unless a harness, or increased head support, is required. Cushions should be selected and used during the assessment of the chair. A firm base may need to be added.

Posture: The feet should rest comfortably on foot-rests with knees bent so that there is no pressure behind the knee; they may need to be held in place with a strap. If the child is able to propel a chair the position of the wheels is crucial. The hands should rest on the hand rims at the top of the wheel with the elbows bent. If a cushion is inserted behind the child, or the propelling wheels have been set back to increase stability, the optimum position is lost. The brakes should be easy to reach and apply; they may need extended levers to facilitate this. A one-hand controlled chair may be prescribed. This has a double rim controlling the right and left wheels. A detachable pommel may be required for children with cerebral palsy. It is vital to watch the child in action, to observe unwanted postures brought on by activity.

Arm rests: These are required unless the child is being encouraged to balance. They must be at the correct height so that when the child rests his forearms on the padded arm-rests the shoulders are not hunched.

Domestic seat sides have a cut-out at the front and allow the wheelchair to manoeuvre closer to a table.

Manoeuvrability and stability

The weight of the chair and length of the wheel base will affect its manoeuvrability. The chair must be suitable for use in the child's home so that width of doorways and passages should be considered as well as access to toilets and bathroom. The stability of the chair depends on its centre of gravity and weight distribution. When the child is sitting in the chair it should be checked on a 16-degree slope to make sure it will not tip. The centre of gravity changes if the legs need to be elevated. The stability and manoeuvrability will also be affected by the surfaces on which the chair travels.

INDEPENDENCE

It is important that the choice of chair does not hinder the child's ability to transfer between chair and bed, toilet or bath or car seat.

TRANSPORT

If the chair is to be transported, it must be light enough to be lifted, and compact enough to fit into a car boot. If transport is not possible, two chairs will need to be prescribed – one for home and one for school use (Wisbeach et al, 1980).

Types of wheelchairs available may be found in the following books:

Handbook of Wheelchairs, Bicycles and Tricycles (MHM 408). HMSO, London. (This handbook is regularly updated by the DHSS.)

Equipment for the Disabled: Wheelchairs and Outdoor Transport. Obtainable from the National Fund for Research into Crippling Diseases, 2 Foredown Drive, Portslade, Brighton BN4 2BB.

The Disabled Living Foundation is able to supply additional information relating to suppliers from whom descriptive literature is available.

POWERED WHEELCHAIRS

At the present time the DHSS will supply a powered chair for use indoors or in the garden to any person unable to propel himself adequately. If the chair has to be transported between home and school, the DHSS will supply a second battery pack and charger.

Information on powered chairs can be obtained from Vehicle Technical Officers at the DHSS. Several BEC models are available from the DHSS. Their great advantage is their construction in aluminium which is much lighter than steel. The battery pack can be removed from the chair, which folds easily to fit into a car boot.

The standard controller is a joystick arising from the control box which may be situated on either side of the chair. The joystick ball is 1½ inches in diameter and this may be changed for a larger ball up to the size of a tennis ball or a T-shaped bar, or simply a vertical rod about 4 inches long, which may be easier to release.

If the joystick is too heavy to operate, a specialised control box with a separate controller may be fitted (Fig. 13/1). The position may

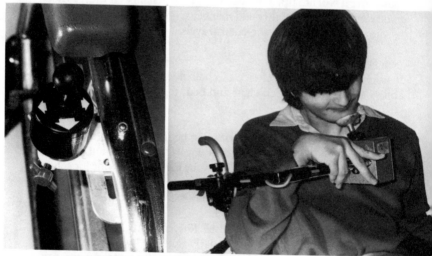

Fig. 13/1 (*left*) Lightweight controller using a joystick ball

Fig. 13/2 (*right*) Chin switch control

be chosen to suit the child, either centrally, on a tray, operated by a chin switch (Fig. 13/2), a squash plate for arm, hand, finger or by foot control. It is particularly useful in the presence of severe muscle weakness. This type of control box replaces the two speeds available from the standard box with proportional control, in which the distance the controller is moved in any direction influences both the speed and direction in which the chair moves. The on/off switch of the control box of a DHSS supplied chair may be push button or a toggle switch which can be extended by attaching a piece of stiff tubing.

The only outdoor powered wheelchair issued by the DHSS is an attendant-operated adult size chair (Model 28B) (Fig. 13/3). This may be issued when the attendant is not strong enough to push a standard wheelchair or where the district is hilly. This chair is large and cannot be folded.

There is a wide variety of powered chairs which can be bought for outdoor use, ranging from the lightweight speedy models to much

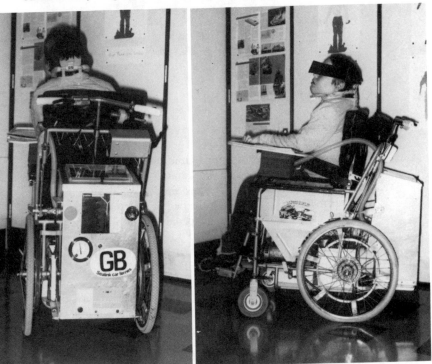

Fig. 13/3 Posterior and lateral views of a model 28B attendant operated powered chair. (This picture shows a patient who is reliant on a ventilator (mounted in enclosed box); the extra battery is carried under the seat)

heavier ones which are a good stepping-stone to driving a car. The main features to be considered when buying an outdoor, powered chair must be stability (Fig. 13/4), range of travel, maintenance, whether it is to be used indoors as well as outdoors, ability to climb kerbs and the need to be transported by car.

Fig. 13/4 Stabilisers on an outdoor powered chair

BICYCLES AND TRICYCLES

This is a vast subject which is well covered and discussed in *With a Little Help* (see References). Bicycles and tricycles provide a form of mobility which most handicapped children enjoy because they can compete with their able-bodied peers and, if adaptation is required, it can often be carried out on a standard model.

On the smallest tricycle where the pedals are attached to the front wheel, the child can be taught to pedal by strapping his feet into moulded plastic footplates attached to the pedals. An attendant-operated push or tow handle attached to the tricycle will help the child to get the feel of pedalling for himself.

Some children have difficulty in keeping their feet in a good position on the pedals. As they push down on the pedal the foot goes into plantar flexion and may then slip off the pedal; if it is strapped into a footplate it becomes very difficult to complete the pedal cycle. This can be overcome by moving the footplate back on the pedal to encourage the forefoot to be used in pushing, or attaching a short iron to the child's leg (Fig. 13/5). The short iron fixes into a footplate screwed to the pedal and this keeps the foot at right angles to the leg and therefore in a good position throughout the circle of movement.

Fig. 13/5 Ankle stabilisation on tricycle pedal using footplate and side steel. The foot is strapped to the footplate

PLAY VEHICLES

Toys designed to sit astride may be adapted for handicapped children. The saddle-seat engine encourages hip abduction. The child sits astride the boiler of the engine and punts himself around with his feet. The front castors are steered by means of a sturdy wooden handle, and the back of the seat simulating the cab is high enough to give the child the feeling of security. The back wheels may be blocked to prevent backward movement. This toy is also sturdy enough to be used as a child's first walking aid.

Go-karts

POWERED

In the powered range, Malden Care make the 'Ralley Special' which is particularly suitable for the child with spina bifida who wants to be able to use it when he is wearing leg orthoses, as it will allow him to sit with his knees straight. Because it is low to the ground the active child will have no difficulty in getting into it from the floor. This is an important consideration for a play vehicle. The Malden 'Monarch' is a go-kart which allows the child to drive it in a conventional chair-sitting position, and it is suitable for a child who has flexion contractures at the knees. Both these vehicles are controlled by a joystick controller which is very light to operate and so it means that a child with poor hand or arm strength should be able to manage it.

The Speedwell 'Supa Kart' is a similar vehicle, but it is steered by means of a steering wheel requiring power and dexterity in the arms and hands.

The Malden 'Mini Kart' is like a tiny motorised tub-chair and is suitable for the child in the $2\frac{1}{2}$–7 year age range. It has an 18-inch long wheelbase and will turn in its own length, which makes it suitable for indoor use. The joystick controller is situated on the front safety bar and can be positioned appropriately for each child.

HAND OPERATED

Hand-operated go-karts include the Theramed 'Row Car' which is propelled and steered by a rowing bar placed centrally, and the Prindus 'Hobcart' which also has a central steering lever controlled by arm and body movement.

Meyra Rehab produce a range of three- and four-wheeled play-mobiles propelled by pedals, tiller bar or hand-pushed wheels.

The 'Scamp' is a hand-operated go-kart with two levers which combine propulsion and steering.

Kettler manufacture a range of foot-pedalled go-karts, and the 'Monza' and 'Tornado' models are both suitable for handicapped children and may prove to be an alternative to a bicycle. They have seat position adjustment and are often used by children who have poor balance.

Some non-powered go-karts may be supplied by the DHSS as an alternative to a bicycle.

ADAPTATION FOR SPECIAL PROBLEMS

Abducted hips in frog plaster

If the child is small it may be possible to use a double pushchair or a Buggy Major and position and hold the child securely with additional straps. The intermediate insert may help to make the child more secure. A bead-bag cushion may be helpful, or the Burnett-MacLaren 'Mould and Hold' Body Support system. The child is positioned in the bead bag within the Major Buggy and then the air is evacuated, forming a firm support around the child.

This sort of adaptation may also be suitable for a child in a hip spica or broomstick plaster.

For the larger child in a frog plaster, R. J. Hayes (Leicester) Limited make a special transporter in which the child is supported and travels in the upright position. This position also makes the transporter suitable for schooling and mealtimes.

The 'Speed Transporter' – a car safety seat on a wheeled transporter – allows a child in two leg plasters, such as a broomstick plaster, to be moved around in the sitting position.

The 'Explorer' is a pushchair for a child in frog-leg or broomstick plasters. The backrest and seat are adjustable and the rear wheels are large enough for the vehicle to be self-propelled. There is also a pram-type handlebar. The 'Explorer' can be supplied with a harness and a play table top, and to aid storing it in a car boot the rear wheels are removable. Some children are unhappy to be transported around busy areas such as a shopping precinct at such a low level, as there is a danger of toes being caught in shopping trolleys and other wheeled vehicles if the plaster holds the legs very wide.

Proning

Sometimes it is impossible to accommodate a child in a conventional vehicle. A simple trolley can be made by attaching a board to a pram chassis, adding a mattress and safety straps, and the child can be pushed around lying prone or supine. A simple indoor solution may be a board with castors attached so that the child may punt himself around on the floor with his hands, or be pulled around by a rope.

If a child needs to be immobilised in the prone position for some time, either in plaster or in order to heal a sore on the buttocks, it helps to ease frustration if he can move himself around. A self-propelled prone trolley can be built using wheelchair propelling wheels at the front and castors at the back. The Chailey 'Prone Trolley' has removable sides to facilitate transfers, and patient-operated brakes. The width and length can be varied to order and the trolley can be dismantled and packed flat for storage and transportation.

Standing

The Yorkhill 'Chariot' is a stand-up box with self-propelling wheels, and castors, designed for children in orthoses to move themselves around in the standing position. It has a large detachable formica tray. There is a range of self-propelling wheel sizes and it can be built for one-arm drive if necessary.

The Papworth electric wheelstand has been developed as a manoeuvrable powered platform for paraplegic children in the upright position wearing orthoses. It has tiller steering, adjustable backrest and a built-in safety belt. This acts as a cut-out, by not allowing the stander to move until the belt is fastened.

It is possible to convert a Buggy Major to carry a child who is unable to sit at all. Sometimes the hips may be so stiff that standing or lying are the only possible positions. A Buggy Major can be adapted by converting the seat into a bag, the base of which is just above the cross-bracing mechanism of the Buggy. A loose baseboard placed inside the bag allows the child to stand facing the back of the seat. A very critical assessment has to be made of the child's weight and height to ensure that the stability of the Buggy is maintained.

ACCESSORIES

Belts and harnesses

All types of wheelchair and wheeled transport should be fitted with a safety strap which should be simple to operate. The waist strap may be made in leather with a conventional buckle, or nylon with a variety of buckles from the simple, threading metal buckle with a sliding centre bar to a choice of car seat-belt-type quick release buckles.

Sometimes a leather belt is contra-indicated for a child with no sensation below the waist as it may cause pressure problems. The position of any stoma should be noted as bad positioning of a belt can cause pressure and bleeding.

Where the child is unable to sit up without supporting himself on the arms of the wheelchair it is possible to make a belt which will help to hold him upright so that he can use both hands. This is made with a length of nylon webbing padded with Evazote (7.5–10cm) closed-cell foam across the front of the rib cage. This is attached to two or three strips of limb elastic which are sewn together at the end of the webbing attached to the vertical back tube of the wheelchair. A very short length of double or treble limb elastic is attached to the opposite back tube with a 'D' ring at its free end. The nylon tail of the long end of the belt is passed through this 'D' ring and pulled back across the padding and fastened with Velcro sewn on to the webbing. In this way the child is held back, but the elastic allows him to lean forward to work at a desk or reach something (Fig. 13/6).

For some older girls this is not satisfactory, and so shoulder loops are made. A strip of limb elastic is passed across the top of the back canvas and attached to the two vertical back tubes of the wheelchair. To the centre of this elastic are stitched two pieces of webbing which

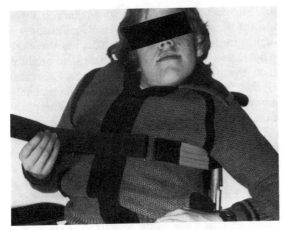

Fig. 13/6 Elasticated chest strap harness

pass over the shoulders and under the arms and are screwed to the vertical back tubes, usually utilising screws holding the back canvas in place. Shoulder straps can be padded with flat Evazote foam tube. The arms are slipped into the shoulder restrainers (Figs. 13/7, 13/8).

There are several harnesses available commercially. The simplest harness will be the most effective. If it is a complicated arrangement it is all too easy not to use it. In children with epilepsy or swallowing difficulties a quick release buckle is essential.

Warmth and protection

The child in a wheelchair needs some form of waterproof protection and something to keep him warm in winter. A flexible PVC rain hood

 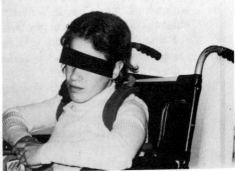

Fig. 13/7 (*left*) Position of the shoulder harness loops on wheelchair
Fig. 13/8 (*right*) Shoulder harness loops holding a girl securely in her chair, yet allowing movement

and cover is available for the Baby Buggy, Buggy Major and Twin Buggy from a firm in the West Midlands. The ALAC will supply a waterproof canvas apron for most sizes of wheelchair, but these are bulky to carry when not in use. Simplantex (Eastbourne) Ltd produce a lightweight proofed nylon, fitted wheelchair apron. They also produce the 'Wheely Mac', a proofed nylon cape which completely covers the occupant and fits right round the chair. There are reinforced holes for the pushing handles, and the cape has a concealed zip-front opening. Two sizes are available – adult and junior. The junior model will fit either a wheelchair or Buggy Major.

The occupant of a wheelchair can get very cold in winter. The wheelchair can be made much warmer by fitting a pure wool sheepskin cover over the seat and backrest. The Deluxe cover and the Cosy Sit are protective covers consisting of a proofed quilted nylon leg bag and seat cover with imitation sheepskin or warm woven lining. These bags are light, warm and showerproof. The zipped opening extends to the feet to make it easy to use. There is a variety of sizes.

WALKING AIDS

It is possible to modify standard walker toys available for young children (see Chapter 1).

The Educational Supply Association produces a walker which combines a long-wheel-based truck and a walking frame. It has a choice of handlebars for the child to propel it.

The adjustable Rollator walker is a tubular steel walker with two wheels at the front and rubber feet at the back to stop it running away. It is propelled by a handle at the top of each side. It can be purchased with a horizontal Cheyne Walk bar between the handles to give the child a good extended arm position for walking (see Fig. 4/10, p. 95). A Rollator walker that can be folded flat makes transportation much easier. This type of walker is available in a range of sizes from small child to adult.

The Cell Barnes Walker Trainer is a metal frame on castors with a leather-cloth seat slung within it. It is suitable for older children who require pelvic support, and is available in various sizes.

A walker can also be based on a tricycle. The 'Supa Pedalong' is of strong steel construction with two wheels at the back and a single wheel and steering handlebar at the front. A saddle is mounted on the cross-bar and a centre board may be fitted to the cross-bar to combat adductor spasm of the hip muscles.

The 'Amesbury Walking Aid' is designed to teach the more

severely handicapped child to walk, and is particularly useful for an athetoid child. It consists of a fully adjustable, padded body support mounted on a framework of tubular steel. It has a large wheelbase with four swivel-lock castors. The handrail encourages an extended arm, and a saddle and centre board may be added to control the amount of weight taken through the legs and any adductor spasm. It is available in two sizes. Unfortunately, it will only fold to a limited extent and so is difficult to transport by car.

The 'Chailey Walker' was developed as a progression from, or as an alternative to the 'Amesbury Walking Aid'. It is a steerable walking aid with swivelling chest/axillae pads which are adjustable for width and height (Fig. 13/9). The hand grips are also adjustable for height, and the walker easily dismantles and packs flat for storage and transportation. The walker supports the user's weight during part of the walking cycle, and the extended arms encourage control of the trunk. If grasp is difficult, leather 'gloves' can be made which hold the child's hands around the hand grips. The ability to collapse the walker means that it can be transported readily in the boot of a car despite the fact that it is sturdy enough to support an athetoid young adult.

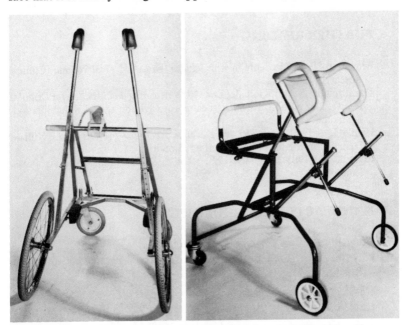

Fig. 13/9 (*left*) The Chailey Walker showing the leather glove to hold hand in position

Fig. 13/10 (*right*) The Cheyne Walker

The 'Cheyne Walker' was developed to provide a means of locomotion for an otherwise immobile child. Such a child may be highly motivated but too severely handicapped to be able to use other walking aids. For example he may be unable to provide himself with balance support due to poor grasp, instability at the shoulder, involuntary movements or a combination of these factors. The walker has a four-wheel base with adjustable trunk support and handlebar (Fig. 13/10). The trunk support is inclined forward at an angle between 25 and 45 degrees from vertical in order to take the child's weight forward and stimulate forward movement, but not taking too much weight from the feet. Arm gaiters may be needed to help maintain grasp.

REFERENCES

Harpin, P. (1981). *With a Little Help*. Muscular Dystrophy Group of Great Britain, London.

Wisbeach, A. et al (1980). Children in wheelchairs. *British Medical Journal*, **1**, 199–201.

FURTHER READING

Brown, J. (1981). Patients in wheelchairs. *British Medical Journal* (Clinical Research), **282**, 638.

Darnbrough, A. and Kinnade, D. (1983). *Motoring and Mobility for Disabled People*, 2nd edition. Royal Association for Disability and Rehabilitation, London.

Hale, G. (ed) (1983). *The New Source Book for the Disabled*. William Heinemann Medical Books Limited, London.

Russell, P. (1983). *The Wheelchair Child*, 2nd edition. Souvenir Press, London.

MANUFACTURERS' ADDRESSES

Baby Buggy; Buggy Major; Intermediate Seat
Newton Aids Ltd, Unit 4, Dolphin Industrial Estate, Southampton Road, Salisbury

Cheyne insert seat for Baby and Major Buggies
ESN Aids, 188 Perrysfield Road, Cheshunt EN8 0TW

PVC Flexihood rain cover for Baby and Major Buggies and Twin Buggies
John Paxton, 1 Florence Road, Sutton Coldfield B73 5NJ

Cindico Traveller
Cindico Ltd, Skerne Road, Driffield YO25 7XH

Postura 'Paedi' Chair
Everest and Jennings Ltd, Princewood Road, Corby NN17 2DX

Jonsport Trolley; Amesbury Walker; Avon Wheelchair
Joncare Meadjess Ltd, Radley Road Industrial Estate, Abingdon
OX14 3RY

Barrett wheelchairs
W. and F. Barrett Ltd, 22 Emery Road, Bristol BS4 5PN

Powerdrive chair
Carters (J. & A.) Ltd, Alfred Street, Westbury BA13 3DZ

Travel chair
Ortho-Kinetics (UK) Ltd, South Hampshire Industrial Park,
Totton, Southampton SO4 3ZZ

BEC powered chair
Biddle Engineering Co Ltd, 103 Stourbridge Road, Halesowen
B63 3UB

Bobcat; Budgie; Disco
T. I. Raleigh Ltd, 177 Lenton Boulevard, Nottingham NG7 2DD

Pashley Picador; Pashley Pickle
W. R. Pashley Ltd, Masons Road, Stratford-upon-Avon CV37 9NL

Thistle tricycles
Tri-Aid Manufacturing Ltd, 29 James Watt Place, College Milton
North, East Kilbride G74 5HG

Play-Mobiles
Meyra-Rehab, Millshaw Park Avenue, Leeds LS11 0LR

Joy Bike; Frog Plaster Transporter; Speed Transporter
R. C. Hayes (Leicester) Ltd, 65A Main Street, Kirby Muxloe,
Leicester LE9 9AN

Flying Dutchman; Row car
Theramed Ltd, PO Box 20, Alton GU34 4BA

Rifton tricycle
Community Playthings, Robertsbridge, East Sussex TN32 5DR

Tricycles and Go-Karts
WRK Developments, Unit 3A Fryers Works, Abercromby Avenue,
High Wycombe HP12 3BW

Malden Go-Karts
Malden Care, Malden House, 579 Kingston Road, London
SW20 8SD

Saddle Seat Engine; Tyre Shape Toy
ESA Creative Learning, Esvian Works, Fairview Road, Stevenage
SG1 0NX

Supa Kart
Speedwell Enterprises, Northampton Avenue, Slough SL1 3BP

Prindus Hob Cart
Prindus, Home Office, Tolworth Tower, Surbiton KT6 7DS

Kett Cars
A. Baveystock and Co Ltd, Teesdale Works, Cooks Road, London
E15 2PL

Burnett MacLaren body support system
Andrew MacLaren Ltd, Station Works, Long Buckby NN6 7PF

Explorer
Gubeley Silver Cross, Leeds LS20 8LP

Yorkhill Chariot
Robert Kellie and Sons Ltd, Rutherford Road, Dryburgh Industrial
Estate, Dundee DD2 3XF

Evazote
Hemisphere Rubber Co, 65 Fairview Road, London SW16 5PX

Crelling harnesses
Crelling Harnesses for the Disabled, 11 The Crescent, Cleveleys
FY5 3LJ

Cosy Sit; Wheely Mac
Simplantex Eastbourne Ltd, 67a Willowfield Road, Eastbourne
BN22 8AR

Deluxe cover
Comfy Products, Providence Place, Bridlington YO15 2QW

Cell Barnes harness; Cell Barnes Walker
Modern Tubular Production Ltd, 188 High Street, Egham
TW20 9EE

Cheyne Walker
Pryor and Howard, Willow Lane, Mitcham CR4 4NA

Chapter 14

Seating for the Chairbound Child

by J. ROCKEY DipCOT *and*
R. L. NELHAM BEng, CEng, MIMechE, MBES

A physically handicapped child who sits in a wheelchair cannot achieve maximum potential if the posture is less than ideal or the supportive pressures are not well distributed. Cushions, harness straps, supportive pads or moulded seat shells may be required to position the child in a comfortable, functional posture with the minimum risk of the development of pressure sores. Different postures may be required for different activities and it is only by consideration of all factors that the most appropriate solution can be reached. The most efficient means of assessing the requirements is by adopting a clinic team approach with the child and parents included as important members of that team.

BIOENGINEERING CONSIDERATIONS

There have been many investigations into the causes of pressure sores and it has now been established that tissue deformation sufficient to occlude capillary blood flow or impede lymphatic drainage will eventually result in tissue ischaemia. Tissue deformation will invariably be caused by a combination of pressure and shear forces since the two rarely exist separately. Shear forces will exist when high friction forces are used to retain a child in a wheelchair or when a high pressure exists adjacent to a low pressure as on a slatted seat. Temperature and humidity also play an important part since wet skin is very much weaker than dry skin and will therefore be more vulnerable to damage (Stewart et al, 1980). An increase in skin temperature will result in an increase in metabolism of the tissues, which will subsequently require an increased blood flow. If the tissues are sufficiently deformed to resist an increase in blood flow then the increased temperature could be a major contributory factor of tissue ischaemia (Fisher et al, 1978). A reduction in skin temperature may result in an increase in relative humidity at the skin surface and this inter-related effect requires a compromise in the choice of suitable materials or designs of seating systems.

Very tight or very loose, and hence creased, clothing, together with the contents of pockets, will have a significant effect on the performance of any support system and may be the cause of tissue damage. Since there are no devices that are currently available for clinical use to measure shear forces, skin temperature or humidity, pressure is used as a guideline in the design and choice of support systems. Pressure transducers are available from several manufacturers and should be used by those responsible for the prescription and design of cushioning and seating systems.

Since pressure is the most easily measured and modified property it is convenient to subdivide seating problems and their solutions into four general categories, namely (i) pressure distribution, (ii) pressure redistribution, (iii) pressure relief and (iv) postural support.

Pressure distribution

In order to avoid tissue deformation it is desirable that the necessary forces to support a child in a wheelchair are well distributed over the available area of support and thus pressures are kept to a minimum. This is usually achieved by the provision of a cushion and in addition to those provided by the DHSS there is a wide range of commercially available designs which incorporate many different materials. Since new cushions are frequently being introduced it is not appropriate to describe specific cushions; it is more helpful to consider the properties of the more common materials used in the construction of the pressure-distributing medium namely, elastic foam, visco-elastic foam, gel, water, air or a particulate material. Table 1 summarises some of the advantages and disadvantages of these materials when used as pressure distributing cushions and more information is provided in a report on wheelchair cushions (Jay, 1983(a) and (b)).

Polyurethane foam fatigues with use quicker than latex rubber foam (Denne, 1978) but all foam cushions need to be checked after approximately one year, dependent upon the properties retained at that time. It is desirable that two-way stretch, water vapour permeable covers are used for these cushions in order not to mask the selected pressure-distributing properties of the foam and to avoid the accumulation of perspiration. This is particularly so if Temper-foam is used since, as well as being visco-elastic, this material has stress-relieving properties which can easily be nullified by the incorrect choice of covering material (Koreska and Albisser, 1975). Waterproof covers are often inelastic and tend to become hard with repeated soaking and drying, leading to a very unsatisfactory sitting surface.

Gel cushions do not generally have a significant effect on skin temperature (Stewart et al, 1980; Fisher et al, 1978) but the waterproof envelope often increases the relative humidity at the skin surface which may be overcome by using a two-way stretch, absorbent cover. Water absorbs more heat and conducts it better than gel and therefore water cushions will have a cooling effect on the skin. As with gel cushions, the waterproof cover tends to increase the relative humidity at the skin surface and the cooling effect of these cushions may be uncomfortable for those with sensation. Some manufacturers provide an insulating layer either built into one side of the cushion or as a slip-on cover but the thickness of this layer may affect the conformity and, hence, pressure-distributing or shear-force reducing properties of the cushion.

Ripple cushions using air as a support medium are not as effective as ripple mattresses since the support area on a cushion is much less than that on a mattress. Air is also used as a support medium in the Roho Balloon Cushion, which is also efficient at reducing shear forces. However, as with gel and water cushions, the impermeable material used to construct these cushions may cause an increase in relative humidity at the skin surface. The insulating properties of air may also cause an increase in skin temperature (Fisher et al, 1978).

Particulate or bead-filled cushions are not suitable for children who have lost sensation since they rely on body movement to distribute the contents away from high pressure areas. This necessitates sensation to determine when sufficient distribution of the beads has occurred because very high localised pressures may result from insufficient distribution. Cushions using expanded polystyrene beads may also cause an increase in skin temperature as a result of the insulating properties of expanded polystyrene.

Pressure redistribution: pressure relief

These two subheadings are grouped together because the techniques used to construct the appropriate support surface are very similar. The aim is to redistribute pressures away from the vulnerable areas, such as the coccyx, sacrum and ischial tuberosities, to the more tolerant areas such as the thighs and sub-trochanteric shelf. This is achieved by shaping a block of foam to the bony structure of the patient and although due consideration should be given to the large range of pressure thresholds that exist from one individual to another,

TABLE 1 Summary of properties of some pressure distributing materials

Pressure distributing material	Advantages	Disadvantages	Comments
Elastic foam (e.g. polyurethane, polyester, latex rubber)	(1) Lightweight (2) Relatively inexpensive (3) Available in various grades and thicknesses (4) Water vapour permeable – a cover may reduce or totally inhibit this property	(1) Fatigues in use – properties need checking after six months. May need replacing after a year. Rubber foam better than plastics (2) Can increase skin temperature	(1) Cover should be used as surface of foam often high friction. Cover should be two-way stretch water vapour permeable
Visco-elastic foam (e.g. Temper-foam).	(1–4) As for elastic foam above (5) Visco-elasticity provides stable sitting surface and allows pressure relief with relatively small movements (6) Temper-foam possesses stress-relieving properties	(1+2) As for elastic foam above (3) Low tensile strength of Temper-foam limits life (4) May lose visco-elastic properties when wet	(1) As for elastic foam above (2) Needs a wheelchair board or a means of preventing it from stretching to fill the wheelchair canvas hammock as this leads to tearing
Gel	(1) No significant effect on skin temperature (2) Viscosity of gel provides a stable sitting surface (3) Vacuum-fitted cover of larger volume than that of gel allows deeper penetration before hammocking occurs (4) Will accommodate lateral movements of user and hence reduce shear forces	(1) Can be heavy (2) Relatively thick cover reduces conformity and leads to hammocking (3) Impermeable cover may increase relative humidity at surface and lead to damp clothing	(1) Leakage of contents may stain clothing and will reduce properties of cushion. May not be possible to refill

Pressure distributing material	Advantages	Disadvantages	Comments
Thixotropic gel	(1) No significant effect on skin temperature (2) Thixotropic gel is fluid under high pressure, solid under low pressure – good pressure distribution and stable sitting surface (3) Vacuum fitted cover of larger volume than that of gel allows deeper penetration before hammocking occurs (4) As for gel	(1–3) As for gel above	(1) As for gel
Water	(1) Can reduce skin temperature (2) Stable sitting surface if water flow restricted (3) Vacuum-fitted cover of larger volume than that of water allows deeper penetration before hammocking occurs	(1) Can be heavy (2) Impermeable cover can increase relative humidity at surface (3) Unstable if water flow not restricted in two dimensions (4) Water/foam combinations stiffer than gel – will not reduce shear forces as much as unrestricted gel	(1) Leakage not likely to stain clothes but may reduce effectiveness of cushion. May not be possible to refill
Air	(1) Lightweight (2) Stable sitting surface if air flow restricted	(1) May increase skin temperature (2) Unstable if single air cell or if air flow unrestricted	(1) Roho balloon cushion reduces shear forces but only if used uncovered. An allergic reaction may occur if cover not used
Particulate (bead-filled cushions)	(1) Lightweight (2) Stable sitting surface (3) Often water vapour permeable	(1) Beads need to be actively dispersed to achieve pressure distribution – not all users capable (2) Skin temperature may be increased if particulate material is an insulator	(1) Very high local pressures may result from inadequately dispersed beads (2) May require the user to have sensation to determine when contents adequately dispersed

the following pressures have been established as guidelines (Motloch et al, 1979):

Posterior thighs	80–100mmHg
Sub-trochanteric shelf	≤60mmHg
Ischial tuberosities	≤40mmHg
Coccyx/sacrum	≤14mmHg

Although construction details vary, the shape of the cushion required to achieve this pressure redistribution is shown schematically in Figure 14/1. In order to avoid shear forces as a result of friction it is desirable that the supporting surfaces of the cushion are kept horizontal and this is only achieved if the cushion is kept flat in use. Therefore, when used in a wheelchair, the cushion is either placed on top of a wooden board or the under surface is curved to fit into the wheelchair canvas hammock.

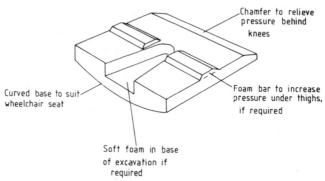

Fig. 14/1 Contoured cushion (diagrammatic)

When a child has a scoliosis, a pelvic tilt will invariably also be present even if spinal bracing is worn. The same techniques for cushion construction may be used to accommodate this pelvic obliquity but the excavated shape will not be symmetrical. As a preventive device, the guideline pressures indicated above are used, but once a sore has developed as a result of the pelvic tilt the pressure on the area of damaged tissue is reduced to zero by ensuring that there is clearance between the cushion and the user at this point.

The simple act of elevating legs on wheelchair elevating leg rests or a wooden wheelchair board may lead to excessive pressures on the sacrum which will necessitate the construction of a contoured cushion to prevent tissue damage in this area. It is essential that two-way stretch materials are used for covering contoured cushions in order that the pressure profiles so carefully established on the uncovered cushion are not altered.

Since pressure measurements can only give an indication of the suitability of any cushion design it is essential that skin inspection is used to establish finally that the choice of design is correct. No wheelchair cushion can distribute seating pressures sufficiently to reduce them to a tolerable level over a long period of time and it is therefore essential that all wheelchair users are encouraged to perform regular 'lift-ups' to relieve pressures completely. The use of a firm foam or highly viscous material will be of help since the slow response to movements results in frequent pressure relief as the user goes about daily tasks. If pressure relief cannot be obtained on a regular basis, a time limit for sitting must be established, based on pressure measurements and skin inspection.

Postural support

Postural support may be required for various reasons. These include:
(a) the establishment of a functional, comfortable posture for hypotonia;
(b) the control of spasm;
(c) the provision of some correction and support for spinal curvature;
(d) temporary support to help moderately handicapped cerebral palsied children to develop voluntary postural control; and
(e) easing the task of handling and management in some cases of fragilitas ossium and severe handicap.

However, postural support cannot be effectively provided until pelvic stability has been achieved, since the trunk cannot be held in the correct position if the pelvis is moving about.

PELVIC STABILITY

The first step in the provision of pelvic stability is often the establishment of a stable base in the chair. This can most easily be achieved by the use of a padded seat board or by placing a wooden board underneath a firm seat cushion.

Pelvic restraint can often be achieved by a strap that encircles the pelvis and pulls down and back at an angle of approximately 45 degrees (Fig. 14/2). This strap is held to the chair by a second strap which is anchored by the wheelchair canvas screws to prevent it from sliding, thus holding the pelvis in the antero-posterior and medio-lateral planes. When the child exhibits hip extension spasms, the pelvic strap may be used with a padded and ramped seat board to induce the required angle of hip flexion, say 100 to 120 degrees –

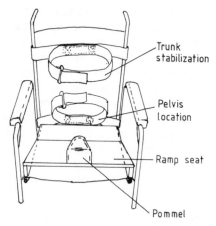

Trunk
stabilization

Pelvis
location

Ramp seat

Pommel

Fig. 14/2 Harness systems
for pelvic control and
postural support together
with a ramp seat board and
pommel

included angle of 60 to 80 degrees–(Motloch, 1977; Dunkel and Trefler, 1977). Excessive hip flexion is avoided since it may lead to total flexion patterns or to orthopaedic, breathing or digestive problems. The posture of a child with cerebral palsy, or with any condition where adductor spasm is present, may be improved by the use of a suitably-sized pommel to widen the sitting base and hence improve pelvic stability. Hip abduction also decreases the tendency to subluxation of the hips. However, care must be taken to ensure that the pommel is not used as the sole means of retaining a child in a chair. The lateral surfaces of the pommel follow the contours of the medial aspects of the thigh in order to apply the abduction forces without inducing large deformation of the tissues. Abduction of the hips will also help to induce a lumbar lordosis and hence extension of the spine for an erect posture. A lumbar support pad will often produce a better posture than that afforded by a flat backrest.

Windswept hips, where one hip is adducted and internally rotated and the other abducted and externally rotated, may be controlled by using adjustable padding and harnessing to apply the force system (Fig. 14/3) (Scrutton, 1978). The pelvic rotation is resisted and the

Fig. 14/3 Forces applied to
correct windswept hips
(after Scrutton, 1978)

previously adducted hip is abducted and externally rotated by keeping the foot in the mid-line of the footplate while pulling or pushing the knee to the side of the chair.

Different combinations of harnessing and padding, together with modifications of these methods of restraining the pelvis may be required to achieve the desired degree of pelvic stability in order that any trunk support that may be required can then be provided.

TRUNK CONTROL

Harness systems may also be used to provide some degree of postural support as shown in Figure 14/2. These have the advantage of being relatively unobtrusive in use and can be partially or totally removed for therapy sessions or for transfer to and from the wheelchair. The addition of shoulder straps may be required to prevent the child from falling or leaning forward over the thoracic strap. In such a case the backrest of the chair may need to be adapted to raise it above the height of the child's shoulders, thus providing a strong anchor point for the shoulder straps and preventing them from pulling down on the shoulders, which may encourage a slumped posture. Slightly more support can be provided by using wider webbing or by adding firm padding to the harnessing.

There are also some modular seating systems being developed which provide moderate support for the cerebral palsied child who is being encouraged to develop voluntary postural control.

More rigid forms of postural support can be provided by wheelchair-mounted pads (Fig. 14/4), padded inserts to wheelchairs

Fig. 14/4 Chair mounted lateral supports

(Fig. 14/5) or intimately moulded seats (Fig. 14/6). If correction of spinal curvature is required the direction of application of the forces to achieve this should be along the line of the ribs (Fig. 14/7a). Forces applied in any other direction (Fig. 14/7b) may deflect and possibly deform the rib cage and cause high localised pressures and shear forces. The resulting discomfort limits the amount of correction that can then be applied. Some wheelchair designs have postural control devices built in and, where these are adjustable, an optimum position can often be obtained.

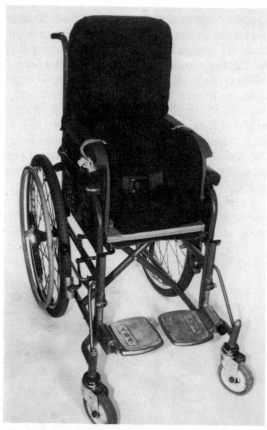

Fig. 14/5 Padded insert for the provision of postural support

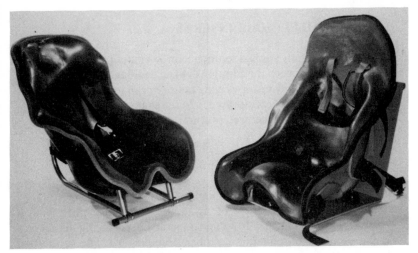

Fig. 14/6 *Left*: Derby moulded seat. *Right*: Chailey moulded seat

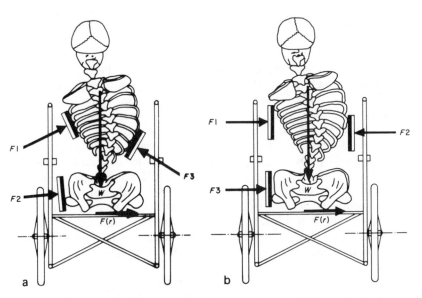

Fig. 14/7(a) *(left)* Correct application of forces to support and correct spinal curvature

Fig. 14/7(b) *(right)* Incorrect application of forces to support and correct spinal curvature

PADDED WHEELCHAIR INSERTS

The most commonly applied solution to problems of postural support in wheelchairs has been the addition of foam padding, with or without a timber support. Foams of varying density or indentation hardness are chosen and suitably sculptured to fit the anatomical features of the child and provide the required postural support or correction.

INTIMATELY MOULDED SEATING SYSTEMS

The success of an intimately moulded support or seating system depends upon the accuracy of fit to the patient's clothed body contours and the universally accepted method of achieving the shape is the vacuum consolidation casting technique. A single or multi-compartment casting bag, consisting of a flexible, elastic membrane containing expanded polystyrene beads, is used to position the patient and to achieve the desired correction of deformity within the limitations of comfort. A vacuum is then applied to the bag so that the shape obtained is made rigid (Nicholls and Strange, 1972; Ring et al, 1978; Germans et al, 1975).

Some seating systems use this principle to produce a definitive seat which allows for regular adjustment of shape. Alternatively, an adhesive is included with the beads to produce a firm, permanent seat (Rose et al, 1979). The surface of this seat tends to be hard and requires upholstering, which complicates the manufacturing process.

The remainder of the moulded seat systems use additional processes to produce the definitive seat. Probably the simplest, and that requiring the least capital equipment, is made from Hexcelite thermoplastic net (Eden, 1978). One layer of Hexcelite is placed over the inside surface of the casting bag to reproduce the patient's shape and additional layers, to increase the strength, are placed on the outside surface of this first layer once it has been removed from the casting bags. The net-type construction allows ventilation of the skin but if required can be lined with an upholstery material which will reduce this effect.

The remaining moulded seating systems rely on the use of plaster of Paris (POP) to duplicate the patient's shape either by pouring liquid POP into the casting bag (Wijkmans, 1978) or by laying several small (or one large) POP bandages into the casting bags (Ring et al, 1978; McQuilton and Johnson, 1981). Hand lay-up, drape forming (McQuilton and Johnson, 1981), or vacuum forming techniques

(Ring et al, 1978; McQuilton and Johnson, 1981; Nelham, 1975), are used to mould thermoplastic foam such as Plastazote or Evazote on to the plaster cast for the lining material of the seat. This is followed by an outer layer of polyethylene or acrylo-nitrile-butadiene-styrene (ABS) to produce a semi-rigid supportive shell. Excess material is removed and the position and shape of the harnessing, together with the attitude of the seat shell, are established during a fitting stage before final finishing and delivery to the patient.

The methods used to fit a seat shell into a wheelchair vary from the use of suitably designed brackets to mount it directly to the wheelchair frame to the production of foam, tubular metal or plastic sub-frames that allow the seat shell to be used in locations other than in a wheelchair (Fig. 14/6). The indications and contra-indications for the supply of moulded seat shells are, as yet, ill defined and it is often only after the patient has been positioned in the vacuum consolidation casting bags that a final decision on the suitability of such a support may be determined.

SHAPEABLE MATRIX

A shapeable matrix material has been developed to allow the production of an adjustable, re-useable moulded seat (Cousins et al, 1982). The material consists of a number of relatively small discreet plastic and metal components which articulate with each other and are assembled in a sheet form prior to shaping into a moulded seat. The articulating surfaces are locked by means of a screw in each of the alternate components once the desired shape has been achieved (Fig. 14/8). Components are removed to enable three-dimensional shapes

Fig. 14/8
Components
of shapeable
matrix

to be produced or to reduce the overall weight when the maximum strength of the structure is not required.

The finished seat is upholstered with standard modules of covered foam to enable the whole seating system to be produced with 'off the shelf' components (Figs. 14/9 and 14/10). As the child grows or a deformity changes the seat shape can be modified by altering the relative positions of the components or can be made larger by adding more components. The matrix material may also be re-used for other patients or can be used to construct any body-contouring equipment such as a cushion.

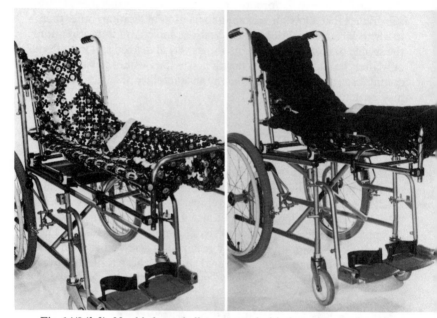

Fig. 14/9 (*left*) Moulded seat shell constructed with shapeable matrix
Fig. 14/10 (*right*) Shapeable matrix seat upholstered with modular sections of padding

SOME DISABILITY RELATED SEATING CONSIDERATIONS

Cerebral palsy (CP)

The floppy CP child is often easier to seat than the spastic or athetoid, for whom it is sometimes extremely difficult to obtain a good posture. It is important to obtain a stable base to the cushion or seating system and to abduct the hips to provide a wide sitting base and to help induce a lumbar lordosis which leads to extension of the spine and ultimately a good posture. Flexion of the hips to resist extension spasms is likely to be required but over-flexion should be avoided in order to prevent a fully flexed posture from being adopted. The seating or positioning of any child with cerebral palsy is a time-consuming occupation since the child will take some time to respond to the new position and is often naturally resistant to any change. It is necessary to ensure that sufficient time is taken to evaluate fully the posture achieved.

Mild rotation spasms can often be controlled by harnessing or a combination of harnessing and padding, but any strong tendency to rotation will be extremely difficult and often impossible to control by seating techniques alone. A moulded seat shell may be the only solution but is unlikely to do more than just support any rotation that is exhibited and although the posture will appear to be very unsatisfactory it may be the best that can be achieved within the constraints of comfort and function.

The child's therapy programme and potential for development of voluntary postural control must be considered when deciding how much postural support to give and it is likely that the CP child will require at least two different seating systems. One to provide a supported posture to allow hand function and education and another which offers less support to stimulate the child's own voluntary postural control. A combination of these two requirements in one seating system is unlikely to produce a satisfactory result.

Spina bifida

Special or contoured cushions are the most frequent provision for children with spina bifida. A moulded seat shell may also be indicated to support a deteriorating spine, in which case it is tempting to support the patient under the axillae. Such support should be avoided if possible; also excessive loading on the rib cage since this may impede respiration. The respiration rate should be checked both before and after the positioning of the child and a check for cyanosis also made. Cyanosis sometimes occurs in the child whose spine is collapsing forward and the only solution is to pull the child back to increase vital capacity. This may be achieved with harnessing and a broad chest pad or a pad fitted between the thighs and the lower rib cage, provided the thighs are not subjected to excessive pressure.

Many children with spina bifida will be incontinent and the method of urine drainage or collection has to be taken into consideration when positioning the child. Excessive hip flexion may cause reverse flow of urine and hence leakage and the route of any catheter used for drainage should not be compromised by posture or pressure.

Bony prominences such as a kyphotic spine should be adequately protected or padded when the child is being cast for a moulded seat. Once the seat has been cast the padding can be removed to check that clearance exists and that no supportive forces are being applied to the bony prominence.

Muscular dystrophy

Children with muscular dystrophy and similar disabilities (such as spinal muscular atrophy) are likely to develop a spinal deformity and should therefore be treated before its onset. The introduction of a lumbar lordosis may be successful in preventing, or at least delaying, the development of a scoliosis, but this cannot be achieved by seating systems alone unless they are reclined by at least 15 degrees, which is not a functional position. The recommended procedure is to fit the patient with a spinal jacket to induce lordosis and then provide whatever cushioning and posture support is required to establish a functional position.

For those who cannot wear a spinal jacket the introduction of a lumbar lordosis may be contra-indicated since it may lead to premature collapse in the anterior direction. A moulded seat may be indicated to provide the child with a lateral support system which can be transferred from a wheelchair to a domestic chair or to a vehicle. A block of Temper-foam may be placed in the vacuum casting bags before the moulded seat is cast and the block transferred to the seat to give the child greater freedom of movement in the moulded seat.

If an electric wheelchair is used it may be desirable to put the control box in the centre to prevent the child from leaning to one side, which may contribute to the development of a scoliosis. As muscle power declines to the point where the joystick control of the wheelchair cannot be operated, touch controls can be fitted which require only slight finger movement to control the direction of the chair.

The maintenance of function is the essential feature of any seating system and if this results in less than an ideal posture it should be accepted. As the power of the trunk muscles declines the lower rib may come into contact with the iliac crest, which will lead to discomfort and a tendency to rotate to alleviate the discomfort. Support is provided to delay the onset of this situation but ultimately it is likely to occur and, again, has to be accepted. The spasmodic and sometimes rapid regression of this condition necessitates frequent revision of the seating requirements, and much experimentation.

Brittle bones (osteogenesis imperfecta, fragilitas ossium)

The main purpose of a seating system, usually a moulded seat shell, for this condition is to enable the child who is severely affected to sit at the normal chronological age and then later on to ease management. The seat shell protects the child from the potentially damaging environment and he can be moved from place to place while in the seat, thus preventing the breakage of bones that can so easily happen during normal everyday activities.

GENERAL POINTS

No seating system can correct a deformity unless an orthosis is prescribed at the same time and the seating system and the orthosis are then used together. The child should not sit in the seating system nor maintain the same posture for more than two hours at a time as this may lead to the development of joint contractures or tissue damage. The child's feet should be well supported unless this is contra-indicated as in some cases of cerebral palsy where hip extension may result. The foot-rest height should be adjusted so that it is not sufficiently high to induce increased pressures on the ischial tuberosities nor too low, which may lead to excess pressure on the distal thighs and hence oedema of the legs, ankles and feet.

Where possible, an asymmetric posture should be avoided and the child should not be expected to adopt a posture that is a drastic change from that experienced prior to the clinic visit. Such changes are often only achieved by a progressive sequence of small changes. If a child has a fixed deformity in one joint the other joints should be kept under observation and mobility encouraged by exercise or passive manipulation.

Some seating systems, particularly moulded seat shells and those requiring wheelchair modifications, may alter the balance of the wheelchair and hence the safety. The stability of the wheelchair should always be checked in use to DHSS specifications after any major modifications to the patient's posture, including elevation of the legs.

CONCLUSIONS

In a perfect world, the assessment of a wheelchair user's requirements and the prescription and supply of the correct equipment would be the responsibility of a trained clinic team. The authors are fortunate to be part of such a team, which includes a doctor, therapist and rehabilitation engineering technician. An orthotist and rehabilitation engineer are consulted as required, as are other relevant disciplines such as social workers. The professional team members must not exclude the child and the parents nor disregard their comments since it is essential to establish the methods of transfer, modes of travel and the family lifestyle.

This 'ideal' clinic team will not be available at many centres but, having gathered those members who are available, it is essential that the clinic is conducted in a relaxed, informal atmosphere in order that the child's 'normal' posture and reactions to changes may be accurately assessed. Failure to do so will result in inefficient seating or a bad posture which will jeopardise the child's chances of reaching his full potential, not to mention the waste of everybody's time.

REFERENCES

Cousins, S. J., Ackerley, K. and Jones, K. N. (1982). *A body support system for the disabled* 75–83. Report 1982, Bioengineering Centre, Roehampton.

Denne, W. A. (1978). *Some properties of sheepskin and polyurethane foam*, 9–12. In *Seating Systems for the Disabled* (ed Ring, N. D.). Biological Engineering Society, London.

Dunkel, R. H. and Trefler, E. (1977). Seating for cerebral palsied children, the Sleek Seat. *Physical Therapy*, 57(5), 524–6.

Eden, S. (1978). *The use of Hexcelite in the manufacture of moulded seat supports*, 21–5. In *Seating Systems for the Disabled* (ed Ring, N. D.). Biological Engineering Society, London.

Fisher, S. V., Szymke, T. E., Apte, S. Y. and Kosiak, M. (1978). Wheelchair cushion effect on skin temperature. *Archives of Physical Medicine and Rehabilitation*, 59, 68–72.

Germans, F. H., Koster, M. W., Kwee, H. H., v.d. Mey, N., Sorejanto, R. and Wijkmans, D. W. (1975). Vacuum dilatency casting for the construction of individually moulded seats, *International Clinical Information Bulletin*, 14(5), 1–9.

Jay, P. (1983a). *Choosing the Best Wheelchair Cushion for Your Needs, Your Chair and Your Lifestyle*. Royal Association for Disability and Rehabilitation, London.

Jay, P. (1983b). *Wheelchair Cushions*. Report to the DHSS Aids Assessment Programme. HMSO, London.

Koreska, J. and Albisser, A. M. (1975). A new foam for the support of the physically handicapped. *Biomedical Engineering*, 10(2), 56–8; 62.

McQuilton, G. and Johnson, G. R. (1981). Cost-effective moulded seating for the handicapped child. *Prosthetics and Orthotics International*, 5, 37–41.

Motloch, W. (1977). Seating and positioning for the physically impaired, *Orthotics and Prosthetics*, 31(2), 11–21.

Motloch, W. et al (1979). *Seating systems for body support and prevention of tissue trauma.* Progress Report 2, Spinal Cord Injury Service, V.A. Hospital Palo Alto, California.

Nelham, R. L. (1975). The manufacture of moulded supportive seating for the handicapped. *Biomedical Engineering,* **10,** 379–81.

Nicholls, P. J. R. and Strange, T. V. (1972). A method of casting severely deformed and disabled patients. *Rheumatology and Physical Medicine,* **11**(7), 356–9.

Ring, N. D., Nelham, R. L. and Pearson, F. A. (1978). Moulded supportive seating for the disabled. *Prosthetics and Orthotics International,* **2,** 30–4.

Rose, G. K. et al (1979). *Annual Progress Report* No. 5, 100–9. ORLAU, The Robert Jones and Agnes Hunt Orthopaedic Hospital, Oswestry, Salop, England.

Scrutton, D. (1978). Chapter in *The Care of the Handicapped Child* (ed Apley, J.). Clinics in Developmental Medicine, Spastics International Medical Publications, William Heinemann Medical Books Limited, London.

Stewart, S. F. C., Palmieri, V. and Cochran, G. V. B. (1980). Wheelchair cushion effect on skin temperature, heat flux and relative humidity. *Archives of Physical Medicine and Rehabilitation,* **61,** 229–33.

Wijkmans, D. W. (1978). *The TNO-vacuum-formfixation system,* 32–7. In *Seating Systems for the Disabled* (ed Ring, N. D.). Biological Engineering Society, London.

FURTHER READING

Noble, P. C. (1981). *The Prevention of Pressure Sores in Persons with Spinal Cord Injuries,* Monograph No. 11. World Rehabilitation Fund Inc, New York.

ACKNOWLEDGEMENT

Figures 14/1, 14/2, 14/7a, 14/7b, 14/9 and 14/10 first appeared in Nelham, R.L. (1984). 'Principles and practice in the manufacture of seating for the handicapped.' *Physiotherapy,* **70,** 54–8. They are reproduced by permission of the editor.

Chapter 15

Rehabilitation Engineering

by N. D. RING MA, MSc, CEng, MIMechE *and*
A. W. S. BROWN MSc, MBES

The contribution of engineering to the rehabilitation of disabled people can be traced back many thousands of years. Indeed, it is recorded that one Egyptian mummy was found to have an artificial leg, although this may well have been supplied after death to complete the body before its journey into the next life. Nevertheless, technology has been used for many centuries to aid the doctor in his desire to rehabilitate his patient to the highest level of independence.

The formal use of the term rehabilitation engineering goes back only to the 1960s. At that time bioengineering was in its infancy and the discipline of rehabilitation engineering emerged as that branch of bioengineering associated with the treatment of the disabled. Its aim is to help the handicapped person to achieve maximum independence personally, socially and in employment.

THE ROLE OF THE REHABILITATION ENGINEER

The inclusion of the rehabilitation engineer in the multidisciplinary team at an early stage is vital. His contribution as he works alongside his medical, paramedical and education colleagues will inevitably vary from case to case, but his potential contribution is relevant at all stages of the rehabilitation programme. In *assessment* baseline data are recorded; in *training* he may provide or modify equipment which will assist in the development of a particular function; in *treatment* he may provide equipment to supplement or complement natural body functions or to allow an increased level of independence to be achieved.

Traditionally, engineers work from a specification of the problem to be solved and the performance to be attained within the solution. This principle applies as much to the field of rehabilitation as it does to space technology. The major difference is that in rehabilitation the engineer's colleagues are not, in general, 'technically trained', i.e. they are not engineers. For this reason the engineer should be involved at the earliest possible opportunity in order to be able to help define the problem and then propose solutions using engineering principles and technology of which his colleagues may be unaware. This applies both to low-level technology, such as may be required for the management of incontinence, and to the sophisticated technology applicable to, say, the provision of synthetic speech to help a child with communication problems.

THE REHABILITATION ENGINEERING PROCESS

It will be helpful to understand the stages by which a piece of equipment is produced to solve a particular problem. They are as follows:

1. Definition of the problem and proposal of a solution
2. Specification
3. Design
4. Development of the one-off piece of equipment
5. Instruction in its use
6. Assessment of effectiveness
7. Design for production
8. Manufacture
9. Market.

When a child is assessed it may become clear that he has some functional problem which is amenable to solution only by some external aid. Consider, for example, a boy with severe athetoid cerebral palsy. He may be unable to urinate standing up due to his poor lower limb co-ordination. If he sits on the lavatory he may be unable to direct the flow of urine into the lavatory bowl because of his poor posture and upper limb control. Thus, the solutions available are either for him to wear a nappy or for his mother or other escort to hold him in an appropriate position, whether standing or seated. While these may be acceptable for the younger child they are clearly not so for an older boy. The first stage is to suggest a solution: in this case a chute or funnel which will reliably catch the stream of urine when the boy is seated on the toilet and direct it into the pan.

Stage two is to draw up a specification. In the case cited this is comparatively simple, the only addition to the performance specification being that the funnel, or deflector, should be completely safe in terms of material, shape and performance. If the boy exhibits a strong hip extensor spasm the deflector must not cause him any damage. The detailed specification and design go hand-in-hand in this case, the design being very simple (Fig. 15/1). For reasons of hygiene and

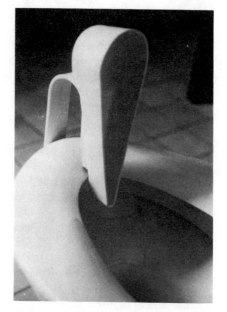

Fig. 15/1 Urine deflector
mounted on conventional
toilet seat

simplicity of construction the deflector in this solution is moulded
from sheet plastic. An integral plastic spring-clip holds the deflector
on the lavatory seat and allows easy release in the event of hip extensor
spasm.

Once a device has been made it should be assessed at two levels.
First, does it satisfy the particular need? Second, can it be generalised
to help others? If so the final stages of the engineering process can be
carried out, namely, design for production, manufacturing and
marketing. No rehabilitation engineer should be satisfied until this
full process has been completed and it is his responsibility to ensure
that each stage of the process is completed effectively.

PROSTHETICS

Although a prosthesis is the term given to any replacement part of the
body, whether eye, tooth, hip or leg, this section will focus only on
artificial limbs.

Any article worn on the body has to be considered carefully to
ensure its compatibility with the body, particularly at the contact
surface. Thus, the socket of an artificial limb is critical since it
provides the link between an animate member, the stump, and an
inanimate object, the prosthesis. The socket must be capable of

transmitting load, of providing a stable and secure attachment and of exhibiting the right degree of compliance to ensure that the stump does not become damaged or irritated. Further, the materials used must be able to withstand normal body fluids such as sweat and, perhaps, urine without excessively reducing heat loss from the stump, which would lead to discomfort.

Other engineering considerations are weight, reliability and ease of putting on and taking off (donning and doffing) of the prosthesis. Cosmesis, in particular, has several aspects. First, the limb should have a pleasing visual appearance, both statically and in its movement patterns. Second, its surface 'feel' should be soft; a hard surface is conspicuous when knocked against, or by, another object. Third, it should be quiet in operation. Finally, it should be inconspicuous when worn under normal clothing. (Failure to achieve these aspects leads to attention being drawn to the limb wearer.)

Power source and control

As a result of the tragedy of the early 1960s associated with the drug thalidomide, much publicity was given to externally powered artificial arms. These made use of a portable power supply in the form of a battery or cylinder of compressed gas. Because of their complex design it was often assumed that these arms must be 'better'. However, it is important to balance the 'blinding' effect of technology with the practical aspects of functional living.

Any artificial arm, if it is functional as opposed to being purely a sleeve-filler, must have both a source of energy and the ability to control the flow of this energy. Traditionally this has involved the amputee wearing a shoulder harness from which cables pass to each joint. Through these cables motion and force are transmitted from the shoulder girdle to the various joints so both the energy and the control are available directly from the wearer and, which is most important, he has a remarkable amount of 'feel' through the cable. In contrast, the externally powered arm has an external source (such as a battery) and the flow of energy is controlled through, say, switches. Thus, any 'feel' has to be introduced artificially through the hardware and the relationship between this 'fed-back' information and the arm's performance has to be learnt. While this is possible, the extra hardware involved in achieving it and the difficulty of realising a really good relationship between the hardware and the child, makes this approach substantially unsuccessful, particularly where several motions of the arm are required simultaneously. In the majority of cases the additional weight, the unreliability and the appearance lead the children to reject the limbs in favour of other means.

The one exception is, perhaps, the use of the myoelectric signals available from residual muscles. The voltage level generated by a contracting muscle is approximately proportional to muscle tension. By using this voltage to cause an electric motor to move the fingers of a prosthetic hand it is possible to have close control over the speed of closure and the gripping force. This technique, which uses a signal related to force, is less successful for the proximal joints, such as the elbow, since control of position (as opposed to force) then becomes more significant.

The reasons for choice of a particular energy source and control system (for externally-powered artificial arms) are beyond the scope of this book. Compressed carbon dioxide was favoured until the mid-seventies but, with the advent of microelectronics and the lighter electro-magnetic materials, electrical sources now tend to be more appropriate.

ORTHOTICS

There are certain aspects of an orthosis which should be considered from an engineering standpoint. Some of these, such as fit, weight and ease of 'donning and doffing' are similar to the prosthetic cases and will not be discussed; however, considerable advance has been made in other aspects of this field in recent years which are worthy of consideration.

With the introduction of lighter and more durable materials has come the development of a number of different forms of bracing system, having features which make them far more acceptable to the patient than has been the case in the past. Not the least important of these features is the cosmetic one, since this ensures a much wider acceptance of some forms of obvious physical disability by the community, reduces to some extent the stigma of physical handicap and improves the confidence and self-respect of the disabled person.

Combined with this cosmetic benefit has come the ability to design an orthosis far more critically to match the individual child's need. For instance, the stiffness of an orthosis can now be 'fine tuned' (see Fig. 12/2, p. 229) to give controlled resistance at, say, the ankle in the ankle-foot orthosis (AFO) (Engen, 1971). However, with the greater freedom of choice which the clinician now enjoys comes the responsibility of ensuring that adequate safety standards are maintained. It is therefore necessary to have some means of assessing the type and magnitude of the forces which the orthoses should be designed to support, and to draw up manufacturing guidelines and performance specifications accordingly. Unfortunately, this is a field in which very little empirical information is available. Even in situations where traditional designs and methods of manufacture can be employed, using modern, lightweight materials of considerable strength, there is no means presently available of ensuring that optimal strength-to-weight ratios are obtained.

One of the roles of the rehabilitation engineer is to set up programmes of appropriate clinically based research to attempt to obtain the information necessary and to make it available to manufacturers. This research should also test and evaluate existing designs in order to highlight the advantages and disadvantages of each, and to suggest practical ways in which such equipment can be improved, standardised, or manufactured more quickly, cheaply and efficiently.

Gait analysis

Many clinicians express the desire to assess and record a patient's gait pre- and postoperatively. Several parameters could be recorded, but it is only relevant to record those which can be used meaningfully by the clinician if a complex and expensive research study is to be avoided. The analysis associated with the above project on orthotics describes gait in terms of timing and methods of ambulation, as well as recording normal activity. Crutch-assisted locomotion is a particularly energy-consuming procedure, and it is important to ensure that orthotic designs assist and, where possible, take into account, the patient's independent mobility.

There are several methods available for the analysis of gait. These include direct observation, measurements made from sequential still-frame ciné or multiple exposure static photographs (Fig. 15/2) or the examination of freeze-frame video records using digital methods on a computer. Analysis of gait can also be applied to other groups such as amputees, stroke patients and sportsmen.

In addition to direct observation, there are various sophisticated electronic devices which have been developed to track the motion or record relative angles of individual body segments. The majority of these make use of active or passive visual, infra red or ultrasonic targets attached to points of interest on the subject. Electronic equipment is used to detect and follow the motion or angle of each target. On-line computing facilities are required for the automatic acquisition, reduction, storage and display of three-dimensional target trajectory data from video cameras.

Fig. 15/2 Multiple exposure photography used in gait analysis

The position of the subject's centre of gravity, the interaction of his feet with the floor, and the forces and timing associated with this interaction can also be important factors in the analysis of gait. Floor interaction forces are typically obtained by means of force plates set into the surfaces over which the subject is required to walk, or by means of limb load monitors in the form of specially instrumented footwear. Events of particular interest, such as heel-strike (HS) and toe-off (TO) can be obtained with foot switches, or by using arrays of electronic contacts positioned along the walkway.

VEHICLES

Next to the inability to speak the lack of independent mobility is probably the greatest restriction to a life of independence. Thus every effort should be made to provide a suitable means of mobility, compatible with the child's disability, which provides him with maximum freedom.

Although independent mobility includes the use of prostheses or orthoses it is wheeled mobility which is discussed. (See Chapter 13, and other relevant sections.) This wheeled mobility should be subdivided into three categories, namely vehicles required for (a) transport for functional living; (b) recreation; and (c) therapy. Clearly one vehicle may come into all three categories but the needs of the child in each category must be considered.

INCONTINENCE

The management of incontinence has been discussed in Chapter 5: this section is concerned with the engineering aspects of aids and appliances.

Most incontinence appliances are designed to deal with urine once it has left the body. Their function is to catch urine, without leakage, at whatever flow rates and volumes the body expels it and to channel it away to a place of storage to be dealt with later.

It is much easier to attach appliances to the male than to the female anatomy and as a result there are no satisfactory female urinals on the market. Disposable absorbent pads are often the best solution available to the incontinent woman and come in a range of shapes and sizes. They do not cope very well with high flow rates of urine and there is much research effort directed at improving their performance. They are also bulky, although pads are beginning to come on to the market containing the so-called 'hydrogels'. These materials occupy very little volume when they are dry and are capable of absorbing many times their own volume in urine.

For males, a sheath appliance with a drainage bag attached to the leg or wheelchair is often the simplest solution. The sheath is usually secured around the penis using a skin adhesive; much improved adhesives have appeared on the market in recent years so that sheaths can be worn undisturbed for several days. However, soreness of the penile tissue can still be a problem as the skin is continually bathed in urine. Pubic pressure urinals, incorporating a drainage bag, are rather more cumbersome but are re-usable and may be especially useful when the penis is too small for a sheath to be attached effectively. The outer cone of the urinal often has an inner sheath or diaphragm to impede leakage.

There has been a renewed interest in the use of electrical stimulators to promote continence in recent years. Techniques based on electrical stimulation continue to be the subject of much research but they are not yet well understood and few people currently benefit from them. Similarly, development work continues on implanted urethral cuffs designed to simulate the function of a healthy sphincter, but they are not widely used at present. There are also a number of external devices which supplement the function of the urethral sphincter rather more crudely.

A brief description of the construction and working of many incontinence aids and appliances (except stoma appliances) will be found in *Directory of Aids* available from the Association of Continence Advisors, 346 Kensington High Street, London W14 8NS.

DISORDERS OF MOVEMENT AND CONTROL

Patients whose disabilities relate to spasticity, or to uncontrolled or spontaneous involuntary limb and postural movement patterns, encounter distinct and serious barriers to independence (see Chapters 6 and 7). Their problems of daily living are multiple, including mobility, communication, feeding, toileting and control of the environment. The engineer's task is to contribute to overcoming these problems by the design of equipment or by modifying the environment.

Frequently these cases, typified by the athetoid cerebral palsied patients, present some voluntary component of movement, superimposed upon an often overwhelming spontaneous, uncontrolled and unpredictable pattern, which results in almost total lack of useful function. There is no cure for the condition, but several approaches are possible to improve a child's independence.

Biofeedback training (BFT)

There is evidence to suggest that some of the above patients can be assisted by suitable training, or by supplementing their natural sensory mechanisms with auxiliary feedback information in the form of some processed visual, vibratory or auditory representation of their actual movements. There are numbers of augmented sensory feedback techniques which have been investigated at various rehabilitation engineering centres in attempts to deal with certain specific disorders of control or movement. These include the development of devices to assist in the control of posture, head attitude, joint position, curvature of the spine, balance, uniformity of gait and drooling.

The theory behind BFT arises from the recognition that human performance is degraded if response is delayed by more than a few hundredths of a second following initiation. Thus if a child who exhibits poor head control has to rely on his parent or therapist to tell him to hold his head upright whenever it falls to one side, he is unable easily to reverse the neuromuscular activity which caused or allowed this 'fall' since too long a delay has occurred between the event and the corrective command. By fitting a head attitude monitor it is possible to give the child some instantaneous augmented feedback in the form of, for example, a tone whose frequency increases as his head moves from a vertical position (Fig. 15/3). Such a device not only trains the child to make corrective responses but can also be used as a permanent and inconspicuous device by building the device into, for example, lightweight headphones which are now socially acceptable due to the modern pop culture.

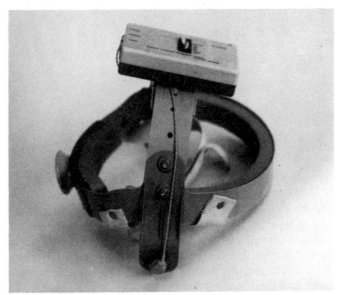

Fig. 15/3 Head position trainer with adjustable threshold for tilt angle

Involuntary limb movements

Techniques are also available for direct mechanical assistance, where appropriate. These generally endeavour to eliminate or compensate for involuntary components of movement, while allowing intentioned components to remain relatively unhindered. Most of these attempts are directed towards improving hand or arm function to assist in writing, feeding, or in the operation of external devices such as wheelchairs, communication aids or environmental control equipment (Fig. 15/4).

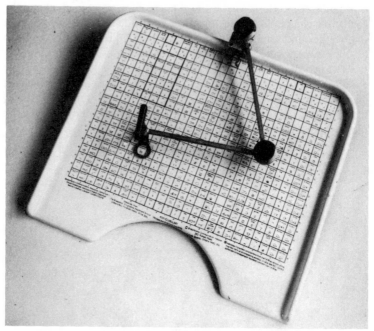

Fig. 15/4 Pointer using viscous dampers to assist communication

Assistance usually takes the form of a body-worn or table-mounted bracing system, incorporating some mechanical device to provide resistance to certain components of movement. If this resistance is in the form of friction it has the disadvantages of having to be pre-set to a given force level and also that the force required to initiate movement is greater than that required to maintain it. However, viscous devices, similar to the anti-slam devices fitted to doors, provide resistance approximately proportional to the velocity of movement. Thus they allow slow, intentioned motion to proceed unhindered, while filtering out the more rapid spontaneous or involuntary components. Table-mounted equipment is to be preferred to body-worn since the latter tends to tire the patient, and is difficult to conceal under clothing.

In order to provide aids which assist a patient in making optimal use of his residual voluntary facilities an appropriate knowledge of the movement characteristics of the individual is required. There is a need for his unrestrained movements to be monitored, together with the ways in which they are modified by his attempts to perform particular tasks. These measurements can yield specific design information for the construction of aids such as those described and can also provide a means of evaluating the ultimate benefit of the aid to the patient.

At Chailey, an ultrasonic method is used to track the unrestricted motion of the hand or fingertip. The data thus obtained can be used to identify certain features in the involuntary movement characteristics of different patients. This study is not yet complete, but it will enable equipment of general applicability to a wide range of patients to be designed and constructed. Additionally, by obtaining a mathematical representation of the motion characteristics of a wide variety of patients, it is hoped that a correlation with clinical descriptions can be obtained, and used to classify the nature and extent of physical disabilities.

This technique also provides a means of assessing the optimal placement and type of control interface to be used by a patient to operate equipment such as electronic communication, environmental control or mobility aids.

This study is not confined to the investigation of involuntary movement patterns only, but also includes an examination of involuntary force characteristics. This work involves the recording of isometric force patterns produced by the patients when performing video-based tracking tasks.

DISORDERS OF COMMUNICATION

A communication disorder is undoubtedly one of the most frustrating disabilities. It frequently afflicts individuals who have normal intellectual capacities and yet who are unable to communicate even their most basic needs, thoughts, emotions or ideas to others. Considerable progress has been made in recent years in this field and, with the ready availability of modern electronic technology at an ever-decreasing cost, a promising future, with genuine prospects of useful and gainful employment, is becoming available to large numbers of severely physically handicapped people.

Improvements and rationalisations of methods of communication and the introduction of new methods of expression, such as the Blissymbol system and the Makaton vocabulary, (which have developed in parallel and have been shown to complement each other with remarkable effect) go hand in hand with technological progress. Although the majority of electronic aids provide painfully slow rates of communication, an often unavoidable drawback occasioned by the poor control ability of the disabled person, the inherent 'intelligence' offered by microprocessor technology can improve the situation significantly.

The range of equipment now available is very wide, in terms of both capability and price. Thus it is vital that great care is taken in assessing a child as described in Chapter 17, in order to establish both his communication ability and his physical capabilities as they relate to communication. For instance, is his seating adequate to hold him in a good position to use equipment? Has he the ability to operate switches if required and, if so, where should they be positioned? Is he capable of learning an encoded input system, similar to Morse code, if this is necessary for the selection of letters on a display?

When selecting particular equipment many features should be considered: portability, reliability, ease of operation, cost and service back-up. As more complex systems are considered the assessor must be sufficiently self-disciplined not to be carried away by the elegance of the technology but to satisfy himself that the device is genuinely most suitable for the requirements of the particular child!

The rate of communication is frequently the first priority. The most rapid method of selection is by 'direct access', e.g. pointing to a letter or symbol board by hand or by using a head-mounted pointer or torch (Figs. 15/5, 15/6, 15/7). This can then be extended, if required, to incorporate sensors so that the letter indicated is simultaneously displayed on a screen. However, taking this step may have significant financial implications.

There are now several purpose-made microprocessor based communication aids available commercially. They tend to be expensive, and service back-up may be costly, inadequate and unreliable. The main reason for this is the relatively small quantity produced of any particular item, with the result that there is only a limited number of qualified technologists familiar with the intricacies of such specialised devices. The 'home computer', on the other hand, can be made to simulate the majority of these devices if appropriate programs are written, and this equipment is usually readily obtainable

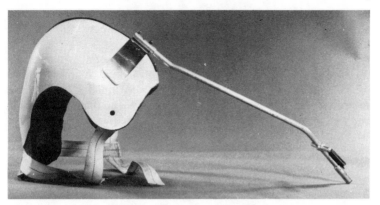

Fig. 15/5 Head mounted pointer

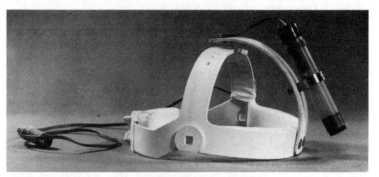

Fig. 15/6 Head mounted torch

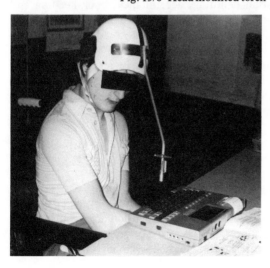

Fig. 15/7
The head-mounted
pointer in use!

at a fraction of the price of a comparable specialised aid. In addition, service facilities are more widely available for the majority of these machines.

One of the most exciting research areas at present is that of the production of artificial speech. Current talking machines allow considerable room for improvement in voice quality, particularly regarding the reproduction of the juvenile and female voices in equipment where an unlimited vocabulary is required. However, the flexibility of vocabulary, portability, economy of power consumption and intelligibility are all improving steadily, and there can be little doubt that the solutions to the above criticisms are close at hand.

ENVIRONMENTAL CONTROL, RECREATION, EDUCATION AND EMPLOYMENT

Microcomputer systems also offer a degree of flexibility seldom found in 'dedicated' or purpose-built electronic aids in that they can be made to perform a multiplicity of functions such as the remote control of television sets, lights, telephones, doors and domestic heating merely by running computer programs appropriate to the particular tasks. In addition, they can provide functions such as recreation in the form of television games and the presentation of reading material, control of electronic toys and the synthesis of music.

The well-established advances in computer aided learning are also available to the disabled person, as are the facilities of word processing, information handling, accountancy, book-keeping and stock control. All these combine to allow a severely physically disabled individual access to a variety of intellectually and financially rewarding opportunities for employment.

The microcomputer will not only revolutionise almost all aspects of life for the able-bodied, but is also likely to improve the lot of the disabled person to such an extent that he will be able to compete on equal terms in the career of his choice.

INTERFACES

One of the most neglected aspects of electronic aids concerns their control by disabled users. Most equipment is developed on the assumption that some sort of patient operated actuator, which can be represented by one or more switches, a joystick or other input device, is available. The exact nature of this actuator, which is fundamental to the patient's efficient or optimal use of the equipment, is seldom given the consideration it requires. It is frequently the case that an otherwise well conceived and engineered design is discarded by the user after a short period of frustration, merely because the type of input, and the mode in which it was tested were inappropriate for his capabilities. The specific means of input to the aid are personal to the user and will frequently have to be specially constructed. In addition, the system software in a microprocessor-based system which is written to accept an input signal from this device, should be personalised for the particular user, possibly by means of some programmed assessment session. This specially developed program can then form an integral part of all programs to be used by the patient on his equipment. As long as there is some provision made in the software for the normal variation in the user's capabilities, there is no need for the assessment to be performed more than once.

If the matching of a particular aid to a patient has been carried out with care and attention the same input device may be used to operate both a communication aid and an electric wheelchair. This might take the form of a joystick which is capable of controlling the direction and speed of a scanning light on a communication board in one use and the direction and speed of the wheelchair in another. In each case there could be a proportional relationship between displacement of the joystick from a centre position and the speed of the output, and between the direction of displacement and the direction of motion.

The cost and portability of self-contained microcomputer systems are improving rapidly, and it is now possible to provide a disabled person with a portable, battery powered unit appropriately programmed to act purely as a matching device between him and other equipment. This means that a disabled person can, through his personalised input computer, operate another unmodified computer system running standard programmes, and thus control other equipment which was not originally designed to accommodate his specific disability.

AIDS TO DAILY LIVING

Frequently an aid is thought of purely in the context of a disabled person, separating that person from so-called 'normal' people. In reality, an aid is a tool or device for making difficult tasks easier, or impossible tasks possible.

An aid must be acceptable in its appearance, functional in its use and cost effective.

The key person through whom a child receives an aid is frequently his therapist. The role of engineer in prescribing aids is to help the team define the need in terms which are amenable to solution, to use his knowledge of different aspects of technology, to support and discuss possible solutions and to design and manufacture an aid which satisfies the broad specification agreed between the child, the therapist and himself. A cheaply-made device which conveys the principles of operation and can be used to check critical dimensions can be invaluable in saving time and money by giving opportunity for the design to be modified before the definitive aid is made.

Once the aid is completed it is the engineer's responsibility to evaluate it. Does it satisfy the requirements? Are there other children who could benefit from a similar device? Could it, with some modifications, be applied to a wider range of functional disability? Is it relevant to produce a small batch for trial as a forerunner to production and marketing? Such questions must be faced squarely and answered responsibly if the effort expended is going to be cost effective in terms of both time and money.

REHABILITATION ENGINEERING SERVICES

In this chapter it has been convenient to consider various aspects of rehabilitation engineering as engineering topics. The danger of such treatment of the subject is that the hardware can appear to take precedence over the child. That must never occur. In considering rehabilitation engineering services as part of a total treatment facility, the individual child and his particular needs must always be uppermost.

Any rehabilitation engineering service must be comprehensive in character and integrated in operation. The comprehensive nature allows a close working relationship between the various engineering disciplines – mechanical, electronics, materials science and so on – and its integration with the medical, paramedical and other supporting disciplines is essential for its success.

Rehabilitation engineering movement advisory panel (REMAP)

There are a number of REMAPs distributed throughout the UK who are able to solve one-off problems experienced by handicapped people. Membership of the panels varies but consists largely of 10–15 volunteers from industry, universities and colleges, social services and the health service. These engineers, technicians, therapists and social workers investigate solutions to individual problems and modify existing equipment or design and manufacture devices as required. The panels are organised on a regional basis and the National Organiser is based at the Royal Association for Disability and Rehabilitation (RADAR), 25 Mortimer Street, London W1N 8AB, from whom details of local REMAPs may be obtained.

REFERENCE

Engen, T. J. (1971). *Instruction Manual for Fabrication and Fitting of Below-knee Polypropylene Orthosis.* Department of Orthotics, TIRR, Houston, Texas.

FURTHER READING

Brown, A. W. S. (1978). *The electronic measurement of limb movement and function.* In *Baclofen: Spasticity and Cerebral Pathology* (ed Jukes, A. M.) Cambridge Medical Publications, Northampton.

Cooper, I. S. (1969). In *Involuntary Movement Disorders.* Hoeber Medical Division, Harper and Row, New York.

Foulds, R. A. (1980). *Communication rates for non-speech expression as a function of manual tasks and linguistic constraints,* 83–7. Proceedings of the International Conference on Rehabilitation Engineering, National Research Council, Ottawa.

Goldenberg, E. P. (1979). *Special Technology for Special Children.* University Park Press, Baltimore.

Largent, P. and Waylett, J. (1975). Follow-up study on upper extremity bracing of children with severe athetosis. *American Journal of Occupational Therapy,* **26**, 341.

Morasso, P. and Tagliasco, V. (1983). Analysis of human movements: spatial localisation with multiple perspective views. *Medical and Biological Engineering and Computing,* **21**, 74–82.

Morgan, M. H. (1981). Ataxia – its causes, measurement and management. *International Rehabilitation Medicine,* **2**, 126–32.

Rosen, M. J., Dunfee, D. E. and Edelstein, B. D. (1979). *Suppression of Abnormal Intention Tremor by Application of Viscous Damping.* Proceedings of the 4th Congress of the International Society of Electrophysiology and Kinesthesiology, Boston.

Rosen, M. J. and Goodenough-Trepagnier, C. (1982). Communication systems for the non-vocal motor handicapped: practical prospects. *IEEE Engineering and Medical Biology Magazine,* **1** (4), 31–5.

Schofield, J. (1981). *Microcomputer Based Aids for the Disabled.* British Computer Society Monographs on Informatics.

Vanderheiden, G. C. (1976). *Non-Vocal Communication Resource Book.* University Park Press, Baltimore.

Wooldridge, C. P. and Russell, G. (1976). Head position training with the cerebral palsied child: an application of biofeedback techniques. *Archives of Physical Medicine and Rehabilitation*, 57, 407–14.

Chapter 16

Education

by H. PARROTT CertEd, DipspecEd
and N. J. GARDNER BSc, MEd(EdPsych)

The aim of this chapter is to look at how special education is provided for physically handicapped pupils and the factors affecting choice. Special education has a short history in this country. The first provision for the physically handicapped was made in 1851. The emphasis was very much towards the offering of training for a trade, and education took second place. Well into this century, the pattern remained the same. Chailey Heritage, started in 1903 by Dame Grace Kimmins, was first and foremost a craft school, a title which it still carries today. Education for the handicapped was begun by charitable organisations and individual enterprise, Government intervention being at first in the form of support and later providing a framework upon which the provision, which is now statutory, could be maintained. A look at the legislation over the last 60 years is necessary in order to see the present pattern.

In 1921 the Education Act recognised four categories of handicap – the blind, deaf, defective (comprising physical and mental disability) and epileptic. The parents of any children within these categories were required to see that their children attended a suitable special school until the age of 16 and it was the responsibility of the local education authorities (LEA) to provide the schools. Interestingly enough, they were empowered to provide continuing education over the age of 16.

By the time of the Education Act of 1944, the education authorities were required to meet the needs of children with special needs within their general duty in both primary and secondary education. It also became the responsibility of the authorities to ascertain which children required special educational 'treatment'. Thus was formed a new framework which categorised children according to handicap. This pattern remained until the most recent of the Acts (1981) which decategorised: it was felt that categorisation acted as a barrier to education. Placing a multi-handicapped child was exceedingly difficult in the presence of definitions which were dependent upon, for example, an IQ score or physical disability. The system was in danger of strangling itself and the need for special provision was increasing. There was, according the Department of Education and Science (DES) figures, an increase of nearly 100 000 children in special schools between 1945 and 1977.

The factors affecting the choice of provision may well depend upon the severity of the handicap – but perhaps more positively, the provisions available should relate to the special educational needs of the child. Before describing the provision, however, the procedure of establishing the need of a child for a form of special education will be explained.

The 1944 Act described formal procedures for discovering handicapped children within local education authorities. Parents could be fined for not complying with the request that their child should be seen by a medical officer who would advise as to whether a child suffered from 'any disability of mind or body' and to what degree. The LEA noted the report of the medical officer and the teacher or 'other persons' and made the decision regarding special education. The LEA then had the two duties of notifying the parents and providing the 'treatment'. A certificate was produced, signed by the medical officer. The medical model was complete, consisting of the categories of disability and the term 'treatment'. Although the system became less formal over a period of time, there was an increasing awareness that much was left to be desired. The outcome of the arguments and discussions that took place was the DES circular 2/75 *The Discovery of Children Requiring Special Education and the Assessment of their Needs*. This described the need for a multidisciplinary approach.

It is wholly admirable that now the assessment of a child's needs is not dependent upon one or two people's reports and comments, but that the multidisciplinary approach has been adopted. The Education Act 1981 lays down that for every child for whom a form of special education is deemed necessary a 'statement' will be drawn up describing the needs and the proposals for meeting those needs. This statement will be under constant review. It is now accepted that a number of people become involved in the discovery and assessment of the child with special needs. Perhaps most important of all are the parents of the child whose wishes, knowledge and feelings have not always been satisfactorily used for the good of the child; indeed, the 1981 Act has been called the Parents' Charter. Others involved from the outset include hospital staff, the family doctor, the health visitor, the social worker, voluntary agencies, educational welfare officer, educational psychologist, inspectors and advisers in special education, school medical officers, medical consultants, teachers and the members of the child guidance clinics. Some of these will have information necessary to form a recommendation as to the part that will be played by special education in its many forms. The emphasis in the statement will obviously be dependent upon the child's needs which may well be multiple, but the responsibility to provide lies in the hands of the LEA. Reference is also made in the Act to a 'named person' whose task will be to guide parents through the process of assessing needs and looking at the available provision.

SPECIAL EDUCATIONAL PROVISION

The child with special educational needs may be placed in:
1. An ordinary class with the support of a teacher's aide.
2. An ordinary class with withdrawal to a resource base.
3. An ordinary class with part time in a special class.
4. A special class full time.
5. A day special school part time.
6. A day special school full time.
7. A residential special school.
8. Hospital and a hospital school, or
9. The child may stay at home and have a home tutor.

Local authorities may not be able to provide all these resources but it is up to them to seek suitable provision. If local provision is inadequate, it is the local authorities' responsibility to seek suitable provision elsewhere. The advantages of working closely, and at best, hand in hand with health and social services departments and voluntary bodies can readily be seen.

The needs

The decision must now be reached regarding the matching of need to provision. The Warnock Report (1978) suggests that special educational needs require:

the provision of special means of access to the curriculum through special equipment, facilities or resources, modification of the physical environment or specialist teaching techniques; the provision of special or modified curricula; particular attention to the social structure and emotional climate in which education takes place.

and special education is:

> effective access on a full or part time basis to teachers with appropriate qualifications or substantial experience of both; effective access on a full or part time basis to other professionals with appropriate training; and an educational and physical environment with necessary aids, equipment and resources appropriate to the child's needs

It can be seen then that the emphasis has moved away from the categories previously mentioned to the fact that a child who has need of some form of special education deserves to have it wherever it can be given to the best advantage: the fact that a child is, for example, physically handicapped, must not in itself be a barrier against his receiving education within an ordinary school. The decision as to where a child is to be educated must be made by realising all the child's needs and seeing where they can best be satisfied. In the case of the physically handicapped child this decision will be made by looking at the regional provision of physiotherapy and occupational therapy, speech therapy and so on, in accordance with the 'Statement'.

If a special school, where these facilities are readily available, is going to be the best solution, then it should be recommended. The wishes of the parents and the proximity of the school to the home should also be taken into account. Residential schooling may obviously play an important role in some cases. Having reached the decision of where the education is going to be best received, it is up to that establishment, in conjunction with the authority, to provide it. The child will be reviewed annually and, in this way, close contact will be maintained with all parties. The staff of the establishment however, are the people who will be carrying out the recommended plan.

CURRICULUM

In many cases the special schools for the physically handicapped have a curriculum development problem which is faced by no other school, namely that of educating children representing every aspect of the intellectual range and age range from 2 years of age, from the severely handicapped child who would have come into the category ESN(severe) to the child who is hoping to continue his studies through further education.

At the present time, the majority of children found within schools for the physically handicapped have a specific learning problem as well as having a physical handicap. In this respect the special school is becoming more specialised, especially in the field of educating the multiply-handicapped child, whose needs are physical, intellectual, emotional and social. Discrimination can be positive and the special school has a secure future. Its success will be dependent upon its ability to manage the changes that are likely to occur both in the type of handicap and in the role that the school is to play. As has been suggested, the role of the special school is becoming more clearly defined as more children are educated within the ordinary system. This of course brings with it a great many difficulties related to the management of the curriculum, the way in which the children are taught and the balance made within the school between education and 'training'. This balance is one that must be studied very carefully in the school providing for the handicapped child, for whom the educational input is but one cog within the wheel of development.

Many people become involved in the assessment of the handicapped child before a decision is made regarding special education, and the pattern is certainly reproduced once the child is at his special school. The physically handicapped child is not at school solely for academic education; he will need regular physiotherapy, perhaps speech therapy also. He may have medical needs which require him to attend various clinics or undergo major surgery. In addition, the timetable will include independence training sessions which will perhaps take him away from the classroom setting. All these factors must be taken into account when planning the child's curriculum.

The importance of a regular reviewing system can readily be seen. Without discussion between the disciplines involved, correct priorities are difficult to ascertain. Emphasis must be placed upon each area of development at the correct time and departmental records and observations are an essential part of the reviewing procedure. As the physically handicapped child reaches the last few years of his school life, planning for the future becomes more important and once again the need for an interdisciplinary approach is fundamental to the work. Regular contact with further education establishments, social services and the specialist careers service will ensure that relevant work is being carried out within the school and realistic plans are being made for the individual young person's future.

SPECIAL EDUCATIONAL NEEDS

The 1981 Education Act defines a child with special educational needs as one who has a learning difficulty which is significantly greater than the majority of children of his age, or has a disability which prevents or hinders him making effective use of the educational facilities which are generally provided in schools. As has been stated, LEAs have a duty to ensure that special educational provision is made for children who have special needs and, where possible, this should be provided in ordinary schools. It is therefore important to consider the types of learning difficulty which are commonly encountered in physically handicapped pupils.

It is convenient to divide the physically handicapped into two main categories when considering their educational needs: (1) those in which there is no brain damage such as limb deficiency or arthrogryposis; and (2) those who have neurological damage such as spina bifida with hydrocephalus, or cerebral palsy.

Children in the first category have a primary physical handicap and this may prevent them from making effective use of ordinary educational facilities. They may have problems of access, both to the physical environment, and to the curriculum of an ordinary school. They may therefore require modifications to the school and/or the curriculum and may need aids to enable them to make full use of the resources on offer, such as a microcomputer with adapted switching mechanisms (see Chapter 17). Provided that these needs are met the children will not show a greater incidence of learning difficulties than the school population in general.

Children with neurological damage, however, may have complex handicaps so that, in addition to their physical disabilities, they may have general or specific intellectual impairment, sensory deficits, perceptual deficits and possibly speech and language disorders. Such children require specialist assessment of their educational needs and they are more likely to need special teaching. An outline of their specific educational problems will be found in the appropriate chapters.

When considering a child's special educational needs, a useful distinction can also be made between those with congenital disorders, e.g. spina bifida, and those whose conditions have a later onset, e.g. road traffic accident victims. Children in the latter category will have had some period of normal learning, and this can give them an enormous advantage over those with congenital conditions (depending upon the severity of the central nervous system (CNS) damage).

The largest groups of physically handicapped children suffer from congenital abnormalities which involve neurological damage, e.g. cerebral palsy and spina bifida. The following discussion on educational attainments will concentrate on *this* group of children, their basic educational attainments in reading, writing and arithmetic and possible remedial methods will be considered. Children with neurological damage are likely to have problems of attention and concentration and these difficulties will affect their attainments in all subjects and must therefore be taken into account when planning any educational programmes.

Reading

Reading is of central importance to most areas of the school curriculum and, consequently, reading attainment has been studied in some detail. Rutter et al (1970) noted that a significant number of children with physical disorders were retarded in reading. Furthermore, although the amount of school missed was similar for those with and those without neurological disorders, the rate of specific reading retardation was nearly twice as great in the group with neurological damage. The authors concluded that neurological damage had direct effects upon reading ability. Cope and Anderson (1977) studied the reading attainments of physically handicapped pupils in units and special schools and found that a high proportion of pupils in both types of provision were significantly backward in reading. Further analysis of the results shows that children of below average intelligence and poor visual/perceptual skills are considerably at risk of being retarded in reading wherever they are educated, whereas, although the evidence is not conclusive, it appears that mildly handicapped children of average ability are unlikely to have serious difficulty in learning to read.

Attempts have been made to try to isolate the disabilities which cause reading problems. However, in view of the complex nature of the reading task this has not so far yielded definitive results. For example, it is assumed that visual and auditory discrimination are component skills of reading but the absolute level of these skills that are necessary for an individual to be able to learn to read successfully is not known. Many studies have, however, demonstrated clearly the relationship between language facility and reading ability. Spina bifida children may have comparatively good verbal skills and this ability will help the child to learn to read. Other factors such as ocular defects, poor visual discrimination and figure/ground problems may hinder the acquisition of reading skills.

How these problems affect reading may best be understood by examining the strategies used by fluent readers who adopt a flexible approach, switching from one strategy to another depending on, for example, what is being read. It is clear that well-developed sensory-motor organisation will help the reader in adopting this flexible approach. Wedell (1973) has pointed out that although neurologically damaged children may have limited levels of sensory organisation these may be sufficient for the child to learn to read, provided he is taught how to use them and as long as his language development is also adequate. He points out that if these two factors are not present, then the sensory organisation skills may well become more crucial to the success or failure of learning to read. Continuous assessment of a child's progress should be undertaken so that, if a child is failing, changes to the teaching method or material can be made as necessary. For instance, a child with visual perceptual difficulties may not learn from the look-and-say approach and may therefore require a phonic approach in order to make the best use of relatively good auditory skills.

Writing

Many physically handicapped children have problems with hand-writing either due to gross motor difficulties or to other specific problems. These children may never write competently and will require alternative means of recording their work such as a typewriter. Children who write very slowly and form letters poorly may benefit from learning to type in addition to writing.

Research findings indicate that neurologically damaged children are likely to have difficulties in learning to write. Wedell (1973) and Anderson and Spain (1977) have suggested that the problem of fine motor control is the main underlying cause of poor handwriting. Anderson also states that poor perceptual and visuo-motor difficulties probably hinder the child from making the correct spatial judgements that are necessary in writing.

In many ordinary schools, children learn to write by copying and so regard writing as the same as any other pattern copying task where the end result is more important than the means. Thus, children develop their own idiosyncratic ways of forming letters. Those who have handwriting problems benefit from being specifically taught to write by emphasis on the arm and hand movements necessary for correct letter formation.

Number work

It appears that a large proportion of physically handicapped children have difficulties with arithmetic. Indeed, Anderson (1973) found that 78 per cent of neurologically damaged children were rated by their teachers as having significantly more difficulty in their number work than with their reading. More recently research conducted with spina bifida children has found in indications that these children, even when of average ability and only mildly handicapped, have definite problems with arithmetic compared to a non-handicapped control group (Halliwell et al, 1980).

Gaddes (1980) has identified difficulties in language, reading and spatial imagery as leading to slow progress in acquiring numeracy. The problems of poor spatial imagery can be understood in terms of the Piagetian model of child development. In the pre-operational stage, thinking is characterised by perceptual rather than by conceptual processes, so that a child at this stage will depend on his visual perception to a very large extent when making quantitative judgements. In the early stages, modern teaching of mathematics is largely concerned with teaching the child to make judgements of quantity independently of, for example, spatial arrangements. Activities to teach this concept include sorting, grading and counting objects, and visual, perceptual, perceptuo-motor and fine motor skills are all required for the successful execution of such tasks. It is evident, therefore, that children with these problems may well experience difficulties in the early stages of learning mathematics. They may be helped by verbal descriptions of the tasks to aid their acquisition of number concepts.

As the child progresses, he will be required to record his work, and difficulties in sensory and motor organisation may cause further problems in his setting out of sums, arranging of figures in the appropriate columns and in remembering the correct sequence in which to carry out the required computations. In addition to the problems of sensory and motor organisation, it must be remembered that many neurologically damaged children have attentional difficulties. Heskell (1972) has emphasised the significance of these factors in determining a child's level of attainment in arithmetic.

REMEDIAL METHODS

The previous sections have described the types of specific difficulty which neurologically damaged pupils may have in learning the three

Rs. None of these difficulties should suggest that a child cannot be taught basic skills but rather that, in order to make satisfactory progress, structured systematic teaching will be required. The problems of motivation in these children have been noted and it will benefit the child if his learning difficulty can be diagnosed as soon as possible, so that he is not allowed to 'fail' for a long period before help is offered.

It would seem advisable, when considering educational attainment, that remediation should concentrate on a child's performance of the educational tasks. For example, it may have been noted that a child has difficulty in word matching: remediation should aim, therefore, to improve the child's discrimination of words and letters. Many programmes are available which claim to remediate specific problems such as visuo-perceptual skills and eye-hand co-ordination difficulties. However, the evidence of the effectiveness of these programmes is inconclusive, particularly with regard to their effects on educational attainment. It appears that gains in specific areas, such as visual discrimination, do not necessarily generalise to other skills, e.g. reading, without specific training.

Teaching physically handicapped children with specific difficulties should, in general, follow the same principles described for other children with learning difficulties. Many books are available which describe how to teach systematically: an example is Ainscow and Tweddle (1979) who outline how to assess and teach children with learning difficulties using an objective approach.

General principles of remediation of learning problems

1. Early diagnosis and assessment.
2. Clear definition of what the child is to learn.
3. Breakdown of the task to be learned into small parts so that each part can be taught separately.
4. Decide how and when the child will be taught and by whom.
5. Evaluate the effectiveness of the teaching by regular assessment of the child's progress.

The role of the therapist within the special school is of great importance. A satisfactory line of communication is the secret of success in this field as with all others and the team approach cannot be over-emphasised as there will be many areas in which professionals will work together: the occupational therapist and teacher with perceptual and hand function problems; the rehabilitation engineer who will be involved in seating, positioning and the provision of aids towards learning; and the speech therapist with language and speech development programmes.

In discussion on regular and frequent occasions, the goals for the individual can be described and worked towards, thus achieving the necessary balance, ensuring as normal a development as possible, and securing the knowledge that the child is not 'missing out' an area of development because of emphasis being put on the wrong aspect at the wrong time. It is 'normal' for a child of, say, 7 to spend the major part of any term-time day in the classroom with a teacher. There is, therefore, a strong argument for as many of the child's necessary therapeutic programmes as possible to be built into the classroom work. There are naturally times when a child may be satisfactorily withdrawn from the classroom, but these should be kept to an absolute minimum for the sake of the child's overall development.

THE PRE-SCHOOL AND SCHOOL CHILD

For all children with physical or sensory disabilities or showing signs of learning or behavioural difficulties, early education is the key to their individual development and the prevention or mitigation of later disturbances (Warnock, 1978).

There is little doubt that parents can act as the main educators of children, but it is well recognised that this situation may be extremely difficult when a child has a severe physical handicap, and parents will need strong support from professionals. The Warnock Report recommends extensive use of peripatetic teachers to assist the parents and hopes that such teachers would be able to act as assessor, parent-trainer, the main contact with other disciplines, as well as being the teacher of the child in the home. The report further suggests that this teacher should be based within a special school, thus being able to reflect the aims and objectives within the educational system of the school in which the child may be placed.

Early education of the child with disability must not be seen as taking place purely within the confines of the special school and, wherever possible, efforts should be made to offer the child the opportunity of being in an ordinary playgroup, providing that the situation within that group is satisfactory in terms of attitude, staffing, facilities and equipment.

Because of the child's disability, there will be certain aspects of early learning which may have to be taught in a highly controlled situation, rather than naturally learned by the child. This is particularly the case with children whose mobility and hand function is affected. In such cases the advantages of the parents being involved are great and therapists need to work with the parents and teacher. It is not always practical for a pre-school child with a disability to be managed successfully within a nursery school, and there is no doubt that a special school, with all its facilities, may be the most satisfactory place for a pre-school playgroup. In such cases the child's needs and functions can be assessed by all concerned, and structured programmes of early learning skills, function and mobility developed.

In a multidisciplinary organisation it is of the utmost importance that the child is not over-stressed in terms of areas of achievement, for example, in the classroom and in the therapy departments. The involvement of any department is bound to be of substantial importance in relation to the young person's overall development. But as the therapists are assisting the child's ability to learn as a child without a disability learns, the assessment of that ability and the functions that will assist the process are at the centre of the plan.

If one is aiming to achieve a placement in the mainstream educational system for a particular child – and this will be the case in some situations – then this aim, once realistically stated by all concerned, must be worked towards wholeheartedly. There may be particular necessities that must be looked at regarding, for example, access and facilities within the proposed school. Therapists have an important role to play here and can act as the co-ordinators between the two establishments, special and mainstream. There must also be liaison between the teaching and ancillary staff throughout the preparation time. This liaison must not be lost once such a move has been made: a programme of therapy must continue once the child has moved; the physical problems that a child has to live with will not disappear when he is at an ordinary school.

The work carried out within the field of special education is based on the needs of the individual; the size of the special school itself can therefore be of distinct advantage. Small class groups enable the teacher to provide material and time for one child's specific needs to a greater extent than can generally be managed in the mainstream of education. There must, however, be a general aim of any educational establishment which states the philosophy of the curriculum, and it is the responsibility of the school to make clear in such a statement the basic needs of the children. From the general aim will be born the individual goals for the children.

Any educational system is primarily concerned with the preparation of children for their future and the work of the special education field is certainly no exception to this rule. In fact, the problems of the future for children with special educational needs are probably greater than those, for example, without a physical or intellectual handicap. It follows that, especially when the time comes to prepare the child for leaving school, a great deal of thought must be given to the curriculum content and, again, the importance of interdisciplinary thinking and action comes to the fore.

The systematic, criterion-related methods of teaching have been briefly touched upon earlier and, although it is not the purpose of this chapter to give more than a cursory examination of methods used, it may be of advantage to indicate the manner in which such a system may be operated for a particular section of the school. This will highlight two factors: the objectives approach, and the needs of the school-leaver.

THE SCHOOL-LEAVER

The school-leaver's curriculum of work at the special school is directed towards the preparation for leaving. All would agree that children should be prepared to approach their future in a purposeful and creative way so that their lives may have significance and personal satisfaction. A major problem lies in the fact that it is difficult to measure success, so the importance of objectives can readily be seen. The objectives are steps towards an aim and may be measured. The more short-term the objective, the easier it is to measure and the greater is the opportunity for the child to succeed. The pupil will know what is expected of him and precisely when he has completed the task. Through this method work can be carefully planned, recorded and evaluated. A balanced curriculum will contain four main areas around which all work may be presented: (1) skills; (2) subjects; (3) experiences; and (4) attitudes.

The Schools' Council publication, *The Curriculum in Special Schools*, emphasises the usefulness of noting in a straightforward manner the possible input that any subject will have in respect of the objectives defined. Thus the leavers' preparation programme will contain elements of the teaching of skills and subjects and enable the student to develop his attitudes as well as having useful experiences related, for example, to possible future employment.

A further way in which the process may be tackled is to develop a 'core' curriculum for the school-leaver, containing the essential aspects of learning. The core might for example contain: (1) literacy and numeracy skills; (2) therapeutic and physical developmental skills; (3) practical communication skills; and (4) learning process skills. The acquisition of the skills supplied through the core curriculum will then enable the student to apply them within the limitations of his capabilities, in the areas of individual interests, work experience, personal and social conduct and daily living activities. The student thus achieves in practical situations, having been taught that he has the ability to achieve in a specific area. The greater the sense of achievement, the more progress a student will make. Continual assessment of the young person's progress and evaluation of the work will ensure that the curriculum is both effective and related to his individual needs, and these are to be related to the possibilities open to him once he has left school, in other words they are related to the original aim.

It must be accepted that it is not possible or perhaps desirable to measure all aspects of a young person's development in such a clear-cut manner. The personal observations of the teacher are an invaluable part of the recording process. The teacher must be very careful, however, to be as clear as possible when recording an observation. The statement, 'Johnny was a nuisance to everyone today' is not useful. The observation that Johnny spilt his drink on five occasions may be of great value. The first tells more about the teacher than the child.

In conclusion, it may be said that there is a distinct danger of underestimating children's abilities in the absence of a well-balanced curriculum. If the *abilities* of the children receiving special education, in whatever form, are stressed, then the *disabilities* will become more easily accepted by the child and the confidence with which that young person tackles a new situation may happily surprise everyone, including the child.

REFERENCES

Ainscow, M. and Tweddle, D. A. (1979). *Preventing Classroom Failure: An Objectives Approach*. John Wiley and Sons Ltd, Chichester.

Anderson, E. M. (1973). *The Disabled Schoolchild. A Study of Integration in Primary Schools*. Methuen, London.

Anderson, E. M. and Spain, B. (1977). *The Child with Spina Bifida*. Methuen, London.

Cope, C. and Anderson, E. M. (1977). *Special Units in Ordinary Schools: An Exploratory Study of Special Provision for Disabled Children*. Institute of Education, University of London.

Department of Education and Science (1978). *Special Educational Needs*. Report of the Committee of Enquiry into the Education of Handicapped Children and Young People (The Warnock Report). HMSO, London.

Gaddes, W. H. (1980). *Learning Disabilities and Brain Function*. Springer-Verlag, New York.

Halliwell, M. D., Carr, J. G. and Pearson, A. M. (1980). The intellectual and educational functioning of children with neural tube defects. *Kinderchirurgie*, **31**, 375–81.

Heskell, S. H. (1972). *Arithmetical Disabilities in Programmed Instruction: A Remedial Approach*. C. C. Thomas, Illinois.

Rutter, M., Tizard, J. and Whitmore, K. (eds)(1970). *Education, Health and Behaviour*. Longman, London.

Wedell, K. (1973). *Learning and Perceptuo-motor Disabilities in Children*. John Wiley and Sons Ltd, Chichester.

FURTHER READING

Anderson, E. M. and Clarke, L. (1982). *Disability in Adolescence*. Methuen London.

Brennan, W. K. (1974). *Shaping the Education of Slow Learners*. Routledge and Kegan Paul, London.

Brennan, W. K. (1979). *Curricular Needs of Slow Learners*. Evans Bros and Methuen Educational, London.

Brennan, W. K. (1982). *Changing Special Education*. Oxford University Press, Oxford.

Department of Education and Science (1980). *Special Needs in Education*. HMSO, London.

Department of Education and Science (1981). *The School Curriculum*. HMSO, London.

Hegarty, S. and Lucas, D. (1981). *Educating Pupils with Special Needs in the Ordinary School*. NFER Publishing Co Ltd, Windsor.

Swann, W. (1981). *A Special Curriculum?* Oxford University Press, Oxford.

Tansley, A. E. and Gulliford, R. (1960). *The Education of Slow-Learning Children*. Routledge and Kegan Paul, London.

Chapter 17

Augmentative Communication Systems

by V. MOFFAT LCST *and* A. W. S. BROWN MSc, MBES

Communication is among the most basic of human needs. The severely speech impaired and physically handicapped child is unable to communicate by speech or gesture. He may be able at best to signal yes/no by nodding and shaking his head or smiling and frowning. His needs may be anticipated by parent or teacher, or the 'listener' may resort to a 'Twenty Questions' form of yes/no answer, which is exhausting for the child, time consuming for the questioner and frustrating for both.

Alternative methods of non-speech communication systems are being used by the severely speech impaired to augment or supplement their speech. It is to be remembered that speech must always accompany any system, and that children are encouraged to vocalise or speak at all times.

It is important that the child is referred as early as possible because there are many pre-training skills that it is necessary to establish before any system can be used.

ASSESSMENT

An interdisciplinary approach to assessment is essential, and often the child will need long-term assessment over a period of perhaps weeks rather than days to ensure that the most appropriate system is introduced.

General aspects of assessment

It is important to assess:
(a) Present method of communication, whether it be facial expression, gesture, vocalisation, speech or alphabet.
(b) Motivation to communicate and general level of alertness.
(c) Interaction with parents and their attitude to the system.
(d) Reliable yes/no response.
(e) Physical capabilities for signing or indication, i.e. hand function; head, foot or eye control.
(f) Mobility.

Formal aspects of assessment

1. Developmental level.
2. Comprehension of language.
3. Expressive language.
4. Psychological assessment for intellectual level.
5. Hearing acuity.
6. Visual acuity and eye movements.

Suitability for a symbol system

If the child is being considered for a symbol system, further investigations will have to be made to test ability to:

Classify objects
Recognise pictures
Match picture to picture
Match picture to symbol
Match symbol to symbol
Recognise colours
Have knowledge of size, spacing, direction and position.

Through the assessment the most appropriate method of communication is selected for the child's present needs, and also some prediction should be made of his future requirement.

COMMUNICATION SYSTEMS

Communication systems show a developmental progress of visual concepts from recognising real objects to using the alphabet or word. The child may use one or more communication systems to augment his speech (Fig. 17/1).

1. Indicating concrete objects to convey requests
2. Indicating symbolic toys
3. *Indicating picture boards*: Photographs or drawings can be used to communicate needs and ideas. It may then be appropriate to progress to line drawings as a pre-symbol stage.
4. *Symbol systems*: Blissymbols enable more abstract and complex communication than previous methods. The word is always written above the symbol and therefore the 'listener' does not have to learn the system. The most severely physically handicapped person can usually find a method of indicating the symbols as long as he has good inner language, adequate vision and visual

Fig. 17/1 Child using two systems – Makaton and Blissymbolics – to augment her speech

Fig. 17/2 Use of chin switches to operate POSSUM typewriter

perception and is well motivated to use the system. These methods of indication can be by hand, eye, head-pointer, mouth-stick or electronic scanning devices.

5. *Signing systems*: British Sign Language (BSL), American Indian (Amer-Ind), Makaton, Paget-Gorman. These systems require relatively good hand function, and the 'listener' usually needs some training to understand the signs. It may be a useful system for children whose visual perceptual problems make symbols inappropriate.

6. *Alphabet*: Spelling boards, word boards, typing, patient operated selector mechanisms (POSSUM), Microwriter, Canon Communicator, SPLINK, are some examples of the numerous electronic aids that are available. The child may use one of these aids in addition to retaining another system for more immediate communication.

POSSUM gives a range of systems from basic learning skills and environmental controls to communication, text processors and typewriting (Fig. 17/2).

Microwriter is a portable writing device that can be used by a wide range of disabled people whose handicap prevents them from writing or communicating effectively. It is easily operated by controlling six keys, spaced for operation by the fingers of one hand. The keys are depressed in a pattern to represent letters and the letters then appear on a small linear display. The Microwriter has a memory for 8000 characters and can be readily interfaced with a printer, television monitor or computer, and can also be fitted to a cassette player (for storage of information) and a voice synthesiser (Fig. 17/3).

The Canon Communicator is a hand-held communication aid for use by the severely speech impaired and by those who have difficulty with writing. It has a mini-keyboard similar in form to the keyboard of a typewriter. There is a keyguard for those with severe motor control problems.

SPLINK (Speech Link) is a communication aid for the speech disabled, used in conjunction with a standard television receiver. A message is sent from the wordboard to the processor unit, either by means of a connecting cable or by infra red link, so that when the wordboard is touched an audible 'bleep' is produced from the loudspeaker on the television set and the appropriate word appears on the screen. 950 words plus the alphabet can be held on the television screen providing a visual memory for the user. Editing facilities are provided to allow amendment or correction of the last entry on the screen, and a number of commonly used phrases such

Fig. 17/3 Learning code to use adapted microwriter

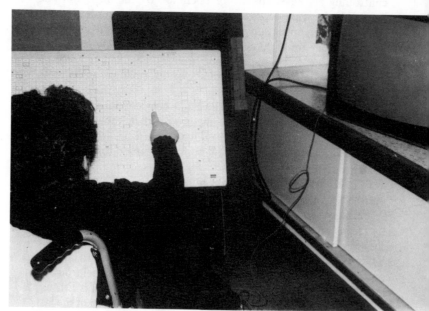

Fig. 17/4 Student demonstrating the use of SPLINK as a communication aid

Fig. 17/5 Student operating Phonic Mirror Handivoice

as 'How are you?' can be produced at a single touch. Several wordboards can be used with one microprocessor/television system enabling group use (Fig. 17/4).

7. *Artificial speech*: The Phonic Mirror/Handivoice devices allow patients to communicate through the medium of artificial speech, using an internally stored vocabulary of words, phrases and phonemes (Fig. 17/5). Access to the stored vocabulary can be by means of either a direct selection keyboard in one version, or through the use of a numeric code selected directly on a keyboard or by sequential scanning using external patient-operated switches in the other version.

These are representative of a number of similar devices such as the Vocaid and Convaid machines, which are now available. There are as yet few examples of such equipment that are capable of synthesising a child's voice, although this is likely to improve.

8. *Microprocessor-based communication aids* of various types are appearing regularly and, indeed, the SPLINK, Microwriter and the speech output devices mentioned above are examples of these. Many programmes to assist communication, which can be used

with the variety of the now freely available 'home computers', are also being produced, although the quality, versatility and usefulness of many of these can be disappointing. Small computers, such as the Epson HX-20, which integrate the features of display, keyboard or switch input, mass storage by means of magnetic tape and the capability of communicating electronically with other computers in a single, portable, battery powered unit offer great promise in this field.

NON-SPEECH COMMUNICATION SYSTEMS

Blissymbolics

This system originated from the work of Charles K. Bliss whose war experiences in his native Austria led him to create a communication system that could be understood internationally. As a refugee in China he realised that the Chinese had difficulty in understanding each other's dialects, but were able to read because their script was based on standardised concept-related symbols. He therefore developed a system based on meaning rather than sounds and published the first edition of his book *Semantography* in 1949.

In 1971 a multi-disciplinary team at the Ontario Crippled Children's Centre, Toronto, began investigation into alternative methods of communication for children with cerebral palsy. They realised the potential of Blissymbolics.

The symbols are concept-related pictographs (they look like the things they represent) and ideographs (they represent ideas), and have the advantage that they are meaning-based and so can be used to expand language concept (Fig. 17/6).

The vocabulary chart provides a constant visual reinforcement, and users are stimulated to vocalise as they locate symbols. (*Introductory Information: The Bliss Symbol Communication System* – see page 318.)

Sigsymbols

A sigsymbol is a simple and bold outline drawing standing for a whole word. It is either representational or conceptually linked with an established signing system. Such symbols have been used in teaching the severely mentally handicapped in a wide variety of activities and games, all broadly concerned with the development of language and communication. The sign linkage of the present version of sigsymbols is with British Sign Language (BSL).

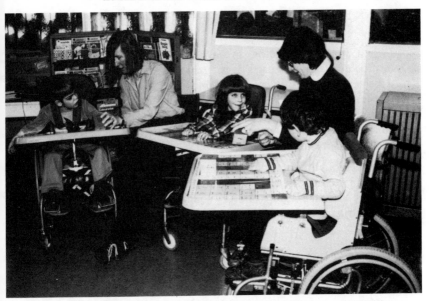

Fig. 17/6 A group session showing nurse and speech therapist working with young Blissymbol users

There are other symbol systems, for example REBUS (Clark et al, 1974) and Premack (Deich and Hodges, 1977).

SIGNING SYSTEMS

British Sign Language (BSL) is a naturally evolving language of the deaf, which is now widely used to assist communication for the mentally handicapped. It does not have the English spoken word order, so the deaf have to arrange the signs to spoken word order and use finger spelling to communicate with the hearing population.

The Makaton Vocabulary: This started in the 1970s as a signing system for deaf, mentally handicapped adults. The signs are taken from the British Sign Language of the Deaf and consist of a specially selected vocabulary, considered to be most essential and useful in providing basic communication. It is structured in stages of increasing complexity and follows the normal pattern of language development.

Amer-Ind Gestural Code: This is a hand code developed by the American Indians 15 000–20 000 years ago. It is based on concepts, and 80 per cent of the signs can be interpreted by the non-instructed viewer. It is not a language, having neither grammatical nor structural rules.

Paget-Gorman Sign System: In 1934 this system was devised to help deaf people learn language. It is based on American-Indian signs of which each group of ideas has its own basic sign and each is further identified by additional gesture, e.g. 'animal' is a basic gesture, with the other hand adding further gesture to make a pig. All the ambiguities of syntax are clarified and the system obviates the need to use finger spelling.

Cued Speech: This was developed in 1965–6 as a language tool used with the profoundly deaf. It provides a mental model of language so that the listener is aware of every sound in every word. The hand is used during speech to clarify the ambiguities of lip reading.

THE EFFECTIVENESS OF SYSTEMS

Picture boards provide only a limited amount of information.

Manual signing systems require adequate hand function and a knowledge of the system on the part of the receiver.

Symbol systems can be used by the child and the 'listener' as the word is written above the symbol; they are concept based and therefore there are no limitations on information. The symbol charts can be adapted easily to a variety of electronic displays or eye-coding techniques.

The alphabet/word systems are limited to the child who has the ability to read and spell.

Interim measure

The system may be used as an interim measure until speech is intelligible or until the child can progress to the next system. The *aim* is for the severely speech impaired child to progress through the systems and ultimately to use the alphabet or word (Fig. 17/7).

Speech as opposed to system

It has been found that the vocalisation of the child may be reduced initially while he is learning the new system, but more often it is discovered that, once the pressure of speaking is reduced by having an alternative method of communication, the child relaxes and communication improves.

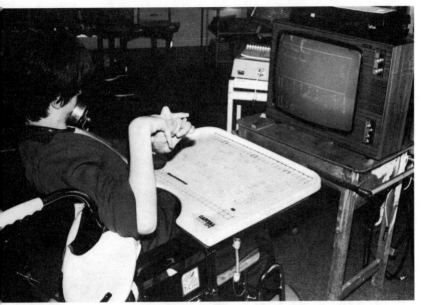

Fig. 17/7 Student using chin switch to operate Apple Computer using SPLINK wordboard to aid spelling

Training the child to use the system

1. Good positioning: it is essential that the child is positioned correctly, if using a symbol system, so that he has maximum head and trunk control for indication.
2. Motivation: motivate the child to want to communicate by giving him experiences and choices.
3. Develop a reliable yes/no response.
4. Train indication by hand-, head- or eye-pointing.
5. Train basic auditory and visual perceptual skills.
6. Train eye contact for the child using a signing system.
7. Link photographs and pictures to symbols.
8. Use symbols/signs during learning of other skills.

Training staff to use the system

Lastly, remember the child must have someone with whom to communicate, and it is essential that the family and all staff should be trained to use the relevant system. The system should be used at all times by members of staff, and the child should have the display board – in the case of symbols – attached to his wheelchair or person.

AUGMENTATIVE COMMUNICATION CENTRES

Several specialised centres have been set up in England and Wales to provide assessment and prescription of communication aids. These centres are mainly concerned with adult patients, but there is a growing interest in the needs of children. The centres are under the auspices of the DHSS.

REFERENCES

Clark, C. R., Davies, C. D. and Woodcock, R. W. (1974). *Standard REBUS Glossary*. Distributed in the UK by Educational Evaluation Enterprises, Awre, Newnham Gloucestershire.

Deich, R. and Hodges, P. (1977). *Language Without Speech*. Human Horizons Series. Souvenir Press, London.

The booklet *Introductory Information: The Bliss Symbol Communication System* may be obtained from Living and Learning, Duke Street, Wisbech PE13 2AE.

USEFUL ADDRESSES

The Co-ordinating Group for Communication Systems
c/o The Wolfson Centre, Mecklenburgh Square London WC1N 2AP

Information of the various systems mentioned in the text may be sought from the following:

Blissymbolics
Blissymbolics Communication Resource Centre
The South Glamorgan Institute of Higher Education, Western Avenue, Llandaff, Cardiff CF5 2YB

Makaton Vocabulary
The Makaton Vocabulary Development Project, 31 Firwood Drive, Camberley GU15 3QD

Paget-Gorman Sign System
106 Marell Avenue, Oxford OX4 1NA

British Sign Language
The Royal National Institute for the Deaf, 105 Gower Street, London WC1E 6AH

Cued Speech
The National Centre for Cued Speech, 66–68 Upper Richmond Road, London SW15 2RP

Amer-Ind
7 Chester Close, Lichfield WS13 7SX

Information on Communication Aids is obtainable from:

POSSUM
POSSUM Typewriter Systems, Middlegreen Trading Estate, Middlegreen Road, Langley, Slough SL3 6DF

Microwriter
Foundation for Communication for the Disabled, c/o Microwriter Ltd, 31 Southampton Row, London WC1B 5HJ

Canon Communicator
Mr A. Berg (General Manager), Calculator Division, Canon Business Machines (UK) Ltd, Waddon House, Stafford Road, Croydon CR9 4DP

SPLINK
Mr J. Piper, Tools for Living, Middlewood, 45 Croft Road, Broadhaven, Haverfordwest SA62 3HY

Phonic Mirror Handivoice: HC 110/HC 120
Mr Richard Brendel, P.C. Werth Ltd, Audiology House, 45 Nightingale Lane, London SW12 8SU

Chapter 18

Care Procedures and Replacing the Family

by P. RUSSELL BA

RESIDENTIAL CARE: THE LEGAL BASIS

Despite the growing emphasis on community care and support for the concept of parents as partners, there will always be some children who will need to live away from home at least for a time. Residential care can be a positive experience and may be a means for ensuring that severely disabled children do receive the services they need. If of good quality, it will take account of the need for forward planning based on interdisciplinary assessment; preparation for child, natural parents and the carers; the provision of services geared both to special needs and the concept of 'normalisation' which is a key factor in community care and, eventually, to progress on either to a return home, to adult services or to more independent living in various ways.

Children living in NHS accommodation will probably have been placed under health legislation relating to the provision of services or *treatment* appropriate to their needs. They may be the subject of care proceedings by their local authority and their length of stay may be more related to problems in finding alternative provision in the community than to their continuing need for health services in an NHS residential setting. Children in residential special schools will be so placed by the education authority under the procedures of the Education Act 1981. If they are unable to spend holiday periods with their families they will normally be in the care of the local authority and will spend their holiday periods with substitute families or in a variety of residential settings.

Children who are placed in voluntary or local authority children's homes come under a confusing variety of legislation, which – as the 1974 Harvie Report noted – has left many unprotected by the procedures of the successive Child Care Acts and sometimes isolated from mainstream children's services.

In 1963 the Children and Young Persons Act introduced a number of preventive and rehabilitative measures for children coming into the care of the local authority. Children's regional planning committees were required to be set up and a system of community homes established in each region. The local authority Social Services Act of 1970 integrated several departments, including the children's department, into the new social services departments and central responsibility was passed to the Department of Health and Social Security (DHSS). In 1980 a number of earlier statutes relating to children in care were consolidated in the Child Care Act 1980 which introduced a 'welfare principle' in Section 18, namely that:

> In reaching any decision relating to a child in their care, a local authority shall give first consideration to the need to safeguard and promote the welfare of the child throughout his childhood and shall so far as practicable ascertain the wishes and feelings of the child regarding the decision and give due consideration to them, having regard to his age and understanding.

Under this Act, local authorities have a statutory duty to assess, review a child's situation and, depending on the type of residential home in which a child is placed, have to follow the relevant regulations. A child placed in a community home will come under the Community Homes Regulations 1972, in voluntary homes under the Administration of Children's Homes Regulations 1951, and in private homes under regulations to be issued under the Children's Homes Act 1982. All children have the ultimate protection of Section 1 of the Children and Young Persons Act 1933 against wilful ill-treatment, neglect, etc, by anyone having charge or custody of that child. But it should be emphasised that mentally disordered or disabled children placed in private or voluntary residential care homes *without* the protection of a care order (which is common practice where the child is placed under the Mental Health Act 1983 or the Health Services and Public Health Act 1968) do not have the same protection as children in care who come under the regulations itemised above. The Harvie Study Group recommended that handicapped children in residential homes (and nursing homes or mental nursing homes) should be protected by regulations similar to the Community Homes Regulations. In practice some local authorities do treat *all* children as if they were in care and regularly review and assess. But the position of handicapped children in private or voluntary homes, which may be distant from their place of origin, must give rise for concern and should be seen as a priority area for community health services and local authorities. It should be emphasised that many private and voluntary homes offer an excellent and appropriate specialist health service advice, staff support and in-service training and finding appropriate provision for the child's adult life.

Some independent homes accommodate children through private arrangements with their families. If the child is not in the care of a local authority, the arrangement will be treated like private fostering which is covered by the Foster Children Act 1980, which brings together relevant sections of a number of acts. Long-term fostering comes under the same legislation, although short-term fostering as respite care may be subject to mental health legislation.

A growing number of severely handicapped children are being integrated into ordinary community homes. Some voluntary organisations, like the North West Division of Dr Barnardo's, have also pioneered work in this direction, which may have important consequences for staff training and support. Such integration mirrors the increasing number of severely handicapped children living in their own homes and highlights a need for broad-based community services to support the carers.

FOSTERING

In the past few years, increasing numbers of severely handicapped children have been successfully placed with long-term foster parents. Although special fostering will place considerable demands upon both the family and supporting professionals, the success of the new initiative has important consequences for children who might otherwise have spent most of their childhood in institutional care. The majority of children so placed are carefully 'matched' to selected foster parents. The market place approach to foster family recruitment, using local newspapers, radio programmes and voluntary organisations, seems to have been very successful in finding the new families. Such recruitment policies break away from traditional social services department practice and look for individual parents for individual children. There is some evidence that such foster parents may be 'atypical'. They may be single or married, older, have a particular interest in handicap or be anticipating a challenge to their own professional and personal abilities.

The majority of social services departments or voluntary organisations providing this service run structured training courses (which also offer an opportunity for potential foster parents to change their minds if the challenge seems too great). Such courses will look at the implications of disability, offer practical management skills for coping with incontinence, behaviour problems or specific aids, and link the new parents into existing voluntary and statutory services for families with handicapped children. Many foster parents will need to maintain positive contact with a child's natural parents, with the relevant local special school, and in some instances (as with the National Children's Home's Avon scheme) they may be regarded as *professional* foster parents and work directly to the social services on a contract basis.

Caring for a handicapped child is never cheap. Additional heating charges, modifications to household equipment or premises, transport and other practical resources may be needed. However, substitute families have the advantage of feeling no guilt about having a handicapped child. They must have a good relationship with named individuals in their local social services department, and they are generally anxious to work positively with local health and education services.

The number of long-term foster placements is probably still quite small, but there has been a major growth in short-term respite, foster care schemes throughout the country. Many of the respite schemes have in turn indicated strategies for preparing children for future placements, training foster families and ways forward in meeting special needs in ordinary housing.

ADOPTION

In the United States as well as the United Kingdom, there has been an increase in the number of adoptions of handicapped children. To some extent this reflects the lack of normal babies and small children available for adoption, but it also indicates the commitment by many families to accepting a child who is 'different' and a recognition that this is a positive challenge and not a negative experience. Preparation for successful adoption has to be carefully planned and supported. The adoption agency 'Parents for Children', specialising in placement of often very severely handicapped children, has highlighted the need for sensitive identification of children and potential parents, for an evolutionary approach moving carefully forward from the first introduction, and recognising the need to work with the present care staff or nurses who will have to cope with any failure in placement. While it has been argued that children may be at risk if a planned relationship does not materialise, 'Parents for Children' demonstrates how a coherent policy can cope with disappointment and learn from past experiences.

There is still some residual doubt about whether every child can be placed in an adoptive home, if their earlier institutional experiences and disabilities are such that they find adaptation virtually impossible. The London Borough of Camden has taken an initiative in putting three such children (with multiple and mental handicaps) into an ordinary house with carers who are a blend of foster parent and residential child care worker. The children will remain together in the house that is their home, and if care changes are necessary will change staff and not their home. Co-operation with local authority housing departments and with housing associations will clearly be of major importance in achieving a greater shift to community care, since locality and type of housing may be major factors in facilitating a normal life style for the child and parent.

In February 1982, Section 32 of the Children Act 1975 was implemented in order to introduce schemes of allowances for adopters. Section 32 arose from a recognition that some children available for adoption will place special needs and demands upon their adoptive families. Without additional resources, such adoptions might be impossible. Schemes for payment of allowances vary in different parts of the United Kingdom, and their first seven years of operation are being monitored by the National Children's Bureau on behalf of the DHSS.

AN ORDINARY LIFE

The majority of disabled young people will want to live in the same way as their able-bodied peers – in an ordinary house in an ordinary street. In recent years there have been major developments in the provision of small group homes (usually run by social services' departments or voluntary organisations, but with a significant number established as part of an 'out-reach' service by hospitals). Group homes may be literally self-supporting, with regular visits from relevant professionals and volunteers. The residents will go out to day centres, adult training centres or to sheltered or open employment, and may have assistance from a local authority home help if required. A growing number of young people have higher dependency needs, however, and group homes may therefore have minimal staffing (sometimes through volunteers or tenants who have duties to perform in place of rent). Initially group homes were largely developed for mobile mentally handicapped people, but residential provision for severely physically disabled people is now following the same model. The cost of maintaining group homes is usually low with regard to other forms of residential care, but the provision of flexible support has caused difficulties and group homes need to be perceived as part of a wider strategy for helping disabled people in the community.

More severely disabled young people not willing or able to remain with their natural parents may live in a variety of ways. Some, with adequate preparation and suitable adaptations, may be able to manage their own flats. Local authority housing departments and housing associations are generally very co-operative, and the availability of improvement and intermediate grants makes it possible to adapt and update a range of accommodation for wheelchair use. Some disabled people will live in hostels at least until they have developed adequate self-care skills and are willing and able to move to more independent living. Some hostels, or residential homes, will be provided by the voluntary sector, and organisations like the Leonard Cheshire Foundation have extensive experience in providing high quality residential care.

Wherever a young person lives, he is likely to be affected by a new philosophy which looks to achieving not only a high standard of physical environment and personal care, but also a sense of autonomy, informed choice and self-respect. For good quality residential care does not only depend on bricks and mortar, but on acceptance of the disabled person's rights as an individual: the right to personal relationships with the opposite sex, choice of meal and bedtimes, privacy and participation in decision making. All have implications not only for the disabled young person but for the professionals working with him before and after the transition to adult life.

A minority of disabled young people will remain in hospital care either because they are literally ill and need specialist treatment or because they may have lacked opportunities for independence training and forward planning which have been available to their peers. The transition to adult from children's services at 16 in the NHS, 18 in the local authority and 19 for education can cause major problems unless careful plans are made. Assessment and preparation for adult life need to begin at an early stage in adolescence and hospital children are at particular disadvantage if they are distanced from their place of origin and family contacts. Because these children are often not in the care of a local authority and subject to regular reviews and assessment, planning may pose a major problem unless the *hospital* social worker takes the initiative.

The children's regional planning committee of the London boroughs treats *all* handicapped children living away from home as if they were the subject of care orders and this procedure offers a constructive model for planning for the future of children currently living in NHS provision.

RESIDENTIAL EDUCATION

A considerable number of handicapped children spend part, or indeed all, of their education in residential special schools. Although many are run by local education authorities (LEAs), a significant number are run by voluntary organisations like the Spastics Society or Invalid Children's Aid Association. The latter usually provide very specific services which are not available elsewhere.

Placements in residential special schools are almost invariably financed by the LEA. In certain cases the reason for such a placement may be primarily social in order to avoid family stress and breakdown and the necessity to take the child into care if he was placed in social services residential provision.

The Education Act 1981 makes it clear that 16–19-year-olds who are registered as pupils at a school are entitled to continuing education *in school* during that period. The law on further education is currently being revised and the rights to places in either local authority or independent further educational provision are unclear. An increasing number of LEAs are making provision in ordinary colleges of further education, but the unsuitability of many premises, with poor access to lecture rooms and toilet facilities, often causes problems.

A number of older disabled children and young people may choose to have a period of residential education in the post-16 period either in a residential school or in a further education establishment of some kind. Examples of the provision available include Hereward College, run by Coventry education authority, which provides a range of academic subjects leading to a variety of qualifications and possible progression to higher education or professional courses elsewhere. There are several courses available for the less able 16–19-year-olds offering assessment and a range of mobility and social skills training schemes, as well as further education. These demonstrate the need of a 'bridge' between school and adult life for many of the most severely disabled young people.

Financial support for residential further education may be difficult. Education authorities may give discretionary grants, but some look to social services departments to cover the residential living component of such courses. In these circumstances disputes can develop about what constitutes care or education. Mandatory grants are available for disabled students wishing to attend university, like all other young people. However, many disabled students will need an additional input of support and physical care in their everyday lives at university and may need to look to their social services department for financial support in achieving this help. The use of Community Service Volunteers seems to be very successful, but adequate consultation with the desired university and the National Bureau for Handicapped Students well in advance of application may minimise the extra help needed. Some universities and polytechnics are better equipped than others to help disabled people and have accessible academic facilities and specially adapted accommodation.

HOSPITAL CARE

If children need to live in hospital or other NHS units, they should have consistent care, a domestic style environment, access to education (usually through the hospital school) and regular review. In a 1981 circular, the Secretary of State requested regional health authorities to assess children living in hospital regularly in conjunction with the local authority with a view to more appropriate accommodation in the community. Hospital social workers will have a key role in ensuring that such links are made and also in maintaining a positive relationship with parents.

The majority of children living in hospital are not in the care of a local authority, often because of anxiety about weakening potentially fragile family relationships. However, the use of voluntary reception into care under Section 2 of the 1980 Act (with counselling for the parents) may be a way forward in ensuring that children are not 'forgotten' and in ensuring that the excellent developmental gains often achieved in hospital can lead to a more flexible and 'ordinary' lifestyle in the community. A number of hospitals are participating in preparation for fostering schemes and the role of hospital-based professionals (including paediatricians, psychologists, physiotherapists and nurses) may be critical in demonstrating that community care is possible.

The development of the community mental handicap nurse as an 'outreach' service is one instance of health service skills being disseminated wider in the community. Numbers of such appointments are now being provided through joint finance and the change in these arrangements as set out in Health Circular HC(83)6, *Health Service Development: Care in the Community and Joint Finance*, demonstrates the way forward.

FURTHER READING

Adcock, M. and White, R. (1977). *The Assumption of Parental Rights and Duties: An Exploration of Issues Relating to Children in Care*. British Agencies for Adoption and Fostering.

Brearley, P. (1980). *Admission to Residential Care*. Tavistock Publications Limited, London.

Curtis, S. (1983). *Looking at Handicap: Information on Ten Medical Conditions*. British Agencies for Adoption and Fostering, London.

Dingwall, R. (1982). *Care Proceedings: A Practical Guide for Social Workers, Health Visitors and Others*. Basil Blackwell, Oxford.

Kerrane, A. et al (1980). *Adopting Older and Handicapped Children: A Consumer's View of the Preparation, Assessment, Placement and Post-placement Support Services*. Barnardo's, Barkingside.

Parker, R. A. (ed)(1980). *Caring for Separated Children: Plans, Procedures and Priorities*. Macmillan Publishers Limited, London.

Russell, P. (1980). *Fostering Handicapped Children: An Overview*. Included in the Proceedings of a Symposium on *Foster Care: A Team Work Service*, held at Oxford under the auspices of the National Foster Care Association.

Shearer, A. (1980). *Handicapped Children in Residential Care: A Study in Policy Failure*. Bedford Square Press, London.

Spaulding, K. (1978). *Opening New Doors: Finding Families for Older and Handicapped Children*. British Agencies for Adoption and Fostering, London.

Triseliotis, J. (ed)(1980). *New Developments in Foster Care and Adoption*. Routledge and Kegan Paul, London.

The National Children's Bureau publishes the following titles:
Booklist 31 – *Fostering Children with Special Needs*
Booklist 33a – *Children in Care*
Booklist 42 – *Physically Handicapped Children*
Booklist 57 – *Special Education*
Booklist 94 – *Fostering Children with Special Needs*

USEFUL ADDRESSES

National Children's Bureau, 8 Wakley Street, London EC1V 7QE
British Agencies for Adoption and Fostering, 11 Southwark Street, London SE1 1SY

Chapter 19

Social Integration, Sexuality and Sex Education

by S. DORNER MA

FRIENDSHIPS AT SCHOOL

It is probably a truism to state that the great majority of physically handicapped teenagers want to have friends, but it is a statement which highlights one of the major difficulties encountered in adolescence by the physically handicapped.

Within the context of school, the picture is fairly encouraging. The overwhelming majority of teenagers report friendships, occasionally with one friend only, but usually with more. Not surprisingly, it is those with problems such as speech defects who are most vulnerable to lack of friends except where the school specialises in such handicaps. Even so, such self-reporting must be interpreted with some caution since it has been shown that teachers at both special and ordinary schools quite often see handicapped pupils as tending to be rather solitary (Anderson and Clarke, 1982). Further, the description 'not much liked by other children' is applied more frequently to them than to able-bodied pupils.

FRIENDSHIPS OUTSIDE SCHOOL

Clearly, however, the fact that handicapped youngsters usually have friends at school does not resolve the issue of social integration and studies which have looked at friendships outside school reveal a disturbing problem (Dorner, 1977; Anderson and Clarke, 1982). Both these studies show a striking contrast between the friendships outside school of the able-bodied and the physically handicapped. Less than 10 per cent of the former see no friends outside school, while figures for the latter range from 30 to 60 per cent, depending on the type of school attended (Anderson and Clarke, 1982). Dorner (1976) found that 40 per cent of spina bifida adolescents had *no* friends outside school or college.

While it may be argued, with some justification, that the prospects for social integration are greater for those whose handicaps do not involve impaired mobility, it remains the case that lack of opportunity, problems of shyness or low self-esteem, or other difficulties, such as incontinence, result in considerable social problems even for those who are relatively or completely mobile.

LONELINESS

Social isolation must be distinguished from loneliness, the latter being essentially a subjective experience that affects individuals, at least to some extent, independently of the frequency of their social contacts. Some very isolated people may not feel lonely and the degree of social contact they maintain is often a matter of choice. Handicapped youngsters do not, in general, appear to feel that they have such choice. They feel strongly, and rightly, that their opportunities for social contact are very restricted. It is therefore not surprising that loneliness is a common problem in adolescence for the handicapped.

Loneliness is given as the most common reason for misery or unhappiness in handicapped youngsters. This, in itself, tends to create a kind of vicious circle since unhappiness often leads either to a need to withdraw or to reduced social 'attractiveness' in the eyes of peers or to both consequences.

SOCIAL INTEGRATION AND TYPE OF SCHOOL

This is a complicated topic and it has been the subject of close investigation (Warnock Report 1978) and recent legislation (Education Act 1981). It is essential to underline here that handicapped teenagers are emphatic that they do not want their friendships or opportunities for social contact to be restricted to other handicapped young people. It follows that, in this sense, handicapped youngsters' social needs are more readily met if they can attend mainstream schools and there is now fairly clear evidence that handicapped teenagers at ordinary schools are more able to maintain social contact outside school than those at special schools. (Special residential schools, in contrast, are probably more able to prevent feelings of loneliness during term time.) While it may well be agreed that ordinary schools do facilitate greater social integration, certain other points must be made.

In the first place, social integration is *still* a problem for one-third or more of those at ordinary schools. Secondly, most, if not all, special schools encourage part-time attendance wherever possible at local ordinary schools and attempt to foster other opportunities for social contact with the able-bodied through social functions and clubs. Thirdly, for the foreseeable future, full-time special education will be both necessary and advisable for many handicapped children and adolescents. It would be unrealistic, given present circumstances, to think otherwise. Special schools need to, and are, attempting to address themselves to the problem of greater social integration.

THE WISH TO 'BELONG'

It would be a mistake to regard the issue of social integration as being defined simply in terms of frequency of social contact with able-bodied peers and absence of feelings of loneliness, important as these are. Just as important, it can be argued, is the need of the handicapped youngster to feel he or she is esteemed and accepted rather than merely tolerated and patronised by able-bodied young people. Articulate handicapped teenagers argue powerfully for their right to be treated as 'just like anyone else'. This appears to be a very reasonable wish to feel they belong. Many with visible handicaps are conscious of the readiness with which they come to be labelled and stigmatised on the basis of their physical difficulties and may over-compensate as a consequence. Those whose handicaps are not visible may go to considerable and, sometimes, unhelpful lengths to deny the existence of their handicap in their efforts to be the same as their peers. However they resolve the problem, the need to belong reflects the wider issue of social and cultural attitudes towards the handicapped, which are beyond the scope of this chapter, but which the handicapped adolescent feels keenly.

SOCIAL INTEGRATION AFTER SCHOOL-LEAVING

From the limited systematic work that has been done, it seems fairly clear that the position of older adolescents does not change significantly. Indeed, it sometimes happens that social contact generally becomes *less* frequent, particularly for the more severely handicapped and that opportunities to mix with able-bodied peers, far from increasing, become less easy; leaving school occurs at a time when the peer group begins to alter in structure to accommodate to the formation of heterosexual couple-relationships.

Work, too, has a social aspect, but various surveys have shown that there is a high number of handicapped teenagers unable to find work. Apart from the familiar problems for unemployed youth, lack of work means lack of opportunity to meet people in a work situation. Thus the potential of work situations to foster social integration is unused.

Up to this point, discussion has proceeded as if a handicapped young person's social relationships occur independently of his family context. Clearly this is not the case. One of the major functions of the family is to foster social integration. Anecdotally and clinically, at least, there is a significant number of families striving energetically to ensure that the physically-handicapped family member is integrated as much as possible into family social activities. This is true not only of parents but of siblings, especially older brothers or sisters, and of members of the extended family. At the same time it must be acknowledged that some parents themselves are so affected by the problems of going out that they, too, come to lead a restricted social life (Dorner, 1975). In this study, over 40 per cent of parents felt their own social life was limited because of difficulties in arranging to go out.

APPROACHES TO INTERVENTION

Lack of social integration continues to be a central problem for most handicapped youngsters and it has been suggested that the problem operates at four levels.
1. Limited actual social contact with the able-bodied.
2. Subjective feelings of loneliness.
3. A need to 'belong' to the peer group.
4. Social attitudes towards the handicapped.
Clearly there is scope for both statutory and voluntary agencies to work together to meet some of these needs. Indeed, there are encouraging signs that a variety of interventions are now being tried.

The most useful type of intervention appears to use a structure based on fostering *social* interaction through clubs for the physically handicapped and able-bodied. Perhaps the best known agency organising such activities is PHAB (Physically Handicapped and Able-Bodied). However, both the Spastics Society and the Association for Spina Bifida and Hydrocephalus (ASBAH), to name but two, have become energetically involved in such activities. One of the goals of these clubs is to reduce the sense of alienation experienced by so many physically handicapped youngsters, but they also provide informally an opportunity for them to ventilate their feelings in discussion with the sympathetic, skilled staff who run these clubs.

Some programmes are under way which formalise these discussions so that group meetings are built into the overall plan of social activity. Often, these are planned as residential courses which combine social activity, group discussions and, perhaps, formal talks on relevant topics, e.g. work opportunities, independent living, from appropriate professionals.

Interventions of this kind appear to be more useful than purely psychological intervention. While counselling or psychotherapy may occasionally be helpful to individual patients, personal experience indicates that, in general, handicapped teenagers are far from enthusiastic when offered formal psychological help. Attempts that have been made to establish 'clinics' for such youngsters have often been characterised by poor attendance rates. A study by Bywater (1981) showed that only two out of 27 youngsters suffering from cystic fibrosis welcomed the idea of counselling, and this is almost certainly characteristic of teenagers suffering from other physically-handi-capping conditions. Counselling may, however, be of value to parents, and any planned intervention needs to take account of the fact that a handicapped youngster's family is an invaluable social resource. It is an understandable consequence of parental concern over the years that over-involved relationships in the family may have been established and, where this has occurred, family counselling is definitely indicated.

SEXUALITY AND SEX EDUCATION

The personal and social context

The term *handicapped* is very broad and the nature of the handicap or disability clearly affects the process of personal and social develop-ment of which sexuality forms a part. Where the defect is congenital, the handicapped adolescent, his family, and his social group will have been grappling for many years with the difficult problem of psychosocial adaptation. Where the defect has been acquired recently, adaptation is affected by profound grief and anger over the lost function or capacity. Such youngsters are often very different in personality from the striking passivity and low self-esteem of those who have experienced the effect of handicap throughout their lives.

Intellectual handicap, whether mild or severe, also affects personality adaptation, particularly in the areas of personal and social maturity, and this demands special intervention and help in the area of sexuality. Similarly there are specific problems for those with sensory handicap whose adjustment may well have suffered from the persistent effects of limited inter-personal communication.

Psychosocial adjustment

It is important for any professional involved in a programme of sex education for handicapped adolescents to be aware of the broader problems of psychosocial adjustment that have been outlined earlier. Having no friends clearly implies having no friends of the opposite sex. Anderson and Clarke (1982) studied a mixed group of 15-year-olds with spina bifida or cerebral palsy. Of the handicapped group 80 per cent had little or nothing to do with the opposite sex compared with only 27 per cent of able-bodied controls of the same age. Further, whereas 45 per cent of controls had, or were having, steady boy or girl friends, this was true for only 14 per cent of the handicapped group. Dorner (1977) showed a similar picture.

Both studies emphasise that the wish to establish an intimate relationship with a member of the opposite sex is very common. Not surprisingly, this is particularly important for older teenagers (16 and over) and there is an overwhelming preference that boy or girl friends should be able-bodied. This reflects the wish of handicapped teenagers to be 'just like anyone else'. Again, it is vital for any programme of sex education to recognise clearly the strength of the handicapped teenager's aspiration to be just like any other person. It is also essential to recognise how limited the opportunities are for the handicapped to learn about sex at first hand. This statement covers the whole range of first-hand experience from dating to actual sexual intercourse. Anderson and Clarke (1982) found that only 25 per cent of their handicapped group had been out with someone of the opposite sex, compared with 75 per cent of able-bodied controls, and that the experience of dating by the handicapped group was much more likely to have been with just one boy or girl. Further, and importantly, it was much less likely that kissing had occurred in the relationship. In Dorner's study of older teenagers, physical intimacy was often similarly lacking and, out of 46 teenagers with spina bifida, only one experience of sexual intercourse by a girl aged 19 was acknowledged. This was a disaster, not surprisingly, and led to a suicidal attempt. Figures from Schofield's study (1968) reveal a strikingly different picture of the proportion of able-bodied teenagers having had sexual intercourse by the age of 19 years.

In summary, sexuality and sex education cannot be detached from the general personal and social predicament of handicapped teenagers, for whom developing sexuality becomes yet another plank nailed to the apparently insurmountable fence dividing them from normality. Any form of programme of sex education must provide an opportunity for feelings of distress and anger brought about by the presence of this barrier to be fully ventilated.

Sexual information and knowledge

The barrier between the handicapped and the able-bodied reduces these teenagers' knowledge of sex. Schofield's study (1968) showed that most normal teenagers (62 per cent of boys and 44 per cent of girls) derived most of their information about sex from their peers. This is clearly not the case for handicapped teenagers, most of whom learned about sex either from their parents, their schools or other residential institutions.

The way in which the nature of the handicap affects placement affects the way in which teenagers learn about sex, since handicapped adolescents attending ordinary schools are more likely to learn about sex from their peers. The main point, however, is that, because their source is different, what handicapped teenagers learn about sex is likely to be different from the knowledge gleaned by the able-bodied. It is true that this may protect those who are disabled from some of the anxiety-arousing adolescent mythology about sex (for example the dire effects of masturbation), but it is also true that they are then, at a time of life when it is generally acknowledged that much learning must take place away from parents, vulnerable to the personal viewpoints or indeed prejudices of parents or parents' substitutes such as teachers or nurses.

Certainly, in talking to handicapped teenagers, one finds that a good deal of their own sex education has been of the birds-and-bees variety or euphemistic in some other way. Further, there has often been an assumption that the whole area of sexuality is of theoretical relevance only, especially for those with severe disability because the opportunity for actual sexual experience will not arise.

Although adolescents with physical handicap are indeed relatively very inexperienced, the picture for adults is not the same, and research and clinic experience reveal reasonable numbers of severely handicapped young people able to establish sexually intimate relationships. One important practical issue here is the need to ensure that a handicapped young person has adequate knowledge not only of conception, but also of contraception. Many disabled teenagers have only the vaguest knowledge about the latter – for example, 'I know there is something called the Pill.'

I have so far underlined the dangers of viewing sexuality related to handicap as an issue isolated from other aspects of handicap. This is also true of the specific question of sexual information. There are some conditions, such as those involving damage to the spinal cord, which directly affect sexual function. A review of sexual function in spinal-cord injured patients (Griffiths et al, 1973) estimated the proportion of such patients with intact sexual function as between 7 and 20 per cent depending on the nature of the lesion. While sex education for such directly affected groups clearly needs to take account of their condition, experience suggests strongly that many handicapped youngsters have major worries about sexual function even when there is no physiological or neurological reason. Lack of any systematic general knowledge about their condition is a striking finding in research into the problems of handicapped teenagers and implies lack of specific knowledge about whether or not sexual performance will be impaired. Worries about genetic transmission are also prevalent and, again, are based more on fantasy than on reality. Typically, disabled young people either seriously over-estimate or under-estimate the genetic risks involved.

CONCLUSIONS

Any programme of sex education for the disabled has to take account of their overall psychological and social predicament, particularly their feelings of wanting to be like their able-bodied peers and the resultant apathy, despair or anger when this cannot happen. The flexible use of group discussion which includes sympathetic able-bodied teenagers is helpful in generating discussion about personal relationships as the context in which more specific discussion about sexual relationships can take place. The success of PHAB groups proves that the number of such sympathetic able-bodied youngsters is considerable.

There is a need for general information, not purely sexual information. Few disabled teenagers know enough about their condition to know how their sexual activities may or may not be affected. Lack of opportunity and anxiety often prevents them from trying to find out. Again, some of this information may be given on a group basis, but there is also a need for individual advice and counselling to be made available to take account of the private anxieties that many such teenagers are likely to have and the particular nature of the handicap and its severity. The need for individual counselling, in my experience, usually arises best as a natural development from group discussion. As in most good counselling, the pace must be acceptable to the client, not rigidly set by the counsellor.

The language of sex education is crucial. Except in the case of some of the very severely intellectually retarded young people, the language of sex already exists. It is a vernacular language. In general, sex education is more likely to succeed if the language is simple. Four-letter words, used technically not pejoratively, have more likelihood of being understood and to be more familiar than four-syllable expressions.

The personal attitudes to sex education of the adults in the handicapped teenager's network are important (Cole et al, 1973). Any sex education programme may well demand that parents, educators, doctors, nurses and others will be faced with their own prejudices, embarrassment, anxieties and conflicts about sexuality.

Where teenagers live at home or are in frequent contact with their parents, the parents, too, will need the opportunity to express their feelings and attitudes. In the same way, staff discussions are an essential ingredient of successful sex education. Powerful opposition to the acceptance of sexuality in the handicapped is often aroused in institutions responsible for their care. Unless such opposition is fully discussed and reasonably resolved, failure is almost inevitable. The Association to Aid Sexual and Personal Relationships of Disabled People (SPOD), 286 Camden Road, London N7 0BJ may be able to offer specialist consultation as well as advisory leaflets.

REFERENCES

Anderson, E. M. and Clarke, L. (1982). *Disability in Adolescence*. Methuen, London.

Bywater, E. M. (1981). Adolescents with cystic fibrosis: psycho-social adjustment. *Archives of Disease in Childhood*, 56, 538–43.

Cole, T., Childgren, R. and Rosenberg, P. (1973). A new programme of sex education and counselling for spinal cord injured adults and health care professionals. *Paraplegia*, 2, 111–24.

Dorner, S. (1975). The relationships of physical handicap to stress in families with an adolescent with spina bifida. *Developmental Medicine and Child Neurology*, 17 (6), 767–76.

Dorner, S. (1976). Adolescents with spina bifida. *Archives of Disease in Childhood*, 51, 439–44.

Dorner, S. (1977). Sexual interest and activity in adolescents with spina bifida. *Journal of Child Psychology and Psychiatry*, 18, 229.

Griffiths, R., Tomko, U. A. and Timms, R. (1973). Sexual function in spinal cord injured patients. *Archives of Physical Medicine and Rehabilitation*, 54, 539–43.

Schofield, M. (1968). *The Sexual Behaviour of Young People*. Penguin, Harmondsworth.

ACKNOWLEDGEMENT

The section *Sexuality and Sex Education* (p. 333) first appeared under the title 'Sexuality and Sex Education for the Handicapped Teenager' in the *Journal of Maternal and Child Health*, September 1980. It is reproduced by permission of the publishers, Barker Publications Limited, Richmond TW9 1PX.

Chapter 20

Adolescence and the Young Adult

by F. G. SHEPPARD DipVG, P. RUSSELL BA
and Y. SNIDER AIMSW

Normal parental expectation is that school is largely preparation for earning a living, preferably in a skilled occupation in which planned training and prospects for advancement are evident. Parents of a handicapped child often, but not always, become conditioned to settling for 'something in which he will be happy'. (What proportion of the population as a whole achieve this?)

Ideally, job choice should be commensurate with the abilities and aptitudes of the individual, but the *level* of the work may be decided by such factors as intellectual ability and attainment, geographical location, economic climate, and so on. It normally follows that doing something well brings its own satisfaction so, with anyone entering employment, from the outset the emphasis should be on ability. Obviously other factors need to be considered, but one must start by looking for job satisfaction.

What are these other factors where the handicapped young person is concerned?

Social acceptability: This means more than just having social graces, important though they are. It means care with personal hygiene – even a mildly unpleasant smell is unacceptable to fellow workers. It means communicating at a reasonably adult level. It means consistently showing willingness and perseverance – workmates soon tire of making allowances, and they find immaturity difficult to accept.

Independence at work: Special care must be taken to ensure that the work is organised to facilitate this and to reduce fetching and carrying by others to a minimum, e.g. beginning and end of day, use of toilet, help in the canteen.

Mobility, in the place of work and travelling to and from: where the former is concerned, too rarely do employers avail themselves of the facility offered by the Manpower Services Commission to adapt premises and/or equipment up to a cost of £5000. Specially adapted vehicles are available, but are costly and cannot be obtained until the young person is 17. If possible, driving lessons and test should be hurdles that are passed before taking up employment: assistance with fares to work is available, but the sheer effort of trying to cope with public transport can be too much.

Personality: Mary Greaves (1969) in her study *Work and Disability* states: Everyone I have spoken to with wide experience of disabled people in employment has without exception and without prompting by me pointed out that the most important single factor in the whole chain of factors leading to employment and retention of employment is the personality of the individual. This is of more importance than intelligence or the degree of disability, and is of equal importance with the degree of acquired skill.

The chance of obtaining employment in the competitive open market may be enhanced by courses of further education or training, but just to 'take a course' is not enough – there must be the motivation and determination to benefit from it. In all walks of life there are those who obtain qualifications, sometimes professional, and then find that these are not immediately followed by an appointment to the careers of their choice.

For the handicapped student, however, there can be additional benefits. A charge often levelled against those leaving residential special schools is that they sometimes fail to think out the likely consequences of their actions – or inaction! The more adult environment of further education or training establishments should help to remedy this. Adjustment to the new environment may produce great pressure, well described by Judith Holman (1981) who points out the need for counselling and a named person to whom the student can go when experiencing difficulties. Schools need to assist their students to recognise that in work or college it will be their responsibility to make their needs known, and that it signifies maturity and not inadequacy to do so. In addition, such courses help to engender a more positive approach to the use of leisure time – sometimes enforced leisure.

More will be said later about the possible alternatives to open employment, but special mention should be made of the value of colleges offering the opportunity for assessment prior to taking a vocational course. This can help offset the disadvantage a handicapped young person suffers compared with his non-handicapped peers who have more knowledge of the world of work by virtue of greater opportunity to observe and talk about occupations in their locality and perhaps to try out some during school-based work experience. Similar assessments are available at some employment rehabilitation centres, possibly followed by training courses elsewhere. However, it must be remembered that the problem of employment of handicapped persons is basically one of fitting an individual or a minority group into an environment designed for a majority group.

Increasingly, provision for the handicapped is improving in local technical colleges. Where the potential student is likely to be home-based this affords the opportunity to make local friends, integrate into the local community after perhaps many years away from home, develop leisure activities and a sense of belonging. However, local further education provision is inevitably patchy, and the respective merits of day versus residential provision can be difficult to assess.

What of the future? Are the expectations of parents and handicapped young people changing in view of the long-term decline in the national economy? How important is more further education and/or training – and for what? Is open employment no longer to be seen as the ultimate goal when parents and siblings are unemployed? Will parental support need a change of emphasis towards sheltered employment or residential placement? Special schools and further education and training establishments need to be active in advising their students in the light of these factors.

The current position is that possibly 30 per cent of disabled people are unemployed – double the rate for the non-handicapped, and nearly 1 in 2 *severely* disabled workers is unemployed. Some 13 666 places were provided in sheltered employment in 1980–1, but there were a further 12 000 places needed. Traditionally, the provision of sheltered employment has been in the form of Remploy factories and sheltered workshops, but now that such a large proportion of the working population is employed by public bodies, there could be some experimenting in the employment of different disabilities and perhaps some remodelling of the actual structure of employment.

For example, two comparatively recent innovations are the introduction of *sheltered industrial groups* (SIGs) and the concept of *job sharing*. SIGs now provide about 20 per cent of all jobs in sheltered employment and are mainly run by local authorities in what were formerly known as 'enclaves' for disabled people working in ordinary employment but under special supervision. In addition to the advantages of integrating disabled workers with the non-handi-capped, SIGs require a much lower subsidy – only about one-third of the average subsidy of sheltered workshops. A development of this type of thinking has been the Pathway Scheme, run by the Royal Society for Mentally Handicapped Children and Adults. Under this scheme a mentally handicapped person is placed with an employer who can be reimbursed with the first three months' wages of the trainee, who is supported by a 'foster worker' paid a weekly honorarium of £4.00. In 1980 the per capita placement cost was £1031, which included pre-employment training and subsequent supervision.

Job-sharing received official backing in July 1982 when the Government announced a scheme under which a grant is payable to employers 'where the splitting of a job results in the recruitment of an unemployed person who is claiming benefit. It could also be paid to help to avoid someone becoming redundant and claiming benefit.' The concept of job-sharing has been operating in the USA on a growing scale since the 1970s, and some local authorities and other employers in this country have instituted formal policies of job-sharing.

Discrimination in favour of handicapped people could be of considerable benefit to those whose disablement causes them to tire quickly and be unable to manage a full working day.

Re-training

Re-training is likely to be an increasing feature of the future, not only within trades and occupations, but also involving complete changes in direction. There is a shift from employment in manufacturing industries as automation advances, and more people are employed in the service industries. In recent years Government-aided training and re-training courses have changed to meet the changing needs of industry, and it is hoped that future provisions will be increasingly sensitive to those needs. But this calls, too, for flexibility and adaptability on the part of the employee – disabled or not – and his schooling should aim to develop these attributes. The years – and indeed weekly hours – spent in employment are likely to diminish rapidly, and correspondingly the need for work outside the formal employment sector will increase. Meaningful – and perhaps profitable – hobbies and leisure activities will need to be more to the fore to take up some of the slack left by reduced hours in employment. In some cases, and perhaps in some periods of the working life, this type of work may replace formal employment as it does already in some establishments and communities such as CARE Villages, etc. Here again there is the need for education to play its part in the preparation for these various aspects of adult life.

THE TRANSITION TO ADULT LIFE

The adolescent period is usually one of turmoil for all families, but for those with a handicapped member it may be a crisis period and one in which fragile mutual support is finally broken down and residential care sought. The 16–19 age-group highlights the many anomalies in our caring services. First there is a lack of 'co-terminosity' in those agencies involved in care. A child becomes an adult at 16 in the Health Service, at 18 for social services and at 19 (if he is lucky) in education. Thus in a period of three years parents may lose a long-trusted paediatrician, access to respite care for *children*, and the informed guidance of the school and its associated advisory and specialist services.

In a sense adolescence is a new problem. Traditionally, many severely handicapped young people entered residential care, usually hospital based. Now the philosophy of normalisation (together with a belief that community care is right) and the virtual disappearance of beds in long-stay hospitals have brought about a 'sea change'. Not only are the young people themselves different, since they have expectations of a quality of life commensurate with their education, but social services have to meet a major challenge at a time when resources are decreasing. Parents also are 'different'. The new generation is articulate, has been involved in planning new services and also has different expectations for its own life. Few families now follow the traditional patterns of child rearing, with the wife remaining at home and financially dependent upon the husband. There are many more single parent families (where any burden of care is a problem doubled); many jobs require mobility and, indeed, many women anticipate that they will return to careers interrupted by a time-limited period of family life.

Partnership with parents is a concept much publicised and highly valued in the development of services for handicapped *children* and their families. Partnership can take many forms, but it will frequently involve participation in the actual assessment and treatment of the child. It may involve regular programmes of work and is likely to make demands (as well as offering rewards) in the day-to-day routine of family life. Perhaps it is fair to review the working relationship with professionals when the child becomes a young *adult*. First, is it right that parents should be expected to act as co-therapists well beyond the age when they would wish to be involved with parent-teacher associations or similar activities with their other children? Second, is it actually right to expect the young person to accept parents in this way? Third, should parents have the right to cease actively and physically to care (in the sense of offering total care) unless they are guaranteed respite services and time for their own lives?

Such arguments do not presuppose that parents wish to discard their responsibilities. Rather, they reflect the fact that greatly improved education and other services lead to different expectations in the young person and his parents. Many young people will indeed wish to stay in their family home. But perhaps our assumptions are biased by the convenience of this form of community care and overlook the very real problems which will be encountered. Social services must assume a critical and major role in adolescence. While handicapped young people and their families may have perceived education and health services as the key agencies in the earlier years, local authority support systems and residential care become of growing importance in this transitional period.

One major need for parents of young people in this age-group is a home-making service. A survey of services for the mentally handicapped in Coventry found that few families of mentally handicapped people received such domiciliary services as meals on wheels, home helps, and incontinence laundry services. While the survey identified 313 young people as being eligible and indeed in need of short-term care, only eight short-stay places were available (six of these being in a voluntary home). Such services as the Crossroads Care Attendants Scheme for physically handicapped people are also essential for handicapped young people moving into group homes. They may be critical factors in the success of *adult* fostering and boarding-out placements.

The majority of families do not look for long-term residential facilities until they themselves feel unable to cope effectively. Rather, as a study by a social worker in West Sussex revealed, families have 'no deep-seated longing for luxury provision, but for the very cost-effective extension of short-term and day-care facilities'. Without the latter, it is likely that many families will indeed break down or alternatively that parents will press early for residential solutions in order to assure themselves that 'he will be all right after I'm gone'. An additional plus factor in providing good quality and readily available day-care and short-term care is that both may form social skills and independence training which will in turn permit placement in sheltered housing or hostels rather than more expensive high-dependency units. Many physically disabled young people can live quite independently, with appropriate aids, but may need special training to function effectively. In both cases parents will also need help in 'letting go' and bridging the gap in their own lives which such a move will make.

SCHOOL LEAVERS: REALISTIC AIMS FOR FUTURE PLACEMENT

For many young people open employment and/or living at home is impossible, and the alternative of residential accommodation is required. Ideally, discussion within the family should take place during the last 2 or 3 years of school life and social services should be involved in planning for the future. A variety of provision exists and may be summarised as follows:

		Sponsorship
A. *Further education and training*		
	1. Higher education – university or polytechnic (if accessible to disabled people)	Local education authority (LEA)
	2. Open university	
	3. Specialist technical colleges for the disabled	LEA
	4. Specialist units for further education in particular disabilities, e.g. Spastics Society, Shaftesbury Society	LEA
	5. Vocational training. Specialist colleges, e.g. Queen Elizabeth Training College	Manpower services commission (MSC)
B. *Sheltered employment*		
	1. Remploy or local authority work centre	MSC
	2. Residential sheltered work centres	Social services department (SSD)
	3. Direct work placement	MSC/Careers officers
C. Residential care for severely handicapped, e.g. Cheshire Foundation, Servite House		SSD
D. Independence training in basic skills and general development		LEA/SSD
Assessment units, e.g. Banstead Place		

It has to be remembered that to move from home to residential adult care is a profound culture shock; even moving from residential school to an adult setting takes an enormous amount of adjustment. Very few youngsters have any concept of what such units are like and this makes preparation difficult. It helps if a group – such as a class group – can visit a variety of adult units in the way that non-handicapped school-leavers visit factories, offices and other places of work. Obviously some units, like some work places, will be inappropriate for those visiting them, but they will give the youngsters some ideas and some basis for realistic discussion.

Finding the right unit (or choice of units) for an individual is very difficult because so many elements need to be considered. These include:

Geographical location: The unit needs to be within reach of the people important to the young person – family/foster home/friends. In this connection it is important to consider how motivated everyone is to maintain links in the face of possible difficulties and whether the onus would be on the youngster or on the family/friends.

Age limits: Some units will not consider young people before the age of 18 or 19, so plans which involve continuing, or further education may have to be made.

Maturity: Units may be 'paternalistic' and offer a lot of support to new, young and immature residents, or require a degree of maturity in their residents unlikely to be found in the average school-leaver.

Level of work: This varies from the offer of diversional activities, if wanted, to units which survive because residents work to economically viable standards. In between are units which offer 'real' work without undue pressure and those where the work is of a diversionary nature but compulsory. Some units have minimal choice of work; The Grange, Bookham, for instance is entirely devoted to needle trades.

Nursing/orderly care: Some units can provide a high level of trained nursing care and will cater for serious disablement, others provide a good deal of 'beginning and end of day' help via untrained staff. At the other end of the scale there are units who need the residents to be virtually independent. Some have nurse help, but the resident must be responsible for seeking it out.

Exclusions: Certain medical conditions such as epilepsy may be excluded.

Leisure time: Leisure pursuits may be built in, but more often there is an expectation that residents will be able to plan and fill their own leisure hours.

Holidays: If the unit closes completely for holidays and the family cannot provide, then it is wise to plan with the young people where they might take a holiday. It would be sensible to let them have experience of a holiday in the chosen centre prior to starting in residence. Probably the best guide to places is *Holidays for the Physically Handicapped* published by the Royal Association for Disability and Rehabilitation.

Social work support: It goes without saying that if it is necessary to introduce a new social worker as the young person moves this should be achieved in plenty of time and that, if appropriate, the whole family should have the information.

Sponsorship: The unit must either belong to a local authority or attract sponsorship from that authority.

The difficulties can be formidable, particularly in finding the unit which combines the degree of care needed with the type of work which is acceptable for the severely handicapped who have good academic potential.

When the choice has been narrowed down to two or three units, visits and short stays are necessary. It is vital that work is done on problem areas between these visits. A youngster may demonstrate that he has insufficient experience to manage, for example, his budgeting; or the unit may need an explanation that a complaint from a boy with spina bifida about a painless redness below the knee might mean a fracture.

The young need thorough discussion before leaving school about the professionals from whom they should seek help and, if possible, an introduction to them. In the case of young people without much family support, a social worker is vital and should be introduced well in advance of a move (if a change of worker is involved). It must be remembered that the chosen residential unit is not necessarily for life, and indeed it may be necessary to move from one unit to another dependent on changing needs and progressive condition.

REFERENCES

Greaves, M. (1969). *Work and Disability*. Disabled Living Foundation and RADAR, London.

Holman, J. (1980). Disabled school leavers. *Concern*, **38**, 29–32. (Winter 1980–81.)

Holidays for the Handicapped. Published annually by the Royal Association for Disability and Rehabilitation (RADAR) London.

BIBLIOGRAPHY

Ability not Disability: Handbook for Careers Officers (1981). Published by the Institute of Careers Officers.

USEFUL ADDRESSES

Institute of Careers Officers
2nd Floor, Old Board Chambers
37A High Street, Stourbridge DY8 1TA

Association of Crossroads Care Attendants Schemes Ltd
94a Coton Road
Rugby CV21 4LN   0788 73653

Banstead Place (Assessment Centre)
Park Road, Banstead, Surrey SM7 3EE   Burgh Heath 56222

Cheshire Foundation (Head Office)
26–29 Mansel Street, London SW1P 2QN   01-828 1822

Dorincourt Sheltered Workshop
Oaklawn Road, Leatherhead KT22 0BT   Oxshott 2599

Enham Village Centre
The White House, Enham-Alamein
Andover Hampshire SP11 6HJ   0264 51551

The Grange Training Centre
Rectory Lane, Bookham KT23 4DY   Bookham 52608

Hereward College
Branston Crescent, Tile Hill Lane
Coventry CV4 9SW   0203 461231

Love Walk Hostel for Disabled Women Workers
10 Love Walk, London SE5 8AE   01-703 3632

Papworth Village Industries
Papworth Hall, Papworth Everard
Cambridge CB3 8RF   (Huntingdon) 0480 830341

Portland Training College for the Disabled
Nottingham Road, Mansfield NG18 4TJ   (Blidworth) 06234 2141

Queen Elizabeth Training College
Leatherhead Court, Leatherhead KT22 0BN   Oxshott 2204

Remploy (Head Office)
415 Edgware Road, London NW2 6LR   01-452 8020

Royal Society for Mentally Handicapped Children and Adults
123 Golden Lane, London EC1Y 0RT   01-253 9433

St Loyes College (for training the disabled for industry and commerce)
Topsham Road, Exeter EX2 6EP   0392 55426

Searchlight Workshops
Claremont Road
Newhaven East Sussex BN9 0NQ   07912 4007

Servite House Headquarters
17 The Boltons, London SW10 9SX   01-370 3311

Shaftesbury Society
112 Regency Street, London SW1P 4AX   01-834 2656

Woodlarks Workshop Trust
Lodge Hill Road, Farnham GU10 3RB   0252 714041

Chapter 21

Aids to Daily Living

by J. ROCKEY DipCOT

The following tables attempt to draw together suitable aids for enabling activities of daily living to be more effectively performed by the child himself/herself, or, in some cases, to provide assistance for the carer. There is also a table of suggestions for the adaptation of clothing to enable the wearer to cope more efficiently with fastenings etc.

Throughout the book there are additional sections on aids, and in many instances they have been linked with the illustrations in this chapter.

POSITIONS FOR PLAY

Equipment	Disability
Wedge. Corner seat Side-lying board (Fig. 21/1) Flexistand (see Fig. 6/8, p. 140); standing table	Cerebral palsy
Low well-padded trolley	Spina bifida
Wooden nursery chair on castors with tray/table Overhead gantry with slings or springs (Fig. 21/2)	Limb deficiency Arthrogryposis Spinal muscular atrophy
Chairs of various types (see Fig. 1/5, p. 42)	All disabilities

Fig. 21/1 Side-lying board

Fig. 21/2 Overhead gantry with arm slings on elastic to aid hand function in arthrogryposis

FEEDING

Equipment	Adaptation	Disability
Assisted:		
Position important		Cerebral palsy
Many spoons available	Horn or polycarbonated spoon can be angled (Fig. 21/3)	
Straight-sided bowl		
Non-slip mat		
Self:		
Use Peto bar for non-dominant hand (see Fig. 6/7, p. 137)		Cerebral palsy
If sufficiently motivated a viscous damped feeding aid or cam-operated feeder can be used for older CP children (Fig. 21/3)		
Rocker feeder (Fig. 21/4)		Arthrogryposis
Pivot bar (Fig. 9/5, p. 183)		
Stump slip-on cutlery (Fig. 11/3, p. 206)		Limb deficiency
Drinking		
Two-handled cups		All disabilities
Glass with detachable handles (Fig. 21/5)		
Plastic tubing for straw		
Straw with non-return valve		
(Pat Saunders valved straw)		

Fig. 21/3 Cam-operated feeder: angled polycarbonate spoon: horn spoon

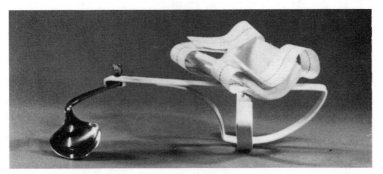

Fig. 21/4(a) Rocker feeder – for children who have minimal muscle power in the arms and stiff elbow joints

Fig. 21/4(b)
Rocker feeder
in action

Fig. 21/5 Doidy cup: glass with detachable handles: mug with straw

PERSONAL HYGIENE

Activity	Equipment	Adaptation	Disability
Toileting	Potty chair with trunk support and handrail (see Fig. 1/5, p. 42)	Straps; harness Back cut out	Cerebral palsy Neuromuscular disorders Spina bifida
	Commercially moulded toilet seat	Individual moulded toilet seat	Cerebral palsy Neuromuscular disorders Arthrogryposis
	Handrails to assist transfer Raised toilet seat		Cerebral palsy Spina bifida
	Steps up to lavatory		Limb deficiency
Cleansing	Folding horizontal bar for older child leaves hands free for cleansing (Fig. 21/6)		Spina bifida Cerebral palsy Arthrogryposis Limb deficiency
	Toilet paper secured under knob of seat Bidet for home use Hand-held toilet aid Toilet paper on heel		Upper limb amelia
Washing	Flannel mitt Suction soap holder; suction sponge and loofah; liquid soap dispenser; tap turner		Limb deficiency Cerebral palsy Arthrogryposis

see Fig. 1/5, p. 42

Activity	Equipment	Adaptation	Disability
Bathing	Bubble bath. Non-slip shapes or strips. Shallow bath insert (Fig. 21/7) Chailey swimming/bath aid (Fig. 21/8) Bath boards; bath seats; rails		All disabilities
Drying	Large bath sheet to roll in		All disabilities
Cleaning teeth	Electric toothbrush Toothbrush holder (Fig. 21/9)		Limb deficiency Arthrogryposis
Shaving	Battery/electric shaver mounted on to wall under a mirror		Limb deficiency Arthrogryposis
Menstruation	Tampon inserter (Fig. 21/10) Stick-on pads		Limb deficiency Arthrogryposis
Hair care	Shower attachment or in bath; shampoo dispenser Long-handled or angled comb or brush		Limb deficiency
Lifting	Hoists		Dependent children

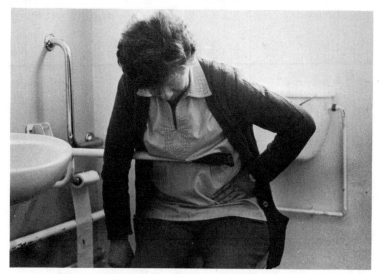

Fig. 21/6 Folding horizontal bar for stability on the toilet

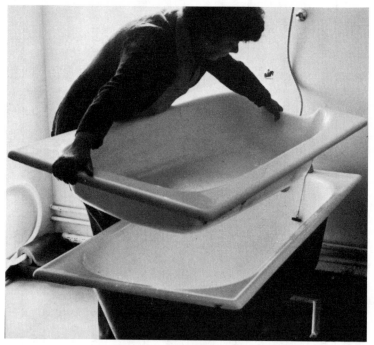

Fig. 21/7 Shallow bath insert

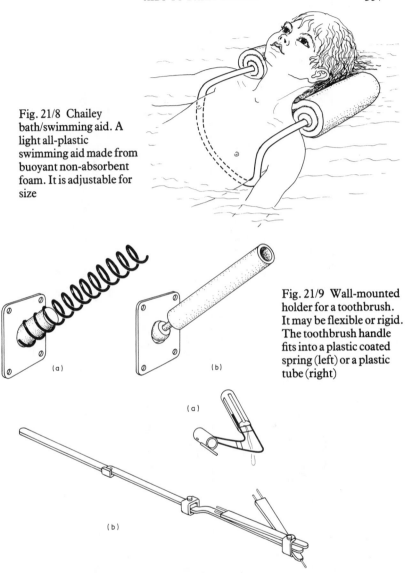

Fig. 21/8 Chailey bath/swimming aid. A light all-plastic swimming aid made from buoyant non-absorbent foam. It is adjustable for size

Fig. 21/9 Wall-mounted holder for a toothbrush. It may be flexible or rigid. The toothbrush handle fits into a plastic coated spring (left) or a plastic tube (right)

(a)

(b)

(a)

(b)

Fig. 21/10 Tampon inserter. Two small stainless steel prongs fit deeply into the lower end of the grooves of a 'Lil-lets' tampon thus preventing body contact during use. The angle of the prongs allows safe insertion, and a small stainless steel pin facilitates removal via the looped cord attached to the tampon. The prongs alone (a) can be provided for fitting to an appropriate handle or a complete device with a folding handle and range of sizes of prong to fit the appropriate tampon (b)

GENERAL ACTIVITIES

Activity	Equipment	Adaptation	Disability
Reach	Croupier stick Lazy tongs		All disabilities
Access to home/school	Ramps	Arranged through OTs in social services departments in conjunction with local housing/school authorities	All disabilities
Travelling by car/train	Car seats; harness Sufficient room for stowing wheelchairs		All disabilities
Transferring	Sliding board or rotating front seat Hoist		All disabilities
Educational: writing/painting	Raised angled desk tops Angled wheelchair trays	Plastic tubing over pencils/paintbrushes for mouth writers Orthodontic pencil holders rarely necessary	Limb deficiency Arthrogryposis

Activity	Equipment	Adaptation	Disability
Cutting with scissors	One-handed and spring-loaded scissors (Fig. 21/11)		Cerebral palsy Arthrogryposis Limb deficiency Muscular dystrophy
Securing paper	Magnets and metal sheet		
Ruling		Magnets attached to ruler and metal sheet under	
Communication	Electric typewriters POSSUM and various electronic equipment (see Chapter 17)	Individual switches to operate the equipment	All disabilities with poor hand function

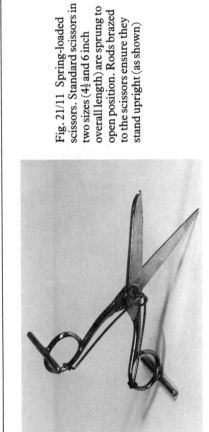

Fig. 21/11 Spring-loaded scissors. Standard scissors in two sizes (4½ and 6 inch overall length) are sprung to open position. Rods brazed to the scissors ensure they stand upright (as shown)

CLOTHING

Article	Aid	Adaptation	Disability
Socks	Dressing stick with S-shaped hook; mouth- or hand-piece; length of stick critical Sock gutter	Loops with inner core of string	Limb deficiency Arthrogryposis Cerebral palsy Spina bifida
Shoes	Long-handled shoe horn	Slip-on for normal lower limbs Moulded insoles into shop shoes Trainers with Velcro fastening Shop shoes on prostheses (not possible for child to put on)	Limb deficiency Arthrogryposis Cerebral palsy
Shoe laces	'No bows' Elastic shoe laces		All disabilities
Under pants		Loops in front of side seams at waist or leg depending on disability	Limb deficiency Arthrogryposis Spina bifida
Trousers	Dressing stick Dressing stick	Lengthen fly to centre crutch seam Insert key ring into tab of zip Waist fastening Velcro through slide ring and back	All disabilities

Item	Aids	Features	Disabilities
	Dressing stick	Loops at waist (in front of side seams) Zips at lower end of trousers for ease of getting over shoes when in prostheses or orthoses, or wearing a drainage bag	Spina bifida Arthrogryposis
Skirts	Dressing stick and suction hooks on wall	Loops in front of side seams Elasticised waist band Velcro fastening at waist as trousers Wrap around skirts	Limb deficiency Arthrogryposis All disabilities
Bras	Dressing stick and suction hooks on wall	Crossed shoulder straps No fastening Front opening	
Vests/T-shirts		Loose	
Shirts/blouses/dress	Button sticks do up Mouth to undo Dressing stick for Velcro	Loose Stitch half-way up opening	
Outdoor clothing	Poncho/cloak		Spina bifida Cerebral palsy
Quilted leg bags			All disabilities in wheelchairs

Select Bibliography

This bibliography is in addition to references and further reading in other chapters.

Bobath, B. and Bobath, K. (1975). *Motor Development in the Different Types of Cerebral Palsy*. William Heinemann Medical Books Limited, London.

Downie, P. A. (ed)(1982). *Cash's Textbook of Neurology for Physiotherapists*, 3rd edition. Faber and Faber, London.

Dubowitz, V. (1978). *Muscle Disorders in Childhood*. W.B. Saunders Co, Philadelphia.

Espir, M. L. E. and Rose, C. F. (1980). *The Basic Neurology of Speech*, 3rd edition. Blackwell Scientific Publications Limited, Oxford.

Holle, B. (1977). *Motor Development in Children: Normal and Retarded*. Blackwell Scientific Publications Limited, Oxford.

Holt, K. (1977). *Developmental Paediatrics*. Volume in the Postgraduate Paediatric Series (Apley, J. (gen ed)). Butterworths, London.

Hosking, G. (1982). *An Introduction to Paediatric Neurology*. Faber and Faber, London.

Menelaus, M. B. (1980). *The Orthopaedic Management of Spina Bifida Cystica*, 2nd edition. Churchill Livingstone, Edinburgh.

Nettles, O. R. (1979). *Counselling Parents of Children with Handicaps*. Tappenden Print Company Limited, Crawley, Sussex.

Reynell, J. (1970). *Children with Physical Handicaps*. In *The Psychological Assessment of Mental and Physical Handicaps*, (ed Mittler, P.). Methuen, London.

Select List of Useful Organisations

These organisations which are listed are only a few of the many who offer information, advice and counselling. In addition the following book will be a useful source reference.

Directory for the Disabled edited by A. Darnbrough and D. Kinrade. Published by Woodhead-Faulkner, Cambridge CB2 3PF. (Regularly updated.)

Voluntary Council for Handicapped Children
National Children's Bureau, 8 Wakley Street
London EC1V 7QE   01-278 9441

Invalid Children's Aid Association
126 Buckingham Palace Road
London SW1W 9SB   01-730 9891

Physically Handicapped and Able Bodied (PHAB)
42 Devonshire Street
London W1N 1LN   01-637 7475

Lady Hoare Trust for Physically Disabled Children
7 North Street, Midhurst
West Sussex GU29 3DJ   073081 3696

National Bureau for Handicapped Students
40 Brunswick Square
London WC1N 1AZ   01-278 3459

Royal Association for Disability and Rehabilitation (RADAR)
25 Mortimer Street
London W1N 8AB   01-637 5400

Disabled Living Foundation
346 Kensington High Street
London W14 8NS   01-602 2491

Rehabilitation Engineering Movement Advisory Panels (REMAP)
Thames House North, Millbank
London SW1P 4QG   01-834 4444

Association to Aid Sexual and Personal Relationships
of Disabled People (SPOD)
286 Camden Road
London N7 0BJ   01-607 8851

British Sports Association for the Disabled
Stoke Mandeville Stadium, Harvey Road
Aylesbury, Buckinghamshire HP21 8PP   0296 84848

Riding for the Disabled Association
Avenue R, National Agricultural Centre
Kenilworth, Warwickshire CV8 2LY   (Coventry) 0203 56107

The International Cerebral Palsy Society
5a Netherhall Gardens
London NW3 5RN   01-794 9761

Spastics Society
12 Park Crescent
London W1N 4EQ   01-636 5020

Western Cerebral Palsy Centre
Bobath Centre, 5 Netherhall Gardens
London NW3 5RN   01-794 6084

Spinal Injuries Association
5 Crowndale Road
London NW1 1TU   01-388 6840

Association for All Speech Impaired Children (AFASIC)
Room 14, Toynbee Hall
28 Commercial Street, London E1 6LS   01-247 1497

Muscular Dystrophy Group of Great Britain
35 Macaulay Road
London SW4 0QP   01-720 8055

The Compassionate Friends
5 Lower Clifton Hill
Bristol BS8   0272 292778

Association for Spina Bifida and Hydrocephalus (ASBAH)
Tavistock House North
Tavistock Square, London WC1H 9HJ   01-388 1382

British Epilepsy Association
Crowthorne House, Bigshotte
New Wokingham Road, Wokingham RG11 3AY(Crowthorne) 0344 773122

The National Deaf Children's Society
45 Hereford Road
London W2 5AH   01-229 9272

Royal National Institute for the Deaf
105 Gower Street
London WC1E 6AH   01-387 8033

Friedreich's Ataxia Group
12c Worplesdon Road
Guildford GU2 6RW   0483 503133

Colostomy Welfare Group
38/39 Eccleston Square (2nd Floor)
London SW1V 1PB   01-828 5175

Ileostomy Association of Great Britain and Ireland
Central Office, Amblehurst House
Chobham, Woking
Surrey GU24 8PZ   (Chobham) 09905 8277

Medic-Alert Foundation
11–13 Clifton Terrace
London N4 3JP   01-263 8596

Toy Libraries Association
Seabrook House, Wyllyotts Manor
Darkes Lane, Potters Bar EN6 2HL   Potters Bar 44571

Scottish Information Service for the Disabled
19 Claremont Crescent
Edinburgh EH7 4QD   031-556 3882

Scottish Sports Association for the Disabled
c/o Fife Institute of Physical Recreational Education
Viewfield Road, Glenrothes, Fife KY6 2RA   0592 771700

Scottish Paraplegic Association
3 Cargill Terrace
Edinburgh EH5 3ND   031-552 8459

Scottish Spina Bifida Association
190 Queensferry Road
Edinburgh EH4 2BN   031-332 0743

Scottish Council for Spastics
22 Corstophine Road
Edinburgh EH12 6DD   031-337 2804

Index